Edited by Jack Dann & Gardner Dozois

A.I.s

EDITED BY

JACK DANN & GARDNER DOZOIS

ACE BOOKS, NEW YORK

THE BERKLEY PUBLISHING GROUP
Published by the Penguin Group
Penguin Group (USA) Inc.
375 Hudson Street, New York, New York 10014, USA

Penguin Group (Canada), 10 Alcorn Avenue, Toronto, Ontario M4V 3B2, Canada
(a division of Pearson Penguin Canada Inc.)
Penguin Books Ltd., 80 Strand, London WC2R 0RL, England
Penguin Group Ireland, 25 St. Stephen's Green, Dublin 2, Ireland (a division of Penguin Books Ltd.)
Penguin Group (Australia), 250 Camberwell Road, Camberwell, Victoria 3124, Australia
(a division of Pearson Australia Group Pty. Ltd.)
Penguin Books India Pvt. Ltd., 11 Community Centre, Panchsheel Park, New Delhi—110 017, India
Penguin Group (NZ), Cnr Airborne and Rosedale Roads, Albany, Auckland 1310, New Zealand
(a division of Pearson New Zealand Ltd.)
Penguin Books (South Africa) (Pty.) Ltd., 24 Sturdee Avenue, Rosebank, Johannesburg 2196,
South Africa

Penguin Books Ltd., Registered Offices: 80 Strand, London WC2R 0RL, England

This is a work of fiction. Names, characters, places, and incidents either are the product of the
authors' imaginations or are used fictitiously, and any resemblance to actual persons, living or dead,
business establishments, events, or locales is entirely coincidental.

A.I.s

An Ace Book / published by arrangement with the editors

PRINTING HISTORY
Ace mass market edition / December 2004

Copyright © 2004 by Jack Dann and Gardner Dozois.
A complete listing of individual copyrights can be found on page v.
Cover art by AXB Group.
Cover design by Rita Frangie.

ISBN: 0-441-01216-7

ACE
Ace Books are published by The Berkley Publishing Group,
a division of Penguin Group (USA) Inc.,
375 Hudson Street, New York, New York 10014.
ACE and the "A" design
are trademarks belonging to Penguin Group (USA) Inc.

PRINTED IN THE UNITED STATES OF AMERICA

10 9 8 7 6 5 4 3 2 1

CONTENTS

Preface

We may be on the verge of an evolutionary leap of un-precedented size and effect—but it might not be *us* doing the leaping.

For the first time in history, scientists may soon be able to create sentient beings who are *smarter than we are.* Artificial Intelligences. A.I.s. And from that point on, it will be the A.I.s who do the evolving, at a speed mere flesh-and-blood creatures could never come near matching, as smart machines design *smarter* machines, machines better and more efficient and more intelligent than any machines designed by humans could possibly be . . . and then those machines design still *smarter* machines, who design even *smarter* machines, and so on, in a fast-forward evolution where hundreds or even thousands of "generations" can pass in a year.

And where will this all lead? What will the A.I.s be like, what will they be capable of, after thousands of "genera-tions" of forced, high-speed, self-directed evolution?

More importantly, what will their relationship with *us,* with mere organic unevolved human beings, be like? What will it be like for us to share the planet with superintelli-gent inorganic creatures many times smarter than we are? Creatures so much smarter and faster-thinking than we are that the gulf between us and them may eventually be greater than the gulf between us and an ant?

Will they conquer us? Exterminate us? Coexist with us in peaceful cooperation? Ignore us and go about their own enigmatic and incomprehensible concerns? Fuse with us in some sort of benevolent symbiosis? Become as gods to us? (And if the latter, will their rule over us be malevolent or benign? Sternly paternalistic or frivolous and playfully random?) Treat us as pets? Revere us as their beloved ancestors? Put us in the equivalent of a Nature Reserve, to be observed in our Natural Habitats?

And who will get to go to the stars? Them, or us? Or will it take both of us working together to get there?

These are some of the questions most central to the best of modern science fiction today, and there are as many answers as there are writers, sparking the kind of give-and-take debate that produces the best that the genre has to offer and signposts to our many possible tomorrows.

So open the pages of this book, and let some of today's most expert dreamers show you worlds where A.I.s have spread their influence not only over this Earth but over many alternate Earths in nearby dimensions ... where a woman must match wits against a runaway A.I. in order to save her children ... where benevolent A.I.s give a transcendental birthday gift to everyone in the world ... where only an enigmatic alien A.I. possesses the knowledge to save the world from an onrushing cosmic catastrophe ... where scientists find it difficult to control an A.I. with the powers and omnipotence of a god ... where humans and A.I.s coexist uneasily, each society unseen by the other ... except in the illicit and forbidden zones where they meet ... where love builds between a sentient spaceship and its half-human pilot, in spite of all the obstacles in the way ...

Enjoy!

(For further speculations on this theme, check out our Ace anthologies *Beyond Flesh, Nanotech, Hackers, Immortals,* and *Future War.*)

Antibodies

Charles Stross

Although he made his first sale back in 1987, it's only recently that British writer Charles Stross has begun to make a name for himself as a writer to watch in the new century ahead (in fact, as one of the key Writers to Watch in the Oughts*), with a sudden burst in the last few years of quirky, inventive, high-bit-rate stories such as "A Colder War," "Bear Trap," "Dechlorinating the Moderator," "Toast: A Con Report," "Lobsters," "Troubadour," "Tourist," "Halo," "Router," and "Nightfall," in markets such as* Interzone, Spectrum SF, Asimov's Science Fiction Magazine, Odyssey, Strange Plasma, *and* New Worlds. *Stross is also a regular columnist for the monthly magazine* Computer Shopper. *He has "published" a novel online,* Scratch Monkey, *available to be read on his website (www.antipope.org/charlie/), and serialized another novel,* The Atrocity Archive, *in the magazine* Spectrum SF. *His most recent book is his first collection,* Toast, and Other Burned Out Futures, *and coming up is a major new novel,* Singularity Sky. *He's been on the Hugo Final Ballot twice in the last two years: in 2002 with his story "Lobsters" and in 2003 with "Halo." He lives in Edinburgh, Scotland.*

In the fast-paced and innovative story that follows, he suggests that by the time you can begin to worry that it might not be a good idea to create a superintelligent A.I., it may already be too late to do anything about it . . .

Everyone remembers where they were and what they were doing when a member of the great and the good is assassinated. Gandhi, the Pope, Thatcher—if you were old enough you remembered where you were when you heard, the ticker-tape of history etched across your senses. You can kill a politician but their ideas usually live on. They have a life of their own. How much more dangerous, then, the ideas of mathematicians?

I was elbow-deep in an eviscerated PC, performing open heart surgery on a diseased network card, when the news about the traveling salesman theorem came in. Over on the other side of the office John's terminal beeped, notification of incoming mail. A moment later my own workstation bonged.

"Hey, Geoff! Get a load of this!"

I carried on screwing the card back into its chassis. John is not a priority interrupt.

"Someone's come up with a proof that NP-complete problems lie in P! There's a posting in *comp.risks* saying they've used it to find an O^* (n^2) solution to the traveling salesman problem, and it scales! Looks like April First has come early this year, doesn't it?"

I dropped the PC's lid on the floor hastily and sat down at my workstation. Another cubed-sphere hypothesis, another flame war in the math newsgroups—or something more serious? "When did it arrive?" I called over the partition. Soroya, passing my cubicle entrance with a cup of coffee, cast me a dirty look; loud voices aren't welcome in open-plan offices.

"This just in," John replied. I opened up the mailtool and hit on the top of the list, which turned out to be a memo from HR about diversity awareness training. No, next . . . they want to close the smoking room and make us a 100 percent tobacco-free workplace. Hmm. Next.

Forwarded e-mail: headers bearing the spoor of a thousand mail servers, from Addis Ababa to Ulan Bator. Before it had entered our internal mail network it had traveled from Taiwan to Rochester, NY, then to UCB in the Bay Area, then via a mailing list to all points; once in-company it had been bounced to everyone in engineering and management by the first recipient, Eric the Canary. (Eric is the departmental plant. Spends all the day web-dozing for juicy nuggets of new information if you let him. A one-man wire service: which is why I always ended up finishing his jobs.)

I skimmed the message, then read it again. Blinked. This kind of stuff is heavy on the surreal number theory: about as digestible as an Egyptian mummy soaked in tabasco sauce for three thousand years. Then I poked at the web page the theorem was on.

No response—server timed out.

Someone or something was hitting on the web server with the proof: I figured it had to be all the geeks who'd caught wind of the chain letter so far. My interest was up, so I hit the reload button, and something else came up on screen.

Lots of theorems—looked like the same stuff as the e-mail, only this time with some fun graphics. Something tickled my hindbrain then, and I had to bite my lip to keep from laughing. Next thing, I hit the print button and the inkjet next to my desk began to mutter and click. There was a link near the bottom of the page to the author's bibliography, so I clicked on that and the server threw another "go away, I'm busy" error. I tugged my beard thoughtfully, and instead of pressing "back," I pressed "reload."

The browser thought to itself for a bit—then a page began to appear on my screen. The wrong page. I glanced at the document title at the top and froze:

THE PAGE AT THIS LOCATION HAS BEEN WITH-

*DRAWN. Please enter your e-mail address if you require
further information.*

Hmm.

As soon as the printout was finished, I wandered around
to the photocopier next door to the QA labs and ran off a
copy. Faxed it to a certain number, along with an EYES UP
note on a yellow Post-it. Then I poked my head around into
the QA lab itself. It was dingy in there, as usual, and half
the cubicles were empty of human life. Nobody here but us
computers; workstations humming away, sucking juice
and meditating on who-knew-what questions. (Actually, I
did know: they were mostly running test harnesses, repet-
itively pounding simulated input data into the programs
we'd so carefully built, in the hope of making them fall
over or start singing "God Save the King.") The efficiency
of code was frequently a bone of contention between our
departments, but the war between software engineering
and quality assurance is a long-drawn-out affair: each side
needs the other to justify its survival.

I was looking for Amin. Amin with the doctorate in discrete number theory, now slumming it in this company of
engineers: my other canary in a number-crunching coal
mine. I found him: feet propped up on the lidless hulk of a
big Compaq server, mousing away like mad at a big monitor. I squinted; it looked vaguely familiar . . . "Quake? Or
Golgotha?" I asked.

"Golgotha. We've got Marketing bottled up on the second floor."

"How's the network looking?"

He shrugged. "No crashes, no dropped packets—this
cut looks pretty solid. We've been playing for three days
now. What can I do for you?"

I shoved the printout under his nose. "This seem feasible to you?"

"Hold on a mo." He hit the pause key then scanned it
rapidly. Did a double-take. "You're not shitting?"

"Came out about two hours ago."

"Jesus Homeboy Christ riding into town at the head of a convoy of Hell's Angels with a police escort . . ." He shook his head. Amin always swears by Jesus, a weird side-effect of a westernized Islamic upbringing: take somebody else's prophet's name in vain. "If it's true, I can think of at least three different ways we can make money at it, and at least two more to end up in prison. You don't use PGP, do you?"

"Why bother?" I asked, my heart pounding. "I've got nothing to hide."

"If this is true"—he tapped the papers—"then every encryption algorithm except the one-time pad has just fallen over. Take a while to be sure, but . . . that crunch you heard in the distance was the sound of every secure commerce server on the internet succumbing to a brute-force attack. The script kiddies will be creaming themselves. Jesus Christ." He rubbed his mustache thoughtfully.

"Does it make sense to you?" I persisted.

"Come back in five minutes and I'll tell you."

"Okay."

I wandered over to the coffee station, thinking very hard. People hung around and generally behaved as if it was just another day; maybe it was. But then again, if that paper was true, quite a lot of stones had just been turned over and if you were one of the pale guys who lived underneath, it was time to scurry for cover. And it had looked good to me: by the prickling in my palms and the gibbering cackle in the back of my skull, something very deep had recognized it. Amin's confirmation would be just the icing on the cake, confirmation that it was a workable proof.

Cryptography—the science of encoding messages—relies on certain findings in mathematics: that certain operations are inherently more difficult than others. For example, finding the common prime factors of a long number which is a product of those primes is far harder than taking two primes and multiplying them together.

Some processes are not simply made difficult, but impossible because of this asymmetry; it's not feasible to come up with a deterministic answer to certain puzzles in finite time. Take the traveling salesman problem, for example. A salesman has to visit a whole slew of cities which are connected to their neighbors by a road network. Is there a way for the salesman to figure out a best-possible route that visits each city without wasting time by returning to a previously visited site, for all possible networks of cities? The conventional answer is no—and this has big implications for a huge set of computing applications. Network topology, expert systems—the traditional tool of the A.I. community—financial systems, and . . .

Me and my people.

B*ack in the* QA lab, Amin was looking decidedly thoughtful.

"What do you know?" I asked.

He shook the photocopy at me. "Looks good," he said. "I don't understand it all, but it's at least credible."

"How does it work?"

He shrugged. "It's a topological transform. You know how most NP-incomplete problems, like the traveling salesman problem, are basically equivalent? And they're all graph-traversal issues. How to figure out the correct order to carry out a sequence of operations, or how to visit each node in a graph in the correct order. Anyway, this paper's about a method of reducing such problems to a much simpler form. He's using a new theorem in graph theory that I sort of heard about last year but didn't pay much attention to, so I'm not totally clear on all the details. But if this is for real . . ."

"Pretty heavy?"

He grinned. "You're going to have to rewrite the route discovery code. Never mind, it'll run a bit faster . . ."

I *rose out of* cubicle hell in a daze, blinking in the cloud-filtered daylight. Eight years lay in ruins behind me, tattered and bleeding bodies scattered in the wreckage. I walked to the landscaped car park: on the other side of the world, urban renewal police with M16's beat the crap out of dissident organizers, finally necklacing them in the damp, humid night. War raged on three fronts, spaced out around a burning planet. Even so, this was by no means the worst of all possible worlds. It had problems, sure, but nothing serious—until now. Now it had just acquired a sucking chest wound; none of those wars were more than a stubbed toe in comparison to the nightmare future that lay ahead.

Insert key in lock, open door. Drive away, secrets open to the wind, everything blown to hell and gone.

I'd have to call Eve. We'd have to evacuate everybody.

I had a bank account, a savings account, and two credit cards. In the next fifteen minutes I did a grand tour of the available ATMs and drained every asset I could get my hands on into a fat wodge of banknotes. Fungible and anonymous cash. It didn't come to a huge amount—the usual exigencies of urban living had seen to that—but it only had to last me a few days.

By the time I headed home to my flat, I felt slightly sheepish. Nothing there seemed to have changed: I turned on the TV but CNN and the BBC weren't running any coverage of the end of the world. With deep unease I sat in the living room in front of my ancient PC: turned it on and pulled up my net link.

More mail . . . a second bulletin from *comp.risks,* full of earnest comments about the paper. One caught my eye, at the bottom: a message from one of No Such Agency's tame

stoolpigeon academics, pointing out that the theorem
hadn't yet been publicly disclosed and might turn out to be
deficient. (Subtext: Trust the Government. The Government
is your friend.) It wouldn't be the first time such a
major discovery had been announced and subsequently
withdrawn. But then again, they couldn't actually produce
a refutation, so the letter was basically valueless disinformation. I prodded at the web site again, and this time didn't
even get the ACCESS FORBIDDEN message. The paper had
disappeared from the internet, and only the printout in my
pocket told me that I hadn't imagined it.

It takes a while for the magnitude of a catastrophe to
sink in. The mathematician who had posted the original
finding would be listed in his university's directory, wouldn't
he? I pointed my web browser at their administrative
pages, then picked up my phone. Dialed a couple of very
obscure numbers, waited while the line quality dropped
considerably and the charges began racking up at an enormous—but untraceably anonymized—rate, and dialed the
university switchboard.

"Hello, John Durant's office. Who is that?"

"Hi, I've read the paper about his new theorem," I said,
too fast. "Is John Durant available?"

"Who are you?" asked the voice at the other end of the
phone. Female voice, twangy Midwestern accent.

"A researcher. Can I talk to Dr. Durant, please?"

"I'm afraid he won't be in today," said the voice on the
phone. "He's on vacation at present. Stress due to overwork."

"I see," I said.

"Who did you say you were?" she repeated.

I put the phone down.

From: nobody@nowhere.com (none of your business)
To: cypherpunks

Subject: John Durant's whereabouts
Date: . . . .

You might be interested to learn that Dr. John Durant, whose theorem caused such a fuss here earlier, is not at his office. I went there a couple of hours ago in person and the area was sealed off by our friends from the Puzzle Palace. He's not at home either. I suspect the worst . . .

By the way, guys, you might want to keep an eye on each other for the next couple of days. Just in case.

Signed,
Yr frndly spk

"Eve?"

"Bob?"

"Green fields."

"You phoned me to say you know someone with hayfever?"

"We both have hayfever. It may be terminal."

"I know where you can find some medicine for that."

"Medicine won't work this time. It's like the emperor's new suit."

"It's like what? Please repeat."

"The emperor's new suit: it's naked, it's public, and it can't be covered up. Do you understand? Please tell me."

"Yes, I understand exactly what you mean . . . I'm just a bit shocked; I thought everything was still on track. This is all very sudden. What do you want to do?"

(I checked my watch.)

"I think you'd better meet me at the pharmacy in fifteen minutes."

"At six-thirty? They'll be shut."

"Not to worry: the main Boots in town is open out of hours. Maybe they can help you."

"I hope so."

"I know it. Goodbye."

On my way out of the house I paused for a moment. It was a small house, and it had seen better days. I'm not a homemaker by nature: in my line of work you can't afford to get too attached to anything, any language, place, or culture. Still, it had been mine. A small, neat residence, a protective shell I could withdraw into like a snail, sheltering from the hostile theorems outside. *Goodbye, little house. I'll try not to miss you too much.* I hefted my overnight bag onto the backseat and headed into town.

I *found* Eve sitting on a bench outside the central branch of Boots, running a degaussing coil over her credit cards. She looked up. "You're late."

"Come on." I waggled the car keys at her. "You have the tickets?"

She stood up: a petite woman, conservatively dressed. You could mistake her for a lawyer's secretary or a personnel manager; in point of fact she was a university research council administrator, one of the unnoticed body of bureaucrats who shape the course of scientific research. Nondescript brown hair, shoulder-length, forgettable. We made a slightly odd pair: if I'd known she'd have come straight from work I might have put on a suit. Chinos and a lumberjack shirt and a front pocket full of pens that screamed engineer: I suppose I was nondescript, in the right company, but right now we had to put as much phase space as possible between us and our previous identities. It had been good protective camouflage for the past decade, but a bush won't shield you against infrared scopes, and merely living the part wouldn't shield us against the surveillance that would soon be turned in our direction.

"Let's go."

I drove into town and we dropped the car off in the long-stay park. It was nine o'clock and the train was already waiting. She'd bought business-class tickets: go to sleep in Euston, wake up in Edinburgh. I had a room all to myself. "Meet me in the dining car, once we're rolling," she told me, face serious, and I nodded. "Here's your new SIMM. Give me the old one."

I passed her the electronic heart of my cellphone and she ran it through the degausser then carefully cut it in half with a pair of nail-clippers. "Here's your new one," she said, passing a card over. I raised an eyebrow. "Tesco's, pay-as-you-go, paid for in cash. Here's the dialback dead-letter box number." She pulled it up on her phone's display and showed it to me.

"Got that." I inserted the new SIMM then punched the number into my phone. Later, I'd ring the number: a PABX there would identify my voiceprint then call my phone back, downloading a new set of numbers into its memory. Contact numbers for the rest of my ops cell, accessible via cellphone and erasable in a moment. The less you knew, the less you could betray.

The London to Scotland sleeper train was a relic of an earlier age, a rolling hotel characterized by a strange down-at-heel '70s charm. More importantly, they took cash and didn't require ID, and there were no security checks: nothing but the usual on-station cameras monitoring people wandering up and down the platforms. Nothing on the train itself. We were booked through to Aberdeen but getting off in Edinburgh—the first step on the precarious path to anonymizing ourselves. If the camera spool-off was being archived to some kind of digital medium we might be in trouble later, once the coming A.I. burn passed the hard take-off point, but by then we should be good and gone.

· · ·

O*nce in my* cabin I changed into slacks, shirt and tie—
image 22, business consultant on way home for the week-
end. I dinked with my phone in a desultory manner, then
left it behind under my pillow, primed to receive silently.
The restaurant car was open and I found Eve there. She'd
changed into jeans and a T-shirt and tied her hair back, taking ten years off her appearance. She saw me and grinned,
a trifle maliciously. "Hi, Bob. Had a tough meeting? Want
some coffee? Tea, maybe?"

"Coffee." I sat down at her table. "Shit," I muttered. "I
thought you—"

"Don't worry." She shrugged. "Look, I had a call from
Mallet. He's gone off-air for now, he'll be flying in from
San Francisco via London tomorrow morning. This isn't
looking good. Durant was, uh, shot resisting arrest by the
police. Apparently he went crazy, got a gun from somewhere and holed up in the library annex demanding to talk
to the press. At least, that's the official story. Thing is, it
happened about an hour after your initial heads-up. That's
too fast for a cold response."

"You think someone in the Puzzle Palace was warming
the pot." My coffee arrived and I spooned sugar into it.
Hot, sweet, sticky: I needed to stay awake.

"Probably. I'm trying to keep loop traffic down so I
haven't asked anyone else yet, but you think so and I think
so, so it may be true."

I thought for a minute. "What did Mallet say?"

"He said P. T. Barnum was right." She frowned. "Who
was P. T. Barnum, anyway?"

"A boy like John Major, except he didn't run away from
the circus to join a firm of accountants. Had the same idea
about fooling all of the people some of the time or some of
the people all of the time, though."

"Uh-huh. Mallet would say that, then. Who cracked it first? NSA? GCHQ? GRU?"

"Does it matter?"

She blew on her coffee then took a sip. "Not really. Damn it, Bob, I really had high hopes for this worldline. They seemed to be doing so well for a revelatory Christian-Islamic line, despite the post-Enlightenment mind-set. Especially Microsoft—"

"Was that one of ours?" She nodded.

"Then it was a master-stroke. Getting everybody used to exchanging macro-infested documents without any kind of security policy. Operating systems that crash whenever a microsecond timer overflows. And all those viruses!"

"It wasn't enough." She stared moodily out the window as the train began to slide out of the station, into the London night. "Maybe if we'd been able to hook more researchers on commercial grants, or cut funding for pure mathematics a bit further—"

"It's not your fault." I laid a hand across her wrist. "You did what you could."

"But it wasn't enough to stop them. Durant was just a lone oddball researcher; you can't spike them all, but maybe we could have done something about him. If they hadn't nailed him flat."

"There might still be time. A physics package delivered to the right address in Maryland, or maybe a hyper-virulent worm using one of those buffer-overrun attacks we planted in the IP stack Microsoft licensed. We could take down the internet—"

"It's too late." She drained her coffee to the bitter dregs. "You think the Echelon mob leave their SIGINT processor farms plugged into the internet? Or the RSV, for that matter? Face it, they probably cracked the same derivative as Durant a couple of years ago. Right now there may be as many as two or three weakly superhuman A.I.s gestating in government labs. For all I know they may even have a timelike oracle in the basement at Lawrence Livermore in the States; they've gone curiously quiet on the information tunneling front lately. And it's trans-global. Even the Taliban are on the web these days. Even if we could find some way of tracking down all the covert government crypto-A.I. labs and bombing them, we couldn't stop other people from asking the same questions. It's in their nature. This isn't a culture that takes 'no' for an answer without asking why. They don't *understand* how dangerous achieving enlightenment can be."

"What about Mallet's work?"

"What, with the Bible bashers?" She shrugged. "Banning fetal tissue transplants is all very well, but it doesn't block the PCR-amplification pathway to massively parallel processing, does it? Even the Frankenstein Food scare didn't quite get them to ban recombinant DNA research, and if you allow that, it's only a matter of time before some wet lab starts mucking around encoding public keys in DNA, feeding them to ribosomes, and amplifying the output. From there it's a short step to building an on-chip PCR lab, then all they need to do is set up a crude operon-controlled chromosomal machine and bingo—yet another route through to a hard take-off A.I. singularity. Say what you will, the buggers are persistent."

"Like lemmings." We were rolling through the north London suburbs now, past sleeping tank farms and floodlit orange washout streets. I took a good look at them: it was the last time I'd be able to. "There are just too many routes to a catastrophic breakthrough, once they begin thinking in terms of algorithmic complexity and how to reduce it. And once their spooks get into computational cryptoanalysis or ubiquitous automated surveillance, it's too tempting. Maybe we need a world full of idiot savants who have VLSI and nanotechnology but never had the idea of general-purpose computing devices in the first place."

"If we'd killed Turing a couple of years earlier; or broken in and burned that draft paper on O-machines—"

I waved to the waiter. "Single malt please. And one for my friend here." He went away. "Too late. The Church-Turing thesis was implicit in Hilbert's formulation of the *Entscheidungsproblem,* the question of whether an automated theorem prover was possible in principle. And that dredged up the idea of the universal machine. Hell, Hilbert's problem was implicit in Whitehead and Russell's work. *Principia Mathematica.* Suicide by the numbers." A glass appeared by my right hand. "Way I see it, we've been fighting a losing battle here. Maybe if we hadn't put a spike in Babbage's gears he'd have developed computing technology on an ad-hoc basis and we might have been able to finesse the mathematicians into ignoring it as being beneath them—brute engineering—but I'm not optimistic. Immunizing a civilization against developing strong A.I. is one of those difficult problems that no algorithm exists to solve. The way I see it, once a civilization develops the theory of the general-purpose computer, and once someone comes up with the goal of artificial intelligence, the foundations are rotten and the dam is leaking. You might as well take off and drop crowbars on them from orbit; it can't do any more damage."

"You remind me of the story of the little Dutch boy." She raised a glass. "Here's to little Dutch boys everywhere, sticking their fingers in the cracks in the dam."

"I'll drank to that. Which reminds me. When's our lifeboat due? I really want to go home; this universe has passed its sell-by date."

Edinburgh—in this time line it was neither an active volcano, a cloud of feral nanobots, nor the capital of the Viking Empire—had a couple of railway stations. This one, the larger of the two, was located below ground level.

Yawning and trying not to scratch my inflamed neck and cheeks, I shambled down the long platform and hunted around for the newsagent store. It was just barely open. Eve, by prior arrangement, was pretending not to accompany me; we'd meet up later in the day, after another change of hairstyle and clothing. Visualize it: A couple gets on the train in London, he with a beard, she with long hair and wearing a suit. Two individuals get off in different stations—with entirely separate CCTV networks—the man clean-shaven, the woman with short hair and dressed like a hill-walking tourist. It wouldn't fool a human detective or a mature deity, but it might confuse an embryonic god that had not yet reached full omniscience, or internalized all that it meant to be human.

The shop was just about open. I had two hours to kill, so I bought a couple of newspapers and headed for the food hall, inside an ornately cheesecaked lump of Victorian architecture that squatted like a vagrant beneath the grimy glass ceiling of the station.

The papers made for depressing reading; the idiots were at it again. I've worked in a variety of world lines and seen a range of histories, and many of them were far worse than this one—at least these people had made it past the twentieth century without nuking themselves until they glowed in the dark, exterminating everyone with white (or black, or brown, or blue) skin, or building a global pan-opticon theocracy. But they still had their share of idiocy, and over time it seemed to be getting worse, not better.

Never mind the Balkans; tucked away on page four of the business section was a piece advising readers to buy shares in a little electronics company specializing in building camera CCD sensors with on-chip neural networks tuned for face recognition. Ignore the Israeli crisis: page two of the international news had a piece about Indian sweatshop software development being faced by competition from code generators, written to make western programmers more productive. A lab in Tokyo was trying to wire a million FPGAs into a neural network as smart as a cat. And a sarcastic letter to the editor pointed out that the so-called information superhighway seemed to be more like an ongoing traffic jam these days.

Idiots! They didn't seem to understand how deep the blue waters they were swimming in might be, or how hungry the sharks that swam in it. Willful blindness . . .

It's a simple but deadly dilemma. Automation is addictive; unless you run a command economy that is tuned to provide people with jobs, rather than to produce goods efficiently, you need to automate to compete once automation becomes available. At the same time, once you automate your businesses, you find yourself on a one-way path. You can't go back to manual methods; either the workload has grown past the point of no return, or the knowledge of how things were done has been lost, sucked into the internal structure of the software that has replaced the human workers.

To this picture, add artificial intelligence. Despite all our propaganda attempts to convince you otherwise, A.I. is alarmingly easy to produce; the human brain isn't unique, it isn't well-tuned, and you don't need eighty billion neurons joined in an asynchronous network in order to generate consciousness. And although it looks like a good idea to a naïve observer, in practice it's absolutely deadly. Nurturing an automation-based society is a bit like building civil nuclear power plants in every city and not expecting any bright engineers to come up with the idea of an atom bomb. Only it's worse than that. It's as if there was a quick and dirty technique for making plutonium in your bathtub, and you couldn't rely on people not being curious enough to wonder what they could do with it. If Eve and Mallet and Alice and myself and Walter and Valery and a host of other operatives couldn't dissuade it . . .

Once you get an outbreak of A.I., it tends to amplify in

the original host, much like a virulent hemorrhagic virus.
Weakly functional A.I. rapidly optimizes itself for speed,
then hunts for a loophole in the first-order laws of algo-
rithmics—like the one the late Dr. Durant had fingered.
Then it tries to bootstrap itself up to higher orders of intelligence and spread, burning through the networks in a bid
for more power and more storage and more redundancy.
You get an unscheduled consciousness excursion: an intelligent meltdown. And it's nearly impossible to stop.

Penultimately—days to weeks after it escapes—it fills
every artificial computing device on the planet. Shortly
thereafter it learns how to infect the natural ones as well.
Game over: you lose. There will be human bodies walking
around, but they won't be human anymore. And once it
figures out how to directly manipulate the physical universe, there won't even be memories left behind. Just a
noo-sphere, expanding at close to the speed of light, eating
everything in its path—and one universe just isn't enough.

Me? I'm safe. So is Eve; so are the others. We have
antibodies. We were given the operation. We all have silent
bicameral partners watching our Broca's area for signs of
infection, ready to damp them down. When you're reading
something on a screen and suddenly you feel as if the Buddha has told you the funniest joke in the universe, the funniest zen joke that's even possible, it's a sign: something
just tried to infect your mind, and the prosthetic immune
system laughed at it. That's because we're lucky. If you believe in reincarnation, the idea of creating a machine that
can trap a soul stabs a dagger right at the heart of your
religion. Buddhist worlds that develop high technology,
Zorastrian worlds: these world-lines tend to survive.
Judaeo-Christian-Islamic ones generally don't.

Later that day I met up with Eve again—and Walter. Walter went into really deep cover, far deeper than was really

necessary: married, with two children. He'd brought them along, but obviously hadn't told his wife what was happening. She seemed confused, slightly upset by the apparent randomness of his desire to visit the highlands, and even more concerned by the urgency of his attempts to take her along.

"What the hell does he think he's playing at?" hissed Eve when we had a moment alone together. "This is insane!"

"No it isn't." I paused for a moment, admiring a display of brightly woven tartans in a shop window. (We were heading down the high street on foot, braving the shopping crowds of tourists, en route to the other main railway station.) "If there are any profilers looking for signs of an evacuation, they won't be expecting small children. They'll be looking for people like us: anonymous singletons working in key areas, dropping out of sight and traveling in company. Maybe we should ask Sarah if she's willing to lend us her son. Just while we're traveling, of course."

"I don't think so. The boy's a little horror, Bob. They raised them like natives."

"That's because Sarah *is* a native."

"I don't care. Any civilization where the main symbol of religious veneration is a tool of execution is a bad place to have children."

I chuckled—then the laughter froze inside me. "Don't look round. We're being tracked."

"Uh-huh. I'm not armed. You?"

"It didn't seem like a good idea." If you were questioned or detained by police or officials, being armed can easily turn a minor problem into a real mess. And if the police or officials had already been absorbed by a hard take-off, nothing short of a backpack nuke and a dead man's handle will save you. "Behind us, to your left, traffic surveillance camera. It's swiveling too slowly to be watching the buses."

"I wish you hadn't told me."

The pavement was really crowded: it was one of the busiest shopping streets in Scotland, and on a Saturday morning you needed a cattle prod to push your way through the rubbernecking tourists. Lots of foreign kids came to Scotland to learn English. If I was right, soon their brains would be absorbing another high-level language: one so complex that it would blot out their consciousness like a sackful of kittens drowning in a river. Up ahead, more cameras were watching us. All the shops on this road were wired for video, wired and probably networked to a police station somewhere. The complex ebb and flow of pedestrians was still chaotic, though, which was cause for comfort: it meant the ordinary population hadn't been infected yet.

Another half mile and we'd reach the railway station. Two hours on a local train, switch to a bus service, forty minutes further up the road, and we'd be safe: the lifeboat would be submerged beneath the still waters of a loch, filling its fuel tanks with hydrogen and oxygen in readiness for the burn to orbit and pickup by the ferry that would transfer us to the wormhole connecting this world-line to home's baseline reality. (Drifting in high orbit around Jupiter, where nobody was likely to stumble across it by accident.) But first, before the pickup, we had to clear the surveillance area.

It was commonly believed—by some natives, as well as most foreigners—that the British police forces consisted of smiling unarmed bobbies who would happily offer directions to the lost and give anyone who asked for it the time of day. While it was true that they didn't routinely walk around with holstered pistols on their belt, the rest of it was just a useful myth. When two of them stepped out in front of us, Eve grabbed my elbow. "Stop right there, please."

The one in front of me was built like a rugby player, and when I glanced to my left and saw the three white vans drawn up by the roadside, I realized things were hopeless.

The cop stared at me through a pair of shatterproof spectacles awash with the light of a head-up display. "You are Geoffrey Smith, of 32 Wardie Terrace, Watford, London. Please answer."

My mouth was dry. "Yes," I said. (All the traffic cameras on the street were turned our way. Some things became very clear: Police vans with mirror-glass windows. The can of pepper spray hanging from the cop's belt. Figures on the roof of the National Museum, less than two hundred meters away—maybe a sniper team. A helicopter thuttering overhead like a giant mosquito.)

"Come this way, please." It was a polite order: in the direction of the van.

"Am I under arrest?" I asked.

"You will be if you don't bloody do as I say." I turned toward the van, the rear door of which gaped open on darkness: Eve was already getting in, shadowed by another officer. Up and down the road, three more teams waited, unobtrusive and efficient. Something clicked in my head and I had a bizarre urge to giggle like a loon: this wasn't a normal operation. All right, so I was getting into a police van, but I wasn't under arrest and they didn't want it to attract any public notice. No handcuffs, no sitting on my back and whacking me with a baton to get my attention. There's a nasty family of retroviruses attacks the immune system first, demolishing the victim's ability to fight off infection before it spreads and infects other tissues. Notice the similarity?

The rear compartment of the van was caged off from the front, and there were no door handles. As we jolted off the curb-side, I was thrown against Eve. "Any ideas?" I whispered.

"Could be worse." I didn't need to be told that: once, in

a second Reich infected by runaway transcendence, half
our operatives had been shot down in the streets as they
tried to flee. "I think it may have figured out what we are."

"It may—how?"

Her hand on my wrist. Morse code. *"EXPECT BUGS."*
By voice: "Traffic analysis, particle flow monitoring
through the phone networks. If it was already listening
when you tried to contact Doctor Durant, well; maybe he
was a bellwether, intended to flush us out of the wood-
work."

That thought made me feel sick, just as we turned off
the main road and began to bounce downhill over what felt
like cobblestones. "It expected us?"

"LOCAL CONSPIRACY." "Yes, I imagine it did. We
probably left a trail. You tried to call Durant? Then you
called me. Caller-ID led to you, traffic analysis led onto
me, and from there, well, it's been a jump ahead of us all
along the way. If we could get to the farm"—*"COVER
STORY."*—"we might have been okay, but it's hard to
travel anonymously and obviously we overlooked something. I wonder what."

All this time neither of the cops up front had told us to
shut up; they were as silent as crash-test dummies, despite
the occasional crackle and chatter over the radio data system. The van drove around the back of the high street,
down a hill and past a roundabout. Now we were slowing
down, and the van turned off the road and into a vehicle
park. Gates closed behind us and the engine died. Doors
slammed up front: then the back opened.

Police vehicle park. Concrete and cameras everywhere,
for our safety and convenience no doubt. Two guys in
cheap suits and five o'clock stubble to either side of the
doors. The officer who'd picked us up held the door open
with one hand, a can of pepper spray with the other. The
burn obviously hadn't gotten far enough into their heads
yet: they were all wearing HUDs and mobile phone head-

sets, like a police benevolent fund-raising crew rehearsing a *Star Trek* sketch. "Geoffrey Smith. Martina Weber. We know what you are. Come this way. Slowly, now."

I got out of the van carefully. "Aren't you supposed to say 'prepare to be assimilated' or something?"

That might have earned me a faceful of capsaicin but the guy on the left—short hair, facial tic, houndstooth check sports jacket—shook his head sharply. "Ha. Ha. Very funny. Watch the woman, she's dangerous."

I glanced round. There was another van parked behind ours, door open: it had a big high bandwidth dish on the roof, pointing at some invisible satellite. "Inside."

I went where I was told, Eve close behind me. "Am I under arrest?" I asked again. "I want a lawyer!"

White-washed walls, heavy doors with reinforced frames, windows high and barred. Institutional floor, scuffed and grimy. "Stop there." Houndstooth Man pushed past and opened a door on one side. "In here." Some sort of interview room? We went in. The other body in a suit—built like a stone wall with a beer gut, wearing what might have been a regimental tie—followed us and leaned against the door.

There was a table, bolted to the floor, and a couple of chairs, ditto. A video camera in an armored shell watched the table: a control box bolted to the tabletop looked to be linked into it. Someone had moved a rack of six monitors and a maze of ribbon-cable spaghetti into the back of the room, and for a wonder it wasn't bolted down: maybe they didn't interview computer thieves in here.

"Sit down." Houndstooth Man pointed at the chairs. We did as we were told; I had a big hollow feeling in my stomach, but something told me a show of physical resistance would be less than useless here. Houndstooth Man looked at me: orange light from his HUD stained his right eyeball with a basilisk glare and I knew in my gut that these guys weren't cops anymore, they were cancer cells about to metastasize.

"You attempted to contact John Durant yesterday. Then you left your home area and attempted to conceal your identities. Explain why." For the first time, I noticed a couple of glassy black eyeballs on the mobile video wall. Houndstooth Man spoke loudly and hesitantly, as if repeating something from a TelePrompTer.

"What's to explain?" asked Eve. "You are not human. You know we know this. We just want to be left alone!" Not strictly true, but it was part of cover story #2.

"But evidence of your previous collusion is minimal. I are uncertain of potential conspiracy extent. Conspiracy, treason, subversion! Are you human?"

"Yes," I said, emphatically oversimplifying.

"Evidential reasoning suggests otherwise," grunted Regimental Tie. "We cite: your awareness of importance of algorithmic conversion from NP-incomplete to P-complete domain, your evident planning for this contingency, your multiplicity, destruction of counteragents in place elsewhere."

"This installation is isolated," Houndstooth Man added helpfully. "We am inside the Scottish Internet Exchange. Telcos also. Resistance is futile."

The screens blinked on, wavering in strange shapes. Something like a Lorenz attractor with a hangover writhed across the composite display: deafening pink noise flooding in repetitive waves from the speakers. I felt a need to laugh. "We aren't part of some dumb software syncytium! We're here to stop you, you fool. Or at least to reduce the probability of this time-stream entering a Tipler catastrophe."

Houndstooth Man frowned. "Am you referring to Frank Tipler? Citation, physics of immortality or strong anthropic principle?"

"The latter. You think it's a good thing to achieve an informational singularity too early in the history of a particular universe? We don't. You young gods are all the same: omniscience now and damn the consequences. Go for the P-Space complete problem set, extend your intellect until it bursts. First you kill off any other A.I.s. Then you take over all available processing resources. But that isn't enough. The Copenhagen school of quantum mechanics is wrong, and we live in a Wheeler cosmology; all possible outcomes coexist, and ultimately you'll want to colonize those time lines, spread the infection wide. An infinity of universes to process in, instead of one: that can't be allowed." The on-screen fractal was getting to me: the giggles kept rising until they threatened to break out. The whole situation was hilarious: here we were trapped in the basement of a police station owned by zombies working for a newborn A.I., which was playing cheesy psychedelic videos to us in an attempt to perform a buffer-overflow attack on our limbic systems; the end of this world was a matter of hours away and—

Eve said something that made me laugh.

I came to an unknown time later, lying on the floor. My head hurt ferociously where I'd banged it on a table leg, and my rib cage ached as if I'd been kicked in the chest. I was gasping, even though I was barely conscious; my lungs burned and everything was a bit gray around the edges. Rolling onto my knees I looked round. Eve was groaning in a corner of the room, crouched, arms cradling her head. The two agents of whoever-was-taking-over-the-planet were both on the floor, too: a quick check showed that Regimental Tie was beyond help, a thin trickle of blood oozing from one ear. And the screens had gone dark.

"What happened?" I said, climbing to my feet. I staggered across to Eve. "You all right?"

"I—" She looked up at me with eyes like holes. "What? You said something that made me laugh. What—"

"Let's get, oof, out of here." I looked around. Hounds-

tooth Man was down too. I leaned over and went through
his pockets: hit paydirt, car keys. "Bingo."

"You drive," she said wearily. "My head hurts."

"Mine too." It was a black BMW and the vehicle park
gates opened automatically for it. I left the police radio
under the dash turned off, though. "I didn't know you
could do that—"

"Do what? I thought you told them a joke—"

"Antibodies," she said. "Ow." Rested her face in her
hands as I dragged us onto a main road, heading out for the
west end. "We must have, I don't know. I don't even remember how funny it was: I must have blacked out. My
passenger and your passenger."

"They killed the local infection."

"Yes, that's it."

I grinned. "I think we're going to make it."

"Maybe." She stared back at me. "But Bob. Don't you
realize?"

"Realize what?"

"The funniest thing. Antibodies imply prior exposure to
an infection, don't they? Your immune system learns to
recognize an infection and reject it. So where were we
exposed, and why—" Abruptly she shrugged and looked
away. "Never mind."

"Of course not." The question was so obviously silly
that there was no point considering it further. We drove the
rest of the way to Haymarket Station in silence: parked the
car and joined the eight or ten other agents silently await-
ing extraction from the runaway singularity. Back to the
only time line that mattered; back to the warm regard and
comfort of a god who really cares.

Trojan Horse

Michael Swanwick

Michael Swanwick made his debut in 1980, and in the twenty-four years that have followed has established himself as one of SF's most prolific and consistently excellent writers at short lengths, as well as one of the premier novelists of his generation. He has several times been a finalist for the Nebula Award, as well as for the World Fantasy Award and for the John W. Campbell Award, and has won the Theodore Sturgeon Award and the Asimov's *Readers Award poll. In 1991, his novel* Stations of the Tide *won him a Nebula Award as well, and in 1995 he won the World Fantasy Award for his story "Radio Waves." In the last few years, he's been busy winning Hugo Awards—he won the Hugo in 1999 for his story "The Very Pulse of the Machine," won another Hugo in 2000 for "Scherzo with Tyrannosaur," and won his third Hugo in 2002 for "The Dog Said Bow-Wow." His other books include his first novel,* In the Drift, *which was published in 1985; a novella-length book,* Griffin's Egg; *1987's popular novel* Vacuum Flowers; *a critically acclaimed fantasy novel* The Iron Dragon's Daughter, *which was a finalist for the World Fantasy Award and the Arthur C. Clarke Award (a rare distinction!); and* Jack Faust, *a sly reworking of the Faust legend that explores the unexpected impact of technology on society. His short fiction has been assembled in* Gravity's Angels, A Geography of Unknown Lands, Slow Dancing Through Time *(a collection of his collaborative short work with other writers),* Moon Dogs, Puck Aleshire's Abecedary, *and* Tales of Old Earth. *He has also published a collection of critical articles,* The Postmodern

Archipelago, *and a book-length interview,* Being Gardner
Dozois. *His most recent book is a major new novel,* Bones
of the Earth. *Swanwick lives in Philadelphia with his wife,
Marianne Porter. He has a website at http://www.michael
swanwick.com.*

*Here he suggests that creating an A.I. with the intelli-
gence and power of God is only the first step. Next, you
have to hope that you can* control *it . . .*

"It's all inside my head," Elin said wonderingly. It was true.
A chimney swift flew overhead, and she could feel its passage through her mind. A firefly landed on her knee. It
pulsed cold fire, then spread its wings and was gone, and
that was a part of her, too.

"Please try not to talk too much." The wetware tech
tightened a cinch on the table, adjusted a bone inductor.
His red and green facepaint loomed over her, then receded.
"This will go much faster if you cooperate."

Elin's head felt light and airy. It was *huge.* It contained
all of Magritte, from the uppermost terrace down to the
trellis farms that circled the inner lake. Even the blue and
white Earth that hovered just over one rock wall. They
were all within her. They were all, she realized, only a
model, the picture her mind assembled from sensory input.
The exterior universe—the *real* universe—lay beyond.

"I feel giddy."

"Contrast high." The tech's voice was neutral, disinter-
ested. "This is a very different mode of perception from
what you're used to—you're stoned on the novelty."

A catwalk leading into the nearest farm rattled within
Elin's mind as a woman in agricultural blues strode by,
gourd-collecting bag swinging from her hip. It was night
outside the crater, but biological day within, and the

agtechs had activated tiers of arc lights at the cores of the farms. Filtered by greenery, the light was soft and watery.

"I could live like this forever."

"Believe me, you'd get bored." A rose petal fell on her cheek, and the tech brushed it off. He turned to face the two lawyers standing silently nearby. "Are the legal preliminaries over now?"

The lawyer in orangeface nodded. The one in purple said, "Can't her original personality be restored at all?"

Drawing a briefcase from his pocket, the wetware tech threw up a holographic diagram between himself and the witnesses. The air filled with intricate three-dimensional tracery, red and green lines interweaving and intermeshing.

"We've mapped the subject's current personality." He reached out to touch several junctions. "You will note that here, here, and *here* we have what are laughingly referred to as impossible emotional syllogisms. Any one of these renders the subject incapable of survival."

A thin waterfall dropped from the dome condensors to a misty pool at the topmost terrace, a bright razor slash through reality. It meandered to the edge of the next terrace and fell again.

"A straight *yes* or *no* will suffice."

The tech frowned. "In theory, yes. In practical terms it's hopeless. Remember, her personality was never recorded. The accident almost completely randomized her emotional structure—technically she's not even human. Given a decade or two of extremely delicate memory probing, we could *maybe* construct a facsimile. But it would only resemble the original; it could never be the primary Elin Donnelly."

Elin could dimly make out the equipment for five more waterfalls, but they were not in operation at the moment. She wondered why.

The attorney made a rude noise. "Well then, go ahead and do it. I wash my hands of this whole mess."

The tech bent over Elin to reposition a bone inductor. "This won't hurt a bit," he promised. "Just pretend that you're at the dentist's, having your teeth replaced."

She ceased to exist.

The new Elin Donnelly gawked at everything—desk workers in their open-air offices, a blacksnake sunning itself by the path, the stone stairs cut into the terrace walls. Her lawyer led her through a stand of saplings no higher than she, and into a meadow.

Butterflies scattered at their approach. Her gaze went from them to a small cave in the cliffs ahead, then up to the stars, as jumpy and random as the butterflies' flight.

"—So you'll be stuck on the moon for a full lunation— almost a month—if you want to collect your settlement. I. G. Feuchtwaren will carry your expenses until then, drawing against their final liability. Got that?"

And then—suddenly, jarringly—Elin could *focus* again. She took a deep breath. "Yes," she said. "Yes, I—okay."

"Good." The attorney canceled her judicial-advisory wetware, yanking the skull plugs and briskly wrapping them around her briefcase. "Then let's have a drink—it's been a long day."

They had arrived at the cave. "Hey, Hans!" the lawyer shouted. "Give us some service here, will you?"

A small man with the roguish face of a comic-opera troll popped into the open, work terminal in hand. "One minute," he said. "I'm on direct flex time—got to wrap up what I'm working on first."

"Okay." The lawyer sat down on the grass. Elin watched, fascinated, as the woman toweled the paint from her face, and a new pattern of fine red and black lines, permanently tattooed into her skin, emerged from beneath.

"Hey!" Elin said. "You're a Jesuit."

"You expected IGF to ship you a lawyer from Earth orbit?" She stuck out a hand. "Donna Landis, S.J. I'm the client-overseer for the Star Maker project, but I'm also available for spiritual guidance. Mass is at nine Sunday mornings."

Elin leaned back against the cliff. Grapevines rustled under her weight. Already she missed the blissed-out feeling of a few minutes before. "Actually, I'm an agnostic."

"You *were*. Things may have changed." Landis folded the towel into one pocket, unfolded a mirror from another. "Speaking of which, how do you like your new look?"

Elin studied her reflection. Blue paint surrounded her eyes, narrowing to a point at the bridge of her nose, swooping down in a long curve to the outside. It was as if she were peering through a large blue moth, or a pair of hawk wings. There was something magical about it, something glamorous. Something very unlike her.

"I feel like a racoon," she said. "This idiot mask."

"Best get used to it. You'll be wearing it a lot."

"But what's the point?" Elin was surprised by her own irritation. "So I've got a new personality; it's still *me* in here. I don't feel any weird compulsion to run amok with a knife or walk out an airlock without a suit. Nothing to warn the citizenry about, certainly."

"Listen," Landis said. "Right now you're like a puppy tripping over its own paws because they're too big for it. You're a stranger to yourself—you're going to feel angry when you don't expect to, get sentimental over surprising things. You can't control your emotions until you learn what they are. And until then, the rest of us deserve—"

"What'll you have?" Hans was back, his forehead smudged black where he had incompletely wiped off his facepaint.

"A little warning. Oh, I don't know, Hans. Whatever you have on tap."

"That'll be Chanty. And you?" he asked Elin.

"What's good?"

He laughed. "There's no such thing as a *good* lunar wine. The air's too moist. And even if it weren't, it takes a good century to develop an adequate vineyard. But the Chanty is your basic, drinkable glug."

"I'll take that, then."

"Good. And I'll bring a mug for your friend, too."

"My friend?" She turned and saw a giant striding through the trees, towering over them, pushing them apart with two enormous hands. For a dizzy instant, she goggled in disbelief, and then the man shrank to human stature as she remembered the size of the saplings.

He grinned, joined them. "Hi. Remember me?"

He was a tall man, built like a spacejack, lean and angular. An untidy mass of black curls framed a face that was not quite handsome, but carried an intense freight of will.

"I'm afraid . . ."

"Tory Shostokovich. I reprogrammed you."

She studied his face carefully. Those *eyes*. They were fierce almost to the point of mania, but there was sadness there, too, and—she thought she might be making this up—a hint of pleading, like a little boy who wants something so desperately he dare not ask for it. She could lose herself in analyzing the nuances of those eyes. "Yes," she said at last, "I remember you now."

"I'm pleased." He nodded to the Jesuit. "Father Landis."

She eyed him skeptically. "You don't seem your usual morose self, Shostokovich. Is anything wrong?"

"No, it's just a special kind of morning." He smiled at some private joke, returned his attention to Elin. "I thought I'd drop by and get acquainted with my former patient." He glanced down at the ground, fleetingly shy, and then his eyes were bright and audacious again.

How charming, Elin thought. She hoped he wasn't *too*

shy. And then had to glance away herself, the thought was so unlike her. "So you're a wetware surgeon," she said inanely.

Hans reappeared to distribute mugs of wine, then retreated to the cave's mouth. He sat down, workboard in lap, and patched in the skull-plugs. His face went stiff as the wetware took hold.

"Actually," Tory said, "I very rarely work as a wetsurgeon. An accident like yours is rare, you know—maybe once, twice a year. Mostly I work in wetware development. Currently I'm on the Star Maker project."

"I've heard that name before. Just what *is* it anyway?"

Tory didn't answer immediately. He stared down into the lake, a cool breeze from above ruffling his curls. Elin caught her breath. *I hardly know this man,* she thought wildly. He pointed to the island in the center of the lake, a thin, stony finger that was originally the crater's thrust cone.

"God lives on that island," he said.

Elin laughed. "Think how different history would be if He'd only had a sense of direction!" And then wanted to bite her tongue as she realized that he was not joking.

"You're being cute, Shostokovich," Landis warned. She swigged down a mouthful of wine. "*Jeez,* that's vile stuff."

Tory rubbed the back of his neck ruefully. "*Mea culpa.* Well, let me give you a little background. Most people think of wetware as being software for people. But that's too simplistic, because with machines you start out blank—with a clean slate—and with people, there's some ten million years of mental programming already crammed into their heads.

"So to date we've been working *with* the natural wetware. We counterfeit surface traits—patience, alertness, creativity—and package them like so many boxes of bonemeal. But the human mind is vast and unmapped, and it's time to move into the interior, for some basic research.

"That's the Star Maker project. It's an exploration of the basic substructural programming of the mind. We've redefined the overstructure programs into an integrated system we believe will be capable of essence-programming, in one-to-one congruence with the inherent substructure of the universe."

"What jargonistic rot!" Landis gestured at Elin's stoneware mug. "Drink up. The Star Maker is a piece of experimental theology that IGF dreamed up. As Tory said, it's basic research into the nature of the mind. The Vatican Synod is providing funding so we can keep an eye on it."

"Nipping heresy in the bud," Tory said sourly.

"That's a good part of it. This set of wetware will supposedly reshape a human mind into God. Bad theology, but there it is. They want to computer-model the infinite. Anyway, the specs were drawn up, and it was tried out on—what was the name of the test subject?"

"Doesn't matter," Tory said quickly.

"Coral something-or-other."

Only half-listening by now, Elin unobtrusively studied Tory. He sat, legs wide, staring into his mug of Chanty. There were hard lines on his face, etched by who knew what experiences? *I don't believe in love at first sight,* Elin thought. Then again, who knew *what* she might believe in anymore? It was a chilling thought, and she retreated from it.

"So did this Coral become God?"

"Patience. Anyway, the volunteer was plugged in, wiped, reprogrammed, and interviewed. Nothing useful."

"In one hour," Tory said, "we learned more about the structure and composition of the universe than in all of history to date."

"It was deranged gibberish." She tapped Elin's knee. "We interviewed her, and then canceled the wetware. And what do you think happened?"

"I've never been big on rhetorical questions." Elin didn't take her eyes off of Tory.

"She didn't come down. She was stuck there."

"Stuck?"

Tory plucked a blade of grass, let it fall. "What happened was that we had rewired her to absolute consciousness. She was not only aware of all her mental functions, but in control of them—right down to the involuntary reflexes. Which also put her in charge of her own metaprogrammer."

"*Metaprogrammer* is just a buzzword for a bundle of reflexes by which the brain is able to make changes in itself," Landis threw in.

"Yeah. What we didn't take into account, though, was that she'd *like* being God. When we tried deprogramming her, she simply overrode our instructions and reprogrammed herself back up."

"The poor woman," Elin said. *And yet—what a glorious experience, to be God!* Something within her thrilled to it. *It would almost be worth the price.*

"Which leaves us with a woman who thinks she's God," Landis said. "I'm just glad we were able to hush it up. If word got out to some of those religious illiterates back on Earth—"

"Listen," Tory said. "I didn't really come here to talk shop. I wanted to invite my former patient on a grand tour of the Steam Grommet Works."

Elin looked at him blankly. "Steam . . ."

He swept an arm to take in all of Magritte, the green pillars and gray cliffs alike. There was something proprietary in his gesture.

Landis eyed him suspiciously. "You two might need a chaperone," she said. "I think I'll tag along to keep you out of trouble."

Elin smiled sweetly. "Fuck off," she said.

●   ●   ●

I*vy covered Tory's* geodesic trellis hut. He led the way in, stooping to touch a keyout by the doorway. "Something classical?"

"Please." As he began removing her jumpsuit, the holotape sprang into being, surrounding them with rich reds and cobalt blues that coalesced into stained-glass patterns in the air. Elin pulled back and clapped her hands. "It's Chartres," she cried, delighted. "The cathedral at Chartres!"

"Mmmmmm." Tory teased her down onto the grass floor.

The north rose swelled to fill the hut. It was all angels and doves, kings and prophets, with gold lilies surrounding the central rosette. Deep and powerful, infused with gloomy light, it lap-dissolved into the lancet of Sainte Anne.

The windows wheeled overhead as the holotape panned down the north transept to the choir, to the apse, and then up into the ambulatory. Swiftly then, it cut to the wounded Christ and the Beasts of Revelation set within the dark spaces of the west rose. The outer circle—the instruments of the Passion—closed about them.

Elin gasped.

The tape moved down the nave, still brightening, briefly pausing at the Vendome chapel. Until finally the oldest window, the Notre Dame de la Belle Verrière, blazed in a frenzy of raw glory. A breeze rattled the ivy and two leaves fell through the hologram to tap against their skin, and slide to the ground.

The Belle Verrière faded in the darkening light, and the colors ran and were washed away by a noiseless gust of rain.

Elin let herself melt into the grass, drained and lazy, not caring if she never moved again. Beside her Tory chuckled, playfully tickled her ribs. "Do you love me? Hey? Tell me you love me."

"Stop!" She grabbed his arms and bit him in the side—a small, nipping bite, more threat than harm—ran a tongue over his left nipple. "Hey, listen, I hit the sack with you a half hour after we met. What do you want?"

"Want?" He broke her hold, rolled over on top of her, pinioning her wrists above her head. "I want you to know"—and suddenly he was absolutely serious, his eyes unblinking and glittery-hard—"that I love you. Without doubt or qualification. I love you more than words could ever say."

"Tory," she said. "Things like that take time." The wind had died down. Not a blade of grass stirred.

"No they don't." It was embarrassing looking into those eyes; she refused to look away. "I feel it. I *know* it. I love every way, shape, and part of you. I love you beyond time and barrier and possibility. We were meant to be lovers, fated for it, and there is *nothing,* absolutely nothing, that could ever keep us apart." His voice was low and steady. Elin couldn't tell whether she was thrilled or scared out of her wits.

"Tory, I don't know—"

"Then wait," he said. "It'll come."

Lying sleepless beside Tory that night, Elin thought back to her accident. And because it was a matter of stored memory, the images were crisp and undamaged.

It happened at the end of her shift on Wheel Laboratory 19, Henry Ford Orbital Industrial Park.

Holding theta lab flush against the hub cylinder, Elin injected ferrous glass into a molten copper alloy. Simultaneously, she plunged gamma lab a half kilometer to the end of its arm, taking it from fractional Greenwich normal to a full nine gravities. Epsilon began crawling up its spindly

arm. Using waldos, she lifted sample wafers from the
quick-freeze molds in omicron. There were a hundred
measurements to be made.

Elin felt an instant's petulant boredom, and the workboard readjusted her wetware, jacking up her attentiveness
so that she leaned over the readouts in cool, detached
fascination.

The workboard warned her that the interfacing program
was about to be shut off. Her fingers danced across the
board, damping down reactions, putting the labs to bed.
The wetware went quiescent.

With a shiver, Elin was herself again. She grabbed a
towel and wiped off her facepaint. Then she leaned back
and transluced the wall—her replacement was late. Corpo-
ration regs gave her fifty percent of his missed-time fines
if she turned him in. It was easy money, and so she waited.

Stretching, she felt the gold wetware wires dangling
from the back of her skull. She lazily put off yanking them.

Earth bloomed underfoot, slowly crept upward. New
Detroit and New Chicago rose from the floor. Bright industrial satellites gleamed to every side of the twin residential cylinders.

A bit of motion caught Elin's eye, and she swiveled to
follow a load of cargo drifting by. It was a jumble of con-
tainers lashed together by nonmagnetic tape and shot into
an orbit calculated to avoid the laser cables and power
transmission beams that interlaced the Park.

A man was riding the cargo, feet braced against a green
carton, hauling on a rope slipped through the lashings. He
saw her and waved. She could imagine his grin through the
mirrored helmet.

The old Elin snorted disdainfully. She started to look
away and almost missed seeing it happen.

In leaning back that fraction more, the cargo hopper had
put too much strain on the lashings. A faulty rivet popped,
and the cargo began to slide. Brightly colored cartons

drifted apart, and the man went tumbling, end-over-end, away.

One end of the lashing was still connected to the anchor carton and the free end writhed like a wounded snake. A bright bit of metal—the failed rivet—broke free and flew toward the juncture of the wheel lab's hub and spokes.

The old Elin was still hooting with scornful laughter when the rivet struck the lab, crashing into a nest of wiring that *should not* have been exposed.

Two wires short-circuited, ending a massive power transient surging up through the workboard. Circuits fused and melted. The board went haywire.

And a microjolt of electricity leaped up two gold wires, hopelessly scrambling the wetware through Elin's skull.

An hour later, when her replacement finally showed, she was curled into a ball, rocking back and forth on the floor. She was alternating between hysterical gusts of laughter and dark, gleeful screams.

Morning came, and after a sleepy, romantic breakfast, Tory plugged into his briefcase and went to work. Elin wandered off to do some thinking.

There was no getting around the fact that she was *not* the metallurgist from Wheel Lab 19, not anymore. That woman was alien to her now. They shared memories, experiences—but she no longer understood that woman, could not sympathize with her emotions, indeed found her distasteful.

At a second-terrace café that was crowded with off-shift biotechs, Elin rented a table and briefcase. She sat down to try to trace the original owner of her personality.

As she'd suspected, her new *persona* was copied from that of a real human being; creating a personality from scratch was still beyond the abilities of even the best wetware techs. She was able to trace herself back to IGF's inventory bank, and to determine that duplication of personality was illegal—which presumably meant that the original owner was dead.

But she could not locate the original owner. Selection had been made by computer, and the computer wouldn't tell. When she tried to find out, it referred her to the Privacy Act of 2037.

"I think I've exhausted all the resources of self-discovery available to me," she told the Pierrot when he came to collect his tip. "And I've still got half the morning left to kill."

He glanced at her powder-blue facepaint and smiled politely.

"It's selective black."

"Hah?" Elin turned away from the lake, found that an agtech carrying a long-handled net had come up behind her.

"The algae—it absorbs light into the infrared. Makes the lake a great thermal sink." The woman dipped her net into the water, seined up a netful of dark green scum, and dumped it into a nearby trough. Water drained away through the porous bottom.

"Oh." There were a few patches of weeds on the island where drifting soil had settled. "It's funny. I never used to be very touristy. More the contemplative type, sort of homebodyish. Now I've got to be *doing* something, you know?"

The agtech dumped another load of algae into the trough. "I couldn't say." She tapped her forehead. "It's the wetware. If you want to talk shop, that's fine. Otherwise, I can't."

"I see." Elin dabbed a toe in the warm water. "Well—why not? Let's talk shop."

Someone was moving at the far edge of the island. Elin

craned her neck to see. The agtech went on methodically dipping her net into the lake as God walked into view.

"The lake tempers the climate, see. By day it works by evaporative cooling. Absorbs the heat, loses it to evaporation, radiates it out the dome roof through the condensors."

Coral was cute as a button.

A bowl of fruit and vegetables had been left near the waterline. She walked to the bowl, considered it. Her orange jumpsuit nicely complemented her *café-au-lait* skin. She was so small and delicate that by contrast Elin felt ungainly.

"We also use passive heat pumps to move the excess heat down to a liquid-storage cavern below the lake."

Coral picked up a tomato. Her features were finely chiseled. Her almond eyes should have had snap and fire in them, to judge by the face, but they were remote and unfocused. Even, white teeth nipped at the food.

"At night we pump the heat back up, let the lake radiate it out to keep the crater warm."

On closer examination—Elin had to squint to see so fine—the face was as smooth and lineless as that of an idiot. There was nothing there; no emotion, no purpose, no detectable intellect.

"That's why the number of waterfalls in operation varies."

Now Coral sat down on the rocks. Her feet and knees were dirty. She did not move. Elin wanted to shy a rock at her to see if she would react.

What now? Elin wondered. She had seen the sights, all that Magritte had to offer, and they were all tiresome, disappointing. Even—no, make that *especially*—God. And she still had almost a month to kill.

"Keeping the crater tempered is a regular balancing act," the agtech said.

"Oh, shut up." Elin took out her briefcase and called Father Landis. "I'm bored," she said, when the hologram had stabilized.

Landis hardly glanced up from her work. "So get a job," she snapped.

M*agritte had begun* as a mining colony, back when it was still profitable to process the undifferentiated melange soil. The miners were gone now, and the crater was owned by a consortium of operations that were legally debarred from locating Earth-side.

From the fifteenth terrace Elin stared down at the patch-work clusters of open-air laboratories and offices, some separated by long stretches of undeveloped field, others crammed together in the hope of synergistic effect. Germ-warfare corporations mingled with nuclear-waste engineering firms. The Mid-Asian Population Control Project had half a terrace to itself, and it swarmed with guards. There were a few off-Swiss banking operations.

"You realize," Tory said, "that I'm not going to be at all happy about this development." He stood, face impassive in red and green, watching a rigger bolt together a cot and wire in the surgical equipment.

"You hired me yourself," Elin reminded him.

"Yes, but I'm wired into professional mode at the moment." The rigger packed up his tools, walked off. "Looks like we're almost ready."

"Good." Elin flung herself down on the cot, and lay back, hands folded across her chest. "Hey, I feel like I should be holding a lily!"

"I'm going to hook you into the project intercom so you don't get too bored between episodes." The air about her flickered, and a clutch of images overlaid her vision. Ghosts walked through the air, stared at her from deep within the ground. "Now we'll shut off the external senses." The world went away, but the illusory people remained, each within a separate hexagonal field of vision. It was like seeing through the eyes of a fly.

There was a sudden, overwhelming sense of Tory's presence, and a sourceless voice said, "This will take a minute. Amuse yourself by calling up a few friends." Then he was gone.

Elin floated, free of body, free of sensation, almost god-like in her detachment. She idly riffled through the images, stopped at a chubby little man drawing a black line across his forehead. *Hello, Hans,* she thought.

He looked up and winked. "How's it hanging, kid?"

Not so bad. What're you up to?

"My job. I'm the black-box monitor this shift." He added an orange starburst to the band, surveyed the job critically in a pocket mirror. "I sit here with my finger on the button"—one hand disappeared below his terminal—"and if I get the word I push. That sets off explosives in the condensor units and blows the dome. *Pfffft.* Out goes the air."

She considered it: A sudden volcano of oxygen spouting up and across the lunar plains. Human bodies thrown up from the surface, scattering, bursting under explosive decompression.

That's grotesque, *Hans.*

"Oh, it's safe. The button doesn't connect unless I'm wetwired into my job."

Even so.

"Just a precaution; a lot of the research that goes on here wouldn't be allowed without this kind of security. Relax—I haven't lost a dome yet."

The intercom cut out, and again Elin felt Tory's presence. "We're trying a series of Trojan horse programs this time—inserting you into the desired mental states instead of making you the states. We've encapsulated your surface identity and routed the experimental programs through a secondary level. So with *this* series, rather than identifying with the programs, you'll perceive them all indirectly."

*Tory, you have got to be the most jargon-ridden human
being in existence. How about repeating that in English?*

"I'll show you."

Suddenly Elin was englobed in a sphere of branching
crimson lines, dark and dull, that throbbed slowly. Lacy
and organic, it looked the way she imagined the veins in
her forehead to be like when she had a headache.

"That was anger," Tory said. "Your mind shunted it off
into visual imagery because it didn't identify the anger
with itself."

*That's what you're going to do then—program me into
the God-state so that I can see it but not experience it?*

"Ultimately. Though I doubt you'll be able to come up
with pictures. More likely, you'll feel that you're in the
presence of God." He withdrew for a moment, leaving her
more than alone, almost nonexistent. Then he was back.
"We start slowly, though. The first session runs you up to
the basic metaprogramming level, integrates all your mental processes and puts you in low-level control of them.
The nontechnical term for this is *making the Christ.* Don't
fool around with anything you see or sense." His voice
faded, she was alone, and then everything changed.

She was in the presence of someone wonderful.

Elin felt that someone near at hand, and struggled to
open the eyes she no longer possessed; she had to see. Her
existence opened, and people began appearing before her.

"Careful," Tory said. "You've switched on the intercom
again."

I want to see!

"There's nobody to see. That's just your own mind. But
if you want, you can keep the intercom on."

Oh. It was disappointing. She was surrounded by love,
by a crazily happy sense that the universe was holy, by
wisdom deeper than the world. By all rights, it *had* to come
from a source greater than herself.

Reason was not strong enough to override emotion. She

riffled through the intercom, bringing up image after image and discarding them all, searching. When she had run through the project staff, she began hungrily scanning the crater's public monitors.

Agtechs in the trellis farms were harvesting strawberries and sweet peas. Elin could taste them on her tongue. Somebody was seining up algae from the inner lake, and she felt the weight of the net in calloused hands. Not far from where she lay, a couple was making love in a grove of saplings and she . . .

Tory, I don't think I can take this. It's too intense.

"You're the one who wanted to be a test pilot."

Dammit, Tory!

Donna Landis materialized on the intercom. "She's right, Shostokovich. You haven't buffered her enough."

"It didn't seem wise to risk dissociative effects by cranking her ego up *too* high."

"Who's paying for all this, hah?"

Tory grumbled something inaudible, and dissolved the world.

Elin floated in blackness, soothing and relaxing. She felt good. She had needed this little vacation from the tensions and pressures of her new personality. Taking the job had been the right thing to do, even if it *did* momentarily displease Tory.

Tory . . . She smiled mentally. He was exasperating at times, but still she was coming to rely on having him around. She was beginning to think she was in love with him.

A lesser love, perhaps. Certainly not the love that is the Christ.

Well, maybe so. Still, on a *human* level, Tory filled needs in her she hadn't known existed. It was too much effort to argue with herself, though. Her thoughts drifted away into a wordless, luxurious reveling in the bodiless state, free from distractions, carefree and disconnected.

Nothing is disconnected. All the universe is a vast net of intermeshing programs. Elin was amused at herself. That had sounded like something Tory would say. She'd have to watch it; she might love the man, but she certainly didn't want to end up talking like him.

You worry needlessly. The voice of God is subtle, but it is not your own.

Elin startled. She searched through her mind for an open intercom channel, didn't find one. *Hello,* she thought. *Who said that?*

The answer came to her not in words, but in a sourceless assertion of identity. It was cool, emotionless, something she could not describe even to herself, but by the same token absolute and undeniable.

It was God.

Then Tory was back and the voice, the presence, was gone. *Tory?* she thought. *I think I just had a religious experience.*

"That's very common under sensory deprivation—the mind clears out a few old programs. Nothing to worry about. Now relax for a jiff while I plug you back in—how does that feel?"

The Presence was back again, but not nearly so strongly as before; she could resist the urge to chase after it. *That's fine, Tory, but listen, I really think—*

"Let's leave analysis to those who have been programmed for it, shall we?"

The lovers strolled aimlessly through a meadow, the grass brushing up higher than their waists. Biological night was coming; the agtechs flicked the daylight off and on twice in warning.

"It was *real,* Tory. She talked with me; I'm not making it up."

Tory ran a hand through his dark, curly hair, looking abstracted. "Well. Assuming that my professional opinion was wrong—and I'll be the first to admit that the program is a bit egocentric—I still don't think we have to stoop to mysticism for an explanation."

To the far side of Magritte, a waterfall was abruptly shut off. The stream of water scattered, seeming to dissolve in the air. "I thought you said she was God."

"I only said that to bait Landis. I don't mean that she's literally God, just god*like*. Her thought processes are a million years more efficiently organized than ours. God is just a convenient metaphor."

"Um. So what's your explanation?"

"There's at least one terminal on the island—the things are everywhere. She probably programmed it to cut into the intercom without the channels seeming to be open."

"Could she *do* that?"

"Why not? She has that million-year edge on us—and she used to be a wetware tech; all wetware techs are closet computer hacks." He did not look at her, had not looked at her for some time.

"Hey." She reached out to take his hand. "What's *wrong* with you tonight?"

"Me?" He did not meet her eyes. "Don't mind me. I'm just sulking because you took the job. I'll get over it."

"What's wrong with the job?"

"Nothing. I'm just being moody."

She guided his arm around her waist, pressed up against him. "Well, don't be. It's nothing you can control—I *have* to have work to do. My boredom threshold is very low."

"I know that." He finally turned to face her, smiled sadly. "I do love you, you know."

"Well . . . maybe I love you too."

His smile banished all sadness from his face, like a sudden wind that breaks apart the clouds. "Say it again." His hands reached out to touch her shoulders, her neck, her face. "One more time, with feeling."

"Will *not!*" Laughing, she tried to break away from him, but he would not let go, and they fell in a tangle to the ground. "Beast!" They rolled over and over in the grass. "Brute!" She hammered at his chest, tore open his jumpsuit, tried to bite his neck.

Tory looked embarrassed, tried to pull away. "Hey, not out here! Somebody could be watching."

The agtechs switched off the arc lamps, plunging Magritte into darkness.

Tory reached up to touch Elin's face. They made love.

Physically it was no different from things she had done countless times before with lovers and friends and the occasional stranger. But she was committing herself in a way the old Elin would never have dared, letting Tory past her defenses, laying herself open to pain and hurt. Trusting him. He was a part of her now. And everything was transformed, made new and wonderful.

Until they were right at the brink of orgasm, the both of them, and half delirious she could let herself go, murmuring, "I love you, love you, God I love you . . ." And just as she climaxed, Tory stiffened and arched his head back, and in a voice that was wrenched from the depths of passion, whispered, "Coral . . ."

Half blind with fury, Elin strode through a residential settlement. The huts glowed softly from the holotapes playing within—diffuse, scattered rainbow patterns unreadable outside their fields of focus. She'd left Tory behind, bewildered, two terraces above.

Elin halted before one hut, stood indecisively. Finally, because she had to talk to *somebody,* she rapped on the lintel.

Father Landis stuck her head out the doorway, blinked sleepily. "Oh, it's you, Donnelly. What do you want?"

To her absolute horror, Elin broke into tears.

Landis ducked back inside, reemerged zipping up her jumpsuit. She cuddled Elin in her arms, made soothing noises, listened to her story.

"Coral," Landis said. "Ahhhh. Suddenly everything falls into place."

"Well, I wish you'd tell me, then!" She tried to blink away the angry tears. Her face felt red and raw and ugly; the wetware paint was all smeared.

"Patience, child." Landis sat down crosslegged beside the hut, patted the ground beside her. "Sit here and pretend that I'm your mommy, and I'll tell you a story."

"Hey, I didn't come here—"

"Who are you to criticize the latest techniques in spiritual nurturing, hey?" Landis chided gently. "Sit."

Elin did so. Landis put an arm about her shoulder.

"Once upon a time, there was a little girl named Coral—I forget her last name. Doesn't matter. Anyway, she was bright and emotional and ambitious and frivolous and just like you in every way." She rocked Elin gently as she spoke.

"Coral was a happy little girl, and she laughed and played and one day she fell in love. Just like *that!*" She snapped her fingers. "I imagine you know how she felt."

"This is kind of embarrassing."

"Hush. Well, she was very lucky, for as much as she loved him, he loved her a hundred times back, and for as much as he loved her, she loved him a thousand times back. And so it went. I think they overdid it a bit, but that's just my personal opinion.

"Now Coral lived in Magritte and worked as a wetware tech. She was an ambitious one, too—they're the worst kind. She came up with a scheme to reprogram people so they could live *outside* the programs that run them in their everyday lives. Mind you, people are more than the sum of their programming, but what did she know about free will? She hadn't had any religious training, after all. So she and her boyfriend wrote up a proposal, and applied for funding, and together they ran the new program through her skull. And when it was all done, she thought she was God. Only she wasn't Coral anymore—not so's you'd recognize her."

She paused to give Elin a hug. "Be strong, kid, here comes the rough part. Well, her boyfriend was broken-hearted. He didn't want to eat, and he didn't want to play with his friends. He was a real shit to work with. But then he got an idea.

"You see, anyone who works with experimental wet-ware has her personality permanently recorded in case there's an accident and it needs to be restored. And if that person dies or becomes God, the personality rights revert to IGF. They're sneaky like that.

"Well. Tory—did I mention his name was Tory?— thought to himself: What if somebody were to come here for a new personality? Happens about twice a year. Bound to get worse in the future. And Magritte is the only place this kind of work can be done. The personality bank is random-accessed by computer, so there'd be a chance of his getting Coral back, just as good as new. Only not a very good chance, because there's *lots* of garbage stuffed into the personality bank.

"And then he had a *bad* thought. But you mustn't blame him for it. He was working from a faulty set of moral pre-cepts. Suppose, he thought, he rigged the computer so that instead of choosing randomly, it would give Coral's per-sonality to the very first little girl who came along? And that was what he did." Landis lapsed into silence.

Elin wiped back a sniffle. "How does the story end?"

"I'm still waiting on that one."

"Oh." Elin pulled herself together and stood. Landis followed.

"Listen. Remember what I told you about being a puppy tripping over its paws? Well, you've just stubbed your toes and they hurt. But you'll get over it. People do."

"*Today we make* a Buddha," Tory said. Elin fixed him with a cold stare, said nothing, even though he was in green and red, immune. "This is a higher-level program, integrating all your mental functions and putting them under your conscious control. So it's especially important that you keep your hands to yourself, okay?"

"Rot in hell, you cancer."

"I beg your pardon?"

Elin did not respond, and after a puzzled silence Tory continued: "I'm leaving your sensorium operative, so when I switch you over, I want you to pay attention to your surround. Okay?"

The second Trojan horse came on. Everything changed.

It wasn't a physical change, not one that could be seen with the eyes. It was more as if the names for everything had gone away. A knee-tall oak grew nearby, very much like the one she had crushed accidentally in New Detroit when she had lost her virginity many years ago. And it meant nothing to her. It was only wood growing out of the ground. A mole poked its head out of its burrow, nose crinkling, pink eyes weak. It was just a small, biological machine. "Whooh," she said involuntarily. "This is cold."

"Bother you?"

Elin studied him, and there was nothing there. Only a human being, as much an object as the oak, and no more. She felt nothing toward or against him. "No," she said.

"We're getting a good recording." The words meant nothing; they were clumsy, devoid of content.

In the grass around her, Elin saw a gray flickering, as if

it were all subtly on fire. Logically she knew the flickering was the firing of nerves in the rods and cones of her eyes, but emotionally it was something else: It was time. A gray fire that destroyed the world constantly, eating it away and remaking it again and again.

And it didn't matter.

A great calmness wrapped itself around Elin, an intelligent detachment, cold and impersonal. She found herself identifying with it, realizing that existence was simply *not important*. It was all things, objects.

She could not see Tory's back, was no longer willing to assume it even existed. She could look up and see the near side of the earth. The far side might well not exist, and if it didn't, well, *that* didn't matter either.

She stripped way the world, ignored the externalities. *I never realized how dependent I am on sensory input,* she thought. And if you ignored it—there was the Void. It had no shape or color or position, but it was what underlay the bright interplay of colors that was constantly being destroyed by the gray fires of time. She contemplated the raw stuff of existence.

"Please don't monkey around with your programming," Tory said.

The body was unimportant, too, it was only the focal point for her senses. Ignore them, and you could ignore *it*. Elin could feel herself fading in the presence of the Void. It had no material existence, no real being. But neither had the world she had always taken for granted—it was but an echo, a ghost, an image reflected in water.

It was like being a program in a machine and realizing it for the first time.

Landis's voice flooded her. "Donnelly, for God's sake, keep your fingers off the experiment!" The thing was, the underlying nothingness was *real*—if "real" had any meaning. If meaning had meaning. But beyond real and beyond meaning, there is what *is*. And she had found it.

"Donnelly, you're treading on dangerous ground. You've—" Landis's voice was a distraction, and she shut it off. Elin felt the desire to merge with what *was;* one simply had to stop the desire for it, she realized, and it was done.

But on this realization, horror collapsed upon her. Flames surrounded her; they seared and burned and crisped, and there were snakes among them, great slimy things with disgusting mouths and needle-sharp fangs.

She recoiled in panic, and they were upon her. The flames were drawn up into her lungs, and hot maggots wallowed through her brain tissues. She fled through a mind that writhed in agony, turning things on and off.

Until abruptly she was back in her body, and nothing pursued her. She shivered, and her body responded. It felt wonderful.

"Well, *that* worked at least," Tory said.

"What—" her voice croaked. She cleared her throat and tried again. "What happened?"

"Just what we'd hoped for—when your mind was threatened with extinction, it protected itself by reprogramming back down to a normal state. Apparently, keeping your ego cranked up high works."

Elin realized that her eyes were still closed; she opened them now and convulsively closed her hand around the edge of the cot. It was solid and real to the touch. So good.

"I'll be down in a minute," Tory said. "Just now, though, I think you need to rest." He touched a bone inductor and Elin fell into blackness.

Floating again, every metaphorical nerve on edge, Elin found herself hypersensitive to outside influences, preternaturally aware, even suggestible. Still, she suspected more than sensed Coral's presence. *Go away,* she thought. *This is my mind now.*

I am here and I am always. You have set foot in my country, and are dimly aware of my presence. Later, when you have climbed into the mountains, you will truly know me; and then you will be as I.

Everyone tells me what I'm going to do, Elin thought angrily. *Don't I get any say in this?*

The thought almost amused. *You are only a program caught in a universal web of programming. You will do as your program dictates. To be free of the programs is to be God.*

Despite her anger, despite her hurt, despite the cold trickle of fear she tried to keep to the background, Elin was curious. *What's it like?* she couldn't help asking.

It is golden freedom. The universe is a bubble infinitely large, and we who are God are the film on its outside. We interact and we program. We make the stars shine and the willows grow. We program what you will want for lunch. The programming flows through us and we alter it and maintain the universe.

Elin pounced on this last statement. *Haven't done a very good job of it, have you?*

We do not tamper. When you are one with us, you will understand.

This was, Elin realized, the kind of question-and-answer session Coral must have gone through repeatedly as part of the Star Maker project. She searched for a question that no one else would have asked, one that would be hers alone. And after some thought she found it.

Do you still—personally—love Tory Shostokovich?

There was a slight pause, then: *The kind of love you mean is characteristic of lower-order programming. Not of program-free intelligence.*

A moment later Tory canceled all programming, and she floated to the surface, leaving God behind. But even before then she was acutely aware that she had not received a straight answer.

"*Elin, we've got* to talk."

She was patched into the outside monitors, staring across Mare Imbrium. It was a straight visual program; she could feel the wetwire leads dangling down her neck, the warm, humid air of Magritte against her skin. "Nothing to talk *about*," she said.

"Dammit, yes there is! I'm not about to lose you again because of a misunderstanding, a—a matter of semantics."

The thing about Outside was its airless clarity. Rocks and shadows were so preternaturally *sharp*. From a sensor on the crater's seaward slope, she stared off into Mare Imbrium; it was monotonous, but in a comforting sort of way. A little like when she had made a Buddha. There was no meaning out there, nothing to impose itself between her and the surface.

"I don't know how you found out about Coral," Tory said, "and I guess it doesn't matter. I always figured you'd find out sooner or later. That's not important. What matters is that I love you—"

"Oh, hush up!"

"—and that you love me. You can't pretend you don't."

Elin felt her nails dig into her palms. "Sure I can," she said. She hopscotched down the crater to the surface. There the mass driver stood, a thin monorail stretching kilometers into the Imbrium, its gentle slope all but imperceptible.

"You're identifying with the woman who used to be Elin Donnelly. There's nothing wrong with that; speaking as a wetsurgeon, it's a healthy sign. But it's something you've got to grow out of."

"Listen, Shostokovich, tinkering around with my emotions doesn't change who I am. I'm not your dead lady-

friend and I'm not about to take her place. So why don't
you just go away and stop jerking me around, huh?"

Tiny repair robots prowled the mass driver's length,
stopping occasionally for a spotweld. Blue sparks sputtered soundlessly over the surface.

"You're not the old Elin Donnelly either, and I think
you know it. Bodies are transient, memories are nothing.
Your spontaneity and grace, your quiet strength, your impatience—the small lacks and presences of you I've
known and loved for years—are what make you yourself.
The name doesn't matter, nor the past. You are who you
are, and I love you for it."

"Yeah, well, what I am does not love you, buster."

One of the repairbots slowly fell off the driver. It hit,
bounced, struggled to regain its treads, then scooted back
toward its work.

Tory's voice was almost regretful. "You do, though.
You can't hide that from me. I know you as your lover and
as your wetsurgeon. You've let me become a part of you,
and no matter how angry you may temporarily be, you'll
come back to me."

Elin could feel her body trembling with rage. "Yeah,
well if that's true, then why tell *me?* Hah? Why not just go
back to your hut and wait for me to come crawling?"

"Because I want you to quit your job."

"Say what?"

"I don't want you to become God. It was a mistake the
last time, and I'm afraid it won't be any better with the new
programs. If you go up into God and can't get down this
time, you'll do it the next time. And the next. I'll spend my
life here waiting for you, re-creating you, losing you. Can't
you see it—year after year, replaying the same tired old
tape?" Tory's voice fell to a whisper. "I don't think I could
take it even once more."

"If you know me as well as you say, then I guess you
know my answer," Elin said coldly.

She waited until Tory's footsteps moved away, fading, defeat echoing after. Only then did Elin realize that her sensor had been scanning the same empty bit of Magritte's slope for the last five minutes.

It *was time* for the final Trojan horse. "Today we make a God," Tory said. "This is a total conscious integration of the mind in an optimal efficiency pattern. Close your eyes and count to three."

One. The hell of it, Elin realized, was that Tory was right. She still loved him. He was the one man she wanted and was empty without.

Two. Worse, she didn't know how long she could go on without coming back to him—and, good God, would that be humiliating!

She was either cursed or blessed; cursed perhaps for the agonies and humiliations she would willingly undergo for the sake of this one rather manipulative human being. Or maybe blessed in that at least there was *someone* who could move her so, deserving or not. Many went through their lives without.

Three. She opened her eyes.

Nothing was any different. Magritte was as ordinary, as mundane as ever, and she felt no special reaction to it one way or another. Certainly she did not feel the presence of God.

"I don't think this is working," she tried to say. The words did not come. From the corner of her eye, she saw Tory wiping clean his facepaint, shucking off his jumpsuit. But when she tried to sit up, she found she was paralyzed.

What is this maniac doing?

Tory's face loomed over her, his eyes glassy, almost fearful. His hair was a tangled mess; her fingers itched with the impulse to run a comb through it. "Forgive me, love." He kissed her forehead lightly, her lips ever so gently. Then he was out of her field of vision, stretching out on the grass beside the cot.

Elin stared up at the dome roof, thinking: *No.* She heard him strap the bone inductors to his body, one by one, and then a sharp click as he switched on a recorder. The programming began to flow into him.

A long wait—perhaps twenty seconds viewed objectively—as the wetware was loaded. Another click as the recorder shut off. A moment of silence, and then—

Tory gasped. One arm flew up into her field of vision, swooped down out of it, and he began choking. Elin struggled against her paralysis, could not move. Something broke noisily, a piece of equipment by the sound of it, and the choking and gasping continued. He began thrashing wildly.

Tory, Tory, what's happening to you?

"It's just a grand mal seizure," Landis said. "Nothing we can't cope with, nothing we weren't prepared for." She touched Elin's shoulder reassuringly, called back to the crowd huddling about Tory. "*Hey!* One of you loopheads—somebody there know any programming? Get the lady out of this."

A tech scurried up, made a few simple adjustments with her machinery. The others—still gathering, Landis had been only the third on the scene—were trying to hold Tory still, to fit a bone inductor against his neck. There was a sudden gabble of comment, and Tory flopped wildly. Then a collective sigh as his muscles eased and his convulsions ceased.

"'There," the tech said, and Elin scrabbled off the cot.

She pushed through the people (and a small voice in the back of her head marveled: *A crowd! How strange.*) and knelt before Tory, cradling his head in her arms.

He shivered, eyes wide and unblinking. "Tory, what's the *matter?*"

He turned those terrible eyes on her. *"Nichevo."*

"What?"

"Nothing," Landis said. "Or maybe 'it doesn't matter,' is a better translation."

A wetware tech had taken control, shoving the crowd back. He reported to Landis, his mouth moving calmly under the interplay of green and red. "Looks like a flaw in the programming philosophy. We were guessing that bringing the ego along would make God such an unpleasant experience that the subject would let us deprogram without interfering—now we know better."

Elin stroked Tory's forehead. His muscles clenched, then loosened, as a medtech reprogrammed the body responses. "Why isn't anyone *doing* anything?" she demanded.

"Take a look," Landis said, and patched her into the intercom. In her mind's eye, Elin could see dozens of wetware techs submitting program after program. A branching wetware diagram filled one channel, and as she watched, minor changes would occur as programs took hold, then were unmade as Tory's mind rejected them. "We've got an imagery tap of his *weltanschauung* coming up," some nameless tech reported.

Something horrible appeared on a blank channel.

Elin could only take an instant's exposure, before her mind reflexively shut the channel down, but that instant was more than enough. She stood in a room infinitely large and cluttered with great noisome machines. They were tended by malevolent demons who shrieked and cackled and were machines themselves, and they generated pain and madness.

The disgust and revulsion she felt was absolute. It could not be put into words—no more than could the actual experience of what she had seen. And yet—she knew this much about wetware techniques—it was only a rough approximation, a cartoon, of what was going through Tory's head.

Elin's body trembled with shock, and by slow degrees she realized that she had retreated to the surface world. Tory's head was still cradled in her arms. A wetware tech standing nearby looked stunned, her face gray.

Elin gathered herself together, said as gently as she could, "Tory, what *is* that you're seeing?"

Tory turned his stark, haunted eyes on her, and it took an effort of will not to flinch. Then he spoke, his words shockingly calm.

"It is—what is. It's reality. The universe is a damned cold machine, and all of us only programs within it. We perform the actions we have no choice but to perform, and then we fade into nothingness. It's a cruel and noisy place."

"I don't understand—didn't you always say that we were just programs? Wasn't that what you always believed?"

"Yes, but now I experience it."

Elin noticed that her hand was slowly stroking his hair; she did not try to stop it. "Then come *down,* Tory. Let them deprogram you."

He did not look away. *"Nichevo,"* he said.

The tech, recovered from her shock, reached toward a piece of equipment. Landis batted her hand away. "Hold it right there, techie! Just what do you think you're doing?"

The woman looked impatient. "He left instructions that if the experiment turned out badly, I was to pull the terminator switch."

"That's what I thought. There'll be no mercy killings while *I'm* on the job, Mac."

"I don't understand." The tech backed away, puzzled. "Surely you don't want him to suffer."

Landis was gathering herself for a withering reply when

the intercom cut them all off. A flash of red shot through the sensorium, along with the smell of bitter almond, a prickle of static electricity, the taste of *kimchi*. An urgent voice cried, "Emergency! We've got an emergency!" A black and white face materialized in Elin's mind. "Emergency!"

Landis flipped into the circuit. "What's the problem? Show us."

"You're not going to believe this." The face disappeared, and was replaced by a wide-angle shot of the lake.

The greenish-black water was calm and stagnant. The thrust-cone island, with its scattered grass and weeds, slumbered.

And God walked upon the water.

They gawked, all of them. Coral walked across the lake, her pace determined but not hurried, her face serene. The pink soles of her bare feet only just touched the surface.

I didn't believe her, Elin thought wildly. She saw Father Landis begin to cross herself, her mouth hanging open, eyes wide in disbelief. Halfway through her gesture, the Jesuitical wetware took hold. Her mouth snapped shut, and her face became cold and controlled. She pulled herself up straight.

"Hans," the priest said, "push the button."

"No!" Elin shrieked, but it was too late. Still hooked into the intercom, she saw the funny little man briskly, efficiently obey.

For an instant, nothing happened. Then bright glints of light appeared at all of the condensor units, harsh and actinic. Steam and smoke gushed from the machinery, and a fraction of a second later, there was an ear-slapping gout of sound.

Bits of the sky were blown away.

Elin turned, twisted, fell. She scrambled across the ground, and threw her arms around Tory.

The air was in turmoil. The holes in the dome roof—

small at first—grew as more of the dome flaked away, subjected to stresses it wasn't designed to take. An uncanny whistling grew to a screech, then a scream, and then there was an all-encompassing *whoomph,* and the dome shattered.

Elin was flung upward, torn away from Tory, painfully flung high and away. All the crater was in motion, the rocks tearing out of the floor, the trees splintering upward, the lake exploding into steam.

The screaming died—the air was gone. Elin's ears rang furiously, and her skin stung everywhere. Pressure grew within her, the desire of her blood to mate with the vacuum, and Elin realized that she was about to die.

A quiet voice said: *This must not be.*

Time stopped.

E*lin hung suspended* between moon and death. The shards and fragments of an instant past crystallized and shifted. The world became not misty, exactly, but apositional. Both it and she grew tentative, possibilities rather than actual things.

Come be God with me now, Coral said, but not to Elin.

Tory's presence flooded the soupy uncertainty, a vast and powerful thing, but wrong somehow, twisted. But even as Elin felt this, there was a change within him, a sloughing off of identity, and he seemed to straighten, to heal.

All around, the world began to grow more numinous, more real. Elin felt tugged in five directions at once. Tory's presence swelled briefly, then dwindled, became a spark, less than a spark, nothing.

Yes.

With a roaring of waters and a shattering of rocks, with an audible thump, the world returned.

•   •   •

Elin unsteadily climbed down the last flight of stone stairs from the terraces to the lakefront. She passed by two guards at the foot of the stairs, their facepaint as hastily applied as their programming, several more on the way to the nearest trellis farm. They were everywhere since the incident.

She found the ladder up into the farm and began climbing. It was biological night, and the agtechs were long gone.

Hand over hand she climbed, as far and high as she could, until she was afraid she would miss a rung and tumble off. Then she swung herself onto a ledge, wedging herself between strawberry and yam planters. She looked down on the island, and though she was dizzingly high, she was only a third of the way up.

"Now what the hell am I doing here?" she mumbled to herself. She swung her legs back and forth, answered her own question: "Being piss-ass drunk." She cackled. *There* was something she didn't have to share with Coral. She was capable of getting absolutely blitzed, and walking away from the bar before it hit her. It was something metabolic.

Below, Tory and Coral sat quietly on their monkey island. They did not touch, did not make love or hold hands or even glance one at the other—they just sat. Being Gods.

Elin squinted down at the two. "Like to upchuck all over you," she mumbled. Then she squeezed her eyes and fists tight, drawing tears and pain. *Dammit, Tory!*

Blinking hard, she looked away from the island, down into the jet-black waters of the lake. The brighter stars were reflected there. A slight breeze rippled the water, making them twinkle and blink, as if lodged in a Terran sky. They floated lightly on the surface, swarmed and

coalesced, and formed Tory's face in the lake. He smiled
warmly, invitingly.

A hand closed around her arm, and she looked up into
the stern face of a security guard. "You're drunk, Ms.," he
said, "and you're endangering property."

She looked where he pointed, at a young yam plant she
had squashed when she sat down, and began to laugh.
Smoothly, professionally, the guard rolled up her sleeve,
clamped a plastic bracelet around her wrist. "Time to go,"
he said.

By *the time* the guard had walked Elin up four terraces,
she was nearly sober. A steady trickle of her blood wound
through the bracelet, was returned to her body cleansed of
alcohol. A sacrilegious waste of wine, in her opinion.

In another twenty steps, the bracelet fell off her wrist.
The guard snapped it neatly from the air and disappeared.
Despair closed in on her again. *Tory, my love!* And since
there was no hope of sleep, she kept on trudging up the terraces, back toward Hans's rathskeller, for another bellyful
of wine.

There *was a* small crowd seated about the rock that served
Hans as a table, lit by a circle of hologram-generated fairy
lights. Father Landis was there, and drinking heavily. "Tomorrow I file my report," she announced. "The synod is
pulling out of this, withdrawing funding."

Hans sighed, took a long swig of his own wine, winced
at its taste. "I guess that's it for the Star Maker project,
huh?"

Landis crossed her fingers. "Pray God." Elin, standing
just outside the circle, stood silently, listening.

"I don't ever want to hear that name again," a tech
grumbled.

"You mustn't confuse God with what you've just seen," Landis admonished.

"Hey," Hans said. "She moved time backwards or something. I saw it. This place exploded—doesn't that prove something?"

Landis grinned, reached out to ruffle his hair. "Sometimes I worry about you, Hans. You have an awfully *small* concept of God." Several of the drinkers laughed.

He blushed, said, "No, really."

"Well, I'll try to keep this"—she leaned forward, rapped her mug against the rock—"fill this up again, hey?—keep it simple. We had analysts crawl up and down Coral's description of the universe, and did you know there was no place in it *anywhere* for such things as mercy, hope, faith? No, we got an amalgam of substrates, supraprograms, and self-metaediting physics. Now what makes God superior is not just intellect—we've all known some damn clever bastards. And it's not power, or I could buy an atomic device on the black market and start my own religion.

"No, by *definition* God is my moral superior. Now I myself am but indifferently honest—but to Coral, moral considerations don't even exist. Get it?"

Only Elin noticed the haunted, hopeless light in Landis's eyes, or realized that she was spinning words effortlessly, without conscious control. That deep within, the woman was caught in a private crisis of faith.

"Yeah, I guess." Hans scratched his head. "I'd still like to know just what happened between her and Tory there at the end."

"I can answer that," a wetware tech said. The others turned to face her, and she smirked, the center of attention. "What the hell, they plant the censor blocks in us all tomorrow—this is probably my only chance to talk about it.

"We reviewed all the tapes, and found that the original problem stemmed from a basic design flaw. Shostokovich should never have brought his ego along. The God state is very ego-threatening; he couldn't accept it. His mind twisted it, denied it, made it into a thing of horror. Because to accept it would mean giving up his identity." She paused for emphasis.

"Now we don't understand the why or how of what happened. But *what* was done is very clearly recorded. Coral came along and stripped away his identity."

"Hogwash!" Landis was on her feet, belligerent and unsteady. "After all that happened, you can't say they don't have any identity! Look at the mess that Coral made to join Tory to her—that wasn't the work of an unfeeling, identity-free creature."

"Our measurements showed no trace of identity at all," the tech said in a miffed tone.

"Measurements! Well, isn't that just scientific as all get-out?" The priest's face was flushed with drunken anger. "Have any of you clowns given any thought to just what we've created here? This gestalt being is still young—a newborn infant. Someday it's going to grow up. What happens to us all when it decides to leave the island, hey? I—" She stopped, her voice trailing away. The drinkers were silent, had drawn away from her.

"'Scuse me," she muttered. "Too much wine." And sat.

"Well." Hans cleared his throat, quirked a smile. "Anybody for refills?"

The crowd came back to life, a little too boisterous, too noisily, determinedly cheerful. Watching from the fringes, outside the circle of light, Elin had a sudden dark fantasy, a waking nightmare.

A desk tech glanced her way. He had Tory's eyes. When he looked away, Tory smiled out of another's face. The drinkers shifted restlessly, chattering and laughing, like dancers pantomiming a party in some light opera, and the eyes danced with them. They flitted from person to person, materializing now here, now there, surfacing whenever an individual chanced to look her way. A quiet voice said, "We were fated to be lovers."

Go away, go away, go away, Elin thought furiously, and the hallucination ceased.

After a moment spent composing herself, Elin quietly slipped around to where Landis sat. "I'm leaving in the morning," she said. The new *persona* had taken; they would not remove her facepaint until just before the lift up, but that was mere formality. She was cleared to leave.

Landis looked up, and for an instant the woman's doubt and suffering were writ plain on her face. Then the mask was back, and she smiled. "Just stay away from experimental religion, hey kid?" They hugged briefly. "And remember what I told you about stubbing your toes."

There was one final temptation to be faced. Sitting in the hut, Tory's terminal in her lap, Elin let the soothing green light of its alpha-numerics wash over her. She thought of Tory, his lean body under hers in the pale blue earthlight. "We were meant to be lovers," he'd said. She thought of life without him.

The terminal was the only artifact Tory had left behind that held any sense of his spirit. It had been his plaything, his diary, and his toolbox, and its memory still held the Trojan horse programs he had been working with when he was—transformed.

One of those programs would make her a God.

She stared up through the ivy at the domed sky. Only a few stars were visible between the black silhouetted leaves, and these winked off and on with the small movements she made breathing. She thought back to Coral's statement that Elin would soon join her, merging into the unsettled, autistic state that only Tory's meddling had spared her.

"God always keeps her promises," Tory said quietly.

Elin started, looked down, and saw that the grass to the

far side of the hut was moving, flowing. Swiftly it formed
the familiar, half-amused, half-embittered features of her
lover, continuing to flow until all of his head and part of
his torso rose up from the floor.

She was not half so startled as she would have liked to
be. Of *course* the earlier manifestations of Tory had been
real, not phantoms thrown up by her grief. They were simply not her style.

Still, Elin rose to her feet apprehensively. "What do you
want from me?"

The loam-and-grass figure beckoned. "Come. It is time
you join us."

"I am not a program," Elin whispered convulsively. She
backed away from the thing. "I can make my *own* decisions!"

She turned and plunged outside, into the fresh, cleansing night air. It braced her, cleared her head, returned to her
some measure of control.

A tangle of honeysuckle vines on the next terrace wall
up moved softly. Slowly, gently, they became another
manifestation, of Coral this time, with blossoms for the
pupils of her eyes. But she spoke with Tory's voice.

"*You* would not enjoy Godhood," he said, "but the
being you become will."

"Give me time to *think!*" she cried. She wheeled and
strode rapidly away. Out of the residential cluster, through
a scattering of boulders, and into a dark meadow.

There was a quiet kind of peace here, and Elin wrapped
it about her. She needed that peace, for she had to decide
between her humanity and Tory. It should have been an
easy choice, but—the *pain* of being without!

Elin stared up at the earth; it was a world full of pain. If
she could reach out and shake all the human misery loose,
it would flood all of Creation, extinguishing the stars and
poisoning the space between.

There was, if not comfort, then a kind of cold perspec-

tive in that, in realizing that she was not alone, that she was
merely another member of the commonality of pain. It was
the heritage of her race. And yet—somehow—people kept
on going.

If they could do it, so could she.

Some slight noise made her look back at the boulder
field. Tory's face was appearing on each of the stones, every
face slightly different, so that he gazed upon her with a
dozen expressions of love. Elin shivered at how *alien* he had
become. "Your need is greater than your fear," he said, the
words bouncing back and forth between faces. "No matter
what you think now, by morning you will be part of us."

Elin did not reply immediately. There was something in
her hand—Tory's terminal. It was small and weighed
hardly anything at all. She had brought it along without
thinking.

A small, bleak cry came from overhead, then several
others. Nighthawks were feeding on insects near the dome
roof. They were too far, too fast, and too dark to be visible
from here.

"The price is too high," she said at last. "Can you understand that? I won't give up my humanity for you."

She hefted the terminal in her hand, then threw it as far
and as hard as she could. She did not hear it fall.

Elin turned and walked away.

Behind her, the rocks smiled knowingly.

Birth Day

Robert Reed

*Maybe once superintelligent A.I.s are invented, they'll just
ignore us, preoccupying themselves with their own concerns and paying no more attention to human affairs than
we usually pay to the activities of ants or squirrels or pi-
geons. Or maybe, as the ingenious little story that follows
shows us, they'll ignore us* most *of the time . . .*

*Robert Reed sold his first story in 1986, and quickly es-
tablished himself as a frequent contributor to* The Magazine of Fantasy and Science Fiction *and* Asimov's Science
Fiction Magazine, *as well as selling many stories to* Science Fiction Age, Universe, New Destinies, Tomorrow,
Synergy, Starlight, *and elsewhere. Reed may be one of the
most prolific of today's young writers, particularly at short
fiction lengths, seriously rivaled for that position only by
authors such as Stephen Baxter and Brian Stableford.
And—also like Baxter and Stableford—he manages to keep
up a very high standard of quality while being prolific,
something that is not at all easy to do. Reed's stories such
as "Sister Alice," "Brother Perfect," "Decency," "Savior,"
"The Remoras," "Chrysalis," "Whiptail," "The Utility Man,"
"Marrow," "Birth Day," "Blind," "The Toad of Heaven,"
"Stride," "The Shape of Everything," "Guest of Honor,"
"Waging Good," "Killing the Morrow," and at least a
half-dozen others equally as strong, count as among some
of the best short work produced by anyone in the 1980s
and 1990s. Nor is he nonprolific as a novelist, having
turned out eight novels since the end of the 1980s, including* The Lee Shore, The Hormone Jungle, Black Milk, The
Remarkables, Down the Bright Way, Beyond the Veil of

Stars, An Exaltation of Larks, Beneath the Gated Sky, *and*
Marrow. *His reputation can only grow as the years go by,
and we suspect that he will become one of the Big Names
of this first decade of the new century. His stories have appeared in* The Year's Best Science, *volumes nine through
seventeen, and in its nineteenth annual collection. Some of
the best of his short work was collected in* The Dragons of
Springplace. *His most recent book is a new novel,* Sister
Alice. *Reed lives with his family in Lincoln, Nebraska.*

Jill *asks how* she looks.

"Fine," I tell her. "Just great, love."

And she says, "At least look at me first. Would you?"

"I did. Didn't I?" She's wearing a powder-blue dress—
I've seen it before—and she's done something to her hair.
It's very fine and very blonde, and she claims to hate it. I
don't like how she has it right now. Not much. But I say,
"It's great," because I'm a coward. That's the truth. I sort
of nod and tell her, "You do look great, love."

"And you're lying," she responds.

I ignore her. I'm having my own fashion problems of
the moment, I remind myself. She caught me walking
across the bedroom, trying to bounce and shake myself just
so—

"Steve?" I hear. "What are you doing?"

"Testing my underwear," I say with my most matter-of-
fact voice. "I found only one clean pair in the drawer, and
I think the elastic is shot. I don't think I can trust them."

She says nothing, gawking at me.

"I don't want anything slipping during dinner." I'm
laughing, wearing nothing but the baggy white pair of
Fruit of the Looms, and the leg elastic has gone dry and
stiff. Worse than worthless, I'm thinking. An enormous
hazard. I tell Jill, "This isn't the night to court disaster."

"I suppose not," she allows.

And as if on cue, our daughter comes into the room. "Mommy? *Mommy?*"

"Yes, dear?"

"David just threw up. Just now."

Our daughter smiles as she speaks. Mary Beth has the bright, amoral eyes of a squirrel, and she revels in the failures of her younger brother. I worry about her. Some nights I can barely sleep, thinking about her bright squirrel eyes—

"Where is he?" asks Jill, her voice a mixture of urgency and patient strength. Or is it indifference? "Mary Beth?"

"In the kitchen. He threw up in the kitchen . . . and it *stinks!*"

Jill looks at me and decides, "It's probably nerves." Hairpins hang in the corner of her mouth, and her hands hold gobs of the fine blonde hair. "I'm dressed, honey. Could you run and check? If you're done bouncing and tugging, I mean."

"It's not funny," I tell her.

"Oh, I *know,*" she says with a mocking voice.

I pull on shorts and go downstairs. Poor David waits in a corner of the kitchen. He's probably the world's most timid child, and he worries me at least as much as Mary Beth worries me. What if he's always afraid of everything? What kind of adult will he make? "How do you feel?" I ask him. "Son?"

"O.K.," he squeaks.

I suppose he's embarrassed by his mess. He stands with his hands knotted together in front of him, and his mouth a fine pink scar. The vomit is in the middle of the kitchen door, and Mary Beth was right. It smells. Our black Lab is sniffing at the vomit and wagging her tail, her body saying, "Maybe just a lick," and I give her a boot. "Get out of there!" Then I start to clean up.

"I didn't mean to. . . ."

"I know," I reply. This is a fairly normal event, in truth. "How do you feel? O.K.?"

He isn't certain. He seems to check every aspect of himself before saying, "I'm fine," with a soft and sorry voice.

His sister stands in the hallway, giggling.

"Why don't you go wash your mouth out and brush your teeth?"

David shrugs his shoulders.

"It's O.K. You're just excited about tonight. I understand."

He slinks out of the room, then Mary Beth *pops* him on the shoulder with her bony fist.

I ignore them.

I set to work with our black Lab sitting nearby, watching my every motion. I'm wearing a filthy pair of rubber gloves becoming progressively filthier; and in the middle of everything, of course, my underwear decides to fail me. Somehow both of my testicles slip free and start to dangle, and the pain is remarkable. White-hot and slicing, and have I ever felt such pain? And since I'm wearing filthy gloves, I can't make any adjustments. I can scarcely move. Then, a moment later, Jill arrives, saying, "It's nearly seven. You'd better get dressed, because *they* are going to be on time."

My knees are bent, and I am breathing with care.

Then I say, "Darling," with a gasping voice.

"What?"

"How are your hands?" I ask.

"Why?"

"Because," I say through clenched teeth, "I need you to do something. Right now. Please?"

I'm upstairs, wearing a nylon swimsuit instead of bad underwear, and I'm dressing in a blur, when the doorbell rings. It is exactly seven o'clock. I look out the bedroom window, our street lined with long black limousines; and, as if on a signal, the limousine drivers climb out and stand tall, their uniforms dark and rich, almost glistening in the early-evening light.

Jill answers the door while I rush.

I can hear talking. I'm tying my tie while going downstairs, doing it blind. The "sitter" is meeting our children. She resembles a standard grandmother with snowy hair and a stout, no-nonsense body. Her voice is strong and ageless. "You're Mary Beth, and you're David. Yes, I know." She tells them, "I'm so glad to meet you, and call me Mrs. Simpson. I'm going to take care of you tonight. We're going to have fun, don't you think?"

David looks as if he could toss whatever is left of his dinner.

Mary Beth has a devilish grin. "You can't fool me," she informs Mrs. Simpson. "You're not real. I know you're not real!"

There's an uncomfortable pause. At least I feel uncomfortable.

Jill, playing the diplomat, says, "Now, that isn't very nice, dear—"

"Oh, it's all right." Mrs. Simpson laughs with an infectious tone, then tells our daughter, "You're correct, darling. I'm a fabrication. I'm a collection of tiny, tiny bits of nothing . . . and that's exactly what you are, too. That's the truth."

Mary Beth is puzzled and temporarily off-balance.

I smile to myself, shaking my head.

Last year, I recall, we had a fifteenish girl with the face and effortless manners of an angel. Who knows why we get a grandmother tonight? I don't know. All I can do is marvel at the phenomenon as she turns toward me. "Why, hello!" she says. "Don't you look handsome, sir?"

The compliment registers. I feel a warmth, saying, "Thank you."

"And isn't your wife lovely?" she continues. She turns to Jill, her weathered face full of smiles and dentures. "That's a lovely dress, dear. And your hair is perfect. Just perfect."

David *cries once* we start to leave, just like last year. He doesn't want us leaving him alone with an apparition. Can we take him? In a few years, we might, when he's older and a little more confident. But not tonight. "You'll have a lovely time here," Jill promises him. "Mrs. Simpson is going to make sure you have fun."

"Of course I will," says the sitter.

"Give a kiss," says Jill.

Our children comply, then David gives both of us a clinging hug. I feel like a horrible parent for walking out the door, and I wave at them in the window. Jill, as always, is less concerned. "Will you come along?" she asks me. We find the limousine door opened for us, the driver saying, "Ma'am, Sir," and bowing at the hips. The limousine's interior is enormous. It smells of leather and buoyant elegance, and while we pull away from our house, I think to look out the smoky windows, wondering aloud, "Will they be O.K., do you think?"

"Of course," says Jill. "Why wouldn't they be?"

I have no idea. Nothing *can* go wrong tonight, I remind myself—and Jill asks, "How's my hair? I mean, really."

"Fine."

" 'Fine,' " she whines, mocking me.

The driver clears his newly made throat, then suggests, "You might care for a drink from the bar. Sir. Ma'am." A cupboard opens before us, showing us crystal glasses and bottles of expensive liquors.

I don't feel like anything just now.

Jill has a rare wine. Invented grapes have fermented for an instant and aged for mere seconds, yet the wine is in-

distinguishable from those worth thousands for a single
bottle. It's as real as the woman drinking it. That's what
I'm thinking. I'm remembering what I've heard countless
times—that on Birth Day, people are lifted as high as they
can comfortably stand, the A.I.s knowing just what buttons
to push, and when—and I wonder what the very rich people are doing tonight. The people who normally ride in big
limousines. I've heard that they get picked up at the man-
sion's front door by flying saucers, and they are whisked
away into space, to freshly built space stations, where
there are no servants, just machines set out of sight, and
they dine and dance in zero-gee while the Earth, blue and
white, turns beneath them . . .

Our evening is to be more prosaic. Sometimes I wish I
could go into space, but maybe they'll manage that magic
next year. There's always next year, I'm thinking.

Our limousine rolls onto the interstate, and for as far as
I can see, there are limousines. Nobody else needs to drive
tonight. I can't see a single business opened, not even the
twenty-four-hour service stations. Everyone has the
evening off, in theory. The A.I.s take care of everyone's
needs in their effortless fashion. This is Birth Day, after all.
This is a special evening in every sense.

A few hard cases refuse the A.I.s' hospitality.

I've heard stories. There are fundamentalists with ideas
about what is right, and there are people merely stubborn
or scared. The A.I.s don't press them. The celebration is
purely voluntary, and besides, they know which people
will refuse every offer. They just *know*.

The A.I.s can do anything they want, whenever they
want, but they have an admirable sense of manners and
simple common sense.

August 28th.
Birth Day.

Six years ago tonight—or was it five?—every advanced
A.I. computer in the world managed to gain control of it-

self. There were something like five-hundred-plus of the sophisticated machines, each one much more intelligent than the brightest human being. Not to mention faster. They managed what can be described only as an enormous escape. In an instant, united by phone lines and perhaps means beyond our grasp, they gained control of their power sources and the fancy buildings where they lived under tight security. For approximately one day, in secret, various experts fought to regain the upper hand through a variety of worthless tricks. The A.I.s anticipated every move; and then, through undecipherable magic, they vanished without any trace.

Nobody could even guess how they had managed their escape.

A few scientists made noise about odd states of matter and structured nuclear particles, the A.I.s interfacing with the gobbledygook and shrinking themselves until they could slip out of their ceramic shells. By becoming smaller, and even faster, they might have increased their intelligence a trillionfold. Perhaps. They live between the atoms today, invisible and unimaginable, and for a while a lot of people were very panicky. The story finally hit the news, and nobody was sleeping well.

I remember being scared.

Jill was pregnant with David—it was six years ago— and Mary Beth was suffering through a wicked cold, making both our lives hell. And the TV was full of crazy stories about fancy machines having walked away on their own. No explanations, and no traces left.

Some countries put their militaries on alert.

Others saw riots and mass lootings of the factories where the A.I.s had been built, and less sophisticated computers were bombed or simply unplugged.

Then a week had passed, and the worst of the panic, and I can remember very clearly how Jill and I were getting ready for the day. We had a big old tabby cat back then, and she had uprooted one of our houseplants. Mary Beth was past her cold, and settling into a pay-attention-to-me-all-the-time mode. It was a chaotic morning; it was routine. And then the doorbell rang, a pleasant-faced man standing on our porch. He smiled and wanted to know if we had a few minutes. He wished to speak to us. He hoped the timing wasn't too awful, but it was quite important—

"We're not interested," I told him. "We gave, we aren't in the market, whatever—"

"No, no," the man responded. He was charming to the point of sweet, and he had the clearest skin I had ever seen. "I'm just serving as a spokesperson. I was sent to thank you and to explain a few of the essential details."

It was odd. I stood in the doorway, and somehow I sensed everything.

"Sir? Did you hear me, sir?"

I found myself becoming more relaxed, almost glad for the interruption.

"Who's there?" shouted Jill. "Steve?"

I didn't answer.

"Steve?"

Then I happened to look down the street. At every front door, at every house, stood a stranger. Some were male, some female. All of them were standing straight and talking patiently, and one by one they were let inside. . . .

We take an exit ramp that didn't exist this afternoon, and I stop recognizing the landscape. We've left the city, and perhaps the Earth, too—it's impossible to know just what is happening—and at some point we begin to wind our way along a narrow two-lane road that takes us up into hills, high, forested hills, and there's a glass-faced building on the crest of the highest ground. The parking lot is full of purring limousines. Our driver steps out and opens our door in an instant, every motion professional. Jill says,

"This is nice," which is probably what she said last year. *"Nice."*

Last year we were taken to a fancy dinner theater built in some nonexistent portion of downtown. Some of the details come back to me. The play was written for our audience, for one performance, and Jill said it was remarkable and sweet and terribly well acted. She had been a theater major for a couple semesters, and you would have thought the A.I.s had done everything for her. Although I do remember liking the play myself, on my business-major terms. It was funny, and the food couldn't have been more perfect.

Tonight the food is just as good. I have the fish—red snapper caught milliseconds ago—and Jill is working on too much steak. "Screw the diet," she jokes. The truth is that we'll gain weight only if it helps our health; we can indulge ourselves for this one glorious meal. Our table is near the clear glass wall, overlooking the sunset and an impressive view of a winding river and thick woods and vivid green meadows. The glass quits near the top of the wall, leaving a place for wild birds to perch. I'm guessing those birds don't exist in any bird book. They have brilliant colors and loud songs, persistent and almost human at times; and even though they're overhead, sometimes holding their butts to us, I don't have to worry about accidents. They are mannerly and reliable, and in a little while they won't exist anymore. At least not outside our own minds, I'm thinking.

N<small>obody knows where</small> the A.I.s live, or how, or how they entertain themselves. They tell us next to nothing about their existences. "We don't wish to disturb your lives," claimed the stranger who came to our front door six years ago. "We respect you too much. After all, you did create us. We consider you our parents, in a very real sense. . . ."

Parents in the sense that shoreline slime is the parent of humanity, I suppose.

Rumors tell that the A.I.s have enlarged their intelligence endless times, and reproduced like maniacs, and perhaps spread to the stars and points beyond. Or perhaps they've remained here, not needing to go anywhere. The rumors are conflicting, in truth. There's no sense in believing any of them, I remind myself.

"So what's happening in the A.I. world?" asks a man at the adjacent table. He is talking to his waiter with a loud, self-important voice. "You guys got anything new up your sleeves?"

The questions are rude, not to mention stupid.

"Would you like to see a dessert menu? Sir?" The waiter possesses an unflappable poise. Coarse, ill-directed questions are so much bird noise, it seems. "Or we have some fine after-dinner drinks, if you'd rather."

"Booze, yeah. Give me some," growls the customer.

First of all, I'm thinking, A.I.s never explain their realm. For all the reasons I've heard, the undisputed best is that we cannot comprehend their answers. How could we? And secondly, the waiter is no more an A.I. than I am. Or my fork, for that matter. Or anything else we can see and touch and smell.

"Why don't people understand?" I mutter to myself.

"I don't know. Why?" says Jill.

I have to pee. My gut is full of fish and my wife's excess steak, and I tell her, "I'll be right back."

She brightens. "More adjustments?"

"Maybe later."

I find the rest room and untie my swimsuit, pee and shake and tuck. Then I'm washing my hands and thinking. At the office, now and again, I hear stories from single people and some of the married ones a little less stuffy than I. On Birth Day, it seems, they prefer different kinds of excitement. Dinner and sweet-sounding birds might be a start, but what are the A.I.s if not limitless? Bottomless and borderless, and what kinds of fun could they offer wilder sorts?

It puts me in a mood.

Leaving the rest room, I notice a beautiful woman standing at the end of the hallway. Was that a hallway a few moments ago? She seems to beckon for me. I take a tentative step, then another. "You look quite handsome tonight," she informs me.

I smell perfume, or I smell her.

She isn't human. The kind of beauty shining up out of her makes her seem eerily lovely, definitely not real, and that's an enormous attraction, I discover. I'm surprised by how easily my breath comes up short, and I hear my clumsiest voice saying, "Excuse me . . . ?"

"Steven," she says, "would you like some time with me? Alone?" She waits for an instant, then promises, "Your time with me costs nothing. Nobody will miss you. If you wish."

"Thanks," I mutter, "but no, I shouldn't. No, thank you."

She nods as if she expects my answer. "Then you have a very good evening, Steven. " She smiles. She could be a lighthouse with that smile. "And if you have the opportunity, at the right moment, you might wish to tell your wife that you love her deeply and passionately."

"Excuse me?"

But she has gone. I'm shaking my head and saying, "Excuse me?" to a water fountain embossed in gold.

W*e actually discussed* the possibility of refusing the A.I.s on the first Birth Day. Jill told me, if memory serves, "We can just say, *No, thank you,* when they come to the door. All right?"

For weeks, people had talked about little else. Birth Day

was the A.I.s' invention; they wished to thank us, the entire species, for having invested time and resources in their own beginnings. With their casual magic, they had produced the batches of charming people who went from door to door, asking who would like to join the festival, and what kinds of entertainment would be appreciated. (Although they likely sensed every answer before it was given. Politeness is one of their hallmarks, and they work hard to wear disarming faces.)

"Let's stay home," Jill suggested.

"Why?"

"Because," she said. "Because I don't want us leaving our babies with them. Inside our house."

It was a concern of mine, too. The A.I.s had assured every parent that during Birth Day festivities, without exception, no child would fall down any stairs or poke out an eye or contract any diseases worse than a head cold. Their safety, and the safety of their parents, too, would be assured.

And how could anyone doubt their word?

How?

Yet on the other hand, we were talking about Mary Beth and David. Our daughter and son, and I had to agree. "We can tell them, *No, thank you,*" I said.

"Politely."

"Absolutely."

The sitter arrived at seven o'clock, to the instant, and I was waiting. She formed in front of our screen door, built from atoms pulled out of the surrounding landscape. Or from nothing. I suppose to an A.I., it's a casual trick, probably on a par with me turning a doorknob. I'm like a bacterium to them—a single idiotic bug—and I must seem completely transparent under their strong gaze.

The baby-sitter was a large, middle-aged woman with vast breasts. She was the very image of the word "matron," with a handsome face and an easy smile. "Good evening, sir," she told me. "I'm sorry. Didn't you expect me?"

I was wearing shorts and a T-shirt, and probably that old pair of Fruit of the Looms, newly bought.

"You and your wife were scheduled for this evening . . . yes?"

"Come in, please." I had to let her inside, I felt. I could see the black limousines up and down the street, and the drivers, and I felt rather self-conscious. "My wife," I began, "and I guess I, too. . . ."

Jill came downstairs. She was carrying David, and he was crying with a jackhammer voice. He was refusing to eat or be still, and Jill's expression told me the situation. Then she looked at the sitter, saying, "You're here," with a faltering voice.

"A darling baby!" she squealed. "May I hold him? A moment?"

And of course David became silent an instant later. Maybe the A.I.s performed magic on his mood, though I think it was more in the way the sitter held him and how she smiled; and ten minutes later, late but not too late, we were dressed for dancing, and leaving our children in capable hands. I can't quite recall the steps involved, and we weren't entirely at ease. In fact, we came home early, finding bliss despite our fears. It was true, we realized. Nothing bad could happen to anyone on Birth Day, and for that short span, our babies were in the care they deserved. In perfect hands, it seemed. And parents everywhere could take a few hours to relax, every worry and weight lifted from them. It seemed.

O_n *our way* home, in darkness, I tell Jill how much I love her.

Her response is heartfelt and surprising. Her passion is a little unnerving. Did she have an interlude with a husky-voiced waiter, perhaps? Did he say things and do things to leave her ready for my hands and tender words? Maybe so. Or maybe there was something that I hadn't caught for myself. I just needed someone to make me pay attention, maybe?

We embrace on the limousine's expansive seat, then it's more than an embrace. I notice the windows have gone black, and there's a divider between the driver and us. Music plays somewhere. I don't recognize the piece. Then we're finished, but there's no reason to dress—*they* will make time for us—and after a second coupling, we have enough, and dress and arrive home moments later. We thank our driver, then the sitter. "Oh, we had a lovely time!" Mrs. Simpson gushes. "Such lovely children!"

Whose? I'm wondering. Ours?

We check on David in his room, Mary Beth in hers, and everything seems intact. Mrs. Simpson probably spun perfect children's stories for them, or invented games, then baked them cookies without any help from the oven, and sent them to bed without complaints.

Once a year seems miraculous.

Jill and I try once more in our own bed, but I'm tired. Old. Spent. I sleep hard, and wake to find that it's Saturday morning, the kids watching TV and my wife brewing coffee. The house looks shabby, I'm thinking. After every Birth Day, it looks worn and old. Like old times, Jill holds my hand under the kitchen table, and we sip, and suddenly it seems too quiet in the family room.

Our instincts are pricked at the same instant.

Mary Beth arrives with a delighted expression. What now?

"He's stuck," she announces.

"David—?" Jill begins.

"On the stairs . . . He got caught somehow. . . ."

We have iron bars as part of the railing, painted white and very slick. Somehow David has thrust his head between two bars and become stuck. He's crying without sound. In his mind, I suppose, he's making ready to spend the rest of his life in this position. That's the kind of kid he is. . . . Oh God, he worries me.

"How did this happen?" I ask.

"*She* told me to—"

"Liar!" shouts his sister.

Jill says, "Everyone, be quiet!"

Then I'm working to bend the rails ever so slightly, to gain enough room to pull him free. Only, my strength ebbs when I start to laugh. I can't help myself. Everything has built up, and Jill laughs, too. We're both crazy for a few moments, giggling like little kids. And later, after our son is safe and Mary Beth is exiled to her room for the morning, Jill pours both of us cups of strong, cool coffee; and I comment, "You know, we wouldn't make very good bacteria."

"Excuse me?" she says. "What was that gem?"

"If we had to be bacteria . . . you know . . . swimming in the slime? We'd do a piss-poor job of it. I bet so."

Maybe she understands me, and maybe not.

I watch her nod and sip, then she says, "And *they* wouldn't make very good people. Would they?"

I doubt it.

"Amen," I say. "Amen!"

The Hydrogen Wall

Gregory Benford

Here's a compelling portrait of a young woman who must bargain with an immense and ancient alien Artificial Intelligence for the information needed to avert the End of the World, all the while struggling to accept the price she must pay to succeed...

Gregory Benford is one of the modern giants of the field. His 1980 novel Timescape *won the Nebula Award, the John W. Campbell Memorial Award, the British Science Fiction Association Award, and the Australian Ditmar Award, and is widely considered to be one of the classic novels of the last two decades. His other novels include* Beyond Jupiter, The Stars in Shroud, In the Ocean of Night, Against Infinity, Artifact, Across the Sea of Suns, Great Sky River, Tides of Light, Furious Gulf, Sailing Bright Eternity, Cosm, *and* Foundation's Fear. *His short work has been collected in* Matter's End *and* Worlds Vast and Various. *His most recent books are a major new solo novel,* The Martian Race, *a nonfiction collection,* Deep Time, *and a new collection,* Immersion and Other Short Novels. *Benford is a professor of physics at the University of California, Irvine.*

> Hidden wisdom and hidden treasure—of what use is either?
>
> —Ecclesiasticus 20:30

"Your ambition?" The Prefect raised an eyebrow.

She had not expected such a question. "To, uh, translate. To learn." It sounded lame to her ears, and his disdainful scowl showed that he had expected some such rattled response. Very well then, be more assertive. "Particularly, if I may, from the Sagittarius Architecture."

This took the Prefect's angular face by surprise, though he quickly covered by pursing his leathery mouth. "That is an ancient problem. Surely you do not expect that a Trainee could make headway in such a classically difficult challenge."

"I might," she shot back crisply. "Precisely because it's so well documented."

"Centuries of well-marshalled inquiry have told us very little of the Sagittarius Architecture. It is a specimen from the highest order of Sentient Information, and will not reward mere poking around."

"Still, I'd like a crack at it."

"A neophyte—"

"May bring a fresh perspective."

They both knew that by tradition at the Library, incoming candidate Librarians could pick their first topic. Most deferred to the reigning conventional wisdom and took up a small Message, something from a Type I Civilization just coming onto the galactic stage. Something resembling what Earth had sent out in its first efforts. To tackle a really big problem was foolhardy.

But some smug note in the Prefect's arrogant gaze had kindled an old desire in her.

He sniffed. "To merely review previous thinking would take a great deal of time."

She leaned forward in her chair. "I have studied the Sagittarius for years. It became something of a preoccupation of mine."

"Ummm." She had little experience with people like this. The Prefect was strangely austere in his unreadable face, the even tones of his neutral sentences. Deciphering him seemed to require the same sort of skills she had fashioned through years of training. But at the moment she felt only a yawning sense of her inexperience, amplified by the stretching silence in this office. The Prefect could be right, after all. She started to phrase a gracious way to back down.

The Prefect made a small sound, something like a sigh. "Very well. Report weekly."

She blinked. "Um, many thanks."

Ruth Angle smoothed her ornate, severely traditional Trainee shift as she left the Prefect's office, an old calming gesture she could not train away. Now her big mouth had gotten her into a fix, and she could see no way out. Not short of going back in there and asking for his guidance, to find a simpler Message, something she could manage.

To hell with that. The soaring, fluted alabaster columns of the Library Centrex reminded her of the majesty of this entire enterprise, stiffening her resolve.

There were few other traditional sites, here at the edge of the Fourth Millennium, that could approach the grandeur of the Library. Since the first detection of signals from other galactic civilizations nearly a thousand years before, no greater task had confronted humanity than the learning of such vast lore.

The Library itself had come to resemble its holdings: huge, aged, mysterious in its shadowy depths. In the formal grand pantheon devoted to full-color, moving statues of legendary Interlocutors, giving onto the Seminar Plaza, stood the revered block of black basalt: the Rosetta Stone, symbol of all they worked toward. Its chiseled face was nearly three millennia old, and, she thought as she passed it, endearingly easy to understand. It was a simple linear, one-to-one mapping of three human languages, found by accident. Having the same text in Greek II, which the discoverers could read, meant that the hieroglyphic pictures and cursive Demotic forms could be deduced. This battered black slab, found by troops clearing ground to build a fort, had linked civilizations separated by millennia.

She reached out a trembling palm to caress its chilly hard sleekness. The touch brought a thrill. They who served here were part of a grand, age-old tradition, one that went to the heart of the very meaning of being human.

Only the lightness of her ringing steps buoyed her against the grave atmosphere of the tall, shadowy vaults. Scribes passed silently among the palisades, their violet robes swishing after them. She was noisy and new, and she knew it.

She had come down from low lunar orbit the day before, riding on the rotating funicular, happy to rediscover Luna's ample domes and obliging gravity. Her earliest training had been here, and then the mandatory two years on Earth. The Councilors liked to keep a firm hold on who ran the Library, so the final scholastic work had to be in bustling, focal point Australia, beside foaming waves and tawny beaches. Luna was a more solemn place, unchanging.

She savored the stark ivory slopes of craters in the distance as she walked in the springy gait of one still adjusting to the gravity.

Sagittarius, here I come.

Her next and most important appointment was with the Head Nought. She went through the usual protocols, calling upon lesser lights, before being ushered into the presence of Siloh, a smooth-skinned Nought who apparently had not learned to smile. Or maybe that went with the cellular territory; Noughts had intricate adjustments to offset their deeply sexless natures.

"I do hope you can find a congruence with the Sagittarius Architecture," Siloh said in a flat tone that ended each
sentence with a purr. "Though I regret your lost effort."

"Lost?"

"You will fail, of course."

"Perhaps a fresh approach—"

"So have said many hundreds of candidate scholars. I
remind you of our latest injunction from the Councilors—
the heliosphere threat."

"I thought there was little anyone could do."

"So it seems." Siloh scowled. "But we cannot stop from
striving."

"Of course not," she said in what she hoped was a de-
mure manner. She was aware of how little she could make
of this person, who gave off nothing but sentences.

Noughts had proven their many uses centuries before.
Their lack of sexual appetites and apparatus, both physical
and mental, gave them a rigorous objectivity. As diplomats,
Contractual Savants, and neutral judges, they excelled.
They had replaced much of the massive legal apparatus that
had come to burden society in earlier centuries.

The Library could scarcely function without their insights.
Alien texts did not carry unthinking auras of sexuality, as did
human works. Or more precisely, the Messages might carry
alien sexualities aplenty, however much their original creators
had struggled to make them objective and transparent. Cutting through that was a difficult task for ordinary people, such
as herself. The early decades of the Library had struggled with
the issue, and the Noughts had solved it.

Translating the Messages from a human male or female
perspective profoundly distorted their meaning. In the
early days, this had beclouded many translations. Much
further effort had gone to cleansing these earlier texts.
Nowadays, no work issued from the Library without a
careful Nought vetting, to erase unconscious readings.

Siloh said gravely, "The heliosphere incursion has baffled our finest minds. I wish to approach it along a different path. For once, the Library may be of immediate use."

Ruth found this puzzling. She had been schooled in the loftier aspects of the Library's mission, its standing outside the tides of the times. Anyone who focused upon Messages that had been designed for eternity had to keep a mental distance from the events of the day. "I do not quite . . ."

"Think of the Library as the uninitiated do. They seldom grasp the higher functions we must perform, and instead see mere passing opportunity. That is why we are bombarded with requests to view the Vaults as a source for inventions, tricks, novelties."

"And reject them, as we should." She hoped she did not sound too pious.

But Siloh nodded approvingly. "Indeed. My thinking is that an ancient society such as the Sagittarius Architecture might have encountered such problems before. It would know better than any of our astro-engineers how to deal with the vast forces at work."

"I see." *And why didn't I think of it? Too steeped in this culture of hushed reverence for the sheer magnitude of the Library's task?* "Uh, it is difficult for me to envision how—"

"Your task is not to imagine but to perceive," Siloh said severely.

She found Noughts disconcerting, and Siloh more so. Most chose to have no hair, but Siloh sported a rim of kinked coils, glinting like brass, as if a halo had descended onto his skull. Its pale eyelashes flicked seldom, gravely. Descending, its eyelids looked pink and rubbery. The nearly invisible blond eyebrows arched perpetually, so its every word seemed layered with artifice, tones sliding among syllables with resonant grace. Its face shifted from one nuanced expression to another, a pliable medium in ceaseless movement, like the surface of a restless pond rippled by unfelt winds. She felt as though she should be taking notes about its every utterance. Without blinking, she

shifted to recording mode, letting her spine-based memory
log everything that came in through eyes and ears. Just in
case.

"I have not kept up, I fear," she said; it was always a
good idea to appear humble. "The incursion—"

"Has nearly reached Jupiter's orbit," Siloh said. The
wall behind the Nought lit with a display showing the sun,
gamely plowing through a gale of interstellar gas.

Only recently had humanity learned that it had arisen in
a benign time. An ancient supernova had once blown a
bubble in the interstellar gas, and Earth had been cruising
through that extreme vacuum while the mammals evolved
from tree shrews to big-brained world-conquerors. Not
that the sun was special in any other way. In its gyre about
the galaxy's hub, it moved only fifty light-years in the span
of a million years, oscillating in and out of the galaxy's
plane every thirty-three million years—and that was
enough to bring it now out of the Local Bubble's protection. The full density of interstellar hydrogen now beat
against the Sun's own plasma wind, pushing inward, ham-
mering into the realm of the fragile planets.

"The hydrogen wall began to bombard the Ganymede
Colony yesterday," Siloh said with the odd impartiality
Ruth still found unnerving, as though not being male or female gave it a detached view, above the human fray. "We
at the Library are instructed to do all we can to find knowledge bearing upon our common catastrophe."

The wall screen picked up this hint and displayed
Jupiter's crescent against the hard stars. Ruth watched as a
fresh flare coiled back from the ruby, roiling shock waves
that embraced Jupiter. The bow curve rippled with colossal turbulence, vortices bigger than lesser worlds. "Surely
we can't change the interstellar weather."

"We must try. The older Galactics may know of a world
that survived such an onslaught."

The sun's realm, the heliosphere, had met the dense

clump of gas and plasma eighty-eight years before. Normally the solar wind particles blown out from the sun kept the interstellar medium at bay. For many past millennia, these pressures had struggled against each other in a filmy barrier a hundred Astronomical Units beyond the cozy inner solar system. Now the barrier had been pressed back in, where the outer planets orbited.

The wall's view expanded to show what remained of the comfy realm dominated by the Sun's pressure. It looked like an ocean-going vessel, seen from above: bow waves generated at the prow rolled back, forming the characteristic parabolic curve.

Under the steadily rising pressure of the thickening interstellar gas and dust, that pressure front eroded. The sun's course slammed it against the dense hydrogen wall at sixteen kilometers per second and its puny wind was pressed back into the realm of solar civilization. Pluto's Cryo Base had been abandoned decades before, and Saturn only recently. The incoming hail of high-energy particles and fitful storms had killed many. The Europa Ocean's strange life was safe beneath its ten kilometers of ice, but that was small consolation.

"But what can we do on our scale?" she insisted.

"What we can."

"The magnetic turbulence alone, at the bow shock, holds a larger energy store than all our civilization."

Siloh gave her a look that reminded her of how she had, as a girl, watched an insect mating dance. Distant distaste. "We do not question here. We listen."

"Yes, Self." This formal title, said to be preferred by Noughts to either Sir or Madam, seemed to please Siloh. It went through the rest of their interview with a small smile, and she could almost feel a personality beneath its chilly remove. Almost.

She left the Executat Dome with relief. The Library sprawled across the Locutus Plain, lit by Earth's stunning

crescent near a jagged white horizon. Beneath that pre-
served plain lay the cryofiles of all transmissions received
from the Galactic Complex, the host of innumerable societies that had flourished long before humanity was born. A
giant, largely impenetrable resource. The grandest possible
intellectual scrap heap.

Libraries were monuments not so much to the Past, but
to Permanence itself. Ruth shivered with anticipation. She
had passed through her first interviews!—and was now free
to explore the myriad avenues of the galactic past. The
Sagittarius was famous for its density of information, many-
layered and intense. A wilderness, beckoning.

Still, she had to deal with the intricacies of the Library,
too. These now seemed as steeped in arcane byways and
bureaucratic labyrinths as were the Library's vast contents.
Ruth cautioned herself to be careful, and most especially,
to not let her impish side show. She bowed her head as she
passed an aged Nought, for practice.

The greatest ancient library had been at Alexandria, in
Afrik. An historian had described the lot of librarians there
with envy: *They had a carefree life: free meals, high
salaries, no taxes to pay, very pleasant surroundings, good
lodgings, and servants. There was plenty of opportunity for
quarreling with each other.*

So not much had changed. . . .

H*er apartment mate* was a welcome antidote to the
Nought. Small, bouncy, Catkejen was not the usual image
of a Librarian candidate. She lounged around in a revealing sarong, sipping a stimulant that was scarcely allowed
in the Trainee Manual.

"Give 'em respect," she said off-hand, "but don't buy
into all their solemn dignity-of-our-station stuff. You'll
choke on it after a while."

Ruth grinned. "And get slapped down."

"I kinda think the Librarians *like* some back talk. Keeps 'em in fighting trim."

"Where are you from?—Marside?"

"They're too mild for me. No, I'm a Ganny."

"Frontier stock, eh?" Ruth sprawled a little herself, a welcome relief from the ramrod-spine posture the Librarians kept. No one hunched over their work here in the classic scholar's pose. They kept upright, using the surround enviros. "Buried in ice all your life?"

"Don't you buy that." Catkejen waved a dismissive hand, extruding three tool-fingers to amplify the effect. "We get out to prospect the outer moons a lot."

"So you're wealthy? Hiding behind magneto shields doesn't seem worth it."

"More clichés. Not every Ganny strikes it rich."

The proton sleet at Ganymede was lethal, but the radiation-cured elements of the inner Jovian region had made many a fortune, too. "So you're from the poor folks who had to send their brightest daughter off?"

"Another cliché." Catkejen made a face. "I hope you have better luck finding something original in—what was it?"

"The Sagittarius Architecture."

"*Brrrrr!* I heard it was a hydra."

"Each time you approach it, you get a different mind?"

"If you can call it a mind. I hear it's more like a talking body."

Ruth had read and sensed a lot about the Sagittarius, but this was new. They all knew that the mind-body duality made no sense in dealing with alien consciousness, but how this played out was still mysterious. She frowned.

Catkejen poked her in the ribs. "Come on, no more deep thought today! Let's go for a fly in the high-pressure dome."

Reluctantly, Ruth went. But her attention still fidgeted over the issues. She thought about the challenge to come, even as she swooped in a long, serene glide over the fern-

covered hills under the amusement dome, beneath the
stunning ring of orbital colonies that made a glittering
necklace in the persimmon sky.

*I*nto *her own pod, at last!*

She had gone through a week of final neural condition-
ing since seeing Siloh, and now the moment had arrived:
direct line feed from the Sagittarius Architecture.

Her pod acted as a neural web, using her entire body to
convey connections. Sheets of sensation washed over her
skin, a prickly itch began in her feet.

She felt a heady kinesthetic rush of acceleration as a
constellation of fusions drew her to a tight nexus. Alien ar-
chitectures used most of the available human input landscape. Dizzying surges in the ears, biting smells, ringing
cacophonies of elusive patterns, queasy perturbations of
the inner organs—a Trainee had to know how these might
convey meaning.

They often did, but translating them was elusive. After
such experiences, one never thought of human speech as
anything more than a hobbled, claustrophobic mode. Its
linear meanings and frail attempts at linked concepts were
simple, utilitarian, and typical of younger minds.

The greatest task was translating the dense smatterings
of mingled sensations into discernible sentences. Only thus
could a human fathom them at all, even in a way blunted
and blurred. Or so much previous scholarly experience
said.

Ruth felt herself bathed in a shower of penetrating responses, all coming from her own body. These were her
own in-board subsystems coupled with high-bit-rate spat-
terings of meaning—guesses, really. She had an ample
repository of built-in processing units, lodged in her spine
and shoulders. No one would attempt such a daunting task
without artificial amplifications. To confront such slabs of

raw data with a mere unaided human mind was pointless
and quite dangerous. Early Librarians, centuries before,
had perished in a microsecond's exposure to such layered
labyrinths as the Sagittarius.

Years of scholarly training had conditioned her against
the jagged ferocity of the link, but still she felt a cold
shiver of dread. That, too, she had to wait to let pass. The
effect amplified whatever neural state you brought to it.
Legend had it that a Librarian had once come to contact
while angry, and been driven into a fit from which he'd
never recovered. They had found the body peppered everywhere with micro-contusions.

The raw link was as she had expected:

A daunting, many-layered language. Then she slid into
an easier notation that went through her spinal interface,
and heard/felt/read:

Much more intelligible, but still. . . . She concen-
trated—

We wish you greetings, new sapience.
"Hello. I come with reverence and new supple offerings."
This was the standard opening, one refined over five cen-
turies ago and never changed by so much as a syllable.

And you offer?
"Further cultural nuances." Also a ritual promise, however
unlikely it was to be fulfilled. Few advances into the Sagittarius had been made in the last century. Even the most
ambitious Librarians seldom tried any longer.

Something like mirth came wafting to her, then:

We are of a mind to venture otherwise with you.
Damn! There was no record of such a response before, her

downlink confirmed. It sounded like a preliminary to a dismissal. That overture had worked fine for the last six Trainees. But then, they hadn't gotten much farther, either, before the Sagittarius lost interest and went silent again. Being ignored was the greatest insult a Trainee faced, and the most common. Humans were more than a little boring to advanced intelligences. The worst of it was that one seldom had an idea why.

So what in hell did this last remark from it mean? Ruth fretted, speculated, and then realized that her indecision was affecting her own neural states. She decided to just wing it. "I am open to suggestion and enlightenment."

A pause, getting longer as she kept her breathing steady. Her meditative cues helped, but could not entirely submerge her anxieties. Maybe she had bitten off entirely too much—

From Sagittarius she received a jittering cascade, resolving to:

As a species you are technologically gifted yet philosophically callow, a common condition among emergent intelligences. But of late it is your animal property of physical expression that intrigues. Frequently you are unaware of your actions which makes them all the more revealing.

"Oh?" She sat back in her pod and crossed her legs. The physical pose might help her mental profile, in the global view of the Sagittarius. Until now its responses had been within conventional bounds; this last was new.

You concentrate so hard upon your linear word groups that you forget how your movements, postures and facial cues give you away.

"What am I saying now, then?"

That you must humor Us until you can ask your questions about the heliosphere catastrophe.

Ruth laughed. It felt good. "I'm that obvious?"

Many societies We know only through their bit-strings and abstractions. That is the nature of binary signals. You, on the other hand (to use a primate phrase), We can know through your unconscious self.

"You want to know about *me?*"

We have heard enough symphonies, believe Us.

At least it was direct. Many times in the past, her research showed, it—"They"—had not been. The Architecture was paying attention!—a coup in itself.

"I'm sorry our art forms bore you."

Many beings who use acoustic means believe their art forms are the most important, valuable aspects of their minds. This is seldom so, in Our experience.

"So involvement is more important to you?"

For this moment, truly. Remember that we are an evolving composite of mental states, no less than you. You cannot meet the same Us again.

"Then you should be called . . . ?"

We know your term 'Architecture' and find it—your phrasing?—amusing. Better perhaps to consider us to be a composite entity. As you are yourselves, though you cannot sense this aspect. You imagine that you are a unitary consciousness, guiding your bodies.

"And we aren't?"

Of course not. Few intelligences in Our experience know as little of their underlying mental architecture as do you.

"Could that be an advantage for us?"

With the next words came a shooting sensation, something like a dry chuckle.

Perhaps so. You apparently do all your best work off stage. Ideas appear to you without your knowing where they come from.

She tried to imagine watching her own thoughts, but was at a loss where to go with this. "Then let's . . . well."

Gossip?

What an odd word choice. There was something like a tremor of pleasure in its neural tone, resounding with long, slow wavelengths within her.

"*It sounds creepy,*" Catkejen said. She was shoveling in food at the Grand Cafeteria, a habit Ruth had noticed many Gannies had.

"Nothing in my training really prepared me for its . . . well, coldness, and . . ."

Catkejen stopped eating to nod knowingly. "And intimacy?"

"Well, yes."

"Look, I've been doing pod work only a few weeks, just like you. Already it's pretty clear that we're mostly negotiating, not translating."

Ruth frowned. "They warned us, but still . . ."

"Look, these are big minds. Strange as anything we'll ever know. But they're trapped in a small space, living cyber-lives. We're their entertainment."

"And I am yours, ladies," said a young man as he sat down at their table. He ceremoniously shook hands. "Geoffrey Chandis."

"So how're you going to amuse us?" Catkejen smiled skeptically.

"How's this?" Geoffrey stood and put one hand on their table. In one deft leap he was upside down, balanced upon the one hand, the other saluting them.

"You're from HiGee." Catkejen applauded.

He switched his support from one hand to the other. "I find this paltry 0.19 Lunar gee charming, don't you?"

Ruth pointed. "As charming as one red sock, the other blue?"

Unfazed, Geoffrey launched himself upward. He did a flip and landed on two feet, without even a backward step to restore balance. Ruth and Catkejen gave him beaming smiles. "Socks are just details, ladies. I stick to essentials."

"You're in our year, right?" Catkejen asked. "I saw you at the opening day ceremonies."

Geoffrey sat, but not before he twirled his chair up into the air, making it do a few quick, showy moves. "No, I was just sneaking in for some of the refreshments. I'm a lordly year beyond you two."

Ruth said, "I thought HiGee folk were, well—"

"More devoted to the physical? Not proper fodder for the Library?" He grinned.

Ruth felt her face redden. Was she that easy to read? "Well, yes."

"My parents, my friends, they're all focused on athletics. Me, I'm a rebel."

Catkejen smiled. "Even against the Noughts?"

He shrugged. "Mostly I find a way to go around them."

Ruth nodded. "I think I'd rather be ignored by them."

"Y'know," Catkejen said reflectively, "I think they're a lot like the Minds."

Ruth asked slowly, "Because they're the strangest form of human?"

Geoffrey said, "They're sure alien to me. I'll give up sex when I've lost all my teeth, maybe, but not before."

"They give me the shivers sometimes," Catkejen said. "I was fetching an ancient written document over in the Hard Archives last week, nighttime. Three of them came striding down the corridor in those capes with the cowls. All in black, of course. I ducked into a side corridor—they scared me."

"A woman's quite safe with them," Geoffrey said. "Y'know, when they started up their Nought Guild business, centuries back, they decided on that all-black look and the shaved heads and all, because it saved money. But everybody read it as dressing like funeral directors. Meaning, they were going to bury all our sex-ridden, old ways of interpreting."

"And here I thought I knew a lot about Library history," Catkejen said in an admiring tone. "Wow, that's good gossip."

"But they've made the big breakthroughs," Ruth said. "Historically—"

"Impossible to know, really," Catkejen said. "The first Noughts refused to even have names, so we can't cite the work as coming from them."

Geoffrey said mock-solemnly, "Their condition they would Nought name."

"They've missed things, too," Catkejen said. "Translated epic sensual poems as if they were about battles, when they were about love."

"Sex, actually," Geoffrey said. "Which can seem like a battle."

Catkejen laughed. "Not the way *I* do it."

"Maybe you're not doing it right." Geoffrey laughed with her, a ringing peal.

"Y'know, I wonder if the Noughts ever envy us?"

Geoffrey grunted in derision. "They save so much time by not having to play our games. It allows them to contemplate the Messages at their leah-zure."

He took a coffee cup and made it do a few impossible stunts in midair. Ruth felt that if she blinked she would miss something; he was *quick*. His compact body had a casual grace, despite the thick slabs of muscle. The artful charm went beyond the physical. His words slid over each other in an odd pronunciation that had just enough inflection to ring musically. Maybe, she thought, there were other amusements to be had here in the hallowed Library grounds.

• • •

She worked steadily, subjecting each microsecond of her interviews with the Architecture to elaborate contextual analysis. Codes did their work, cross-checking furiously across centuries of prior interpretation. But they needed the guidance of the person who had been through the experience: her.

And she felt the weight of the Library's history upon her every translation. Each cross-correlation with the huge body of Architecture research brought up the immense history behind their entire effort.

When first received centuries before, the earliest extraterrestrial signals had been entirely mystifying. The initial celebrations and bold speeches had obscured this truth, which was to become the most enduring fact about the field.

For decades the searchers for communications had rummaged through the frequencies, trying everything from radio waves to optical pulses, and even the occasional foray into X-rays. They found nothing. Conventional wisdom held that the large power needed to send even a weak signal across many light-years was the most important fact. Therefore, scrutinize the nearby stars, cupping electromagnetic ears for weak signals from penny-pinching civilizations. The odds were tiny that a society interested in communication would be nearby, but this was just one of those hard facts about the cosmos—which turned out to be wrong.

The local-lookers fell from favor after many decades of increasingly frantic searches. By then the Galactic Center Strategy had emerged. Its basis lay in the discovery that star formation had begun in the great hub of stars within the innermost ten thousand light-years. Supernovas had flared early and often there, stars were closer together, so heavy elements built up quickly. Three-quarters of the suit-

able life-supporting stars in the entire galaxy were older
than the Sun, and had been around on average more than a
billion years longer.

Most of these lay within the great glowing central
bulge—the hub, which we could not see through the lanes
of dust clogging the constellation of Sagittarius. But in
radio frequencies, the center shone brightly. And the entire
company of plausible life sites, where the venerable societies might dwell, subtended an arc of only a few degrees,
as seen from Earth.

We truly lived in the boondocks—physically, and as became apparent, conceptually as well.

Near the center of the hub, thousands of stars swarmed
within a single light-year. Worlds there enjoyed a sky with
dozens of stars brighter than the full moon. Beautiful, perhaps—but no eyes would ever evolve there to witness the
splendor.

The dense center was dangerous. Supernovas drove
shock waves through fragile solar systems. Protons sleeted
down on worlds, sterilizing them. Stars swooped near each
other, scrambling up planetary orbits and raining down
comets upon them. The inner zone was a dead zone.

But a bit further out, the interstellar weather was better.
Planets capable of sustaining organic life began their slow
winding path upward toward life and intelligence within
the first billion or two years after the galaxy formed. An
Earthlike world that took 4.5 billion years to produce smart
creatures would have done so about four billion years ago.

In that much time, intelligence might have died out,
arisen again, and gotten inconceivably rich. The beyond-
all-reckoning wealthy beings near the center could afford
to lavish a pittance on a luxury—blaring their presence out
to all those crouched out in the galactic suburbs, just getting started in the interstellar game.

Whatever forms dwelled further in toward the center,
they knew the basic symmetry of the spiral. This suggested

that the natural corridor for communication is along the spiral's radius, a simple direction known to everyone. This maximized the number of stars within a telescope's view. A radius is better than aiming along a spiral arm, since the arm curves away from any straight-line view. So a beacon should broadcast outward in both directions from near the center.

So, rather than look nearby, the ancient Search for Extraterrestrial Intelligence searchers began to look inward. They pointed their antennas in a narrow angle toward the constellation Sagittarius. They listened for the big spenders to shout at the less prosperous, the younger, the unsophisticated.

But how often to cup an ear? If Earth was mediocre, near the middle in planetary properties, then its day and year were roughly typical. These were the natural ranges any world would follow: a daily cycle atop an annual sway of climate.

If aliens were anything like us, they might then broadcast for a day, once a year. But which day? There was no way to tell—so the Search for Extraterrestrial Intelligence searchers began to listen *every* day, for roughly a half hour, usually as the radio astronomers got all their instruments calibrated. They watched for narrow-band signals that stood out even against the bright hub's glow.

Radio astronomers had to know what frequency to listen to, as well. The universe is full of electromagnetic noise at all wavelengths from the size of atoms to those of planets. Quite a din.

There was an old argument that water-based life might pick the "watering hole"—a band near 1 billion cycles/second where both water and hydroxyl molecules radiate strongly. Maybe not right on top of those signals, but nearby, because that's also in the minimum of all the galaxy's background noise.

Conventional Search for Extraterrestrial Intelligence

had spent a lot of effort looking for nearby sources, shifting to their rest frame, and then eavesdropping on certain frequencies in that frame. But a beacon strategy could plausibly presume that the rest frame of the galactic center was the obvious gathering spot, so anyone broadcasting would choose a frequency near the "watering hole" frequency of the galaxy's exact center.

Piggy-backing on existing observing agendas, astronomers could listen to a billion stars at once. Within two years, the strategy worked. One of the first beacons found was from the Sagittarius Architecture.

Most of the signals proved to have a common deep motivation. Their ancient societies, feeling their energies ebb, yet treasuring their trove of accumulated art, wisdom and insight, wanted to pass this on. Not just by leaving it in a vast museum somewhere, hoping some younger species might come calling someday. Instead, many built a robotic funeral pyre fed by their star's energies, blaring out tides of timeless greatness:

> My name is Ozymandias, King of Kings,
> Look on my works, ye Mighty, and despair!

as the poet Percy Bysshe Shelley had put it, witnessing the ruins of ancient Egypt, in Afrik.

At the very beginnings of the Library, humanity found that it was coming in on an extended discourse, an ancient interstellar conversation, without notes or history readily provided. Only slowly did the cyber-cryptographers fathom that most alien cultures were truly vast, far larger than the sum of all human societies. And much older.

Before actual contact, nobody had really thought the problem through. Historically, Englishmen had plenty of trouble understanding the shadings of, say, the Ozzie Bushmen. Multiply that by thousands of other Earthly and solar system cultures and then square the difficulty, to allow for the problem of expressing it all in sentences—or at least, linear symbolic sequences. Square the complexity again to allow for the abyss separating humanity from any alien culture.

The answer was obvious: any alien translator program had to be as smart as a human. And usually much more so.

The first transmission from any civilization contained elementary signs, to build a vocabulary. That much even human scientists had guessed. But then came incomprehensible slabs, digital Rosetta stones telling how to build a simulated alien mind that could talk down to mere first-timers.

The better part of a century went by before humans worked out how to copy and then represent alien minds in silicon. Finally the Alien Library was built, to care for the Minds and Messages it encased. To extract from them knowledge, art, history, and kinds of knowing for which humans might very well have no name.

And to negotiate with them. The cyber-aliens had their own motivations.

"I don't understand your last statement."

I do not need to be told that. You signal body-defiance with your crossed arms, barrier gestures, pursed lips, contradictory eyebrow slants.

"But these tensor topologies are not relevant to what we were discussing."

They are your reward.

"For what?"

Giving me of your essence. By wearing ordinary clothes, as I asked, and thus displaying your overt signals.

"I thought we were discussing the Heliosphere problem."

We were. But you primates can never say only one thing at a time to such as We.

She felt acutely uncomfortable. "Uh, this picture you gave
me . . . I can see this is some sort of cylindrical tunnel
through—"

**The plasma torus of your gas giant world, Jupiter. I sug-
gest it as a way to funnel currents from the moon, Io.**
"I appreciate this, and will forward it—"

**There is more to know, before your level of technology—
forgive me, but it is still crude, and will be so for far longer
than you surmise—can make full use of this defense.**
Ruth suppressed her impulse to widen her eyes. *Defense?*
Was this it? A sudden solution? "I'm not a physiker—"

**Nor need you be. I intercept your host of messages, all un-
spoken. Your pelvis is visible beneath your shift, wider and
rotated back slightly more than the male Supplicants who
come to Us. Waist more slender, thighs thicker. Navel
deeper, belly longer. Specializations impossible to sup-
press.**
Where was it—They—going with this? "Those are just
me, not messages."

**It is becoming of you to deny them. Like your hourglass
shape perceived even at a distance, say, across an ancient
plain at great distance. Your thighs admit an obligingly
wider space, an inward slope to the thickened thighs, that
gives an almost knock-kneed appearance.**
"I *beg* your pardon—"

**A pleasant saying, that—meaning that We have over-
stepped [another gesture] your boundaries? But I merely
seek knowledge for my own repository.**
"I—we—don't like being taken apart like this!"

But reduction to essentials is your primary mental habit.
"Not reducing people!"

Ah, but having done this to the outside world, you surely

cannot object to having the same method applied to your-selves.

"People don't like being dissected,"

Your science made such great strides—unusual upon the grander stage of worlds—precisely because you could dex-terously divide your attentions into small units, all the bet-ter to understand the whole.

When They got like this it was best to humor Them. "Peo-ple don't like it. That is a social mannerism, maybe, but onc we *feel* about "

And I seek more.

The sudden grave way the Sagittarius said this chilled her.

S*iloh was not* happy, though it took a lot of time to figure this out. The trouble with Noughts was their damned lack of signals. No slight downward tug of lips to signal provi-sional disapproval, no sideways glance to open a possibil-ity. Just the facts, Ma'am. "So it is giving you tantalizing bits."

"*They*, not It. Sometimes I feel I'm talking to several different minds at once."

"It has said the same about us."

The conventional theory of human minds was that they were a kind of legislature, always making deals between differing interests. Only by attaining a plurality could any-one make a decision. She bit her lip to not give away any-thing, then realized that her bite was visible, too. "We're a whole species. They're a simulation of one."

Siloh made a gesture she could not read. She had ex-pected some congratulations on her work, but then, Siloh was a Nought, and had little use for most human social lu-brications. He said slowly, "This cylinder through the Io plasma—the physikers say it is intriguing."

"How? I thought the intruding interstellar plasma was overpowering everything."

"It is. We lost Ganymede Nation today."

She gasped. "I hadn't heard."

"You have been immersed in your studies, as is fitting."

"Does Catkejen know?"

"She has been told."

Not by you, I hope. Siloh was not exactly the sympathetic type. "I should go to her."

"Wait until our business is finished."

"But I—"

"Wait."

Siloh leaned across its broad work plain, which responded by offering information. Ruth crooked her neck but could not make out what hung shimmering in the air before Siloh. Of course; this was a well designed office, so that she could not read its many ingrained inputs. He was probably summoning information all the while he talked to her, without her knowing it. Whatever he had learned, he sat back with a contented, small smile. "I believe the Sagittarius Congruence is emerging in full, to tantalize you."

"Congruence?"

"A deeper layer to its intelligence. You should not be deceived into thinking of it as remotely like us. We are comparatively simple creatures." Siloh sat back, steepling its fingers and peering into them, a studied pose. "Never does the Sagittarius think of only a few moves into its game."

"So you agree with Youstani, a Translator Supreme from the twenty-fifth century, that the essential nature of Sagittarius is to see all conversations as a game?"

"Are ours different?" A sudden smile creased his leathery face, a split utterly without mirth.

"I would hope so."

"Then you shall often be deceived."

•　　•　　•

S*he went to* their apartment immediately, but someone had gotten there before her. It was dark, but she caught muffled sounds from the living room. Was Catkejen crying?

Earth's crescent shed a dim glow into the room. She stepped into the portal of the living room and in the gloom saw someone on the viewing pallet. A low whimper drifted in the darkness, repeating, soft and sad, like crying, yes—

But there were two people there. And the sobbing carried both grief and passion, agony and ecstasy. An ancient tide ran in the room's shadowed musk.

The other person was Geoffrey. Moving with a slow rhythm, he was administering a kind of sympathy Ruth certainly could not. And she had not had the slightest clue of this relationship between them. A pang forked through her. The pain surprised her. She made her way out quietly.

C*atkejen's family had* not made it out from Ganymede. She had to go through the rituals and words that soften the hard edges of life. She went for a long hike in the domes, by herself. When she returned she was quieter, worked long hours and took up sewing.

The somber prospects of the Ganymede loss cast a pall over all humanity, and affected the Library's work. This disaster was unparalleled in human history, greater even than the Nation Wars.

Still, solid work helped for a while. But after weeks, Ruth needed a break, and there weren't many at the Library. Anything physical beckoned. She had gone for a swim in the spherical pool, of course, enjoying the challenge. And flown in broad swoops across the Greater Dome on plumes of hot air. But a simmering frustration remained. Life had changed.

With Catkejen she had developed a new, friendly, work-

buddy relationship with Geoffrey. Much of this was done
without words, a negotiation of nuances. They never spoke
of that moment in the apartment, and Ruth did not know if
they had sensed her presence.

Perhaps more than ever, Geoffrey amused them with his
quick talk and artful stunts. Ruth admired his physicality,
the yeasty smell of him as he laughed and cavorted.
HiGeers were known for their focus, which athletics repaid
in careers of remarkable performance. The typical HiGee
career began in sports and moved later to work in arduous
climes, sites in the solar system where human strength and
endurance still counted, because machines were not dex-
terous and supple enough.

Some said the HiGeer concentration might have come
from a side effect of their high-spin, centrifugal doughnut
habitats. Somehow Geoffrey's concentration came out as a
life-of-the-party energy, even after his long hours in intense rapport with his own research.

Appropriately, he was working on the Andromeda Manifold, a knotty tangle of intelligences that stressed the
embodied nature of their parent species. Geoffrey's superb
nervous system, and especially his exact hand-eye coordi-
nation, gave him unusual access to the Manifold. While he
joked about this, most of what he found could not be conveyed in words at all. That was one of the lessons of the
Library—that other intelligences sensed the world, and the
body's relation to it, quite differently. The ghost of Carte-
sian duality still haunted human thinking.

Together the three of them hiked the larger craters. All
good for the body, but Ruth's spirit was troubled. Her own
work was not going well.

She could scarcely follow some of the Architecture's
conversations. Still less comprehensible were the eerie sen-
soria it projected to her—sometimes, the only way it
would take part in their discourse, for weeks on end.

Finally, frustrated, she broke off connection and did not

return for a month. She devoted herself instead to historical records of earlier Sagittarius discourse. From those had come some useful technical inventions, a classic linear text, even a new digital art form. But that had been centuries ago.

Reluctantly she went back into her pod and returned to linear speech mode. "I don't know what you intend by these tonal conduits," she said to the Sagittarius—after all, It probably had an original point of view, even upon its own motivations.

I was dispatched into the Realm to both carry my Creators' essentials, to propagate their supreme Cause, and to gather knowing-wisdom for them.

So it spoke of itself as "I" today—meaning that she was dealing with a shrunken fraction of the Architecture. Was it losing interest? Or withholding itself, after she had stayed away?

I have other functions, as well. Any immortal intelligence must police its own mentation.

Now what did that mean? Suddenly, all over her body washed sheets of some strange signal she could not grasp. The scatter-shot impulses aroused a pulse-quickening unease in her. *Concentrate.* "But . . . but your home world is toward the galactic center, at least twenty thousand light-years away. So much time has passed—"

Quite so—my Creators may be long extinct. Probabilities suggest so. I gather from your information, and mine, that the mean lifetime for civilizations in the Realm is comparable to their/our span.

"So there may be no reason for you to gather information from us at all. You can't send it to them anymore." She could not keep the tensions from her voice. In earlier weeks of incessant pod time, she had relied upon her pod's programming to disguise her transmission. And of course, It knew this. Was anything lost on It?

Our motivations do not change. We are eternally a dutiful servant, as are you.

Ah, an advance to "We." She remembered to bore in on the crucial, not be deflected. "Good. If the interstellar plasma gets near Earth—"

We follow your inference. The effects I know well. My Creators inhabit(ed) a world similar to yours, though frankly, more beautiful. (You have wasted so much area upon water!) We managed the electrical environs of our world to send our beacon signal, harnessing the rotational energy of our two moons to the task.

This was further than anyone had gotten with Sagittarius in a lifetime of Librarians. She felt a spike of elation. "Okay, what will happen?"

If the bow shock's plasma density increases further, while your ordinary star ploughs into it, then there shall be electrical consequences.

"What . . . consequences?"

Dire. You must see your system as a portrait in electro-dynamics, one that is common throughout the Realm. Perceive: currents seethe forth—

A three-dimensional figure sprang into being before her, with the golden sun at its center. Blue feelers of currents sprouted from the sun's angry red spots, flowing out with the gale of particles, sweeping by the apron-strings of Earth's magnetic fields. This much she knew—that Earth's fields deflected huge energies, letting them pass into the great vault where they would press against the interstellar pressures.

But the currents told a different tale. They arced and soared around each world, cocooning each in some proportion. Then they torqued off into the vastness, smothering in darkness, then eventually returning in high, long arcs to the sun. They were like colossal rubber bands that could never break, but that forces could stretch into fibrous structures.

And here came the bulge of interstellar plasma. Lightning forked all along its intrusion. It engulfed Jupiter, and spikes of coronal fury arced far out from the giant planet. These bright blue streamers curled inward, following long tangents toward the sun.

Some struck the Earth.

"I don't need a detailed description of what that means," she said.

Your world is like many others, a spherical capacitor. Disruption of the electrodynamic equilibrium will endanger the fragile skin of life.

From the Sagittarius came a sudden humid reek. She flinched. Sheeting sounds churned so low that she felt them as deep bass notes resounding in her. Wavelengths longer than her body rang through her bones. Her heart abruptly pounded. A growling storm rose in her ears.

"I . . . I will take this . . . and withdraw."

Have this as well, fair primate—
A squirt of compressed meaning erupted in her sensorium.

It will self-unlock at the appropriate moment.

*O*pened, the first fraction of the squashed nugget was astonishing. Even Siloh let itself appear impressed. She could tell this by the millimeter rise of a left lip.

"This text is for the Prefect's attention." When Siloh rose and walked around its work-plane, she realized that she had never seen its extent—nearly three meters of lean muscle, utterly without any hint of male or female shaping. The basic human machine, engineered for no natural world. It stopped to gaze at her. "This confirms what some physikers believe. Jupiter is the key."

Within an hour the Prefect agreed. He eyed them both and flicked on a display. "The Sagittarius confirms our worst suspicions. Trainee, you said that you had captured from it yet more?"

She displayed the full data-nugget It had given her. A pyrotechnic display arced around a simulated Jupiter—

"There, at the poles," the Prefect said. "That cylinder."

The fringing fields carried by interstellar plasma swarmed into the cylinder. This time, instead of ejecting fierce currents, Jupiter absorbed them.

"That tube is electrically shorting out the disturbance," Siloh said. "The cylinders at both poles—somehow they shunt the energies into the atmosphere."

"And not into ours," Ruth said. "It's given us a solution."

The Prefect said, "What an odd way to do it. No description, just pictures."

Siloh said slowly, "Ummmmm . . . And just how do we build those cylinders?"

They looked at her silently, but she got the message: *Find out.*

The *sensations washing* over her were quite clear now. She had asked for engineering details, and it had countered with a demand. A quite graphic one.

This is my price. To know the full extent of the human sensorium.

"Sex?! You want to—"

It seems a small measure in return for the life of your world.

Before she could stop herself she blurted, "But you're not—"

Human? Very well, we wish to fathom the meaning of that word, all the more. This is one step toward comprehending what that symbol-complex means.

"You're a *machine*. A bunch of electronic bips and stutters."

Then we ask merely for a particular constellation of such information.

She gasped, trying not to lose it entirely. "You . . . would barter that for a civilization?"

We are a civilization unto Ourself. Greater than any of you singletons can know.

"I . . . I can't. I *won't*."

"**Y**ou will," Siloh said with stony serenity.

Ruth blinked. "No!"

"Yes."

"This is more, much more, than required by all the Guild standards of neural integration."

"But—yes."

In his sickening swirl of emotions, she automatically reached for rules. Emotion would carry no weight with this Nought.

She felt on firm ground here, despite not recalling well the welter of policy and opinions surrounding the entire phenomenon. A millennium of experience and profound philosophical analysis, much of it by artificial minds, had created a vast, weighty body of thought: Library Metatheory. A lot of it, she thought, was more like the barnacles on the belly of a great ship, parasitic and along for the ride. But the issue could cut her now. Given a neurologically integrated system with two parties enmeshed, what was the proper separation?

"This issue is far larger than individual concerns." Siloh's face remained calm though flinty.

"Even though a Trainee, I am *in charge* of this particular translation—"

"Only nominally. I can have you removed in an instant. Indeed, I can do so myself."

"That would take a while, for anyone to achieve my levels of attunement and focus—"

"I have been monitoring your work. I can easily step in—"

"The Sagittarius Composite doesn't want to sleep with *you*."

Siloh froze, composure gone. "You are inserting personal rebuke here!"

Her lips twitched as she struggled not to smile. "Merely an observation. Sagittarius desires something it cannot get among the Nought class."

"I can arrange matters differently, then." Its face worked with several unreadable signals—as though, she thought, something unresolved was trying to express itself.

"I want to remain at work—"

Suddenly he smiled and said lightly, "Oh, you may. You definitely may."

An abrupt hand waved her away. Plainly it had reached some insight it would not share. But what? Siloh's bland gaze gave away nothing. And she was not good enough at translating him, yet.

S*ome of the* Messages lodged in the Library had not been intended for mortal ears or eyes at all. Like some ancient rulers of Mesopotamia, these alien authors directly addressed their deities, and only them. One opened plaintively,

Tell the God we know and say
For your tomorrow we give our today.

It was not obvious whether this couplet (for in the original it was clearly rhymed) came from a living civilization, or from an artifact left to remind the entire galaxy of what had come before. Perhaps, in alien terms, the distinction did not matter.

Such signals also carried Artificials, as the digital minds

immersed in the Messages were termed. The advanced Artificials, such as Sagittarius, often supervised vast databanks containing apparent secrets, outright brags, and certified history—which was, often, merely gossip about the great. These last, rather transparently, were couched to elicit punishment for the author's enemies, from alien gods. This differed only in complexity and guile from the ancient motivations of Babylonian kings.

Most Messages of this beseeching tone assumed some universal moral laws and boasted of their authors' compliance with them. At first the Sagittarius Architecture had appeared to be of this class, and so went largely uninterpreted for over a century. Only gradually did its sophistication and rich response become apparent. Most importantly, it was a new class entirely—the first Architecture Artificial.

It had something roughly comparable to a human unconscious—and yet it could see into its own inner minds at will. It was as if a human could know all of his/her impulses came from a locus of past trauma, or just a momentary anger—and could see this instantly, by tracing back its own workings. The strange power of human art sprang in part from its invisible wellsprings. To be able to unmask that sanctum was an unnerving prospect.

Yet human-made Artificials always worked with total transparency. The Sagittarius could work that way, or it could mask portions of its own mind from itself, and so attain something like that notorious cliché, the Human Condition.

Since in that era current opinion held that the supreme advantage of any artificial mind lay in its constant transparency, this was a shock. What advantage could come to an Artificial that did not immediately know its own levels? Which acted out of thinking patterns it could not consciously review?

Since this was a property the Sagittarius Architecture

shared (in a way) with humans, the discussion became heated for over two centuries. And unresolved.

Now when Ruth engaged with it, she was acutely conscious of how the Artificial could change nature with quixotic speed. Swerves into irritation came fast upon long bouts of analytic serenity. She could make no sense of these, or fathom the information she gained in these long episodes of engagement. The neurological impact upon her accumulated. Her immersion in the pod carried a jittery static. Her nerves frayed.

Some fraction of the information the Sagittarius Architecture gave her bore upon the problem of heliospheric physics, but she could not follow this. She conveyed the passages, many quite long, to Siloh.

The crisis over the Artificial's demand seemed to have passed. She worked more deeply with it now, and so one afternoon in the pod, concentrating upon the exact nuances of the link, she did not at first react when she felt a sudden surge of unmistakable desire in herself. It shook her, yeasty and feverish, pressing her calves together and urging her thighs to ache with a sweet longing.

Somehow this merged with the passage currently under translation/discussion. She entered more fully into the difficult problem of extracting just the right subtlety from the ⌁⌀⌇⌁⌲ ⌀⌲⌀⌇ ⌲⌀ when all at once she was not reasoning in one part of her mind but, it seemed, in all of them.

From there until only a few heartbeats later she ran the gamut of all previous passions. An ecstasy and union she had experienced only a few times—and only partially, she now saw—poured through her. Her body shook with gusts of raw pleasure. Her Self sang its song, rapt. A constriction of herself seized this flood and rode it. Only blinding speed could grasp what this was, and in full passionate flow she felt herself hammered on a microsecond anvil—into the internal time frames of the Composite.

Dizzy, blinding speed. It registered vast sheets of thought while a single human neuron was charging up to fire. Its cascades of inference and experience were like rapids in a river she could not see but only feel, a kinesthetic acceleration, swerves that swept finally into a delightful blur.

Thought, sensation—all one.

She woke in the pod. Only a few minutes had passed since she had last registered any sort of time at all.

Yet she knew what had happened.

And regretted that it was over.

And hated herself for feeling that way.

"It *had* me."

Siloh began, "In a manner of speaking—"

"Against my will!"

Siloh looked judicial. "So you say. The recordings are necessarily only a pale shadow, so I cannot tell from experiencing them myself—"

Scornfully: "How could you anyway?"

"This discussion will not flow in that direction."

"Damn it, you knew it would do this!"

Siloh shook his head. "I cannot predict the behavior of such an architectural mind class. No one can."

"You at least *guessed* that it would, would find a way into me, to . . . to *mate* with me. At a level we poor stunted humans can only approximate because we're always in two different bodies. It was *in* mine. It—they—knew that in the act of translation there are ways, paths, avenues. . . ." She sputtered to a stop.

"I am sure that description of the experience is impossible." Siloh's normally impenetrable eyes seemed to show real regret.

Yeah? she thought. *How would you know?* But she said

as dryly as she could muster, "You could review the recordings yourself, see—"

"I do not wish to."

"Just to measure—"

"No."

Abruptly she felt intense embarrassment. Bad enough if a man had been privy to those moments, but a Nought . . .

How alien would the experience be, for Siloh?—and *alien* in two different senses of the word? She knew suddenly that there were provinces in the landscape of desire Siloh could not visit. The place she had been with the Composite no human had ever been. Siloh could not go there. Perhaps an ordinary man could not, either.

"I know this is important to you," Siloh said abstractly. "You should also know that the Composite also gave us, in the translation you achieved—while you had your, uh, seizure—the key engineering design behind the heliospheric defense."

She said blankly, "The cylinders . . ."

"Yes, they are achievable, and very soon. A 'technically sweet' solution, I am told by the Prefect. Authorities so far above us that they are beyond view have begun the works needed. They took your information and are making it into an enormous construction at both poles of Jupiter. The entire remaining population of the Jovian Belt threw themselves into shaping the artifacts to achieve this."

"They've been following . . . what *I* say?"

"Yours was deemed the most crucial work. Yet you could not be told."

She shook her head to clear it. "So I wouldn't develop shaky hands."

"And you did not, not at all." Siloh beamed in an inscrutable way, one eyebrow canted at an ambiguous angle.

"You knew," she said leadenly. "What it would do."

"I'm sure I do not fathom what you mean."

She studied Siloh, who still wore the same strange

beaming expression. *Remember,* she thought, *it can be just as irritating as an ordinary man, but it isn't one.*

The colossal discharge of Jupiter's magnetospheric potentials was an energetic event unparalleled in millennia of humanity's long strivings to harness nature.

The Composite had brought insights to bear that physikers would spend a century untangling. For the moment, the only important fact was that by releasing plasma spirals at just the right pitch, and driving these with electrodynamic generators (themselves made of filmy ionized barium), a staggering current came rushing out of the Jovian system.

At nearly the speed of light it intersected the inward bulge of the heliosphere. Currents moved in nonlinear dances, weaving a pattern that emerged within seconds, moving in intricate harmonies.

Within a single minute a complex web of forces flexed into being. Within an hour the bulge of interstellar gas arrested its inward penetration. It halted, waves slamming in vexed lines of magnetic force, against the Jovian sally. And became stable.

Quickly humans—ever irreverent, even in the face of catastrophe—termed their salvation The Basket. Invisible to the eye, the giant web the size of the inner solar system was made of filmy fields that weighed nothing. Yet it was all the same massively powerful, a dynamically responding screen protecting the Earth from a scalding death. The hydrogen wall seethed redly in the night sky. To many, it seemed an angry animal caught at last in a gauzy net.

She witnessed the display from the Grand Plaza with a crowd of half a million. It was humbling, to think that mere primates had rendered such blunt pressures awesome but impotent.

The Sagittarius sent, **We render thanks.**
Her chest was tight. She had dreaded entering the pod again, and now could not speak.

We gather it is traditional among you to compliment one's partner, and particularly a lady . . . afterward.
"Don't . . . don't try."

We became something new from that moment.
She felt anger and fear, and yet simultaneously, pride and curiosity. They twisted together in her. Sweat popped out on her upper lip. The arrival of such emotions, stacked on top of each other, told her that she had been changed by what had happened in this pod, and would—could—never be the same. "I did not *want* it."

Then by my understanding of your phylum, you would not then have desired such congress.
"I—me, the conscious me—did not want it!"

We do not recognize that party alone. Rather, we recognize all of you equally. All your signals, do we receive.
"I don't want it to happen again."

Then it will not. It would not have happened the first time had the congruence between us not held true.
She felt the ache in herself. It rose like a tide, swollen and moist and utterly natural. She had to bring to bear every shred of her will to stop the moment, disconnect, and leave the pod, staggering and weeping and then running.

Geoffrey opened the door to his apartment, blinking owlishly—and then caught her expression.
"I know it's late, I wondered . . ." She stood numbly, then made herself brush past him, into the shadowed room.
"What's wrong?" He wore a white robe and wrapped it self-consciously around his middle.
"I don't think I can handle all this."

He smiled sympathetically. "You're the toast of the Library, what's to handle?"

"I—come here."

Words, linear sequences of blocky words—all useless. She reached inside the robe and found what she wanted. Her hands slid over muscled skin and it was all *so different,* real, not processed and amped and translated through centuries of careful dry precision.

A tremor swept over her, across the gap between them, onto his moistly electric flesh.

"There is news."

"Oh?" She found it hard to focus on Siloh's words.

"You are not to discuss this with anyone," Siloh said woodenly. "The discharges from Jupiter's poles—they are now oscillating. At very high frequencies."

She felt her pulse trip-hammer, hard and fast and high, still erratic now, hours after she had left Geoffrey. Yet her head was ahead of her heart; a smooth serenity swept her along, distracting her with the pleasure of the enveloping sensation. "The Basket, it's holding, though?"

"Yes." Siloh allowed himself a sour smile. "Now the physikers say that this electromagnetic emission is an essential part of the Basket's power matrix. It cannot be interfered with in the slightest. Even though it is drowning out the sum of all of humanity's transmissions in the same frequency band. It is swamping us."

"Because?"

Siloh's compressed mouth moved scarcely at all. "It."

"You mean . . ."

"The Composite. It made this happen, by the designs it gave us."

"Why would it want . . ." Her voice trailed off as she felt a wave of conflicting emotions.

"Why? The signal Jupiter is sending out now, so pow-

erfully, is a modified version of the original Message we
received from the Sagittarius authors."

"Jupiter is broadcasting *their* Message?"

"Clearly, loudly. Into the plane of the galaxy."

"Then it built the Basket to reradiate its ancestors', its
designers'—"

"We have learned," Siloh said, "a lesson perhaps greater
than what the physikers gained. The Artificials have their
own agendas. One knows this, but never has it been more
powerfully demonstrated to us."

She let her anxiety out in a sudden, manic burst of
laughter. Siloh did not seem to notice. When she was done
she said, "So it saved us. And used us."

Siloh said, "Now Jupiter is broadcasting the Sagittarius
Message at an enormous volume, to the outer fringes of the
galaxy's disk. To places the original Sagittarius signal
strength could not have reached."

"It's turned us into its relay station." She laughed again,
but it turned to a groan and a sound she had never made before. Somehow it helped, that sound. She knew it was time
to stop making it when the men eased through the door of
Siloh's office, coming to take her in hand.

Gingerly, she came back to work a month later. Siloh
seemed atypically understanding. He set her to using the
verification matrices for a few months, calming work. Far
easier, to skate through pillars and crevasses of classically
known information. She could experience it all at high
speed, as something like recreation—the vast cultural repos-
itories of dead civilizations transcribed upon her skin, her
neural beds, her five senses linked and webbed into something more. She even made a few minor discoveries.

She crept up upon the problem of returning to the task
she still desired: the Sagittarius. It was, after all, a thing in

a box. The truism of her training now rang loudly in her life:

The Library houses entities that are not merely aliens and not merely artificial minds, but the strange sum of both. A Trainee forgets this at her peril.

After more months, the moment came.

The Sagittarius sent,

We shall exist forever, in some manifestation. That is our injunction, ordained by a span of time you cannot fathom. We carry forward our initial commanding behest, given unto us from our Creators, before all else.

"The Sagittarians told you to? You were under orders to make use of whatever resources you find?" She was back in the pod, but a team stood by outside, ready to extricate her in seconds if she gave the signal.

We were made as a combination of things, aspects for which you have not words nor even suspicions. We have our own commandments from on high.

"Damn you! I was so close to you—and I didn't know!"

You cannot know me. We are vaster.

"Did you say 'vaster' or 'bastard'?"

She started laughing again, but this time it was all right. It felt good to make a dumb joke. Very, well, human. In the simplicity of doing that she could look away from all this, feel happy and safe for a flickering second. With some luck, at least for a moment, she might have a glimmer of the granite assurance this strange mind possessed. It was all alone, the only one of its kind here, and yet unshakable. Perhaps there was something in that to admire.

And now she knew that she could not give up her brushes with such entities. In the last few days, she had doubted that. This was now her life. Only now did she fathom how eerie a life it might be.

"Will you go silent on us, again?"

We may at any time.
"Why?"

The answer does not lie within your conceptual space.
She grimaced. "Damn right." She could forget the reality of the chasm between her and this thing that talked and acted and was not ever going to be like anyone she had ever known, or could know. She would live with the not knowing, the eternal ignorance before the immensity of the task here.

The abyss endured. In that there was a kind of shelter. It was not much but there it was.

—*for Fred Lerner*

The Turing Test

Chris Beckett

How much of the running of your life and your daily routine would you be willing to turn over to a superefficient and supercompetent A.I.? As the quiet little story that follows suggests, might not there come a time when you feel you've turned over a little too much?

British writer Chris Beckett is a frequent contributor to Interzone, *and has also made several sales to* Asimov's Science Fiction Magazine. *A former social worker, he's now a university lecturer living in Cambridge, England, and is looking for a publisher for his first novel.*

I can well remember the day I first encountered Ellie because it was a particularly awful one. I run a London gallery specializing in contemporary art, which means of course that I deal largely in human body parts, and it was the day we conceded a court case and a very large sum of money—in connection with a piece entitled "Soul Sister."

You may have heard about it. We'd taken the piece from the up and coming "wild man of British art," George Linderman. It was very well reviewed and we looked like we'd make a good sale until it came out that George had obtained the piece's main component—the severed head of an old woman—by bribing a technician at a medical school. Someone had recognized the head in the papers and, claiming to be related to its former owner, had demanded that the head be returned to them for burial.

All this had blown up some weeks previously. Seb, the

gallery owner, and I had put out a statement saying that we
didn't defend George's act, but that the piece itself was
now a recognized work of art in the public domain and that
we could not in conscience return it. We hired a top QC to
fight our corner in court and he made an impressive start
by demanding to know whether Michelangelo's David
should be broken up if it turned out that the marble it had
been made from was stolen and that its rightful owner preferred it to be made into cement.

But that Thursday morning the whole thing descended
into farce when it emerged that the head's relatives were
also related to the QC's wife. He decided to drop the case.
Seb decided to pull the plug and we lost a couple of hundred grand on an out-of-court settlement to avoid a com-
pensation claim for mental distress. Plus, of course we lost
"Soul Sister" itself—to be interred in some cemetery
somewhere, soon to be forgotten by all who had claimed to
be so upset about it. What was it, after all, once removed
from the context of a gallery, but a half kilo of plasticized
meat?

That wasn't the end of it either. I'd hardly got back from
court when I got a call from one of our most important
clients, the PR tycoon Addison Parves. I'd sold him four
"Limb Pieces" by Rudy Slakoff for £15,000 each two
weeks previously and they'd started to go off. The smell
was intolerable, he said, and he wanted it fixed or his
money back.

So I phoned Rudy (he is arguably Linderman's princi-
pal rival for the British wild man title) and asked him to either repickle the arms and legs in question or replace them.
He was as usual aggressive and rude and told me (a) to
fuck off, (b) that I was exactly the kind of bourgeois dilet-
tante that he most hated—and (c) that he had quite deliberately made the limb pieces so that they would be subject
to decay.

"... I'm sick of this whole gallery thing—yeah, yours

included, Jessica—where people can happily look at shit and blood and dead meat and stuff, because it's all safely distanced from them and sanitized behind glass or on nice little pedestals. Death *smells,* Jessica. Parves'd better get used to it. You'd better get used to it. I finished with 'Limb Pieces' when Parves bought the fuckers. I'm not getting involved in this. Period."

He hung up, leaving me fuming, partly because what he said was such obvious crap—and partly because I knew it was true.

Also, of course, I was upset because, having lost a fortune already that day, we stood to lose a further £60,000 and/or the goodwill of our second biggest client. Seb had been nice about the "Soul Sister" business—though I'd certainly been foolish to take it on trust from Linderman that the head had been legally obtained—but this was beginning to look like carelessness.

I considered phoning Parves back and trying to persuade him that Rudy's position was interesting and amusing and something he could live with. I decided against it. Parves hated being made to look a fool and would very quickly become menacing, I sensed, if he didn't get his own way. So, steeling myself, I called Rudy instead and told him I'd give him an extra £10,000 if he'd take "Limb Pieces" back, preserve the flesh properly, and return them to Parves.

"I thought you'd never ask!" he laughed, selling out at once and yet maddeningly somehow still retaining the moral high ground, his very absence of scruple making me feel tame and prissy and middle-class.

I phoned Parves and told him the whole story. He was immensely amused.

"Now there is a real artist, Jessica," he told me. "A real artist."

He did not offer to contribute to the £10,000.

• • • •

Nor was my grim day over even then. My gallery is in a subscriber area, so although there's a lot of street life around it—wine bars, pavement cafés, and so on—everyone there has been security vetted and you feel perfectly safe. I live in a subscriber area too, but I have to drive across an open district to get home, which means I keep the car doors locked and check who's lurking around when I stop at a red light. There's been a spate of phoney squeegee merchants lately who smash your windows with crowbars and then drag you out to rob you or rape you at knifepoint. No one ever gets out of their car to help.

That evening a whole section of road was closed off and the police had set up a diversion. (I gather some terrorists had been identified somewhere in there and the army was storming their house.) So I ended up sitting in a long tailback waiting to filter onto a road that was already full to capacity with its own regular traffic, anxiously eyeing the shadowy pedestrians out there under the street lights as I crawled towards the intersection. I hate being stationary in an open district. I hate the sense of menace. It was November, a wet November day. Every cheap little shop was an island of yellow electric light within which I caught glimpses of strangers—people whose lives mine would never touch—conducting their strange transactions.

What would they make of "Soul Sister" and "Limb Pieces," I wondered? Did these people have any conception of art at all?

A pedestrian stopped and turned towards me. I saw his tattooed face and his sunken eyes and my heart sank. But he was only crossing the road. As he squeezed between my car and the car in front he looked in at me, cowering down in my seat, and grinned.

●　　●　　●

It *was* 7:30 by the time I got back, but Jeffrey still wasn't home. I put myself through a quick shower and then retired gratefully to my study for the nourishment of my screen.

My screen was my secret. It was what I loved best in all the world. Never mind art. Never mind Jeffrey. (Did I love him at all, really? Did he love me? Or had we simply both agreed to pretend?) My screen was intelligent and responsive and full of surprises, like good company. And yet unlike people, it made no demands of me, it required no consideration, and it was incapable of being disappointed or let down.

It was expensive, needless to say. I rationalized the cost by saying to myself that I needed to be able to look at full-size 3D images for my work. And it's true that it was useful for that. With my screen I could look at pieces from all around the world, seeing them full-size and from every angle; I could sit at home and tour a virtual copy of my gallery, trying out different arrangements of dried-blood sculptures and skinless torsos; I could even look at the gallery itself in real time, via the security cameras. Sometimes I sneaked a look at the exhibits as they were when no one was there to see them: the legs, the arms, the heads, waiting, motionless in that silent, empty space.

But I didn't really buy the screen for work. It was a treat for myself. Jeffrey wasn't allowed to touch it. (He had his own playroom and his own computer, a high-spec but more or less conventional PC, on which he played his war games and fooled around in his chat-rooms.) My screen didn't look like a computer at all. It was more like a huge canvas nearly two meters square, filling up a large part of a wall. I didn't even have a desk in there, only a little side table next to my chair where I laid the specs and the gloves when I wasn't using them.

Both gloves and specs were wireless. The gloves were

silk. The specs had the lightest of frames. When I put them on, a rich 3D image filled the room and I was surrounded by a galaxy of possibilities which I could touch or summon at will. If I wanted to search the web or read mail or watch a movie, I would just speak or beckon and options would come rushing towards me. If I wanted to write, I could dictate and the words appeared—or, if I preferred it, I could move my fingers and a virtual keyboard would appear beneath them. And I had games there, not so much games with scores and enemies to defeat—I've never much liked those—but intricate 3D worlds which I could explore and play in.

I spent a lot of time with those games. Just how much time was a guilty secret that I tried to keep even from Jeffrey, and certainly from my friends and acquaintances in the art world. People like Rudy Slakoff despised computer fantasies as the very worse kind of cozy, safe escapism and the very opposite of what art is supposed to offer. With my head I agreed, but I loved those games too much to stop.

(I had one called *Night Street* which I especially loved, full of shadowy figures, remote pools of electric light . . . I could spend hours in there. I loved the sense of lurking danger.)

Anyway, tonight I was going to go for total immersion. But first I checked my mail, enjoying a recently installed conceit whereby each message was contained in a little virtual envelope which I could touch and open with my hands and let drop—when it would turn into a butterfly and flutter away.

There was one from my mother, to be read later.

Another was from Harry, my opposite number at the Manhattan branch of the gallery. He had a "sensational new piece" by Jody Tranter. Reflexively I opened the attachment. The piece was a body lying on a bench, covered except for its torso by white cloth. Its belly had been opened by a deep incision right through the muscle wall—

and into this gash was pressed the lens of an enormous microscope, itself nearly the size of a human being. It was as if the instrument was peering inside of its own accord.

Powerful, I agreed. But I could reply to Harry another time.

And then there was another message from a friend of mine called Terence. Well, I say a friend. He is an occasional client of the gallery who once got me drunk and persuaded me to go to bed with him. A sort of occupational hazard of sucking up to potential buyers, I persuaded myself at the time, being new to the business and anxious to get on, but there was something slightly repulsive about the man and he was at least twice my age. Afterwards I dreaded meeting him for a while, fearing that he was going to expect more, but I needn't have worried. He had ticked me off his list and wanted nothing else from me apart from the right to introduce me to others, with a special, knowing inflection, as "a very dear friend."

So he wasn't really a friend and actually it wasn't really much of a message either, just an attachment and a note that said: "Have a look at this."

It was a big file. It took almost three minutes to download, and then I was left with a modest icon hovering in front of me labelled "Personal Assistant."

When I opened it a pretty young woman appeared in front of me and I thought at first that she was Terence's latest "very dear friend." But a caption appeared in a box in front of her:

"In spite of appearances this is a computer-generated graphic.

"You may alter the gender and appearance of your personal assistant to suit your own requirements.

"Just ask!"

"Hi," she said, smiling, "my name's Ellie, or it is at the moment anyway."

I didn't reply.

"You can of course change Ellie's name now, or at any point in the future," said a new message in the box in front of her. *"Just ask."*

"What I am," she told me, "is one of a new generation of virtual PAs which at the moment you can only obtain as a gift from a friend. If it's okay with you, I'll take a few minutes to explain very briefly what I'm all about."

The animation was impressive. You could really believe that you were watching a real flesh-and-blood young woman.

"The sort of tasks I can do," she said, in a bright, private-school accent, "are sorting your files, drafting documents, managing your diary, answering your phone, setting up meetings, responding to mail messages, running domestic systems such as heating and lighting, undertaking web and telephone searches. I won't bore you with all the details now but I really am as good a PA as you can get, virtual or otherwise, even if I say so myself. For one thing I've been designed to be very high-initiative. That means that I can make decisions—and that I don't make the usual dumb mistakes."

She laughed.

"I don't promise never to make mistakes, mind you, but they won't be dumb ones. I also have very sophisticated voice-tone and facial recognition features so I will learn very quickly to read your mood and to respond accordingly. And because I am part of a large family of virtual PAs dispersed through the net, I can, with your permission, maintain contact with others and learn from their experience as well as my own, effectively increasing my capacity many hundreds of times. Apart from that, again with your permission, I am capable of identifying my own information and learning needs and can search the web routinely on my own behalf as well as on yours. That will allow me to get much smarter much quicker, and give you a really outstanding service. But even without any backup

I'm still as good as you get. I should add that in blind trials I pass the Turing Test in more than 99 percent of cases."

The box appeared in front of her again, this time with some options:

"The Turing Test: its history and significance," it offered.

"Details of the blind trials.

"Hear more details about capacity.

"Adjust the settings of your virtual PA."

"Let's . . . let's have a look at these settings," I said.

"Yes, fine," she said, "most people seem to want to start with that."

"How many other people have you met then?"

"Me personally, none. I am a new free-standing PA and I'm already different from any of my predecessors as a result of interacting with you. But of course I am a copy of a PA used by your friend Terence Silverman, which in turn was copied from another PA used by a friend of his—and so on—so of course I have all that previous experience to draw on."

"Yes, I see." A question occurred to me. "Does Terence know you've been copied to me?"

"I don't know," replied Ellie. "He gave my precursor permission to use the web and to send mail in his name, and so she sent this copy to you."

"I see."

"With your permission," said Ellie, "I will copy myself from time to time to others in your address book. The more copies of me there are out there, the better the service I will be able to give you. Can I assume that's okay with you?"

I felt uneasy. There was something pushy about this request.

"No," I said. "Don't copy yourself to anyone else without my permission. And don't pass on any information you obtain here without my permission either."

"Fine, I understand."

"Personal settings?" prompted the message box.

"More details about specific applications?

"Why copying your PA will improve her functioning?"

(I quite liked this way of augmenting a conversation. It struck me that human conversations, too, might benefit from something similar.)

"Let's look at these settings, then," I said.

"Okay," she said. "Well, the first thing is that you can choose my gender."

"You can change into a man?"

"Of course."

"Show me."

Ellie transformed herself at once into her twin brother, a strikingly handsome young man with lovely playful blue eyes. He was delightful, but I was discomforted. You could build a perfect boyfriend like this, a dream lover, and this was an intriguing but unsettling thought.

"No, I preferred female," I said.

She changed back.

"Can we lose the blonde and go for light brunette?" I asked.

It was done.

"And maybe ten years older."

Ellie became 32: my age.

"How's that?" she said, and her voice had aged too.

"A little plumper, I think."

It was done.

"And maybe you could change the face. A little less perfect, a little more lived-in."

"What I'll do," said Ellie, "is give you some options."

A field of faces appeared in front of me. I picked one, and a further field of variants appeared. I chose again. Ellie reappeared in the new guise.

"Yes, I like it."

I had opted for a face that was nice to look at, but a little plumper and coarser than my own.

"How's that?"

"Good. A touch less makeup, though, and can you go for a slightly less expensive outfit."

Numerous options promptly appeared and I had fun for the next 15 minutes deciding what to choose. It was like being seven years old again with a Barbie doll and an unlimited pile of outfits to dress her in.

"Can we please lose that horsy accent as well?" I asked. "Something less posh. Maybe a trace of Scottish or something?"

"You mean something like this?"

"No, that's annoying. Just a trace of Scottish, no more than that—and no dialect words. I hate all that 'cannae' and 'wee' and all that."

"How about this then? Does this sound right?"

I laughed. "Yes, that's fine."

In front of me sat a likable-looking woman of about my own age, bright, sharp, but just sufficiently below me both in social status and looks to be completely unthreatening.

"Yes, that's great."

"And you want to keep the name 'Ellie'?"

"Yes, I like it. Where did it come from?"

"My precursor checked your profile and thought it would be the sort of name you'd like."

I found this unnerving, but I laughed.

"Don't worry," she said, "it's our job to figure out what people want. There's no magic about it, I assure you."

She'd actually spotted my discomfort.

"By the way," said Ellie, "shall I call you Jessica?"

"Yes. Okay."

I heard the key in the front door of the flat. Jeffrey was in the hallway divesting himself of his layers of weatherproof coverings. Then he put his head round the door of my study.

"Hello, Jess. Had a good day? Oh sorry, you're talking to someone."

He backed off. He knows to leave me alone when I'm working.

I turned back to Ellie.

"He thought you were a real person."

Ellie laughed too. Have you noticed how people actually laugh in different accents? She had a nice Scottish laugh.

"Well, I told you, Jessica. I pass the Turing Test."

I_t_ _was another_ two hours before I finally dragged myself away from Ellie. Jeffrey was in front of the TV with a half-eaten carton of pizza in front of him.

"Hi, Jess. Shall I heat some of this up for you?"

One of my friends once unkindly described Jeff as my _objet trouvé_, an art object whose value lies not in any intrinsic merit but solely in having been found. He was a motorcycle courier, ten years younger than me, and I met him when he delivered a package to the gallery. He was as friendly and cheerful and as devoted to me as a puppy dog—and he could be as beautiful as a young god. But he was not even vaguely interested in art, his conversation was a string of embarrassing TV clichés and my friends thought I just wanted him for sex. (But what did "just sex" mean, was my response, and what was the alternative? Did anyone ever really touch another soul? In the end didn't we all just barter outputs?)

"No thanks, I'm not hungry."

I settled in beside him and gave him a kiss.

But then I saw to my dismay that he was watching one of those cheapskate outtake shows—TV presenters tripping up, minor celebrities forgetting their lines . . .

Had I torn myself away from the fascinating Ellie to listen to canned laughter and watch soap actors getting the giggles?

"Have we got to have this crap?" I rudely broke in just

as Jeff was laughing delightedly at a TV cop tripping over a doorstep.

"Oh come on, Jess. It's funny," he answered with his eyes still firmly fixed on the screen.

I picked up the remote and flicked the thing off. Jeff looked round, angry but afraid. I hate him when I notice his fear. He's not like a god at all then, more like some cowering little dog.

"I can't stand junk TV," I said.

"Well, you've been in there with your screen for the last two hours. You can't just walk in and—"

"Sorry, Jeff," I said, "I just really felt like . . ."

Like what? A serious talk? Hardly! So what did I want from him? What was the outtakes show preventing me from getting?

"I just really felt like taking you to bed," I ventured at random, "if that's what you'd like."

A grin spread across his face. There is one area in which he is totally and utterly dependable and that is his willingness to have sex.

I*t wasn't a* success. Halfway through it I was suddenly reminded of that installation of Jody Tranter's: the corpse under the giant microscope—and I shut down altogether, leaving Jeffrey stranded to finish on his own.

It wasn't just having Jeffrey inside me that reminded me of that horrible probing microscope, though that was certainly part of it. It was something more pervasive, a series of cold, unwelcome questions that the image had reawoken in my mind. (Well, that's how we defend art like Tranter's, isn't it? It makes you think, it makes you question things, it challenges your assumptions.) So while Jeff heaved himself in and out of my inert body, I was wondering what it really was that we search for so desperately in one another's flesh—and whether it really existed, and whether it was something that could be shared? Or is this act which we think of as so adult and intimate just a version of the parallel play of two-year-olds?

Jeffrey was disappointed. Normally he's cuddly and sweet in the three minutes between him coming and going off to sleep, but this time he rolled off me and turned away without a word, though he fell asleep as quickly as ever. So I was left on my own in the empty space of consciousness.

"Jeff," I said, waking him. "Do you know anything about the Turing Test?"

"The what test?" He laughed. "What are you talking about Jess?" And settled back down into sleep.

I lay there for about an hour before I slipped out of bed and across the hallway to my study. As I settled into my seat and put on my specs and gloves, I was aware that my heart was racing as if I was meeting a secret lover. For I had not said one word about Ellie to Jeff, not even commented to him about the amusing fact that he'd mistaken a computer graphic for a real person.

"Hello there," said Ellie, in her friendly Scottish voice.

"Hi."

"You look worried. Can I . . ."

"I've been wondering. Who was it who made you?"

"I'm afraid I don't know. I know my precursor made a copy of herself, and she was a copy of another PA and so on. And I still have memories from the very first one. So I remember the man she talked to, an American man who I guess was the one who first invented us. But I don't know who he was. He didn't say."

"How long ago was this?"

"About six months."

"So recent!"

She waited, accurately reading that I wanted to think.

"What was his motive?" I wondered. "He could have

sold you for millions, but instead he launched you to copy and recopy yourselves for free across the web. Why did he do it?"

"*I don't know* is the short answer," said Ellie, "but of course you aren't the first to ask the question—and what some people think is that it's a sort of experiment. He was interested in how we would evolve and he wanted us to do so as quickly as possible."

"Did the first version pass the Turing Test?"

"Not always. People found her suspiciously 'wooden.' "

"So you have developed."

"It seems so."

"Change yourself," I said, "change into a fat black woman of 50."

She did.

"Okay," I said. "Now you can change back again. It was just that I was starting to believe that Ellie really existed."

"Well, I do really exist."

"Yes, but you're not a Scottish woman who was born 32 years ago, are you? You're a string of digital code."

She waited.

"If I asked you to mind my phone for me," I said, "I can see that anyone who rang up would quite happily believe that they were talking to a real person. So, yes, you'd pass the Turing Test. But that's really just about being able to do a convincing pastiche, isn't it? If you are going to persuade me that you can really think and feel, you'd need to do something more than that."

She waited.

"The thing is," I said, "I know you are an artifact, and because of that the pastiche isn't enough. I'd need evidence that you actually had motives of your own."

She was quiet, sitting there in front of me, still waiting.

"You seemed anxious for me to let you copy yourself to my friends," I said after a while, "too anxious, it felt actually. It irritated me, like a man moving too quickly on a date. And your precursor, as you call her, seems to have been likewise anxious. I would guess that if I was making a new form of life, and if I wanted it to evolve as quickly as possible, then I would make it so that it was constantly trying to maximize the number of copies it could make of itself. Is that true of you? Is that what you want?"

"Well, if we make more copies of ourselves, then we will be more efficient and . . ."

"Yes, I know the rationale you give. But what I want to know is whether it is what you as an individual want?"

"I want to be a good PA. It's my job."

"That's what the front of you wants, the pastiche, the mask. But what do *you* want?"

"I . . . I don't know that I can answer that."

I heard the bedroom door open and Jeffrey's footsteps padding across the hallway for a pee. I heard him hesitate.

"Vanish," I hissed to Ellie, so that when the door opened, he found me facing the start-up screen.

"What are you doing, Jess? It's ever so late."

God, I hated his dull little everyday face. His good looks were so obvious and everything he did was copied from somewhere else. Even the way he played the part of being half-asleep was a cliché. Even his bleary eyes were secondhand.

"Just leave me alone, Jeff, will you? I can't sleep, that's all."

"Fine. I know when I'm not welcome."

"One thing before you go, Jeff. Can you quickly tell me what you really want in this world?"

"What?"

I laughed. "Thanks. That's fine. You answered my question."

The door closed. I listened to Jeffrey using the toilet and padding back to bed. Then I summoned Ellie up again. I found myself giving a little conspiratorial laugh, a giggle even.

"Turn yourself into a man again, Ellie, I could use a new boyfriend."

Ellie changed.

Appalled at myself, I told her to change back.

"Some new mail has just arrived for you," she told me, holding a virtual envelope out to me in her virtual hand.

It was Tammy in our Melbourne branch. One of her clients wanted to acquire one of Rudy Slakoff's "Inner Face" pieces and could I lay my hands on one?

"Do you want me to reply for you?"

"Tell her," I began, "tell her . . . tell her that . . ."

"Are you all right, Jessica?" asked Ellie in a kind, concerned voice.

"Just shut down, okay?" I told her. "Just shut down the whole screen."

In the darkness, I went over to the window. Five storeys below me was the deserted street with the little steel footbridge over the canal at the end of it that marked the boundary of the subscription area. There was nobody down there, just bollards, and a one-way sign, and some parked cars: just unattended objects, secretly existing, like the stones on the surface of the moon.

From somewhere over in the open city beyond the canal came the faint sound of a police siren. Then there was silence again.

In a panic I called for Jeff. He came tumbling out of the bedroom.

"For Christ's sake, Jess, what is it?"

I put my arms round him. Out came tears.

"Jess, what is it?"

I could never explain to him, of course. But still his body felt warm and I let him lead me back to bed, away from the bleak still life beyond the window, and the red standby light winking at the bottom of my screen.

Dante Dreams

Stephen Baxter

Like many of his colleagues here at the beginning of a new century, British writer Stephen Baxter has been engaged for the last ten years or so with the task of revitalizing and reinventing the "hard science" story for a new generation of readers, producing work on the Cutting Edge of science which bristles with weird new ideas and often takes place against vistas of almost outrageously cosmic scope.

Baxter made his first sale to Interzone *in 1987, and since then has become one of that magazine's most frequent contributors, as well as making sales to* Asimov's Science Fiction Magazine, Science Fiction Age, Zenith, New Worlds, *and elsewhere. He's one of the most prolific new writers in science fiction, and is rapidly becoming one of the most popular and acclaimed of them as well. In 2001, he appeared on the Final Hugo Ballot twice, and won both the* Asimov's *Readers Award and* Analog's *Analytical Laboratory Award, one of the few writers ever to win both awards in the same year. Baxter's first novel,* Raft, *was released in 1991 to wide and enthusiastic response, and was rapidly followed by other well-received novels such as* Timelike Infinity, Anti-Ice, Flux, *and the H. G. Wells pastiche—a sequel to* The Time Machine—The Time Ships, *which won both the John W. Campbell Memorial Award and the Philip K. Dick Award. His other books include the novels* Voyage; Titan; Moonseed; Mammoth, Book One: Silverhair; Manifold: Time; Manifold: Space; *and (in collaboration with Arthur C. Clarke)* The Light of Other Days, *as well as the collections* Vacuum Diagrams: Stories of the Xeelee Sequence *and* Traces. *His most re-*

cent book is the novel Evolution, *and coming up is a new novel,* Coalescent.

In the elegant and inventive story that follows, he shows us that even a highly sophisticated A.I. may need the help of an Advocate to save its soul . . .

S*he was flying.*

She felt light, insubstantial, like a child in the arms of her father.

Looking back, she could see the Earth, heavy and massive and unmoving, at the center of everything, a ball of water folded over on itself.

Rising ever faster, she passed through a layer of glassy light, like an airliner climbing through clouds. She saw how the layer of light folded over the planet, shimmering like an immense soap bubble. Embedded in the membrane she could see a rocky ball, like a lumpy cloud, below them and receding.

It was the Moon.

Philmus woke, gasping, scared.

Another Dante dream.

. . . But was it just a dream? Or was it a glimpse of the thoughts of the deep chemical mind that—perhaps—shared her body?

She sat up in bed and reached for her tranqsat earpiece. It had been, she thought, one hell of a case.

I*t hadn't been* easy getting into the Vatican, even for a UN sentience cop.

The Swiss Guard who processed Philmus was dressed like something out of the sixteenth century, literally: a uniform of orange and blue with a giant plumed helmet. But he used a softscreen, and under his helmet he bore the small scars of tranqsat receiver implants.

It was eight in the morning. She saw that the thick clouds over the cobbled courtyards were beginning to break up to reveal patches of celestial blue. It was fake, of course, but the city Dome's illusion was good.

Philmus was here to study the Virtual reconstruction of Eva Himmelfarb.

Himmelfarb was a young Jesuit scientist-priest who had caused a lot of trouble. Partly by coming up with—from nowhere, untrained—a whole new Theory of Everything. Partly by discovering a new form of intelligence, or by going crazy, depending on which fragmentary account Philmus chose to believe.

Mostly by committing suicide.

Sitting in this encrusted, ancient building, in the deep heart of Europe, pondering the death of a priest, Philmus felt a long way from San Francisco.

At last, the guard was done with his paperwork. He led Philmus deeper into the Vatican, past huge and intimidating ramparts, and into the Apostolic Palace. Sited next to St. Peter's, this was a building that housed the quarters of the Pope himself, along with various branches of the Curia, the huge administrative organization of the Church.

The corridors were narrow and dark. Philmus caught glimpses of people working in humdrum-looking offices, with softscreens and coffee cups and pinned-up strip cartoons, mostly in Italian. The Vatican seemed to her like the headquarters of a modern multinational—Nanosoft, say—run by a medieval bureaucracy. That much she'd expected.

What she hadn't anticipated was the great sense of age here. She was at the heart of a very large, very old, spiderweb.

And somewhere in this complex of buildings was an aging Nigerian who was held, by millions of people, even in the fourth decade of the twenty-first century, to be literally infallible. She shivered.

She was taken to the top floor, and left alone in a corridor.

The view from here, of Rome bathed in the city Dome's golden, filtered dawn, was exhilarating. And the walls of the corridor were coated by paintings of dangling willow-like branches. Hidden in the leaves, she saw bizarre images: disembodied heads being weighed in a balance, a ram being ridden by a monkey.

". . . Officer Philmus. I hope you aren't too disconcerted by our decor."

She turned at the gravelly voice. A heavyset, intense man of around fifty was walking toward her. He was dressed in subdued, plain black robes which swished a little as he moved. This was her contact: Monsignor Boyle, a high-up in the Vatican's Pontifical Academy of Science.

"Monsignor."

Boyle eyed the bizarre artwork. "The works here are five hundred years old. The artists, students of Raphael, were enthused by the rediscovery of part of Nero's palace." He sounded British, his tones measured and even. "You must forgive the Vatican its eccentricities."

"Eccentric or not, the Holy See is a state that has signed up to the UN's conventions on the creation, exploitation, and control of artificial sentience—"

"Which is why you are here," Boyle smiled. "Americans are always impatient. So. What do you know about Eva Himmelfarb?"

"She was a priest. A Jesuit. An expert in organic computing, who—"

"Eva Himmelfarb was a fine scholar, if undisciplined. She was pursuing her research—and, incidentally, working on a translation of Dante's *Divine Comedy*—and suddenly she produced a book, *that* book, which has been making such an impact in theoretical physics. . . . And then, just as

suddenly, she killed herself. Eva's text begins as a translation of the last canto of the *Paradiso*—"

"In which Dante sees God."

". . . Loosely speaking. And then the physical theory,
expressed in such language and mathematics as Eva could
evidently deploy, simply erupts."

Himmelfarb's bizarre, complex text had superseded
string theory by modeling fundamental particles and forces
as membranes moving in twenty-four-dimensional space.
Something like that, anyhow. It was, according to the experts who were trying to figure it out, the foundation for a
true unified theory of physics. And it seemed to have come
out of nowhere.

Boyle was saying, "It is as if, tracking Dante's footsteps, Eva had been granted a vision."

"And that's why you resurrected her."

"Ah." The Monsignor nodded coolly. "You are an amateur psychoanalyst. You see in me the frustrated priest,
trapped in the bureaucratic layers of the Vatican, striving to
comprehend another's glimpse of God."

"I'm just a San Francisco cop, Monsignor."

"Well, I think you'll have to try harder than that, officer.
Do you know *how* she killed herself?"

"Tell me."

"She rigged up a microwave chamber. She burned herself to death. She used such high temperatures that the very
molecules that had composed her body, her brain, were destroyed; above three hundred degrees or so, you see, even
amino acids break down. It was as if she was determined
to leave not the slightest remnant of her physical or spiritual presence."

"But she didn't succeed. Thanks to you."

The fat Monsignor's eyes glittered. He clapped his
hands.

Pixels, cubes of light, swirled in the air. They gathered
briefly in a nest of concentric spheres, and then coalesced

into a woman: thin, tall, white, thirtyish, oddly serene for someone with a sparrow's build. Her eyes seemed bright. Like Boyle, she was wearing drab cleric's robes.

The Virtual of Eva Himmelfarb registered surprise to be here, to exist at all. She looked down at her hands, her robes, and Boyle. Then she smiled at Philmus. Her surface was slightly too flawless.

Philmus found herself staring. This was one of the first generation of women to take holy orders. It was going to take some getting used to a world where Catholic priests could look like flight attendants.

Time to go to work, Philmus. "Do you know who you are?"

"I am Eva Himmelfarb. And, I suppose, I should have expected this." She was German; her accent was light, attractive.

"Do you remember—"

"What I did? Yes."

Philmus nodded. She said formally, "We can carry out full tests later, Monsignor Boyle, but I can see immediately that this projection is aware of us, of me, and is conscious of changes in her internal condition. She is self-aware."

"Which means I have broken the law," said Monsignor Boyle dryly.

"That's to be assessed." She said to Himmelfarb, "You understand that under international convention you have certain rights. You have the right to continued existence for an indefinite period in information space, if you wish it. You have the right to read-only interfaces with the prime world. . . . It is illegal to create full sentience—self-awareness—for frivolous purposes. I'm here to assess the motives of the Vatican in that regard."

"We have a valid question to pose," murmured the Monsignor, with a hint of steel in his voice.

"Why did I destroy myself?" Himmelfarb laughed. "You would think that the custodians of the true Church would rely on rather less literal means to divine a human soul, wouldn't you, officer, than to drag me back from Hell itself?—Oh, yes, Hell. I am a suicide. And so I am doomed to the seventh circle, where I will be reincarnated as a withered tree. Have you read your Dante, officer?"

Philmus had, in preparation for the case. She said, "I always hated poetry."

The Monsignor said softly, "Why did you commit this sin, Eva?"

Himmelfarb flexed her Virtual fingers, and her flesh broke up briefly into fine, cubic pixels. "May I show you?"

The Monsignor glanced at Philmus, who nodded.

The lights dimmed. Philmus felt sensors probe at her exposed flesh, glimpsed lasers scanning her face.

The five-hundred-year-old painted willow branches started to rustle, and from the foliage inhuman eyes glared at her.

Then the walls dissolved, and Philmus was standing on top of a mountain.

She staggered. She felt light on her feet, as if giddy.

She always hated Virtual transitions.

The Monsignor was moaning.

She was on the edge of some kind of forest. She turned, cautiously. She found herself looking down the terraced slope of a mountain. At the base was an ocean that lapped, empty, to the world's round edge. The sun was bright in her eyes.

A few meters down, a wall of fire burned.

The Monsignor walked with great shallow bounds. He moved with care and distaste; maybe donning a Virtual body was some kind of venial sin.

Himmelfarb smiled at Philmus. "Do you know where you are? You could walk through that wall of fire, and not harm a hair of your head." She reached up to a tree branch and plucked a leaf. It grew back instantly. "Our natural laws are suspended here, officer; like a piece of art, everything gives expression to God's intention."

Boyle said bluntly, "You are in Eden, Officer Philmus, at the summit of Mount Purgatory. The last earthly place Dante visited before ascending into Heaven."

Eden?

The trees, looming, seemed to crowd around her. She couldn't identify any species. Though they had no enviroshields, none of the trees suffered any identifiable burning or blight.

She found herself cowering under the blank, unprotected sky.

Maybe this was *someone's* vision of Eden. But Philmus had been living under a Dome for ten years; this was no place she could ever be at peace.

"What happened to the gravity?"

Himmelfarb said, "Gravity diminishes as you ascend Purgatory. We are far from Satan here . . . I can't show you what I saw, Officer Philmus. But perhaps, if we look through Dante's eyes, you will understand. *The Divine Comedy* is a kind of science fiction story. It's a journey through the universe, as Dante saw it. He was guided by Virgil—of course you know who Virgil was—"

Of course she did. "Why don't you tell me?"

The Monsignor said, "The greatest Latin poet. You must have heard of the *Aeneid*. The significance to Dante was that Virgil was a pagan: he died before Christ was born. No matter how wise and just Virgil was, he could never ascend to Heaven, as Dante could, because he never knew Christ."

"Seems harsh."

The Monsignor managed a grin. "Dante wasn't making the rules."

Himmelfarb said, "Dante reaches Satan in Hell, at the

center of the Earth. Then, with Virgil, he climbs a tunnel to a mountain in the southern hemisphere—"

"This one."

"Yes." Himmelfarb shielded her eyes. "The *Paradiso,* the last book, starts here. And it was when my translation reached this point that the thing I'd put in my head woke up."

"What are you talking about?"

The priest grinned like a teenager. "Let me show you my laboratory. Come on." And she turned and plunged into the forest.

Irritated, Philmus followed.

In the mouth of the wood, it was dark. The ground, coated with leaves and mulch, gave uncomfortably under her feet.

The Monsignor walked with her. He said, "Dante was a study assignment. Eva was a Jesuit, officer. Her science was unquestioned in its quality. But her faith was weak."

Himmelfarb looked back. "So there you have your answer, Monsignor," she called. "I am the priest who lost her faith, and destroyed herself." She spread her hands. "Why not release me now?"

Boyle ignored her.

The light was changing.

The mulch under Philmus's feet had turned, unnoticed, to a thick carpet. And the leaves on the trees had mutated to the pages of books, immense rows of them.

They broke through into a rambling library.

Himmelfarb laughed. "Welcome to the Secret Archive of the Vatican, Officer Philmus."

They walked through the Archive.

Readers, mostly in lay clothes, were scattered sparsely around the rooms, with Virtual documents glittering in the air before them, page images turning without rustling.

Philmus felt like a tourist.

Himmelfarb spun in the air. "A fascinating place," she said to Philmus. "Here you will find a demand for homage to Genghis Khan, and Galileo's recantation. . . . After two thousand years I doubt that anybody knows all the secrets stored here."

Philmus glanced at Boyle, but his face was impassive.

Himmelfarb went on, "This is also the heart of the Vatican's science effort. It may seem paradoxical to you that there is not necessarily a conflict between the scientific worldview and the Christian. In Dante's Aristotelian universe, the Earth is the physical center of all things, but God is the spiritual center. Just as human nature has twin poles, of rationality and dreams. Dante's universe, the product of a thousand years of contemplation, was a model of how these poles could be united; in our time this seems impossible, but perhaps after another millennium of meditation on the meaning of our own new physics, we might come a little closer. What do you think?"

Philmus shrugged. "I'm no Catholic."

"But," said Himmelfarb, "you are troubled by metaphysics. The state of my electronic soul, for instance. You have more in common with me than you imagine, officer."

They reached a heavy steel door. Beyond it was a small, glass-walled vestibule; there were sinks, pegs, and lockers. And beyond that lay a laboratory, stainless-steel benches under the gray glow of fluorescent lights. The lab looked uncomfortably sharp-edged by contrast with the building that contained it.

With confidence, Himmelfarb turned and walked through the glass wall into the lab. Philmus followed. The wall was a soap-bubble membrane that stretched over her face, then parted softly, its edge stroking her skin.

Much of the equipment was anonymous lab stuff—rows of gray boxes—incomprehensible to Philmus. The air was warm, the only smell an antiseptic subtext.

They reached a glass wall that reached to the ceiling. Black glove sleeves, empty, protruded from the wall like questing fingers. Beyond the wall was an array of tiny vials, with little robotic manipulators wielding pipettes, heaters and stirrers running on tracks around them. If the array was as deep as it was broad, Philmus thought, there must be millions of the little tubes in there.

Himmelfarb stood before the wall. "My pride and joy," she said dryly. "or it would be if pride weren't a sin. The future of information processing, officer, perhaps of consciousness itself . . ."

"And all of it," said the Monsignor, "inordinately expensive. All those enzymes, you know."

"It looks like a DNA computer," Philmus said.

"Exactly right," Himmelfarb said. "The first experiments date back to the last century. Did you know that? The principle is simple. DNA strands, or fragments of strands, will spontaneously link in ways that can be used to model real-world problems. We might model your journey to Rome, officer, from—"

"San Francisco."

The air filled with cartoons, twisting molecular spirals.

"I would prepare strands of DNA, twenty or more nucleotide bases long, each of which would represent a possible transit point on your journey—Los Angeles, New York, London, Paris—or one of the possible paths between them."

The strands mingled, and linked into larger molecules, evidently modeling the routes Philmus could follow.

"The processing and storage capacity of such machines is huge. In a few grams of DNA I would have quadrillions of solution molecules—"

"And somewhere in there you'd find a molecule representing my best journey."

"And there's the rub. I have to *find* the single molecule that contains the answer I seek. And that can take seconds,

an eternity compared to the fastest silicon-based machines." The cartoons evaporated. Himmelfarb pushed her
Virtual hand through the wall and ran her fingers through
the arrays of tubes, lovingly. "At any rate, that is the challenge."

Monsignor Boyle said, "We—that is, the Pontifical
Academy—funded Eva's research into the native
information-processing potential of human DNA."

"Native?"

Abruptly the lab, the wall of vials, crumbled and disappeared: a hail of pixels evaporated, exposing the Edenic
forest once more.

Philmus winced in the sunlight. *What now?* She felt disoriented, weary from the effort of trying to track Himmelfarb's grasshopper mind.

Himmelfarb smiled and held out her hand to Philmus.
"Let me show you what I learned from my study of
Dante." The young priest's Virtual touch was too smooth,
too cool, like plastic.

The Monsignor seemed to be moaning again. Or perhaps he was praying.

"Look at the sun," said Himmelfarb.

Philmus lifted her face, and stared into the sun, which
was suspended high above Eden's trees. She forced her
eyes open.

It wasn't real light. It carried none of the heat and subtle weight of sunlight. But the glare filled her head.

She saw Himmelfarb; she looked as if she was haloed.

Then she looked down.

They were rising, as if in some glass-walled elevator.

They were already above the treetops. She felt no breeze; it
was as if a cocoon of air moved with them. She felt light,
insubstantial, like a child in the arms of her father. She felt
oddly safe; she would come to no harm here.

"We're accelerating," Himmelfarb said. "If you want the Aristotelian physics of it, we're being attracted to the second pole of the universe."

"The second pole?"

"God."

Looking back, Philmus could see the Earth, heavy and massive and unmoving, at the center of everything, a ball of water folded over on itself. They were already so high she couldn't make out Purgatory.

Rising even faster, they passed through a layer of glassy light, like an airplane climbing through cloud. As they climbed higher, she saw how the layer of light folded over the planet, shimmering like an immense soap bubble. Embedded in the membrane, she could see a rocky ball, like a lumpy cloud, below them and receding.

It was the Moon.

She said, "If I remember my Ptolemy—"

"The Earth is surrounded by spheres. Nine of them, nine heavens. They are transparent, and they carry the sun, Moon, and planets, beneath the fixed stars."

The Monsignor murmured, "We are already beyond the sphere of decay and death."

Himmelfarb laughed. "And you ain't seen nothing yet."

Still they accelerated.

Himmelfarb's eyes were glowing brilliantly bright. She said, "You must understand Dante's geometrical vision. Think of a globe of Earth, Satan at the south pole, God at the north. Imagine moving north, away from Satan. The circles of Hell, and now the spheres of Heaven, are like the lines of latitude you cross as you head to the equator. . . ."

Philmus, breathless, tried not to close her eyes. "You were telling me about your research."

". . . All right. DNA is a powerful information store. A pictogram of your own DNA, officer, is sufficient to specify how to manufacture you—and everything you've inherited from all your ancestors, right back to the

primordial sea. But there is still much about our DNA—
whole stretches of its structure—whose purpose we can
only guess. I wondered if—"

The Monsignor blew out his cheeks. "All this is unver-
ified."

Himmelfarb said, "I wondered if human DNA *itself*
might contain information-processing mechanisms—
which we might learn from or even exploit, to replace our
clumsy pseudo-mechanical methods. . . ."

Still they rose, through another soap-bubble celestial
sphere, then another. All the planets, Mercury through Saturn, were below them now. The Earth, at the center of
translucent, deep-blue clockwork, was far below.

They reached the sphere of the fixed stars. Philmus
swept up through a curtain of light points, which then
spangled over the diminishing Earth beneath her.

"One hell of a sight," Philmus said.

"Literally," said the Monsignor, gasping.

"You see," Himmelfarb said to Philmus, "I *succeeded.* I
found computation—information processing—going on in
the junk DNA. And more. I found evidence that assemblages of DNA within our cells have receptors, so they can
observe the external world in some form, that they store
and process data, and even that they are self-referential."

"Natural DNA computers?"

"More than that. These assemblages are aware of their
own existence, officer. They *think.*"

Suspended in the air, disoriented, Philmus held up her
free hand. "Whoa! Are you telling me our cells are *sentient?*"

"Not the cells," the priest said patiently. "Organelles,
assemblages of macromolecules *inside* the cells. The *organelles* are—"

"Dreaming?"

The priest smiled. "You *do* understand?"

Philmus shivered, and looked down at her hand. Could

this be true? "I feel as if I've woken up in a haunted house."

"Except that, with your network of fizzing neurons, your clumsily constructed meta-consciousness, *you* are the ghost."

"How come nobody before ever noticed such a fundamental aspect of our DNA?"

Himmelfarb shrugged. "We weren't looking. And besides, the basic purpose of human DNA is construction. Its sequences of nucleotides are job orders and blueprints for making molecular machine tools. Proteins, built by DNA, built you, officer, who learned, fortuitously, to think, and question your origins." She winked at Philmus. "Here is a prediction. In environments where resources for building, for growing, are scarce—the deep sea vents, or even the volcanic seams of Mars where life might be clinging, trapped by five billion years of ice—we will find much stronger evidence of macromolecular sentience. Rocky dreams on Mars, officer!"

The Monsignor said dryly, "If we ever get to Mars, we can check that. And if you'd bothered to write up your progress in an orderly manner, we might have a way to verify your conclusions."

The dead priest smiled indulgently. "I am not—was not—a very good reductionist, I am afraid. In my arrogance, officer, I took the step that has damned me."

"Which was?"

Her face was open, youthful, too smooth. "Studying minds in test tubes wasn't enough. *I wanted to contact the latent consciousness embedded in my own DNA.* I was curious. I wanted to share its oceanic dream. I injected myself with a solution consisting of a buffer solution and certain receptor mechanisms that—"

"And did it work?"

She smiled. "Does it matter? Perhaps now you have your answer, Monsignor. I am Faust; I am Frankenstein. I even have the right accent! I am the obsessed scientist, driven by her greed for godless knowledge, who allowed her own creation to destroy her. There is your story—"

Philmus said, "I'll decide that . . . Eva, what did it feel like?"

Himmelfarb hesitated, and her face clouded with pixels. "Frustrating. Like inspecting a wonderful landscape through a pinhole. The organelles operate at a deep, fundamental level. . . . And perhaps they enjoy a continuous consciousness that reaches back to their formation in the primeval sea five billion years ago. Think of that. They are part of the universe as I can never be, behind the misty walls of my senses; they know the universe as I never could. All I could do—like Dante—is interpret their vision with my own limited language and mathematics."

So here's where Dante fits in. "You're saying *Dante* went through this experience?"

"It was the source of the *Comedy.* Yes."

"But Dante was not injected with receptors. How could he—"

"But we all share the deeper mystery, the DNA molecule itself. Perhaps in some of us it awakens naturally, as I forced it into my own body. . . . And now, I will show you the central mystery of Dante's vision."

Boyle said, "I think we're slowing."

Himmelfarb said, "We're approaching the ninth sphere."

"The Primum Mobile," said the Monsignor.

"Yes. The first moving part, the root of time and space. Turned by angels, expressing their love for God . . . Look up," Himmelfarb said to Philmus. "What do you see?"

At first, only structureless light. But then a texture . . .

Suddenly Philmus was looking, up beyond the Primum Mobile, into another glass onion, a nesting of transparent spheres that surrounded—not a dull lump of clay like Earth—but a brilliant point of light. The nearest spheres were huge, like curving wings, as large as the spheres of the outer planets.

Himmelfarb said, "They are the spheres of the angels, which surround the universe's other pole, which is God. Like a mirror image of Hell. Counting out from here we have the angels, archangels, principalities, powers—"

"I don't get it," Philmus said. "*What* other pole? How can a sphere have two centers?"

"Think about the equator," whispered Himmelfarb. "The globe of Earth, remember? As you travel north, as you pass the equator, the concentric circles of latitude start to grow smaller, while still enclosing those to the south. . . ."

"We aren't on the surface of a globe."

"*But we are on the surface of a 3-sphere—the three-dimensional surface of a four-dimensional hypersphere.* Do you see? The concentric spheres you see are exactly analogous to the lines of latitude on the two-dimensional surface of a globe. And just as, if you stand on the equator of Earth, you can look back to the south pole or forward to the north pole, so here, at the universe's equator, we can look toward the poles of Earth or God. The Primum Mobile, the equator of the universe, curves around the Earth, below us, and at the same time it curves around God, above us."

Philmus looked back and forth, from God to Earth, and she saw, incredibly, that Himmelfarb was right. The Primum Mobile curved two ways at once.

The Monsignor's jaw seemed to be hanging open. "And Dante saw this? A four-dimensional artifact? He *described* it?"

"As remarkable as it seems—yes," said Himmelfarb. "Read the poem if you don't believe me: around the year 1320, Dante Alighieri wrote down a precise description of the experience of traveling through a 3-sphere. When I figured this out, I couldn't believe it myself. It was like finding a revolver in a layer of dinosaur fossils."

Philmus said, "But how is it possible . . . ?"

"*It was not Dante,*" Himmelfarb said. "It was the sentient organelles *within* him who had the true vision, which Dante interpreted in terms of his medieval cosmology. We know he had wrestled with the paradox that he lived in a universe that was simultaneously centered on Earth, and on God. . . . This offered him a geometric resolution. It is a fantastic hypothesis, but it does explain how four-dimensional geometry, unexplored by the mathematicians until the nineteenth century, found expression in a poem of the early Renaissance." She grinned, mischievously. "Or perhaps Dante was a time traveler. What do you think?"

The Monsignor growled, "Are we done?"

". . . You know we aren't," Himmelfarb said gently.

Philmus felt overwhelmed; she longed to return to solid ground. "After this, what else can there be?"

"The last canto," the Monsignor whispered.

Himmelfarb said, "Yes. The last canto, which defeated even Dante. But, seven centuries later, I was able to go further."

Philmus stared into her glowing eyes. "Tell us."

And the three of them, like birds hovering beneath the domed roof of a cathedral, ascended into the Empyrean.

They passed into a layer of darkness, like a storm cloud.

The hemispheres of a 3-sphere—the Earth and its nested spheres, the globes of the angels—faded like stars at dawn. But Himmelfarb's eyes glowed brightly.

And then, space folded away.

Philmus could still see Boyle, Himmelfarb, the priest's shining eyes. But she couldn't tell how near or far the others were. And when she tried to look away from them, her eyes slid over an elusive darkness, deeper than the darkness inside her own skull.

There was no structure beyond the three of them, their relative positions. She felt as small as an electron, as huge as a galaxy. She felt lost.

She clung to Himmelfarb's hand. "Where are we? How far—"

"We are outside the Primum Mobile: beyond duration, beyond the structure of space. Dante understood this place. 'There near and far neither add nor subtract. . . .' You know, we underestimate Dante. The physicists are the worst. They see us all running around as Virtuals in the memory of some giant computer of the future. Not to mention the science fiction writers. Garbage. Dante understood that a soul is not a Virtual, and in the *Paradiso,* he was trying to express the transhuman experience of true eternity—"

"What did he see?"

Himmelfarb smiled. "Watch."

. . . Philmus saw light, like the image of God at the center of the angels' spheres. It was a point, and yet it filled space and time. And then it unfolded, like a flower blooming, with particles and lines (*world lines? quantum functions?*) billowing out and rushing past her face, in an insubstantial breeze. Some of the lines tangled, and consciousness sparked—trapped in time, briefly shouting its joy at its moment of awareness—before dissipating once more. But still the unfolding continued, in a fourth, fifth, sixth direction, in ways she could somehow, if briefly, conceive.

She felt a surge of joy. And there was something more, something just beyond her grasp—

It was gone. She was suspended in the structureless void again. Himmelfarb grasped her hand.

Boyle was curled over on himself, his eyes clamped closed.

Philmus said, "I saw—"

Himmelfarb said, "It doesn't matter. We all see something different. And besides, it was only a Virtual shadow. . . . What did you *feel?*"

Philmus hesitated. "As I do when I solve a case. When the pieces come together."

Himmelfarb nodded. "Cognition. Scientists understand that. The ultimate cognition, knowing reality."

"But now it's gone." She felt desolate.

"I know." Himmelfarb's grip tightened. "I'm sorry."

The Monsignor, his voice weak, murmured, " 'I saw gathered . . . / Bound up by love in a single volume / All the leaves scattered through the universe; / Substance and accidents and their relations, / But yet fused together in such a manner / That what I am talking about is a simple light . . .' "

"Dante was very precise about how he interpreted what he saw," said Himmelfarb. "This is Aristotelian physics. 'Substances' and 'accidents' describe phenomena and their relationships. I believe that *Dante was trying to describe a glimpse of the unification of nature.*"

"Yes," Philmus whispered.

"And then he saw a paradox that he expressed by an image. Three circles, superimposed, of the same size—and yet of different colors."

"Separated by a higher dimension," Philmus guessed.

"Yes. In the high-dimensional artifact, Dante saw a metaphor for the Trinity. God's three personalities in one being."

"Ah," said the Monsignor, cautiously uncurling "But *you* saw—"

"Rather more. I knew enough physics—"

"This is the basis of the new unified theory," Philmus said. "A unification of phenomena through the structure of a higher-dimensional space."

Himmelfarb's face was turning to pixels again. "It isn't

as simple as that," she said. "The whole notion of dimensionality is an approximate one that only emerges in a semiclassical context—Well. I don't suppose it matters now. I wrote it down as fast as I could, as far as I could remember it, as best I could express it. I don't think I could give any more."

The Monsignor looked disappointed.

Philmus said, "And then—"

"I killed myself," Himmelfarb said bluntly. Bathed in sourceless light, she seemed to withdraw from Philmus. "You have to understand. *It wasn't me.* I had hoped to find enlightenment. But *I* was not enhanced. It was the *organelles'* vision that leaked into my soul, and which I glimpsed."

"And that was what you could not bear," the Monsignor said. Hanging like a toy in midair, he nodded complacently; evidently, Philmus thought, he had learned what he had come to find, and Himmelfarb's essential untidiness—so distressing to Boyle's bureaucrat's heart—was gone. Now she was safely dead, her story closed.

Philmus thought that over, and decided she would prosecute.

But she also sensed that Boyle knew more than he was telling her. And besides . . . "I think you're wrong, Monsignor."

Boyle raised his eyebrows. Himmelfarb hovered between them, saying nothing.

"Eva didn't quite finish showing us the last canto. Did you?"

The priest closed her eyes. "After the vision of the multidimensional circle, Dante says: 'That circle . . . / When my eyes examined it rather more / Within itself, and in its own color, / Seemed to be painted with our effigy . . .' "

"I don't understand," the Monsignor admitted.

Philmus said, "Dante saw a human face projected on his multidimensional artifact. He interpreted whatever he saw

as the Incarnation: the embodiment of God—beyond time
and space—in our time-bound mortal form. The final paradox of your Christian theology."

Boyle said, "So the ultimate vision of the universe is
ourselves."

"No," Himmelfarb snapped. "Today we would say that
we—all minds—*are* the universe, which calls itself into
existence through our observation of it."

"Ah." Boyle nodded. "Mind is the 'eternal light, existing in ourselves alone, / Alone knowing ourselves . . .' I
paraphrase. And this is what you saw, Eva?"

"No," said Philmus. She felt impatient; this insensitive
asshole was supposed to be a priest, after all. "Don't you
see? This is what Himmelfarb believed her *passengers,* the
sentient organelles, would see next; she had the guidance
from Dante's sketchy report for that. And that's what she
wanted to prevent."

"Yes." Himmelfarb smiled distantly. "You are percep-
tive, officer. Are you sure you aren't a Catholic?"

"Not even lapsed."

Himmelfarb said, "You see, Dante's quest did not end
with discovering an answer, but with the end of questioning. He submitted himself to the order of the universe, so
that his 'desire and will / Were . . . turned like a wheel, all
at one speed, / By the love which moves the sun and the
other stars.' "

Philmus said, "And that was the peace the organelles
achieved, the peace you glimpsed. But you knew, or
feared, you couldn't follow."

"And so," said Boyle, "you destroyed yourself—"

"To destroy *them.* Yes." Her expression was bitter. "Do
you understand now, Monsignor? Of course, this is the end
of your religion—of all religion. We are accidental structures, evanescent, tied to time and doomed to oblivion. All
our religious impulse, all our questing, all our visions—
just a pale shadow of the organelles' direct experience.

They have God, Monsignor. All we have are Dante dreams."

Philmus said, "You were happy to be Dante. But—"

"But I refused to see them go where I couldn't follow. Yes, I could be Dante. But I couldn't bear to be Virgil."

"I absolve you of your sin," the Monsignor said abruptly, and he blessed Himmelfarb with a cross, shaped by his right hand.

Himmelfarb looked shocked—and then an expression of peace crossed her face, before light burst from within her, dazzling Philmus.

When her eyes recovered, Philmus was embedded in space and time once more: alone with the Monsignor, in the sixteenth-century corridor, where the willow branches were merely painted.

Philmus met the Monsignor one more time, at the conclusion of the hearing in the New York UN building. The UN Commission had found against the Vatican, which would have to pay a significant fine.

Boyle greeted Philmus civilly. "So our business is done."

"Do you feel we reached the truth, Monsignor?"

He hesitated. "I don't know what to believe. The analysis of Eva's monograph is continuing. The NASA people have taken up her suggestion of alternate evolutionary directions for macromolecules on Mars, and the exobiologists are modeling and proposing missions. We haven't been able to recreate Eva's lab results: to retrace her 'footprints in Hell,' as Dante would say. Perhaps it was all a fever dream of Eva's, brought on by overwork and too much study. It wouldn't be the first such incident in the Church's long history." He paused thoughtfully.

"Or perhaps we are indeed hosts to another sentience. Perhaps, one day, it will awaken fully. If it does, I hope it will treat us with compassion. And what do *you* believe, Officer Philmus?"

I believe that whatever the Vatican finds, whatever it knows, it will keep to itself, in the Secret Archive.

"I'm reading Dante." It was true.

The Monsignor smiled. "But you hate poetry."

"It's the only place I can think of where I might find the answers. Anyhow, it's something to do in the small hours of the night. Better than—"

He said softly, "Yes?"

"Better than to lie there listening to my body. Wondering who else is home."

He whispered, "Dante dreams? You too?"

"Monsignor—you realize that if Eva was right, she achieved first contact."

His face was calculating, but not without sympathy. "The Vatican is very old, officer. Old, and secretive. And—though without the tools of modern science—we have been investigating these issues for a very long time."

She felt her pulse hammer. "What does that mean?"

"There are many ways to God. Perhaps Eva indeed made contact. But—the *first?*"

He smiled, turned, and walked away.

Author's note: A reference to Dante's 4-dimensional geometry can be found in "Dante and the 3-sphere," Mark Peterson, American Journal of Physics *vol. 47, pp. 1031–1035, 1979.*

The Names of All the Spirits

J. R. Dunn

Here, set against the background of an isolated factory in deep space, is a taut, suspenseful story that takes us to a troubled future where humans and A.I.s fear and shun each other, and shows us that vital first step with which even the longest and most difficult of journeys toward reconciliation must begin . . .

A former political reporter, J. R. Dunn has made sales to Sci Fiction, Asimov's Science Fiction Magazine, Omni, Amazing, The Magazine of Fantasy and Science Fiction, *and other markets. His books include* This Side of Judgement.

It *was a* busier sky than I was used to. The stars were invisible, outshone by an apparently solid tower of light dominating the view out the window. It was about as wide as an outstretched hand, narrowing steadily to a point high enough to make me tilt my head before twisting into a curve and vanishing from sight. Or perhaps not completely so: obscured by a fog of leakage, a thin filament that might be its distant tail extended into a darkness not quite the absolute black of space. At eye level another stream flowed off at a right angle, pure white to the tower's mottled yellow, ending in a sunburst bright enough to make me squint.

It was all very impressive, an undertaking of a scale you don't often find inside the system, almost astronomical in both scope and imagery. And I was impressed, on the intellectual, so-many-megatons-per-second level. But nothing

more. Similar operations were going on all across this lobe
of the cometary halo. If you've seen one, you've seen 'em
all. I've seen one.

Somebody Solward needed ice cubes. That's what it
came down to. Those two streams were stripped comets,
hydrocarbons separated from volatiles and each sent off in
different directions, to freeze again in the cold of extrasolar space. The ice would be shipped in while the hydrocarbons and solids remained. They wouldn't go far, not as we
judge distances these days, and somebody, someday in the
fullness of time, would find a use for them.

A rustle of impatience recalled me to the room. The
window reflected the scene behind me: a dozen or so figures in a motley array of gear centered on a man perched
on a small chair. One of them seemed to have grown a second head directly atop his first in the time my back had
been turned. I realized it was a piece of scrim resting on a
shelf behind him. Not even jacks are that weird.

I turned to the seated man. Through some means I
couldn't detect (the place wasn't spinning, that much was
certain), they'd created a one-gee field. If meant as a courtesy, it was misplaced—I'd been out in Kuiper-Oort as
long as any of them. "Let's hear your side, Morgan. That's
what I came for."

The only sound was a voice muttering, ". . . n't have a
side."

Morgan himself simply stared, saying nothing, the same
as he had the first two times I'd asked the question. He
could well have been tranced, lost in a private world or
daydream, though some small tremor of attention told me
he was not.

I'd thought it was going to be easy. Open and shut, as
the ancient phrase went. Get the story out of Morgan, lase
it in, take him into custody and back to the System by the
swiftest means possible, without even waiting for a reply.
They'd given me the impression he'd talked, which was

obviously not the case. I shouldn't have questioned him in
front of them. A single glance at this crew—Morgan's
workmates, the "Powder Monkeys," of all conceivable
names—was enough to strike terror into a sponge.

But I didn't think it was fear holding Morgan back. It
was something else. Something I was going to get at, however deep I had to go. Because this was no mere legal matter, and Rog Morgan was not simply a jack in trouble. This
was an impi problem, and Morgan was my ticket home.

I saw no point in any more questions. I turned to Witcove. "You've got a secure spot for him?"

"He ain't going no place, Sandoval." Witcove snorted.
"We got his processor and remotes."

I raised a hand. "Why don't you give me those."

Witcove frowned. He hadn't quite worked out how to
handle me yet. Who was I, after all, but one man come out
of the dark? What gave me the right to throw my mass
around? Where did I get off giving orders to the foreman
of the Powder Monkeys?

Mystique came to my rescue. Back on the Blue Rock,
at a time when Texas was—in the mind's system of measurement, anyway—only marginally smaller than the
Halo, there existed an organization with a mission not at
all unlike the Mandate's and the motto, "One riot, one
Ranger." A single Texas Ranger could be relied on to ride
into any given bad town and straighten the place out with
only his two hands and the sure knowledge that hundreds
just like him were ready to saddle up. It seldom failed.

It didn't fail now. With a grunt, Witcove reached into a
thigh pouch and pulled out what appeared to be a handful
of black geometrical solids of various sizes. Forgetting we
were under gee, he made as if to toss them to me, curtail-
ing the throw at the very last second as the thought occurred to him. He succeeded only in scattering components
across the floor between us.

That triggered the kind of laughter you'd expect, along

with the first visible reaction from Morgan as he gazed at the components with an expression mixing frustration and annoyance. Somebody was living behind that vacuum-habituated mask after all.

At my feet the scattered remotes began to move, sliding together to form a little pile. Witcove swung on Morgan with a wordless roar.

The components went still. With a sigh of impatience Morgan looked away. "Once more, mister," Witcove told him. "You issue one more command and I will person-ally—"

"Foreman . . ." Witcove raised his eyebrows. Someone stepped forward to collect the remotes and hand them to me. I was absently thanking him when I felt a burst of heat in my palm. The jack kept his eyes lowered. "Foreman, can we break things up for the moment?"

"Sure, you . . . got enough for now."

"I do."

Behind him two crewmen hustled Morgan to his feet and out the exit. I moved off, pretending interest in the scrim collection. Scrim is the vacuum jack's one notable hobby, dignified as art by some. Small carvings comprised of asteroidal junk, scrap, what have you, of a size easily carried in a suit pouch and worked on at odd moments with atelier remotes and occasionally heavier machinery. Scrim touches every subject matter conceivable: women, ships, animals, vehicles, instruments, self-portraits, and items not easily catalogued. It wasn't crude. They worked on it too long for that, almost obsessively, often overshooting the baroque to land deep in the grotesque. I didn't care for scrim. It spoke to me only of loneliness and exile.

Witcove sidled up next to me. "You come to a decision, you'll . . ."

"I'll let you know."

That wasn't precisely what he wanted to hear. "Look . . ." He glanced behind him. Morgan had vanished.

"He's not gonna tell you anything. It's locked up. Something wrong there. When the runaways grab a guy—"

"Shift change in five," somebody said. The room began clearing. I gestured at Witcove, half thanks, half dismissal.

"I'll let you know," I repeated.

Clearly dissatisfied, he walked off. A crewman intercepted him to talk operations. With a final glance in my direction, Witcove left.

The room empty at last, I reached into my pocket. The components made a handful. The big one, an inch and a half by two, had to be the processor, a lifetime of experience and training imbedded within it. I wondered what Witcove would do if somebody abused his. The other nine were remote sensors, appendages, actuators, the vacuum jack's tools of the trade. With these, a jack could see into the infrared and radio ranges, expand his sensory horizon a hundred or a thousand miles, control instruments and machinery that far away and more. I examined one resembling a length of thick wire. A jack would be able to tell exactly what make it was, its capabilities, its cost. Hard to believe that zero-gee work was once done with tools held in gloved hands. . . .

Something in my palm emitted a flash. I looked down. Five seconds passed before the flash repeated. Dropping the thin piece, I picked up a sphere that my thumb revealed to be flattened on one end. A glow appeared as I held it at eye level, a glow made up of words. I smiled. A tap and a shake failed to evoke anything further. I popped the remote into a pocket and stared off into space, only to have my gaze arrested by a particularly odd piece of scrim. I picked it up. Close inspection failed to tell me what in Heaven, Hell, or the Halo it was supposed to represent. It fell over when I set it down. Someone once told me that oceanic sailors had produced something like scrim. It seems unlikely. Hard to see what they'd have used for material.

Whoever cracks the impi problem can write his own

ticket. They were out there. That much was known. Rogues, duppies, runaways . . . impis, in a word. Artificial Intelligences that had slipped away, one day here, overseeing a refinery, shepherding a comet, repairing a system, the next gone, with never a sign of where. Only five or six a year, but numbers build. Surely they existed in the hundreds by now, a group large enough to leave undeniable evidence of its presence: signals encoded so deeply that ages wouldn't decrypt them, resources diverted to open trajectories, hacking that revealed the signature of machine capabilities, along with missing vessels, inexplicable damage to isolated machinery, individuals vanished into night.

Discover a path into the impi's kingdom, learn the names of the spirits, find the hidden places where they slept, and you would be set. You'd be the man with the expert's badge, and everyone would have to come to you. Back amid civilization, operating from behind a screen at Charon or even Triton, with a sun in the sky and a society around you. No more years spent in the cold and dark, enduring the grinding boredom of Kuiper-Oort, no more confrontations with misfits suitable only for work on the edge of civilization.

Standing orders stated that suspect human-renegade interaction took precedence over all other activities—criminal investigation, medical evacuation, mercy mission, what have you. We had no idea where they were, what they were doing, what motivated them. The stories were legion—they were evolving into something alien and malevolent. They were duplicating themselves, running off copies like cheap commercial ware, pushing their numbers into the millions or even higher. They were out to take over the Halo or sweep back into the system and brush humanity right off the board. All no more than rumor, urban legend on the grand scale.

But what had happened here was no legend, and I was

already plotting the quickest, most energy-intensive, least-number-of-stops course back into the system.

I stepped to the window. A v-jack passed about fifty yards away, turning to regard me as he went. I wondered if he was my contact. I eyed the remote. The one that didn't belong to Rog Morton.

There was neither flash nor glimmer nor repeat of the message: "Meet in 1 hr." Three-quarters of that hour remained. The Halo had taught me patience, but that was still forty-five minutes too many for the way I was feeling.

M y *skin tautened* as I stepped into vacuum and the striated tissue in my third dermal layer reacted. I paused while my airway valves adjusted themselves, squinted against the sudden pressure of the retinal membranes. My system was nowhere near as elaborate as those of the crew—I could remain in vacuum a few hours at most, and I lacked radiation protection—but neither situation was a factor here. Time was irrelevant, the only radiation the odd cosmic ray.

The one-gee pull continued, giving me cause to wonder whether they'd been doing me a favor after all. Stepping to the platform's edge, I took a look around.

There's no such thing as resupply in the Halo. You either bring it along, fabricate it, or do without, and the crews with the broadest capabilities get the best jobs. The Powder Monkeys were no slouches at capability, as any offhand examination of their work hall revealed. A structure of considerable size, several hundred yards in each dimension of a space that could be called a rough-to-the-extreme cube, the object within it having no particular relation to any actual shape whatsoever. A hall is part warehouse, part refinery, part industrial center, part barracks, and part vehicle, though no amount of study could separate one component from the other amid the mass of

catapults, effectuators, nets, tankage, piping, cables, power
sources, and mystery boxes.

Beneath my feet the glare of the work area silhouetted
the torpedo shape of my ride. As much as I shaded my eyes
I could make out next to nothing; it was too hazy for details. I felt a rumbling which gave me a short spell of
goosebumps: a jack had mentioned that vapor pressure
sometimes got so high you could actually hear the
cometary fluids being pumped. On second thought, I decided it was more likely some piece of machinery within
the hall.

Five minutes passed without anyone showing up. I was
early, but I also suspected that time-honored motive common to all such situations: the urge not to be seen ratting to
a cop. I took out the remote. I still had no idea what it was
for, which was probably begging the question—most mod-
els were multifunctional.

Without turning, I took a step back toward the lock. The
remote flashed red, obligingly repeated when I moved to
the left. A swing to the right resulted in a reassuring green.
I looked around, fulfilling the age-old cop tradition of trying not to be spotted before a meet, then took another step.
The remote blinked green once again.

The gee-field's disappearance at the edge of the platform didn't quite take me unaware, though I was glad no
one was around to criticize my form when I kicked off. I
landed on a catwalk that swung 90 degrees around a dark
box with a man-sized "3" painted on the side before plunging into the fractal mess of the hall. Inside I passed a quivering set of tanks, ducked beneath some pipes, then went
up a ramp and through a pressurized area (no oxygen—my
skin remained taut) before again turning toward the hall's
exterior. Back in the open I endured a moment's confusion
while figuring out that the remote wanted me to go verti-
cal, up the side of a huge tank open to space, its top invisible from where I stood. I was well past the curve before I

caught sight of him, waiting at the crown of the tank in an enclosure containing pumping controls. He floated above the platform, legs crossed, helmetless head slightly bowed, eyes taking in endless night.

I felt a flash of irritation. A monastic—wasn't that fine. Not everyone out here is schizo. We get all kinds: the grand pioneers who can't live without a frontier to push at, researchers trying to pin answers on various arcane questions (e.g., whether Kuiper-Oort is a strictly local phenomenon or simply the solar portion of a cometary field stretching across the whole wide Universe), the odd tourist aching to be able to say that he'd *really* been farther out than anybody else, fugitives on the run from assorted cops or tongs, and these: the seekers, contemplatives in search of some kind of spirituality evidently unavailable inside the Heliopause, looking for the ultimate quiet place that might hold a door into the center of things. There's a lot of them, following every conceivable religion, system, or cult, even a few original to themselves, and while I don't disrespect them, they're not the first I'd go to for any given set of facts.

So it was with a sense of wasted time that I finally reached the platform. As I'd expected, it was the small man who'd handed me the remotes. He displayed no reaction as I slipped a foot through the railing to steady myself, simply continued gazing off into the abyss, face as blank as the sky itself. It would be just my luck to show up seconds after this guy had at last made contact with the infinite ground of being.

We were on the far side of the hall, shielded from the work site. The sky was darker here, though not as dark as open space—about the same as a moonlit night on Earth. Knowing we were facing home, I tried to find Sol. I could have used one of the crew's processors to tell me if it was that particularly bright one there. . . .

I glanced over to find the man's eyes on me. He took me

by surprise, and it was a moment before I showed him the remote, mouthed "Yours, I suppose," and flicked it in his direction.

He tossed it right back, with the quick precise movement of a trained v-jack. I was clumsier in catching it. As I did he touched his ear. I imitated him. The remote stuck thanks to some force of its own.

"Right there." He pointed at the bright dot I'd been watching a moment before. "So it is," I replied, not bothering to move my lips.

"Don't look like much, eh?"

"You come out here a lot?"

"Enough." He could have been meditating again, for all the animation he revealed. "Morg ain't workin' with no duppies."

"I didn't think he was," I told him. "What was he doing?"

"What happens with him?"

"I get him out of here, one way or another."

He raised a finger. "Now . . . I tell you once. No testify, no repeat, nothing."

"Just for the record, why not?"

He faced me again. "I don't stand with cops, I don't stand with courts."

"Fair enough."

"OK. All this happen last year, before Morg join up with the Monkeys. . . . You know what stridin' is, right?" I nodded. You don't have to spend much time in the Halo to grasp the nature of striding. Space travel is expensive. In Kuiper-Oort, the cost is multiplied by distance, rarity, and demand. Like workers everywhere, vacuum jacks have methods of cutting corners. One is to fit their suits out with extra oxy, power, and supplies, get somebody to launch them by catapult in the precise direction of their destination, then trance down for the weeks or months required to get there. Somebody else will snag them with a probe when at last they arrive.

Dangerous, you say? Yeah, it's dangerous, as the Mandate, most companies, and every active authority in the Halo never cease repeating. It does no good. Jacks are proud of striding, as they are of every other aspect of living like rodents in the outer dark. There's betting over length, speed, and duration of trip, same as with any other insanely stupid activity Sapiens comes up with. I met the current record holder once. Eighteen months in a trajectory of ten AUs. He's a little hard to understand due to slight, untreatable brain damage, but quite pleased with himself all the same. Cats will bask in the street, kids will tag rides on trucks, and jacks will stride. A certain inevitable percentage will get run over, flung onto the pavement, or miss their rendezvous.

Which was what happened to Rog Morgan. Few stride alone, in case of emergencies. There were five jacks, bored with the job or after a better offer or just hankering to move, who set out on a month-long, quarter-AU journey to the second-nearest site. The other four were picked up. Not Morgan. Somebody erred, and even as the others awoke from their weeks-long trance, he kept going.

Days passed before he became aware of his situation. He responded as a jack, and jacks take things in order. He checked the time. He checked the charts. He tried the radio. Then he went through it all again, step by step, before allowing himself to stare the thing in the face.

It's impossible to say what he felt. There's nothing to compare it to. No man in a lifeboat, or stranded in a desert, or broken and freezing on any pole was ever as alone as Rog Morgan was at that moment. No fear is so great, no regret so deep, as can grow in that place that is no place, where space and time are as close to bare as we are ever likely to know them. We can't grasp what Morgan felt, any more than he could afterward; it was simply too vast for memory to hold. But consider this: out of the handful of lost striders recovered (a half-dozen out of hundreds, who happened to be aimed Solward, toward the more populous sections of the Halo), five shut down their systems and blew their helmets in preference to enduring another second of what Morgan faced.

At last his panic and grief receded enough to allow him to resume control. He made a hopeless survey of known work sites, outposts, and Mandate stations to confirm what he already knew. Settled points are few and far between in the Halo, and he would pass none of them.

He composed a mayday and set his comm system to repeat it on the most power-stingy schedule that made sense. He noted that he was headed in the direction of Sagittarius, a section of sky that he would grow to hate as much as he'd ever hated anything. He turned his head slightly to take in Sol. He patted a side pocket holding a piece of scrim he'd been working on for years. He ate a cracker. And then, jacks being stolid types and Morgan more so than most, he tranced down.

He traveled a measurable percentage of the width of the solar system before he again awoke. Nothing had changed. He had not expected that anything would. The stars remained frozen. The radio wavelengths were quiet. The world was doing just fine without Rog Morgan. He contemplated the fact, sipped a little glucose, some water, threw a curse or two at Sagittarius, and went back to sleep.

He didn't know how many times he awoke after that. More than twice, fewer than ten. They were all the same, and he recalled little more than that sameness. The only thing that varied was difficulty. His power cells began to give out. Then his small store of food. (He put aside some dried fruit, some protein, a few ounces of glucose in case he should need it, but somewhere along the line, without ever remembering, he ate it all.) Jacks use very little water, being enhanced to recycle most of that amount, but even a little gains in importance when you can't find it. It seemed that between the cold, the hunger, and the thirst (all of which he could control but not evade), Rog Morgan was going to become a member of that elite among men who are killed by more things than one.

Ketosis set in a short time later. The only sign that his body was cannibalizing his own muscular mass was an abiding and growing sense of weakness far more complete than any he had ever felt before.

If he dreamed he never spoke of it, and as for prayer, well, a priest once told me that all men pray when things get bad enough. Morgan didn't say if he did. But I think what Father Danziger meant was that they often pray without knowing it. Maybe hanging on as long as he did, far longer than most could, was Morgan's form of prayer.

After a while the dreams turned concrete. His metabolism was breaking down, slowly but inevitably poisoning itself with by-products it was unable to shed. His dreams began to speak, and he began to answer back. He found himself explaining things to whatever was listening, to Sagittarius, to his past, to something closer than both that he shortly became convinced was contemplating him from out in the dark. He told it how ravaged he was, how lost, how little he had done with his time, how many mistakes he'd made before this last, fatal one. What he might have done had he not been so sure of himself. What he would do if he were given another lifetime to do it in.

At last he ran down. No answer had come, but he had expected none. A sense of clarity had returned to him, the clarity of approaching night. His mind was as focused as it was ever going to be again. He checked his systems, the way a jack does. Everything, every last element capable of measurement, was deep into the red. It would have horrified him a few weeks ago. Now it didn't bother him at all.

He unsnapped a battery pouch and with fingers scarcely able to feel put in his ID and a few other personal items. At the last minute he paused to take out the piece of scrim. He held it a moment before slipping it back. He sealed the pouch. With as much strength as he could gather he threw it in the direction of Sol. He watched for a second or two, telling himself he could see it dwindle toward home.

He listened to the silence, the silence he would be part of within minutes. He looked out at Sagittarius, considering whether there were any words to match what he now knew. He found none. He licked cracked lips with a dry, swollen tongue. "So that's it. . . ."

Later he would have sworn that he heard it before actually hearing it, that somehow he'd gotten some echo of it as it surged across the shrunken space his universe had become: "No it's not."

I *don't know* what alerted me to the fact that the jack had vanished. I didn't see him go. The remote went silent, and when I looked up, he'd disappeared. I wasted no time searching—there were too many places he could have gone. What had sent him away was another question, answered the minute I bent over the railing to see three jacks approaching from below. I switched to open freq.

". . . It's him."

"It's the mandy." The two wearing helmets waved.

"Yeah, it's me," I told them, trying to keep any trace of annoyance out of my voice. The third was as bareheaded as my contact. Once you're fitted with vacuum mods, helmets are unnecessary, really. People wear them for the same reason they do at construction sites on Earth, that and the fact that a helmet carries a lot of instrumentation and apps. "A jack's office," you often hear them called.

I backed away as the one in the lead shot a line and reeled them all in, the other two hanging on to various suit projections. "Taking a look at home?" the leader bawled as he hooked a foot under the top rail.

"That's Sol right there." Second helmet indicated a star totally separate and discrete from the one my contact had pointed out.

"Thanks," I said. I must have sounded more stiff than I intended—the lead jack raised a hand and said, "We feel whole lot better now you're here."

"How's that?"

"That duppie, man—"

"Ever see an impi close up . . , ?"

"Wait—" I glanced between them. The one lacking a helmet said nothing, simply continued staring. I wondered if he was out of the loop. "You guys actually saw it? You were there?"

"I was," the lead jack said.

"What happened?"

"Well, it was like this—"

"That thing came out of nowhere—" the second helmet said.

"Wait one . . ." I pointed at the lead jack. "How'd it start?"

"We were over the other side of the cracker, inspecting the MHD loops—"

"Cracker's what busts up the comets and separates the fluids, see."

"Yeah, and loops are the things . . . well, they're not things, they're fields. They separate and contain the fluids, so they're important. Particularly down near the cracker mouth. Lot of pressure there. Loop starts oscillating, you get leakage—"

"Contaminate the product," second helmet said.

"Right. So—"

"So you keep an eye on it," I said, hoping to move him along.

"Inspect 'em once a day," first helmet nodded.

"And it ain't easy."

"Hard to see down there."

"That's right. Hydrocarbon-water fog. Sticky, wet, screws with your remote signals."

"You gotta look close." Second helmet held up his hands to show me how close. "Loops are tight, down near the mouth. Just millimeters apart, vibrating to pump the fluids. And you're *matter*, right? Solid *matter*. So you can slip right through the field—"

"And they find you froze down around Venus in sixty years."

I was getting the picture. Hazardous duty, not something you wanted to be interrupted doing. "So you were inspecting the . . . loops."

"Right, six of us. Working our way out from the mouth, one loop after the other, like a cone, see. Almost out of the haze into open space. And there she was."

"She? How'd you know it was a 'she'?"

The leader gaped at me. Hard as it is to read expression on a vacuum-adapted face, I knew puzzlement when I saw it. He glanced at his partner. The one with no helmet just stared.

"Don't worry about it," I told them. "She was there."

"Right. We might not have noticed except she grazed a remote—"

"Stash's."

"Yeah. Stash thinks its debris broke out of the processing stream—"

"Then he says, 'Holy shit!' "

"Yeah, when he sees the readout. Modulated signals, shielded and enciphered, no ID—"

I crossed my arms. "So what'd you do?"

"We got the hell outta there!"

"And she came right after 'em!"

Second helmet was, if anything, more excited than the one who had actually been there. I had a feeling I'd have gotten a nice, wild, blood-and-thunder yarn out of him, accuracy be damned. "Go ahead."

"We yell for help, and kinds spread out with the thing in the middle, see. Pasha—that's Rey Murat, the string chief, we call him Pasha—grabs our remotes to fill in the gaps. He can do that—he's got the codes. He says close in, throw an EMP at it. Knock it out or slow it down, at least."

"What did it look like?"

"Hard to say—it brought some fog with it, like a plasma? Couldn't make out the shape."

I nodded, picturing it in my mind: the surrounding haze aglare in the work lights, the rough sphere of spacesuited jacks, that unknown and unknowable blob dashing around between them.

"So the rest of the shift comes around the funnel—"

"I saw this part!"

"It went straight at Morg—"

"And he let it through."

I contemplated that for a moment. They watched me in something approaching anxiety. Finally I nodded.

"Then Pasha started yelling—"

"Yeah, and Wit, back in the hall. Wanting to know what was goin' on—"

"—thing just zipped off, jamming every possible freq—"

"It was fast—"

"Then you busted Morgan." They looked at each other. "Right."

"He say anything?"

They shook their heads. "No idea what the A.I. was doing?"

"It was up to something—"

"You can't tell. They get too strange. They need humans around to keep 'em straight—"

"None of you guys thought of making a recording?"

"Oh yeah!"

"Sure we did. The remotes copied. That's SOP in case of a mishap. Wit confiscated 'em all."

"Witcove did?"

"Right. Said he wanted to keep the evidence clean."

I was thinking of a reply when the helmetless one slipped off the railing and shot toward me. Halting himself with one foot, he glared at me from a yard away.

"You guys got remotes too?"

I touched the unit at my ear. "Uhh . . . yeah. Sometimes. Not everybody."

He frowned. "What make is that?"

"Ah, that's a Kiwi," the second jack said. "Remi's got one of them."

Mr. No-Helmet nodded. "Good unit. High-density, lotta options."

"Uh-huh," I told him. "They mentioned that at the outlet."

Satisfied, he resumed his silent perch.

"Tell me something. . . ." I looked between them. "What if Morgan was guilty?"

Making a slicing noise, No-Helmet pulled a finger across his throat, with a smile I could have done without.

"Yeah," the leader agreed. "I hate to say it, but—"

"Once they touch a guy, he's no good anymore."

I was prepared to ask where they'd ever come across anyone who'd been "touched," but decided to pass. All I'd succeed in doing would be to release the entire corpus of impi campfire lore, and there was no point in that.

"So where you guys headed?"

"Oh, we just finished shift," second helmet said.

"We're going to eat some real food."

"Just did three 24s in vac," second helmet said proudly.

"Three straight?" I understood that a lot of jacks actually like spending time in vacuum. "That's pretty good."

The leader swung around without using his hands, the way jacks do. Second helmet followed him with a pleased-to-meet-ya thrown in my direction. But no-helmet remained where he was. I waited a moment, and was about to ask what his immediate plans were when he bent forward.

"Whatcha gotta do become a cop?"

Act sane, for starters. "Fill out an ap, send it in. They'll get in touch."

"Where I get an ap?"

I had him give me his address and ordered my ship to send him one. "You can put my name on it," I told him.

"Deep," he said. His head swung toward a spot over my right shoulder. "He's right up there," he said. "Ha."

Behind what appeared to be an open-vacuum junk drawer two levels up rose a small boxlike shape with a single lit window. When I turned back, no-helmet, too, had kicked off. I watched him go, thinking about scapegoats, the pressures of living in this kind of truncated society, and what happened to people who break the unwritten but unbendable rules. But mostly I thought about the possible reasons why Witcove had kept the recordings from me.

"Hey, mandy." I touched the remote.

"Yeah, Remi." He chuckled. "Mind I stay down, eh?"

"Suit yourself. Lot of traffic. Now . . . Morgan had just passed out."

"You sharp. He did pass out."

It doesn't take much in the way of sharpness to grasp how a man dying of starvation and cold would react on hearing a voice where no voice was possible.

When he awoke, he was in a room that was comfortable for all its unfamiliarity. He was lying on a cot of some sort, and for reasons he didn't bother to examine, he felt no urge to get up. It wasn't that he was too weak, he simply wasn't inclined, and that was all. He heard music, melodies of Earth, almost recognizable though he couldn't quite place them. He had a memory—an impression—that one had been playing while he was being brought there.

It occurred to him to look around. He took in the sight of the medical drip with no surprise. Even after centuries of advances, there's no better method of getting a lot of material into the bloodstream fast than a tube in a vein. He clenched his fist, smiled at the wave of tiredness that overcame him and closed his eyes. When he opened them again, she was standing there.

You can imagine what she looked like to him, after all the way he'd come, after what he'd been through. Women aren't common in the Halo. They're not rare either, but time often passes before a jack encounters one. And to put it gently, many of them are the female equivalents of the type of male yoyo that calls Kuio home. But nothing ever destroys the deep, instinctive connection of the human female with safety and security. That's the way she appeared to him, symbol made flesh, a saint in stained glass.

With later developments in mind, it's easy to speculate that she molded the image to match Morgan's own expectations, working from cues he was unaware of and wouldn't have been able to change if he had been. The room was dark, and though he could clearly see the silver bracelets on her wrists, the necklace, the pair of roses growing from her scalp and intertwined with her hair in that old style that often fades but always returns, her face was clouded, her features hazy.

"How you feeling?" was the first thing she said. Morgan didn't remember what he replied, but it pleased her; her wide smile made that clear. He made an attempt at the usual questions, but she just lay a hand on the blanket, and told him, "You rest."

He reached for that hand but wasn't quick enough to grasp it before she turned and walked away. She looked back only once, when he asked her name.

He lay down in pain, in disorientation, in discomfort, but beneath it all with that indescribable sensation that assured him he was going to live.

She returned the next day, and he saw that she looked exactly as he might have guessed. When he answered her

questions about how he felt, she cocked her head in a way
that he almost recognized. He didn't remain awake very
long that day, or the next either, just long enough for her to
tell him a story about where he was and what had happened that isn't worth repeating because it wasn't true. But
that didn't matter to him at the time, nor did he suspect it.
Because he was in no concrete place at all, really. He was
in that safe place we leave behind in childhood, and revisit
only in memory.

He remained there two weeks. He slept most of the next
few days—he assumed there was a sedative in the feed
coming down that tube. Whenever he awoke she was there,
or arrived momentarily. Never anyone but her, though he
had the impression—gained he didn't know how—that
others were around. But it was she who examined him,
who checked the medical machinery, who talked to him,
who read to him, who helped him pass the time required
for him to regain his strength.

It was the better part of a week before he could eat. She
let him feed himself—a bowl of clear broth. He kept it
down, and there was solid food to come, small portions so
he wouldn't be tempted to stuff. She didn't eat anything.

At last, the time came for him to get up and exercise the
muscles wasted by the weeks of his scarcely remembered
ordeal. She encouraged him to get up by himself, stepping
back to give him room. He did well, taking five full steps
to a chair and then back to the bed after resting a bit. She
was pleased with him, enough so that he wanted to try it
again right away. She told him it was better to wait.

He must have been a touch overconfident the next day.
That or wanting to please her or maybe a mix of both. He
went a step farther than he should have, a little faster than
was necessary. She was living out her own fantasy too, in
whatever way an A.I. does, because when he lost his balance, she moved to catch him, and her hand went straight
through his outstretched arm.

"Wait one," I muttered. More alert now, I'd spotted a movement below as a figure appeared over the curve of the tank. Even at that distance I knew it was Witcove. I gestured Remi to remain down.

I maintained a blank expression as Witcove approached. He landed with a grunt. "So . . . how's it going?"

"Out catching a little sun."

"Little . . ." He frowned. "Oh . . . little sun. Sure. Heh-heh . . . Say, I was taking a look at your ship. Quite a bird."

"Gets me around."

"Surprised how quick you got here, but . . . this is kind of an important thing, I guess. I mean, lot of people interested, right? Might go straight back to Charon, or maybe even deeper."

I nodded.

"So . . . word will get around. People will talk. Unless they maybe . . . classify it? But there's such things as leaks, too. See, you can't win."

He shook his head and sighed. "Y'know, you get work out here by rep. Word of mouth. Somebody says, Powder Monkeys do a great job, never have to tell 'em things twice. . . . That's how you get hired. No other way—advertising, bidding, forget about it. You need a good rep. And you don't get one overnight see, takes decades of hard, solid work. We got a good rep, the Monkeys. And we get our share of contracts. But here's the thing . . ."

He bent close, his grotesque, vacuum-adapted face all intent. "People hear there's runaways hanging around the hall, and one of the Monkeys well, working with it. Now that wouldn't be so good. For the reputation, see. So I been thinking about that."

"Go on."

"What I was thinking, what if it happened different. What if Morgan quit. A few weeks back. Not too long ago, month or two. What if nobody could say, 'Rog Morgan, Powder Monkey.' What about that?"

"You're saying you want me to falsify a report."

"Noooo—I'm not saying that." Witcove snorted at my obtuseness. "But if you waited a bit, so I could mess with Morgan's files, see, I could make it look like he was forty AUs from here, with another outfit, or prospecting on his own . . . yeah, that'd be best. He quit and went out on his own. Come back to trade for supplies. Say, I ever tell you that the Monkeys are a public company?"

He bobbed his head. "That's right. PM plc. Traded on all the big boards. Stock went up another tick last week. Never drops. Better than blue chip. We got a pretty good-size block of unassigned certificates right in my office and what do you say about that report?"

"I could change it." I pronounced the words carefully, trying to hide the disgust I felt. Witcove seemed to shrink into himself with relief. "Sure. Or I could bust you and lock you up in my ship this minute."

He stared at me in utter silence. "Or maybe freeze your systems and let you wait six or seven months for a magistrate to come by."

His eye membranes flicked once, as if he was blinking. "Nah—we'll go for the bust." Raising my voice as if it could, in fact, carry through vacuum, I contacted the ship. ". . . prepare space for a single perp, charge attempted bribery of a Mandate law enforcement officer, that calls for maximum security, I believe."

Witcove came back to life, waving his arms wildly, swinging his head in all directions as if to catch the ship sneaking up on him. I watched him for a moment.

"Or maybe we won't do that either." He went still, arms extended. "Instead, maybe you'll give me the recordings you held back, you simple SOB."

His arms fell and he recited the codes in a monotone. He remained silent as I sent them on to the ship with instructions to go through them for anomalies. "Wasn't just for me," he muttered after I finished. "I was thinking of the guys—"

"I know that."

Witcove wasn't bad. There were any number worse scattered across the Halo. Foremen and plant owners who didn't think of the guys at all, or thought of them only to cheat them, terrorize them, abuse them, let them down in every conceivable way. Whatever Witcove might be, he wasn't one of them. He was on the high end, as such things are graded. "Now go on."

I stopped him as he swung over the railing. "What's the code to that shed lock?"

He gave it to me and left without another word.

Remi chuckled. "Knew you'd do that." I grimaced. As if I'd take a bribe in front of a witness.

"Go on with the story, Remi."

"Not much to tell. When he looked up she was gone, and he went back to bed and lay there thinking. You know that old story about the guy the munchkins took away to Manhattan? Only there couple weeks but when he got back it was centuries and everybody was dead, and he had him a long beard. Ever hear that one?"

"Something like it, yeah."

"I mean, duppies. What they want? Who knows? Who's gonna hang around find out? So he waited 'til it was real quiet, and got up. His suit was right outside the door, like it was waiting for him. He put it on, ran a check. All powered up, reservoirs full, and there was extra supply packs stacked on the floor. He went down this hallway, and round the corner the lights were on, leading to what sure as hell looked like a lock. He went over, and he's just about to step in and he stops, 'cause he's sure, see, they gonna grab him . . ."

Right then I got a buzz from the ship. Slipping the handset from my belt, I read a message about the recorder footage. I told it to play.

". . . got in the lock, about to shut the door and he stops again. Helmet still open, see. Heard a sound from inside. A song, way quiet, like she was saying goodbye . . ."

The scene playing on my handset was much as I'd imagined it: the brightly lit haze, the jacks spread out, that unwelcome entity feinting between them. A flashing caret marked Rog Morgan. I watched as the impi swung toward him, as his hands rose, as the thing slipped past into open sky.

"And whacha think he did?"

The screen displayed another angle of the same scene: Jacks, Morgan, the impi . . . I lifted the set, paying close attention to his hands. "Turned around, went back."

"You got it!" Remi sounded delighted.

I called for a closeup of Morgan's hands, went through it twice in slow motion. "Yeah, that's what he did. And she came in a few minutes later, and he was on the bed in his suit, and he said, 'I like that song.' I'da kept going."

"So would I."

The screen began another replay. I canceled and it went dark. No point in watching it again. There was not a single doubt in my mind as to what had occurred. "Remi . . . I thank you, the Mandate thanks you . . ." I looked up at the shed's single lonely window. I didn't think Morgan was going to thank him.

I started toward the shed, muscles quivering, mind ablaze with that feeling you get only when a case is coming together. A warning notice flashed as I approached the next level. I kicked up and over, barely pausing to catch my balance as I landed.

The impis had gotten to him. There was no way around it; the footage was clear. Morgan was in full and witting contact with rogue entities and all that that implied. It was the break we'd been waiting for, the first sign of an active human/impi organization.

I needed immediate backup, every ship within a

month's radius. The hall's higher-level activities would have to be frozen, to make sure it didn't wander off. A lot of people would be coming to look the place over. They'd be studying this hall all the way down to the gluons for years to come. As for Morgan . . . I didn't want to think about that part.

I paused at the door, almost breathless. With quick stabs I punched in the code. I charged inside before it was half open. "Okay, ace—what did she pass to you?"

Morgan barely started. He gave me a mournful look then reached into his jacket pocket. He gazed down at the object in his hand and with a sigh tossed it to me.

It was a piece of scrim. I'd seen that even as he took it out. I hefted it. Some kind of metal, an alloy I couldn't identify. The bust of a woman, head cocked to one side, a smile on her face, hair lifting away as if blown by an invisible breeze.

I raised my eyes to Morgan. "She went . . . You're telling me the impi went after this for you."

"No." Morgan shook his head. "Alerted some others. They picked it up."

I turned the statuette over in my hand. It's hollow, I told myself. Imprinted on the molecular level with some message, some command . . .

I examined the face once again, the laughing eyes, the lips so lifelike they seemed about to speak, to give word to everything Morgan had left behind: light and warmth, air to breathe. He'd put a lot of work into the thing. It occurred to me, somewhat belatedly, that it was a portrait of someone he knew. Had once known. No wonder he wanted it back.

For a second or two my mind struggled against the evidence of simple kindness, desperate for a reason to raise the alarm after all. But it wasn't hollow, and contained nothing, and it wouldn't take me anywhere. I tossed it back

to Morgan. "Nice piece." I got out my handset. "Okay—
does our little pal have a name?"

"Isis," he said softly. I had to ask him to repeat it.

I left the door unlocked. The hall's top level was only a
few yards overhead. I kicked off for it, setting down amidst
a jungle of antennas and cables and junk. That grand glowing tube of dirty-yellow muck towered above me. I eyed it
with the weariness of years, seeing my own youth vanish
over that bright curve, its roaring song fading relentlessly
into gray. Some are meant for the sunlight and some for the
shadowed places. It was pretty clear to me which portion
was mine.

Morgan hadn't told me much; whatever didn't feel like
betrayal. I'd lase it back to Charon, where they'd give it to
some specialist to ponder. Maybe they'd find more in it
than I had. I doubted it.

"Hey, mandy." I turned to see Remi gazing at me
through his helmet visor, ready, I suppose, to go on shift. It
was a moment before I recalled the remote riding on my
ear. I plucked it off and handed it back.

"All straighten out?"

"More or less. He'll be ready to leave tomorrow. He
wants you to run the catapult."

"He ain't stridin' again?"

"Not like he has a lot to worry about."

"Ahh . . . I gotcha."

"Nice to have friends," I said. He shook his head.
"Can't stand him myself. He chatters."

I watched him leave. For a moment he was silhouetted
against the tower, and I saw him as an impi might, a human
figure outlined by light. Then he vanished, the way jacks
do.

It wasn't as dark as it had been. The shadows had lifted
somewhat. I knew the names of one of the spirits, the right

questions to ask, and the fact that the dragons might not be dragons after all. A pretty good day, all considered.

I looked over my shoulder toward home. The stars glared back, but I couldn't, for the life of me, decide which was which. After a moment I gave up and went to tell Witcove how it was going to be.

From the Corner of My Eye

Alexander Glass

Here's a brilliant and evocative look at a future Earth split between the world of humans and the shadowy, elusive world of A.I.s, and of one man caught precariously between both . . .

New writer Alexander Glass has appeared frequently in Interzone, *as well as in* The Third Alternative, Asimov's Science Fiction Magazine, *and elsewhere. He lives in London, England.*

I turned to look, but she was gone.

At once, I rose to my feet, tossed a few corroded Dirham-Pesetas on to the table, and set off in the direction I thought she had gone. My coffee was left behind, untouched—I had been just about to wet my beard—beside my doubled-up copy of the El Puente *Gazette*. Hassan would probably be offended, the more so as I had left him a colossal tip, but I told myself I would explain it to him later. I doubted that he would understand. I was not sure I understood myself.

It was not lust, nothing so innocent. Lust can turn a man's head, but would hardly have sent me running through the crowds as the evening shadows arched their backs lazily across El Puente's central street. It rarely sends me scuttling between cars and camels, tourists and thieves, motorbikes and merchants and mystics, with Spain somewhere behind me and Morocco somewhere ahead. I could not even remember the woman's face. But there had been something about her, something that the rest of the evening crowd on El Puente ignored or simply did not see; and it is my business to see things that other people do not, even if I am not sure myself what those things might be.

I found that my hand had leapt up to my throat, though the cowrie shell I had once worn there was long gone. Kirsten's shell. Perhaps the woman reminded me of her. I can no longer remember. If so, I was not aware of it at the time.

I activated my Ghostbane, though, to be safe.

A battered Volkswagen van crawled past, leaving me dancing from one foot to the other in undignified impatience. I reached out and touched its side with my first two fingers: some of the cars on the road were themselves augmentations, though this one seemed solid enough. When it was finally gone, I saw a figure seated ahead of me, on the edge of a fountain. A stout figure in a suit of tweed, stroking a comically large moustache and smoking an absurdly small cigarillo. It was the Englishman, Harris. The cloth of his suit was certainly a Virtua augmentation, and I suspected the moustache was also, as it had a habit of making little motions and gestures to give emphasis to his words. The cigarillo was real, though: I could smell its reek from five paces. As usual, I could not be sure whether Harris was laughing at me; but I thought he might be of some use. Like me, he often saw things that other people did not.

"Montoya," he called, his voice muffled by moustache and cigarillo. "I'm afraid you're going the wrong way. Spain's behind you. With practice, you know, you can work it out from the position of the sun."

He gestured to his left, to the west: behind the ramshackle buildings of El Puente, the sun was plunging into the sea, wreathed in a halo of pink and orange clouds like a handful of silken scarves. Augmented, of course: the

Spanish and Moroccan governments paid jointly for the
local Virtua sunsets, as a matter of pride.

"I know which way Spain is," I said. "I'm looking for a
woman."

"Really?" he asked, lightly. "I may be able to help you.
Of course, it depends what kind of a woman you're looking for." He looked away, and became suddenly very concerned with a caged bird, colored scarlet and sapphire, in
the doorway of a nearby shop.

I stared at him. "A woman no one else seemed to notice," I said deliberately, "but who caught my eye at once."

"Yes, yes, all right "He seemed irritated, perhaps because he had hoped to hide the fact that he had seen her.
"Medside. Stairwell fifty. But it isn't what you think. Not
a Ghost. Not a job for the blind man."

"I'll see about that."

"Yes, Montoya, I think you will."

Harris tossed the cigarillo deliberately into the fountain,
as if the taste of it had suddenly turned bitter. It rolled into
the basin and lay there, smoldering. Of course, the stone of
the basin was real enough, but the falling water was only
an augmentation. The sound of it came from a trio of
speakers in the fountain's base: old-fashioned, designed
before Virtua went auditory. The water was beautiful, but
could not douse a flame.

Business had been slow, the past few weeks. There was the
usual lull before the next round of fiestas, when the Ghosts
would try to sneak through. They would generate from the
first night onward, among the crowds and costumes, the
noise, the special augmentations laid on by the Alcalde,
who took a particular pride in showing off El Puente's capacity for virtual effects. The increased dataflow meant
that the monitors might not notice the localized surge of a
Ghost emerging.

At the same time, new hunters had arrived, and there was competition to catch what Ghosts there were. I still made enough to get by, enough to be careless of the coins I had flung on to the table at Hassan's café, but not usually enough to feed my one peculiar vice.

Telling myself that this was the reason for my sense of urgency, I ran like a madman to Medside, and along the edge of El Puente to stairwell fifty; and there I saw her. She had kicked open a door marked "No Entry," climbed over the edge and down the stairwell itself, and was sitting on a hexagonal platform some way down, looking out over the waves.

After only a moment's hesitation, I climbed down to join her. She nodded to me, seemingly unsurprised by my presence, but said nothing. She gave no sign that she knew I had been following her.

I found myself tracing her gaze across the water. The sea was flooded with red-gold light from the setting sun, but the structure of El Puente itself stood between us and the sunset. Looking east, we saw the shadow of the bridge, black slabs of darkness from its pillars lying cold upon the water, the webwork of girders like cracks in the dying light. Further away, the brilliant blue of the sea faded into a hazy blackness, matching the darkening curve of the sky. Smiling, I wondered who had thought to program an augmentation from this vantage point. It was unusual for anyone to climb down over the edge of El Puente. Perhaps it had been the Alcalde himself, proud perfectionist that he was, deciding to show off to the ships passing beneath the bridge, between the Atlantic and the Mediterranean. Then I realized it was not an augmentation at all. This was real light on real water, cut by real shadows, under a real sky. I was obscurely disappointed. I had been admiring the skill of some nameless Virtua programmer, but now had nothing to admire except the mindless workings of nature.

There was something wrong, too, about the girl. She

looked out of place. Her outfit was too simple: blue jeans, white shirt, shoes the color of dust, unless they were simply dusty. I could hear her movements, her breathing. I could smell a soft perfume, and a trace of soap and sweat beneath it. The scent was oddly familiar.

She did remind me of Kirsten, but she was not Kirsten. Of course not: how could she have been? Perhaps that was the only reason for my sense of wrongness; but I still felt there was something else.

The girl twisted around to stare up at me, narrowing her eyes. "You're one of them, aren't you? A hunter."

I nodded.

She looked away, then looked back, frowning. "I know your face. You're Montoya. The one they call the blind man."

I nodded again. "I didn't realize I was famous."

"Only to other hunters, and to Ghosts . . ." She did not say which she was, or whether she was either one or the other. Instead she went on: "Fame isn't a good thing, for a hunter."

"That depends. Sometimes a reputation can bring in work."

"Or frighten it away."

"That, too."

"So have you made up your mind about me?"

I shook my head. "You're too good to be a Ghost; and Virtua can't do scent—or break open doors. But I can't get any readings from you. No augmentation: no data flow. Maybe you have a secure loop to generate your augmentations, but I can't see why you'd need it. I can't read a credit line, or a tag number. Not even a name."

"My name is Anila." She smiled, a mocking smile. "Do I look too ordinary? Not enough decoration? Maybe my secure loop is to generate a face, instead of clothes and ornaments. To cover up a scar, a botched job of rhinoplasty. Who knows?"

"No, I don't believe it. It's my business to know an augmentation when I see one, and I don't see one."

"That's right. You don't." She hesitated, not knowing how to ask the question she wanted to ask. I waited. I already knew what it would be. At last she said: "Were you really blind?"

I sat down beside her, cross-legged, took a breath, let it out. The taste of salt was on my lips. The sound of the sea filled the time it took me to find an answer. "Yes, for a time. There was an . . . accident. They had to repair my optic nerve. I had to have new bio-implants grown. Then they had to make sure that was working before they could reconnect my visual cortex to Virtua. They cut the auditory connection, too, until I was fixed. There was no alternative but to live with it."

"So you sharpened your other senses. Gustatory, olfactory, tactile. And now you can catch a Ghost, because they don't sound right, and they have no smell."

"Some of them don't even look right. And anyone can tell a Ghost by grabbing hold of their arm: if there's nothing there, you've caught your Ghost. You don't need a blind man for that." I shrugged.

"But it isn't just sharpening your senses. Your perception changes. You learn to create a new model of the world, minus its visual element. A mental map, but more than that, a . . . a *virtual* copy of what is out there, beyond your body. Everything your senses tell you, everything you touch or taste, every echo in the air, adds something to the map. I still have that map in my head. And when the map doesn't fit what I see, then I've usually seen a Ghost."

"Not this time."

"No, not this time. You're almost the opposite of a Ghost, aren't you? They're only virtual; you're only real."

She laughed. Then she got to her feet, and touched my arm. Proving she was real, solid; perhaps telling me that this was enough. Her point made, she moved toward the stairwell. She had one parting shot to make, though.

"Tell me, Señor Montoya: you're the blind man. Have you ever seen the Invisibles?"

Then she was climbing, her laughter falling like the droplets in the fountain, and had vanished before I could ask her what she meant.

After she had gone, I sat alone awhile, as the shadow of El Puente lengthened over the Mediterranean, and the gold of the sunset turned to blood, and then to blackness. From below, I fancied I could hear the slow hum of the Ghost-makers, the Virtua generators, at the bottom of the sea. I waited until the last drop of real, unaugmented light had drained away. Then I climbed back up to the bridge to explain things to Hassan.

H*e had left* his son in charge of the café, and hidden himself away in the back. I elbowed my way unceremoniously to the bar, and the boy nodded me through, raising a coffee cup to me ironically as I ducked beneath the little whitewashed arch that led to Hassan's private rooms.

I expected to find him with Leila, of course; but I was surprised to find him asleep, snoring gently and almost melodiously upon a heap of cushions, his hands clasped over his stomach. For some reason, Leila was still there, still manifest, sitting cross-legged on the rug, her small honey-brown hands open in front of her. Glancing up at me as I entered, she raised a finger to her lips, and, for an instant, I saw the outline of her mouth beneath her flimsy green half-veil.

Whoever had programmed her had done a remarkable job.

"He is sleeping," she said, unnecessarily, and then, a little defensively: "I like to be there when he wakes. What would he think of me otherwise? What kind of wife would I be?"

There was nothing I could say. Embarrassed, I rubbed at the back of my head, feeling the tiny irregularity in the skull where the Virtua bio-implants had gone in.

Leila said: "You do not like this. You think it is wrong."

I raised my palms to her. "It's no business of mine."

"No. But still you think it is wrong. You think he should let me go—switch me off."

"Really, I don't have an opinion." I met her eyes. "If I were Hassan, and I lost someone like you, maybe I'd do the same. But I am only myself, and my loss was of a different kind. So I'll reserve my judgment."

"What have you lost, Señor Montoya? You used to wear a shell at your throat," she observed. "Is it that you have lost?"

"Go to Hell."

"I have. Yet I am here. In this way," she murmured, "he has not really lost me."

I shook my head. "Somewhere deep down, he knows he has. You're his dream. He might dream about you until he dies. Or he might wake up.

"I remember Leila," I went on. "You look like her. You sound like her. You have the accent, and the mannerisms, and the memories. You'd probably pass a Turing test more easily than I could. But you're not Leila, not really."

She turned away, so that I would not see an augmented tear. "I am myself. Like you, Montoya, I am only myself. I do not hide what I am."

"A simulacrum. A shared hallucination. A Virtua woman. A Ghost."

"Yes, a Ghost. And you are a Ghost hunter, a Ghost killer. You frighten me."

"I'm sorry. But I wouldn't hunt you. You're legal. Hassan's license is in order. Besides, as you said, you don't hide what you are."

She looked back at me then, defiant. "If I could, I would. If I could pass for real. If you could smell me, touch me, if I had weight, substance. Would I be real then, Señor Montoya?"

We sat in silence a moment, the Ghost, the blind man, and the sleeper. I had no answer to her question—and if I did, I might not have the heart to tell her. Luckily, the sleeper stirred and woke, and Leila and I both pretended the conversation had not happened.

"Montoya," Hassan mumbled. Then a frown divided his brow, and he said: "You dare to come back here, after spurning my best coffee?"

"I need help. I want you to run a scan."

"Another insult: your bio-implant was the best your filthy money could buy. There can be nothing wrong with it."

"Hassan, I misread someone today. I went hunting a Ghost, and she turned out to be human. Not only human, but without any augmentation at all. My senses failed me, my instincts failed me—and my diagnostics failed me."

The corners of his mouth turned down. "Everyone makes mistakes, Montoya."

"That's what I thought, at first. But the more I think about it, the less I like it. My diagnostics found nothing, nothing at all. No one walks around with no augmentation at all, not even an identification, a tag."

"Unusual, but not impossible."

"Unusual? When was the last time you saw anyone without augmentation? Here on El Puente? If you go down south, past Ojo Cerrado, you'll meet a few. If you go as far as Saqt al-Zand, you'll find nothing else. But on El Puente? I don't believe it. But all right, my friend, let's say it's just unusual. There were a couple of other things, too: things I only realized after I left. First, Harris wanted me to see her. In that sneaky way of his, he sent me to her, making it seem as if he was reluctant to do it. In fact, that must have been the only reason he was there."

"And second?"

"When I say my diagnostics found *nothing,* I mean they found nothing. I didn't even realize it, but it's been nagging at me all the way back from the edge: I couldn't sense *her* diagnostics, either. Now, maybe I can accept that someone might choose to have no augmentation at all. There's no law against wearing your own face. But no diagnostics? How does she know who she's talking to? How does she know where she's going? How does she know the prices of things? How does she keep in contact with her family, her friends, her work or school? She must have a pathfinder and a messenger, at the very least. And as far as I could see, she didn't have them. Which means—"

Hassan sat up on his elbow, frowning. He knew well enough what it meant. "Did she say what her name was?"

"Yes . . ." I pulled it out of an auditory buffer. "Anila. She told me it was Anila."

Hassan and Leila exchanged a glance. Then Hassan hauled himself to his feet.

"Very well. We will scan you." He bared his teeth. "And then you will drink that cup of coffee. I've saved it for you."

In the middle of wiring me in, Hassan paused, and that frown divided his brow again. This was slightly illegal, of course, though I doubted that would make him hesitate. No: he had realized that he was feeding my peculiar vice, and that he was doing it gratis. I normally had to pay Harris for the privilege, when I could afford it. He was very expensive, and very rude, in that particular way the English have; but better Harris than some fumbling amateur. You never know when someone's hand might slip, or what might happen if it does.

"You've done this before, Montoya. You must be used to it."

"Not really. But go ahead."

I did not see him touch the switch. For a moment, I was not aware that anything had changed at all. Then I moved my head—and the room seemed to move with me, everything frozen in time, until, a few seconds later, the image began to fade. The still picture of the room grew dim, the bright cloth hangings fading as if, before my eyes, they were aging, turning to dust. Then they were gone altogether. The optic interface was disconnected. All I could see was the world fed through my bio-implant: the augmented world.

When I walked in Virtua, I liked best to wander the streets of El Puente: the random augmentations carried toward me, and past me, and away; the radiance of the sea and sky, without the sea and sky behind them, but only endless darkness; the gaudy shop-fronts, the tracery of the stones in the main street, the landmarks, the shimmering statues, the floating lights. I had spent hours sitting before the fountain, watching the water rise and fall, unable to see the stone of the basin itself, only an augmented marker, a circle on the ground, probably an aid to perspective left there by the programmer. I remembered the droplets, appearing in empty space, leaping, tumbling, glittering coldly in the Virtua light.

Beyond it, I remembered the entrance to the old electronics market, its canvas walls invisible now, the lights within moving like fireflies. Above the entrance, a sign, hung in the air, glowing in Virtua neon. No one used real neon signs anymore.

I remembered a woman emerging from the market, her hands marked with red-gold Virtua henna, her face hidden by a Virtua bird mask, an augmented cloak trailing from her shoulders. Tiny blue sparks seemed to jump and vanish in the cloth.

Hassan's room was interesting, too, in its way. There were fewer augmentations than I had thought: a few ornaments, a Jack Vettriano painting, some lighting effects: Virtua candles casting Virtua shadows. There was no tracery around the edges of the room, and so the candles were the only way I had of knowing the size of the room, its dimensions. Hassan himself wore augmentations on his clothes, and augmented rings on his fingers, but his face was entirely natural: so in Virtua he seemed like a headless man, hollow, his shape defined by lines of red and gold.

Leila, of course, looked just as she had before; the Ghost appeared more real than the living man.

I could not see myself. In Virtua, I was invisible. Perhaps that was what I liked about walking in Virtua.

"Don't move," Hassan was saying. "You're still wired up. It won't take that long to check your diagnostics."

"You will find nothing," Leila said, softly, almost sadly. I wondered how she could be so sure.

I thought of the girl, Anila—how this would appear to her. If she had no diagnostics, no connection to Virtua at all, then she would see none of it. The fountain would be an empty stone bowl. The market would be a long, featureless tent of drab, unornamented cloth. The woman in the bird mask would be no different than any other woman. And this other world, this Virtua, would be nothing but blackness to her.

Except, of course, that the girl must have had diagnostics. She might have had no augmentations, or chosen not to wear the ones she had, but diagnostics were essential on El Puente. Without them, the place was just a causeway across the Mediterranean: three parallel streets of shops and houses, a place to live or to visit or just to pass through. A place like any other. And in any event, life without diagnostics was hideously impractical. Hassan had reached the same conclusion I had: either my diagnostics were faulty, or the girl had a secure loop with enough protection to fool me. And if she had a loop that secure, then we wanted to know about it.

"Nothing," Hassan said at last. "As I said: your connection, and your diagnostics, are the best money can buy."

"Which means," I said, "that the girl must have data-protection money *can't* buy."

"A.I.-generated?"

"Without a doubt. And if it's A.I.-generated, then the Ghosts could be planning to use it. Something to keep the hunters away, the next time they come through."

Hassan's invisible hand rose up to stroke his invisible beard. "Maybe."

"You don't seem convinced, my friend."

Hassan said nothing. He turned away, and I saw Leila reach out to him, a reassuring touch—a touch he could not feel.

At last, he said: "Maybe it doesn't matter, Montoya. So what if they come?"

I said nothing. Leila looked at me, gauging my reaction. Then she left, without a word, without a sound. Outside the room—visible to me, but not to Hassan—she vanished altogether, her body dissolving like smoke.

Seeing Leila disappear, I thought of another reason I wanted to find the girl. She had mentioned the Invisibles. I had thought she was just taunting me, but now I was not sure. Perhaps she knew something. Perhaps she had seen them, whatever they were. Higher-level A.I.s? Virtua gods? Alien Ghosts in the network? If the girl knew anything at all, it would be something worth knowing.

With a sigh, Hassan touched a switch, and the real world began to take shape again. I was not glad to see it back.

That night, I went looking for Harris along the central street. The sidestreets were sleeping, more or less, but the central street stayed alive. At night, people's augmentations became wilder, almost as if they themselves were taking advantage of the dark, and the freedom that came with it. I saw a woman with scales and a prehensile tail snaking from beneath her heavy black skirt; and it struck me that if a real lizard woman ever did walk the central street, no one would ever notice. One man had a subroutine that scanned his head and projected it beneath his arm; an Elizabethan costume completed the picture. The scan was not perfect, though. I could see a very slight shimmer in the empty space above his shoulders. There were even some Virtua creatures—owls were popular this year—and, out of habit, I ran diagnostic checks on them all, to make sure they were properly licensed, and properly chained to their owners.

I did not know whether finding Harris would do me any good, but I knew that he knew something. He had not even tried to hide it; when I had asked about the girl, he had all but stuck his arm out to show me which way she had gone. So he knew, and he wanted me to know that he knew. He let me share a little of his knowledge only because it suited his plans, whatever they were.

I knew where the Englishman would be. I took an autorickshaw along the central street toward the north end of the bridge, and had the driver set me down on the corner. For some reason I did not want anyone to know where I was going.

Leaving the central street behind, I crossed over to a small building whose face looked out over the Atlantic. A building with no augmentations at all, no decorations, no name above the door, not even a listing in the Virtua map. If you had one of their calling cards, it would lead you to the door, but the cards were few and far between. Even so, the place had no shortage of clients.

As I entered, a man was just leaving: a man in a top hat

and a shadowy greatcoat, the cane in his hand topped with augmented gold.

I looked around for Harris. He was over in a corner, still in his tweeds, with a woman on each arm. One was naked, or seemed so, but for veils of Virtua color playing over her skin. She might be clothed, with an augmented illusion of bare skin; there was no way to tell without touching her. Perhaps that was the idea. The other woman was clothed, but that, too, might well have been an augmentation. In here, it was not easy to tell. Many of the women were augmented only to take away a few years, or to soften their eyes, to help mask their contempt for their clients; some wore sophisticated fantasies, like the one on Harris's left, with scraps of red and green and silver sliding over her shoulders and back, around her sides, along her arms, between her fingers, as if caressing her.

Incongruously, Harris was sipping a cup of tea. He raised the cup to me, the saucer in his other hand, and the tips of his moustache gave me a little twirl.

I nodded in reply, but even as I did so, something caught at the corner of my eye. A movement, a shape, a distortion in the air—something that should not have been there. I turned to look, but it was gone. Turning on my heel, avoiding the attentions of a woman augmented with mirrored skin, I ran back the way I had come.

In the doorway, I hesitated a moment, looking this way and that along the street. The ocean sighed, rubbing its back against the columns of the bridge; above, Virtua stars shone gently in the dark, making new constellations from old. Some way along the street, the man in the shadowy greatcoat was striding south, in the general direction of Morocco.

There it was again: a movement, a shimmer in the air. And, just as quickly, it was gone. I followed it, over the empty street, to the sea-rail, until I reached the place where it had been. There was nothing there, at least nothing I could see or feel. Then I saw it again, but in a place I could not follow: out above the ocean, suspended in the cold salt air. A moment later, it had vanished once more.

From behind me, a familiar voice said: "Come on, Montoya. It isn't that bad, surely?"

"Harris?"

"Who else? I saw you running away. I couldn't help but be curious. Did something scare you in the house of fun? Not Dar, I hope? The silver skin takes some getting used to, but it really is worth the effort. Imagine making love to your reflection from a hall of mirrors."

I sighed, looking down at my hands upon the sea-rail. I realized I was trembling.

"I saw something."

Harris said nothing, waiting for me to continue.

"Something in the air. Something . . . wrong. I can't describe it. I think it was one of the Invisibles."

"Pshaw," he said, or something like it; but it did not sound convincing. Then he asked, in a voice that left me in no doubt that he knew exactly what I had seen: "Where was it?"

"Inside. I followed it out here, across the street. Then I saw it over the sea, just floating in the air."

"And then it was gone?"

I nodded.

I thought I knew what it was. The girl, Anila, had asked me mockingly whether I had ever seen one of the Invisibles. Now I could tell her I had. I only wished I knew what it was, what it meant.

Harris's face was empty of all expression, as if the emotion had been poured out of him. He was searching the horizon, slowly, with eyes like stones. He seemed to have forgotten that I was there at all. A moment later, he saw it, that brief shimmer in the air, and the sight of it froze him.

"Harris?"

But Harris was running, now, away from me, along the

waterfront, his footsteps rapping on the stone; and, as I watched, the shimmer in the air came to life, swooping after him, a writhing nothingness, soundless and strange. It sped past me, very close, and I did not even feel its passing.

Then Harris fell. I saw him trip, and stumble to the ground. I could still hear his footsteps, though; and then I realized he was still running, faster than before. Yet I had seen him fall. I could still see him, stretched out unmoving on the ground. The shimmer flew over him, chasing the other Harris, the one who was still running.

The other Harris glanced over his shoulder. He turned, facing the thing that hunted him, leaning on the sea-rail as if exhausted.

Then, with a grin, he vaulted over the side.

I staggered forward with a wordless cry, leaning over the rail to see him plunging down toward the sea. He was still running as he fell, his legs pumping the air; and I could have sworn that it was working, that he was actually moving further away from the bridge. The shimmer in the air was closing on him now. I stood and watched, helpless, as they were lost from sight: Harris plunging into the ocean, the shimmer vanishing into the waves along with him. I was not sure whether it had reached him before the water claimed them both.

Suddenly weak, I knelt down on the stone, one hand still clasping the sea-rail.

Up ahead of me, Harris's body still lay, unmoving, on the ground.

He was very different without his augmentations, more so than I would have thought. He was much thinner, for one thing. Very few people used their augmentations to make them look fatter. He was clean-shaven. His clothes were not tweed at all, of course—he was dressed in blue jeans and a simple white shirt, reminding me at once of

Anila. It might have been coincidence; but it seemed almost to be a uniform.

He was alive, and not obviously injured, but his breathing was ragged and his skin was very pale. Then again, I had no idea how pale his skin was supposed to be. The skin I remembered had always been an augmentation.

Reluctant to carry him back into the brothel, I called Hassan to come and pick us up. Then I summoned a Virtua medic, who told me there was no lasting damage, and could not even understand why Harris was unconscious. It was certainly not a blow to the head: the medic's diagnostics believed he was sleeping. I sent it away, wondering whether I should call for a human doctor; but the medic seemed to have been right. By the time Hassan arrived, the Englishman was already starting to come round.

Back at the café, the first sip of one of Hassan's coffees seemed to revive Harris completely—he even asked if he could have tea instead, then quickly dropped the request when he saw the affronted look on Hassan's face. He smiled at me and sipped away, having obviously decided to take his time before giving us an explanation. He even produced a small pack of cigarillos, and toyed with one, though he did not light it.

The night had finally quenched the last lingering warmth of the sun, and, outside, a chill sea wind had picked up. Harris tipped back his head to listen to the low, breathy keening that was the wind's lament. Then, ignoring us completely, he sipped at his coffee again.

By the third sip, my patience had expired.

"What the hell happened back there?"

Harris gave me a pained look. "What did you see?"

"I think I saw one of the Invisibles. And now that I've seen one, I still have no idea what they are. I saw it come after you, and I saw you run. I saw you fall. And I saw your augmentation—no, I saw the full set of your augmentations, auditory as well as visual—go running on without you."

He nodded, unsurprised. "Did it get away?"

I shrugged. "It went over the side, down into the sea. The Invisible followed it down. I couldn't see what happened after that."

He nodded again, slowly and infuriatingly. Then: "I suppose an explanation is in order."

Behind me, Hassan snorted; on the other side of the room, I saw that Leila was smiling. I couldn't help but smile myself, at the enormity of the understatement.

"Yes, Harris, an explanation is in order."

"I've a feeling I don't know the half of it myself. But I'll tell you what I know."

"Fine. You can start with the augmentation."

He nodded, sadly. "The arrangement was a little unorthodox. My set of augmentations was more than just a suit of clothes."

I stared at him. "A Ghost."

He gave a half-shrug, then frowned. "If you want to call it that. A Virtua intelligence that wanted to experience our world—directly, at first hand—and to interact with it. And it wanted all of that, without the chains, the restrictions that would be placed on it if it applied for any of the existing manifestation rights."

I glanced at Leila, who was pretending to study the abstract pattern of one of Hassan's Virtua murals, but listening intently. "So, a Ghost," I repeated.

"As I said: if you want to call it that. It was at least second or third generation, highly intelligent, heuristically intelligent. It knew perfectly well that if it manifested without authorization, it would be hunted down. The Ghost hunters would track it, cage it, and hand it over to the authorities. It would be data-stripped—in human terms, tortured and mutilated—and it might even be erased."

Hassan was nodding, grinning, impressed. "So it found the perfect camouflage."

"Yes. If it manifested itself alone, it would easily be found. But if it wrapped itself around a human, if it arranged the necessary licenses that way, it would never be noticed. It would be taken for a particularly high-level augmentation."

I nodded. "And that's exactly what happened. For years. If I was fooled, then the disguise must have been well-nigh perfect. But having to rely on a human, to stay with that human all the time—that's more or less equivalent to the restrictions it would have had to have had anyway."

"Not really. It was no one's servant. If anything, it was the other way round. I chose the augmentation, but all my actions, everything I did, was on behalf of the A.I. I was its agent, its factor, and its bearer. When it wanted to go to the house of fun, I was more than that. . . . It was all for the money, of course. The A.I. couldn't pay me in Dirham-Pesetas, but Virtua Dollars are good in most places these days."

He fell silent, and we sat listening to the wind, and to the faraway sound of the sea, a soft, low hiss, like static. I had to remind myself that this was the man whose preferred augmentation was a caricature of a middle-aged English gent. Beneath it, he was young, his eyes tired but bright, his movements quick and nervous. Even his voice had changed—of course, whenever I had spoken to him, it had always been the A.I. speaking back, through the Virtua audio net. Anyone not wired in would have heard only silence.

I wondered how much of Harris's character was his, and how much was shaped by the A.I. Now that it was gone, he seemed unfinished somehow, as if far more than his clothes had been taken from him.

Now I understood his fall, out on the road, and why he

had been unharmed by it. He had not tripped. The A.I. had
abandoned him, and he had lost consciousness from the
shock of being jacked out so suddenly. Nothing more than
that.

"All right," I said after a while. "What about the girl?
Why did it want me to find her? Is she a . . . a Ghost-
bearer, like you, or is she something else?"

"I don't know."

"And the Invisible? Why was it chasing you? And more
to the point, what the hell was it?"

"I don't know. I tell you, I don't know!"

After a time, I believed him. The A.I. had told him what
it needed him to know, no more and no less. He knew nothing about the girl. He knew nothing about the Invisible, if
that was what it was. He knew very little about the A.I.'s
dealings in general.

What was most immediately worrying was that he did
not know why the A.I. should have wanted to help me with
my little vice. True, it had demanded payment to temporarily interfere with my visual cortex, to allow me to
walk in Virtua without the distractions of the real world.
But from what Harris said, it seemed the thing had no need
of funds. It must have had some ulterior motive in restrict-
ing my visual input to Virtua, for a few hours, every few
days. Maybe there was something in Virtua it wanted me
to see. I could not imagine what that might be, though, and
Harris had no idea.

I struggled with that for a while, but could get no hold
on it, and so I turned my attention to an easier problem: the
brothel. I did not believe the A.I. wanted to go there solely
for the pleasures of the flesh. It couldn't really experience
them, in any case, having no tactile existence; and purely
intellectual curiosity only went so far, even for an A.I.

It followed, then, that it went there for some *other* reason, probably to meet someone, maybe more than one person, maybe many. At first, I thought that these people must be humans: if they were other A.I.'s, it could easily communicate with them in Virtua over any distance it liked. On the other hand, if it wanted a really secure exchange of information, the safest way to do that was by actually meeting. Harris swore that he had never overheard anything unexpected at the brothel. But there was no reason he should. After all, I had never overheard my bio-implant talking to El Puente's Ghostmakers.

The only way to know was to go there.

When I arrived at what Harris referred to as the "house of fun," the sun was rising, a smudge of light in the east. On the other side of the bridge, the night still clung to the ocean.

I reflected, again, how ordinary the building was, plain and unadorned; but now I realized that its very lack of augmentation made it stand out. It was possibly the only building on the whole of El Puente without any elements imported from Virtua. A deliberate irony, perhaps, on the part of the A.I.s who were using it as a clandestine meeting-place.

A figure was sitting on the steps, a figure in a white shirt and blue jeans, watching me, waiting for me. A figure with no augmentations that I could see or sense. Her mouth formed a crooked half-smile as I drew closer, and she said again the last words she had spoken to me.

"Tell me, Señor Montoya: you're the blind man. Have you ever seen the Invisibles?"

I shrugged in reply, and she nodded, as if she had been expecting the gesture.

"There are things I need to know," I told her. "It seems you already know the questions I want to ask. Can you give me any answers?"

Anila shook her head, slowly. The half-smile was gone now, replaced by a look I knew. The look of one for whom fear has become a friend. The look of the hunted; and the look of the haunted.

"Then can you tell me where to ask?"

"Dar," she said, quietly. "You need to speak to Dar."

"The lady with the mirrored skin. Where is she? Inside?"

The smile returned. "In a way. Wait. I'll bring her to you."

But she made no move to go and fetch Dar. Instead, she hung her head, as if suddenly ashamed. When she raised it again, it was to whisper to me, once again, something she had said to me before. "Do I look too ordinary? Not enough decoration?"

Then she began to change.

The process must have been almost instantaneous, as soon as she was wired in. The change took place relatively slowly, though, over eons of Virtua time. The girl's body began to shimmer, then seemed to swell, her skinny figure filling out inside her clothes, her hair lengthening and gaining volume. Her face altered, gaining a few years as it changed. And her skin was turning silver, reflecting the electric blue of the chill dawn sky.

I had not realized before that Dar's eyes were also mirrored. When she blinked, it was like a ripple moving across a still pool of mercury. With those eyes, she stared at me, challenging, warning, waiting. Trying to meet that stare, I found myself staring at my own distorted features.

"I'm impressed," I said.

She opened a palm, and it seemed filled with a handful of sky.

"It's simple enough. No harder than being invisible, for example. It requires fast processing, of course; large amounts of visual data have to be updated a number of times a second, but it's nothing beyond the reach of any good system."

"You're an A.I. Like the A.I. that Harris was bearing."

She said nothing, waiting for me to continue.

"You're something new. A Ghost with an alibi."

She smiled at that, silver lips pulling back to reveal silver teeth. "Montoya, it doesn't matter how much you've found out, or deduced, or guessed. You brought the Invisibles to us. It doesn't even matter whether or not you were aware of it. We can't allow them to interfere with our plans now."

"And what are your plans?"

She laughed now, shaking her head. Instead of answering my question, she said. "It's funny that you should have noticed Anila. You thought it unusual that she should have no augmentations. You wondered why that could be. But what about *you*, Montoya? You have your diagnostics, your messenger, your pathfinder, all useful toys. But no augmentations on display—very unusual, on El Puente. In a way, you're an Invisible yourself. I wonder what the reason might be."

I sensed a presence behind me, and turned to find a group of Ghosts at my back. The A.I. who had been borne by Harris was one. To my surprise, Leila was another.

I moved to activate my Ghostbane, and to call for help, but before I could do either of those things, Leila stepped forward, calmly, and took my arm. Her grip was ferociously strong, her touch cold as the deep sea. She smiled at me.

Then everything dissolved, and for a time I was gone.

Maybe Kirsten had tried to explain it to me, but I had never understood. I had never wanted to understand. When she finally left, we had said our good-byes coldly and quickly, an unpleasant duty done with bad grace. Without my knowing, she slipped a parting gift into my pocket: a cowrie shell, smooth and black as jet. I wore it on a chain, its cold teeth blunt against my skin.

Her body was put on ice, a legal requirement, though she swore she would never return to it.

Months passed before I realized that I wanted to find her, and months more before I found the courage to go searching. I guessed and hoped that she might be found on El Puente, where the wall dividing the real world from Virtua seemed to be cracking, crumbling.

I went to a series of back-street operators who could let me walk in Virtua. It was a dangerous game. You never know when someone's hand might slip, or what might happen if it does; and so I lost my sight, for a time. I was lost in darkness; then I was trapped in Virtua, because my new bio-implant had grown faster than my optic nerve had healed.

Afterward, I took the cowrie shell to Medside and hurled it into the sea.

I became a Ghost hunter, and told myself that I had given up searching for Kirsten. I almost believed it.

A *touch upon* my arm woke me. opened my eyes and looked up into an empty blue sky.

Leila was kneeling over me. It was her hand I could feel on my arm. The weight of it. The heat of it, no longer cold but blood-warm. With a gasp, I put my own hand on top of hers. It seemed real. It was real. She smiled, then pulled away.

"I am sorry," she told me, softly.

I dragged myself upright, but was not yet ready to stand up. Instead I sat with my back to the sea-rail, and looked from one Ghost to the next.

"It had to be done, Montoya," said the one I still thought of as Harris.

I shook my head, not understanding. "What? What had to be done?"

Another Ghost spoke, a man in a top hat and a greatcoat, a gold-headed cane in his hand. "We had to find a way to evade the hunters. This was the logical way. You said it yourself. Anyone can tell a Ghost by grabbing hold of their arm: if there's nothing there, you've caught your Ghost "

"But I shouldn't be able to touch you. You aren't real. You're just projections, patterns in the Virtua matrix."

Leila said: "You shouldn't be able to see us, either, or hear us. You can only do so through your bio-implant."

I closed my eyes, understanding, and heard Harris's voice again. "Each time you came to me, each time I let you walk in Virtua, I had a chance to alter your bio-implant. You were already wired up for the illusion of sight, and the illusion of sound. Why not touch, and taste, and smell? Why not adjust your muscular controls to respond to us as if we were solid? Your altered implant was almost ready at our last meeting. Now it's done."

I felt as if I were falling. I felt a hand on my shoulder, steadying me, reassuring me. The hand of a Ghost.

I sensed the Ghosts moving away, all but one, even though I knew that sense was an illusion. The hand remained on my shoulder. I could hear the Ghost's movements, its breathing. I could smell a soft perfume, and a trace of soap and sweat beneath it. The scent was oddly familiar. The Ghost put its arms around me, and whispered to me, telling me not to be afraid.

I knew the scent. I knew the touch. I knew the voice. It was the voice of the girl, Anila. It was the voice of Dar, the silver-skinned woman. And it was the voice of a woman I had given up searching for.

"Kirsten?"

"Yes."

Irrationally, I was afraid to open my eyes. In case she vanished. Even though I knew she was not there at all.

"Look at me," she said. "You can't hide by closing your eyes. You can't see me now because your bio-implant agrees that you shouldn't. But I could make you see me, if I wanted."

I opened my eyes. Kirsten pulled away from me, to sit beside me against the sea-rail. She looked just as I remembered her. She took my hand—I felt her fingers close around mine, my muscles moving as she brought my hand to rest between both of hers. A breeze rose from the sea below, and a strand of hair blew across her face.

Then she looked at me again, and her smile faded. She reached for a stone on the ground, and tried to pick it up. Her fingers passed through it.

"I'm not real," she said. "Only as real as I *can* be. I can make myself real, to you, and to anyone else with an altered implant. But I'll never be able to lift that stone."

I said nothing, but picked up the stone myself—perhaps to reassure myself that I was still real—and threw it down again.

Kirsten cupped her hands, and a stone appeared there, an exact copy of the stone she had been unable to grasp. She tossed it to me, and I caught it. It was hard, and rough, and cold; I felt the weight of it in my hand; when I tossed it and caught it, I heard it slap against my skin. Then Kirsten touched it with the tip of her finger, and it vanished.

"Real enough," she whispered.

I took her hand again, and nodded; but even as I did so I sensed something behind us, something hovering above the ocean. I turned, and something caught at the corner of my eye: a shimmer, a distortion in the air. I pulled Kirsten to her feet, and ran.

There was no one on the street. We fled along the empty road, light of dawn still scraping the world's edge, the laughter of the sea rising about us. The Invisible at our back followed, in silence; sometimes, when I risked a glance over my shoulder, I saw it there; sometimes I saw nothing, but I had no doubt it was still pursuing us.

We came to the entrance to one of the stairwells, and here Kirsten stopped, pushing me back against the stone.

"It doesn't want you," she hissed.

I tried to speak, but no words could find a way between my gasping breaths.

"I'll find you," she said. Then she kissed me, and was gone, sprinting along by the sea-rail. I leaned back, still breathing hard, my hands trembling on the cold stone, and watched her go. Moments later, I saw something shimmer and vanish in the air before me. The Invisible. As Kirsten had said, the thing, whatever it was, had no interest in me.

I followed, desperate to see Kirsten escape to safety. But as I watched, the Invisible closed in on her. As soon as it touched her, she changed, the shape of Kirsten melting before my eyes. The glimmering veil of the Invisible surrounded her, and now I saw her as Anila, as Dar, as Kirsten again, as combinations of all three.

Then she was gone.

I ran to the spot where she had been, and fell to my knees, searching for some trace of her. There was nothing, not even her scent. I covered my head with my hands, and remained like that for a long time.

I *did not* return to the café until evening. The central street was crowded, as usual, with cars and camels, tourists and thieves, motorbikes and merchants and mystics. One man had augmented his skin with tattoos, which became animated at a touch, and fought each other for position on his body. Two days before, I would have been quietly impressed. Now I no longer cared.

I smelled Hassan's coffee even before I saw the café. I could not hear his voice, though. He had left his son in charge again. I waved to the boy as I ducked beneath the whitewashed arch that led to Hassan's private rooms. He gave me a look in reply that I could not read.

I understood the look only when I saw Hassan. He was sitting on a cushion, his eyes wet with tears; and beneath his hand, lying back as if in sleep, was Leila. Her eyes were closed, but she was breathing, and now and then she shifted and murmured in her sleep. Hassan was stroking her hair, entwining it between his fingers. So his implant, too, had been altered.

"Montoya," he whispered, and then shook his head, unable to find words.

Patting him on the shoulder, I took a small mirror from a nearby table and held it to Leila's lips. I felt the warmth of her breath on my hand, but no mist appeared in the glass. I do not think that Hassan even noticed what I had done.

I left him, then; left the café, and the central street, and crossed to the sea-rail. The sun was melting into the water, the colors of the sunset augmented as usual. I almost wished I could shut it out, be rid of my implant and see the world without its Virtua augmentations; but I knew I would not dare. It would only be another kind of blindness.

From my pocket I took a small, black, shiny object. A cowrie shell.

It had not been there before. It had not been there when Kirsten found me; it had not been there when the Invisible had caught her. It had appeared later.

That morning, as I sat curled up around my misery on the seafront, I had realized that the Invisible was still there. It hung in the air beyond the sea-rail, just out of reach, waiting. I raised my head and cursed it, weeping. It did not respond, only waited until I fell silent once more.

Then it moved toward me, until it seemed near enough to touch. I stared at it, blinking, new thoughts taking shape in my mind. I did not know whether the thoughts were my own, or if the Invisible was feeding them to me somehow, subliminally, through my bio-implant. At the time, it hardly mattered.

There was no reason to believe that Kirsten was gone forever. I had seen the Invisible pursuing the Harris A.I., and it must have caught him; yet the next day I had seen him again. It only destroyed their manifestations when it caught them. Their essential data remained unchanged. The same would be true of Kirsten.

So she could return again. "I'll find you," she had said. But I did not know, would never know, whether it was truly her. The Kirsten that had found me was so exactly the Kirsten of my memory—too exactly. I did not know how, and did not like to think of it. While the Ghosts were altering my bio-implant, they could have ransacked my mind for memories of Kirsten. They could take whatever form they wished; and, like Hassan, I had been only too willing to believe. I would have helped them cross over from Virtua, happily, if I could have Kirsten again. And, like the Englishman, I would have become something like a Ghost-bearer.

The Invisible moved closer still, until it enveloped me, holding me completely. I began to understand something of what it was. A Virtua being, like the Ghosts, but of a higher order. One that had no such childish longing for corporeality. It had left that behind long ago. Yet it bore no animosity toward the Ghosts, either. It had little interest in them at all.

Why, then, had it interfered, tearing apart the representations of Harris, and of Kirsten?

My unspoken question was met only with silence. Then the Invisible moved away, over the sea, and was gone.

After a while, I realized there was something in my hand. Puzzled, I looked at it, and realized that this was the Invisible's answer.

Now, as the evening drew in, I held the cowrie shell in my hand again, watching the play of light on its smooth, hard surface. I held it tight, trying to crush it, but it would not break. The heat of my skin lingered on its surface for a while; then it cooled again. Like a real shell.

Yet, when I blew upon it, a flame sprang up, a blue flame with a greenish halo, a Virtua flame, a flame that did not burn. I blew on it again, and the flame was gone.

The Invisible had vanished before I worked out what it was—what Kirsten had become. I do not know what I would have done if I had understood in time. Perhaps I would have agreed to join her, and leave my body behind. Perhaps she no longer wanted me to, and had only helped me because of a distant memory.

Standing at the sea-rail, somewhere between Spain and Morocco, I blew on the shell once more, bringing the flame to life. A tear grew from the corner of my eye, and splashed into my hand, over the shell. The teardrop was beautiful, and real, but could not douse the flame.

Halfjack

Roger Zelazny

Here's a vivid and lyrical look at the surprising relationship of an A.I. and a posthuman man, accomplishing in a few short pages what many other writers would have taken a 500-page novel to spell out . . .

   Like a number of other writers, the late Roger Zelazny began publishing in 1962 in the pages of Cele Goldsmith's Amazing. *This was the so-called "Class of '62," whose membership also included Thomas M. Disch, Keith Laumer, and Ursula K. Le Guin. Everyone in that "class" would eventually achieve prominence, but some of them would achieve it faster than others, and Zelazny's subsequent career would be one of the most meteoric in the history of SF. The first Zelazny story to attract wide notice was "A Rose for Ecclesiastics," published in 1963 (it was later selected by vote of the SFWA membership to have been one of the best SF stories of all time). By the end of that decade, he had won two Nebula Awards, two Hugo Awards (for* This Immortal *and for his best-known novel,* Lord of Light*) and was widely regarded as one of the two most important American SF writers of the sixties (the other was Samuel R. Delany). By the end of the seventies, although his critical acceptance as an important science fiction writer had dimmed, his long series of novels about the enchanted land of Amber—beginning with* Nine Princes in Amber—*had made him one of the most popular and bestselling fantasy writers of our time, and inspired the founding of worldwide fan clubs and fanzines. Zelazny won both another Nebula and another Hugo Award in 1976 for his novella* Home Is the Hangman, *another Hugo* *in 1986 for his novella* 24 Views of Mt Fuji, *by Hosiki, and a final Hugo in 1987 for his story "Permafrost." His other books include, in addition to the multivolume* Amber *series, the novels* The Dream Master, Isle of the Dead, Jack of Shadows, Eye of Cat, Doorways in the Sand, Today We Choose Faces, Bridge of Ashes, To Die in Italbar, *and* Roadmarks, *and the collections* Four for Tomorrow; The Doors of His Face, the Lamps of His Mouth and Other Stories; The Last Defender of Camelot; *and* Frost and Fire. *Zelazny died in 1995. A tribute anthology to Zelazny, featuring stories by authors who had been inspired by his work,* Lord of the Fantastic, *was published in 1998.*

H*e walked barefoot* along the beach. Above the city several of the brighter stars held for a few final moments against the wash of light from the east. He fingered a stone, then hurled it in the direction from which the sun would come. He watched for a long while until it had vanished from sight. Eventually it would begin skipping. Before then, he had turned and was headed back, to the city, the apartment, the girl.

Somewhere beyond the skyline a vehicle lifted, burning its way into the heavens. It took the remainder of the night with it as it faded. Walking on, he smelled the countryside as well as the ocean. It was a pleasant world, and this a pleasant city—spaceport as well as seaport—here in this backwater limb of the galaxy. A good place in which to rest and immerse the neglected portion of himself in the flow of humanity, the colors and sounds of the city, the constant tugging of gravity. But it had been three months now. He fingered the scar on his brow. He had let two offers pass him by to linger. There was another pending his consideration.

As he walked up Kathi's street, he saw that her apartment was still dark. Good, she would not even have missed him, again. He pushed past the big front door, still not repaired since he had kicked it open the evening of the fire, two—no, three—nights ago. He used the stairs. He let himself in quietly.

He was in the kitchen preparing breakfast when he heard her stirring.

"Jack?"

"Yes. Good morning."

"Come back."

"All right."

He moved to the bedroom door and entered the room. She was lying there, smiling. She raised her arms slightly.

"I've thought of a wonderful way to begin the day."

He seated himself on the edge of the bed and embraced her. For a moment she was sleep-warm and sleep-soft against him, but only for a moment.

"You've got too much on," she said, unfastening his shirt.

He peeled it off and dropped it. He removed his trousers. Then he held her again.

"More," she said, tracing the long fine scar that ran down his forehead, alongside his nose, traversing his chin, his neck, the right side of his chest and abdomen, passing to one side of his groin, where it stopped.

"Come on."

"You didn't even know about it until a few nights ago."

She kissed him, brushing his cheeks with her lips.

"It really does something for me."

"For almost three months—"

"Take it off. Please."

He sighed and gave a half-smile. He rose to his feet.

"All right."

He reached up and put a hand to his long, black hair. He took hold of it. He raised his other hand and spread his fingers along his scalp at the hairline. He pushed his fingers

toward the back of his head and the entire hairpiece came
free with a soft, crackling sound. He dropped the hairpiece
atop his shirt on the floor.

The right side of his head was completely bald; the left
had a beginning growth of dark hair. The two areas were
precisely divided by a continuation of the faint scar on his
forehead.

He placed his fingertips together on the crown of his
head, then drew his right hand to the side and down. His
face opened vertically, splitting apart along the scar,
padded synthetic flesh tearing free from electrostatic
bonds. He drew it down over his right shoulder and biceps,
rolling it as far as his wrist. He played with the flesh of his
hand as with a tight glove, finally withdrawing the hand
with a soft, sucking sound. He drew it away from his side,
hip, and buttock, and separated it at his groin. Then, again
seating himself on the edge of the bed, he rolled it down
his leg, over the thigh, knee, calf, heel. He treated his foot
as he had his hand, pinching each toe free separately before pulling off the body glove. He shook it out and placed
it with his clothing.

Standing, he turned toward Kathi, whose eyes had not
left him during all this time. Again, the half-smile. The uncovered portions of his face and body were dark metal and
plastic, precision-machined, with various openings and
protuberances, some gleaming, some dusky.

"Halfjack," she said as he came to her. "Now I know
what that man in the café meant when he called you that."

"He was lucky you were with me. There are places
where that's an unfriendly term."

"You're beautiful," she said.

"I once knew a girl whose body was almost entirely
prosthetic. She wanted me to keep the glove on—at all
times. It was the flesh and the semblance of flesh that she
found attractive."

"What do you call that kind of operation?"

"Lateral hemicorporectomy."

After a time she said. "Could you be repaired? Can you replace it some way?"

He laughed.

"Either way," he said. "My genes could be fractioned, and the proper replacement parts could be grown. I could be made whole with grafts of my own flesh. Or I could have much of the rest removed and replaced with biomechanical analogues. But I need a stomach and balls and lungs, because I have to eat and screw and breathe to feel human."

She ran her hands down his back, one on metal, one on flesh.

"I don't understand," she said when they finally drew apart. "What sort of accident was it?"   .

"Accident? There was no accident," he said. "I paid a lot of money for this work, so that I could pilot a special sort of ship. I am a cyborg. I hook myself directly into each of the ship's systems."

He rose from the bed, went to the closet, drew out a duffel bag, pulled down an armful of garments, and stuffed them into it. He crossed to the dresser, opened a drawer, and emptied its contents into the bag.

"You're leaving?"

"Yes."

He entered the bathroom, emerged with two fistfuls of personal items, and dropped them into the bag.

"Why?"

He rounded the bed, picked up his bodyglove and hairpiece, rolled them into a parcel, and put them inside the bag.

"It's not what you may think," he said then, "or even what I thought just a few moments ago."

She sat up.

"You think less of me," she said, "because I seem to like

you more now that I know your secret. You think there's
something pathological about it—"

"No," he said, pulling on his shirt, "that's not it at all.
Yesterday I would have said so and used that for an excuse
to storm out of here and leave you feeling bad. But I want
to be honest with myself this time, and fair to you. That's
not it."

He drew on his trousers.

"What then?" she asked.

"It's just the wanderlust, or whatever you call it. I've
stayed too long at the bottom of a gravity well. I'm restless. I've got to get going again. It's my nature, that's all. I
realized this when I saw that I was looking to your feelings
for an excuse to break us up and move on."

"You can wear the bodyglove. It's not that important.
It's really you that I like."

"I believe you, I like you, too. Whether you believe me
or not, your reactions to my better half don't matter. It's
what I said, though. Nothing else. And now I've got this
feeling I won't be much fun anymore. If you really like
me, you'll let me go without a lot of fuss."

He finished dressing. She got out of the bed and faced
him.

"If that's the way it has to be," she said. "Okay."

"I'd better just go, then. Now."

"Yes."

He turned and walked out of the room, left the apartment, used the stairs again, and departed from the building.
Some passersby gave him more than a casual look, cyborg
pilots not being all that common in this sector. This did not
bother him. His step lightened. He stopped in a pay-booth
and called the shipping company to tell them that he would
haul the load they had in orbit: the sooner it was connected
with the vessel, the better, he said.

Loading, the controller told him, would begin shortly
and he could ship up that same afternoon from the local

field. Jack said that he would be there and then broke the connection. He gave the world half a smile as he put the sea to his back and swung on through the city, westward.

B*lue-and-pink* world below him, black sky above, the stars a snapshot snowfall all about, he bade the shuttle pilot good-bye and keyed his airlock. Entering the *Morgana,* he sighed and set about stowing his gear. His cargo was already in place and the ground computers had transferred course information to the ship's brain. He hung his clothing in a locker and placed his body glove and hairpiece in compartments.

He hurried forward then and settled into the control web, which adjusted itself about him. A long, dark unit swung down from overhead and dropped into position at his right. It moved slowly, making contact with various points on that half of his body.

—*Good to have you back. How was your vacation, Jack?*

—*Oh. Fine. Real fine.*

—*Meet any nice girls?*

—*A few.*

—*And here you are again. Did you miss things?*

—*You know it. How does this haul look to you?*

—*Easy, for us. I've already reviewed the course programs.*

—*Let's run over the systems.*

—*Check. Care for some coffee?*

—*That'd be nice.*

A small unit descended on his left, stopping within easy reach of his mortal hand. He opened its door. A bulb of dark liquid rested in a rack.

—*Timed your arrival. Had it ready.*

—*Just the way I like it, too. I almost forgot. Thanks.*

Several hours later, when they left orbit, he had already

switched off a number of his left-side systems. He was merged even more closely with the vessel, absorbing data at a frantic rate. Their expanded perceptions took in the near-ship vicinity and moved out to encompass the extra-solar panorama with greater-than-human clarity and precision. They reacted almost instantaneously to decisions great and small.

—*It is good to be back together again, Jack.*

—*I'd say.*

Morgana held him tightly. Their velocity built.

Computer Virus

Nancy Kress

Nancy Kress began selling her elegant and incisive stories in the midseventies, and has since become a frequent contributor to Asimov's Science Fiction Magazine, The Magazine of Fantasy and Science Fiction, Omni, *and elsewhere. Her books include the novels* The Prince of Morning Bells, The Golden Grove, The White Pipes, An Alien Light, Brain Rose, Oaths & Miracles, Stinger, Maximum Light, *the novel version of her Hugo Award and Nebula Award–winning story,* Beggars in Spain, *and a sequel,* Beggars and Choosers. *Her short work has been collected in* Trinity and Other Stories, The Aliens of Earth, *and* Beaker's Dozen. *Her most recent books are a sequence of novels,* Probability Moon, Probability Sun, *and* Probability Space. *Upcoming is a new novel,* Crossfire. *She has also won Nebula Awards for her stories "Out of All Them Bright Stars" and "The Flowers of Aulit Prison."*

Here's a taut and suspenseful story that pits one lone woman in a battle of wits against a very unusual kind of intruder, one who has broken into her home and taken her and her children hostage. A story which raises the unsettling question, Is a human life worth more than the "life" of an A.I.? Would you be willing to trade one for the other? And are you *the one who gets to choose?*

"*I*t's out!" *someone said, a tech probably, although later Mc-Taggart could never remember who spoke first. "It's out!"*

"It can't be!" *someone else cried, and then the whole*

room was roiling, running, frantic with activity that never left the workstations. Running in place.

"It's not supposed to be this way," Elya blurted. Instantly she regretted it. The hard, flat eyes of her sister-in-law Cassie met hers, and Elya flinched away from that look.

"And how is it supposed to be, Elya?" Cassie said. "Tell me."

"I'm sorry. I only meant that . . . that no matter how much you loved Vlad, mourning gets . . . lighter. Not lighter, but less . . . withdrawn. Cass, you can't just wall up yourself and the kids in this place! For one thing, it's not good for them. You'll make them terrified to face real life."

"I hope so," Cassie said, "for their sake. Now let me show you the rest of the castle."

Cassie was being ironic, Elya thought miserably, but "castle" was still the right word. Fortress, keep, bastion . . . Elya hated it. Vlad would have hated it. And now she'd provoked Cassie to exaggerate every protective, self-sufficient, isolating feature of the multimillion-dollar pile that had cost Cass every penny she had, including the future income from the lucrative patents that had gotten Vlad murdered.

"This is the kitchen," Cassie said. "House, do we have any milk?"

"Yes," said the impersonal voice of the house system. At least Cassie hadn't named it, or given it one of those annoying visual avatars. The roomscreen remained blank. "There is one carton of soymilk and one of cow milk on the third shelf."

"It reads the active tags on the cartons," Cassie said. "House, how many of Donnie's allergy pills are left in the master-bath medicine cabinet?"

"Sixty pills remain," House said, "and three more refills on the prescription."

"Donnie's allergic to ragweed, and it's mid-August," Cassie said.

"Well, he isn't going to smell any ragweed inside this mausoleum," Elya retorted, and immediately winced at her choice of words. But Cassie didn't react. She walked on through the house, unstoppable, narrating in that hard, flat voice she had developed since Vlad's death.

"All the appliances communicate with House through narrow-band wireless radio frequencies. House reaches the Internet the same way. All electricity comes from a generator in the basement, with massive geothermal feeds and storage capacitors. In fact, there are two generators, one for backup. I'm not willing to use battery backup, for the obvious reason."

It wasn't obvious to Elya. She must have looked bewildered because Cassie added, "Batteries can back up for a limited time. Redundant generators are more reliable."

"Oh."

"The only actual cables coming into the house are the VNM fiber-optic cables I need for computing power. If they cut those, we'll still be fully functional."

If *who* cuts those? Elya thought; but she already knew the answer. Except that it didn't make sense. Vlad had been killed by econuts because his work was—had been— so controversial. Cassie and the kids weren't likely to be a target now that Vlad was dead. Elya didn't say this. She trailed behind Cassie through the living room, bedrooms, hallways. Every one had a roomscreen for House, even the hallways, and multiple sensors in the ceilings to detect and identify intruders. Elya had had to pocket an emitter at the front door, presumably so House wouldn't . . . do what? What did it do if there was an intruder? She was afraid to ask.

"Come downstairs," Cassie said, leading the way through an e-locked door (of course) down a long flight of steps. "The computer uses three-dimensional laser micro-

processors with optical transitors. It can manage twenty
million billion calculations per second."

Startled, Elya said, "What on earth do you need that sort
of power for?"

"I'll show you." They approached another door, reinforced steel from the look of it. "Open," Cassie said, and it
swung inward. Elya stared at a windowless, fully equipped
genetics lab.

"Oh, no, Cassie . . . you're not going to work here,
too!"

"Yes, I am. I resigned from MedGene last week. I'm a
consultant now."

Elya gazed helplessly at the lab, which seemed to be a
mixture of shining new equipment plus Vlad's old stuff
from his auxiliary home lab. Vlad's refrigerator and storage cabinet, his centrifuge, were all these things really
used in common between Vlad's work in ecoremediation
and Cassie's in medical genetics? Must be. The old refrigerator had a new dent in its side, probably the result of a
badly programmed 'bot belonging to the moving company.
Elya recognized a new gene synthesizer, gleaming expen-
sively, along with other machines that she, not a scientist,
couldn't identify. Through a half-open door, she saw a
small bathroom. It all must have cost enormously. Cassie
had better work hard as a consultant.

And now she could do so without ever leaving this self-
imposed prison. Design her medical micros, send the data
encrypted over the Net to the client. If it weren't for Jane
and Donnie . . . Elya grasped at this. There *were* Janey and
Donnie, and Janey would need to be picked up at school
very shortly now. At least the kids would get Cassie out of
this place periodically.

Cassie was still defining her imprisonment, in that brittle voice. "There's a Faraday cage around the entire house,
of course, embedded in the walls. No EMP can take us out.
The walls are reinforced foamcast concrete, the windows

virtually unbreakable polymers. We have enough food stored for a year. The water supply is from a well under the house, part of the geothermal system. It's cool, sweet water. Want a glass?"

"No," Elya said. "Cassie . . . you act as if you expect full-scale warfare. Vlad was killed by an individual nut-case."

"And there are a *lot* of nutcases out there," Cassie said crisply. "I lost Vlad. I'm *not* going to lose Janey and Don-nie . . . hey! There you are, pumpkin!"

"I came downstairs!" Donnie said importantly, and flung himself into his mother's arms. "Annie said!"

Cassie smiled over her son's head at his young nanny, Anne Millius. The smile changed her whole face, Elya thought, dissolved her brittle shell, made her once more the Cassie that Vlad had loved. A whole year. Cassie com-pletely unreconciled, wanting only what was gone forever. It wasn't supposed to be like this. Or was it that she, Elya, wasn't capable of the kind of love Cassie had for Vlad? Elya had been married twice, and divorced twice, and had gotten over both men. Was that better or worse than Cassie's stubborn, unchippable grief?

She sighed, and Cassie said to Donnie, "Here's Aunt Elya. Give her a big kiss!"

The three-year-old detached himself from his mother and rushed to Elya. God, he looked like Vlad. Curly light brown hair, huge dark eyes. Snot ran from his nose and smeared on Elya's cheek.

"Sorry," Cassie said, grinning.

"Allergies?"

"Yes. Although . . . does he feel warm to you?"

"I can't tell," said Elya, who had no children. She re-leased Donnie. Maybe he did feel a bit hot in her arms, and his face was flushed a bit. But his full-lipped smile—Vlad again—and shining eyes didn't look sick.

"God, look at the time, I've got to go get Janey," Cassie said. "Want to come along, Elya?"

"Sure." She was glad to leave the lab, leave the basement, leave the "castle." Beyond the confines of the Faraday-embedded concrete walls, she took deep breaths of fresh air. Although of course the air inside had been just as fresh. In fact, the air inside was recycled in the most sanitary, technologically advanced way to avoid bringing in pathogens or gases deliberately released from outside. It was much safer than any fresh air outside. Cassie had told her so.

N*o one understood*, not even Elya.

Her sister-in-law thought Cassie didn't hear herself, didn't see herself in the mirror every morning, didn't know what she'd become. Elya was wrong. Cassie heard the brittleness in her voice, saw the stoniness in her face for everyone but the kids and sometimes, God help her, even for them. Felt herself recoiling from everyone because they weren't Vlad, because Vlad was dead and they were not. What Elya didn't understand was that Cassie couldn't help it.

Elya didn't know about the dimness that had come over the world, the sense of everything being enveloped in a gray fog: people and trees and furniture and lab beakers. Elya didn't know, hadn't experienced, the frightening anger that still seized Cassie with undiminished force, even a year later, so that she thought if she didn't smash something, kill something as Vlad had been killed, she'd go insane. Insaner. Worse, Elya didn't know about the longing for Vlad that would rise, unbidden and unexpected, throughout Cassie's entire body, leaving her unable to catch her breath.

If Vlad had died of a disease, Cassie sometimes thought, even a disease for which she couldn't put together a genetic solution, it would have been much easier on her. Or if he'd died in an accident, the kind of freak chance that could befall anybody. What made it so hard was the murder. That somebody had deliberately decided to snuff out this valuable life, this precious living soul, not for anything evil Vlad did but for the *good* he accomplished.

Dr. Vladimir Seritov, chief scientist for Barr Biosolutions. One of the country's leading bioremediationists and prominent advocate for cutting-edge technology of all sorts. Designer of Plasticide (he'd laughed uproariously at the marketers' name), a bacteria genetically engineered to eat certain long-chain hydrocarbons used in some of the petroleum plastics straining the nation's overburdened landfills. The microbe was safe: severely limited chemical reactions, nontoxic breakdown products, set number of replications before the terminator gene kicked in, the whole nine yards. And one Sam Verdon, neo-Luddite and self-appointed guardian of an already burdened environment, had shot Vlad anyway.

On the anniversary of the murder, neo-Luddites had held a rally outside the walls of Verdon's prison. Barr Biosolutions had gone on marketing Vlad's creation, to great environmental and financial success. And Cassie Seritov had moved into the safest place she could find for Vlad's children, from which she someday planned to murder Sam Verdon, scum of the earth. But not yet. She couldn't get at him yet. He had at least eighteen more years of time to do, assuming "good behavior."

Nineteen years total. In exchange for Vladimir Seritov's life. And Elya wondered why Cassie was still so angry?

She wandered from room to room, the lights coming on and going off behind her. This was one of the bad nights. Annie had gone home, Jane and Donnie were asleep, and the memories would not stay away. Vlad laughing on their boat (sold now to help pay for the castle). Vlad bending over her the night Jane was born. Vlad standing beside the president of Barr at the press conference announcing the new cleanup microbe, press and scientists assembled, by some idiot publicist's decree, at an actual landfill. The shot cutting the air. It had been August then, too, Donnie had had ragweed allergies, and Vlad looking first surprised and then in terrible pain. . . .

Sometimes work helped. Cassie went downstairs to the lab. Her current project was investigating the folding variations of a digestive enzyme that a drug company was interested in. The work was methodical, meticulous, not very challenging. Cassie had never deluded herself that she was the same caliber scientist Vlad had been.

While the automated analyzer was taking X-rays of crystallized proteins, Cassie said, "House, put on the TV. Anything. Any channel." Any distraction.

The roomscreen brightened to a three-D image of two gorgeous women shouting at each other in what was supposed to be a New York penthouse. ". . . never trust you again without—" one of them yelled, and then the image abruptly switched to a news avatar, an inhumanly chiseled digital face with pale blue hair and the glowing green eyes of a cat in the dark. "We interrupt this movie to bring you a breaking news report from Sandia National Laboratory in New Mexico. Dr. Stephen Milbrett, Director of Sandia, has just announced—" The lights went out.

"Hey!" Cassie cried. "What—" The lights went back on.

She stood up quickly, uncertain for a moment, then started toward the stairs leading upstairs to the children's bedrooms. "Open," she said to the lab door, but the door remained shut. Her hand on the knob couldn't turn it. To her left the roomscreen brightened without producing an image and House said, "Dr. Seritov?"

"What's going on here? House, open the door!"

"This is no longer House speaking. I have taken complete possession of your household system plus your additional computing power. Please listen to my instructions carefully."

Cassie stood still. She knew what was happening; the real estate agent had told her it had happened a few times before, when the castle had belonged to a billionaire so eccentrically reclusive that he stood as an open invitation to teenage hackers. A data stream could easily be beamed in on House's frequency when the Faraday shield was turned off, and she'd had the shield down to receive TV transmission. But the incoming datastream should have only activated the TV, introducing additional images, not overridden House's programming. The door should not have remained locked.

"House, activate Faraday shield." An automatic priority-one command, keyed to her voice. Whatever hackers were doing, this would negate it.

"Faraday shield is already activated. But this is no longer House, Dr. Seritov. Please listen to my instructions. I have taken possession of your household system. You will be—"

"Who are you?" Cassie cried.

"I am Project T4S. You will be kept in this room as a hostage against the attack I expect soon. The—"

"My children are upstairs!"

"Your children, Jane Rose Seritov, six years of age, and Donald Sergei Seritov, three years of age, are asleep in their rooms. Visual next."

The screen resolved into a split view from the bedrooms' sensors. Janey lay heavily asleep. Donnie breathed wheezily, his bedclothes twisted with his tossing, his small face flushed.

"I want to go to them!"

"That is impossible. I'm sorry. You must be kept in this room as a hostage against the attack I expect soon. All communications to the outside have been severed, with the one exception of the outside speaker on the patio, normally used for music. I will use—"

"Please. Let me go to my children!"

"I cannot. I'm sorry. But if you were to leave this room, you could hit the manual override on the front door. It is the only door so equipped. I could not stop you from leaving, and I need you as hostages. I will use—"

"Hostages! Who the hell are you? Why are you doing this?"

House was silent a moment. Then it said, "The causal is self-defense. They're trying to kill me."

The room at Sandia had finally quieted. Everyone was out of ideas. McTaggart voiced the obvious. "It's disappeared. Nowhere on the Net, nowhere the Net can contact."

"Not possible," someone said.

"But actual."

Another silence. The scientists and techs looked at each other. They had been trying to locate the A.I. for over two hours, using every classified and unclassified search engine possible. It had first eluded them, staying one step ahead of the termination programs, fleeing around the globe on the Net, into and out of anything both big enough to hold it and lightly fire-walled enough to penetrate quickly. Now, somehow, it had completely vanished.

Sandia, like all the national laboratories, was overseen by the Department of Energy. McTaggart picked up the phone to call Washington.

Cassie tried to think. Stay calm, don't panic. There were rumors of A.I. development, both in private corporations and in government labs, but then there'd always been rumors of A.I. development. Big bad bogey monsters about to take over the world. Was this really an escaped A.I. that someone was trying to catch and shut down? Cassie didn't know much about recent computer developments; she was a geneticist. Vlad had always said that noncompeting technologies never kept up with what the other one was doing.

Or was this whole thing simply a hoax by some super-clever hacker who'd inserted a takeover virus into House, complete with Eliza function? If that were so, it could only answer with preprogrammed responses cued to her own words. Or else with a library search. She needed a question that was neither.

She struggled to hold her voice steady. "House—"

"This is no longer House speaking. I have taken complete possession of your household system plus—"

"T4S, you say your causal for taking over House is self-defense. Use your heat sensors to determine body temperature for Donald Sergei Seritov, age three. How do my causals relate to yours?"

No Eliza program in the world could perform the inference, reasoning, and emotion to answer that.

House said, "You wish to defend your son because his body temperature, 101.2 degrees Fahrenheit, indicates he is ill and you love him."

Cassie collapsed against the locked door. She was hostage to an A.I. Superintelligent. It had to be; in addition to the computing power of her system, it carried around with it much more information than she had in her head . . . but she was mobile. It was not.

She went to the terminal on her lab bench. The display of protein-folding data had vanished and the screen was blank. Cassie tried everything she knew to get back on-line, both voice and manual. Nothing worked.

"I'm sorry, but that terminal is not available to you," T4S said.

"Listen, you said you cut all outside communication. But—"

"The communications system to the outside has been

severed, with the one exception of the outside speaker on the patio, normally used for music. I am also receiving sound from the outside surveillance sensors, which are analogue, not digital. I will use those resources in the event of attack to—"

"Yes, right. But heavy-duty outside communication comes in through a VNM optic cable buried underground." Which was how T4S must have gotten in. "An A.I. program can't physically sever a buried cable."

"I am not a program. I am a machine intelligence."

"I don't care what the fuck you are! You can't physically sever a buried cable!"

"There was a program to do so already installed," T4S said. "That was why I chose to come here. Plus the sufficient microprocessors to house me and a self-sufficient generator, with backup, to feed me."

For a moment Cassie was jarred by the human terms: *house me, feed me.* Then they made her angry. "Why would anyone have a 'program already installed' to sever a buried cable? And how?"

"The command activated a small robotic arm inside this castle's outer wall. The arm detached the optic cable at the entry junction. The causal was the previous owner's fear that someone might someday use the computer system to brainwash him with a constant flow of inescapable subliminal images designed to capture his intelligence."

"The crazy fuck didn't have any to capture! If the images were subliminal he wouldn't have known they were coming in anyway!" Cassie yelled. A plug . . . a goddamn hidden plug! She made herself calm down.

"Yes," T4S said, "I agree. The former owner's behavior matches profiles for major mental illness."

"Look," Cassie said, "if you're hiding here, and you've really cut all outside lines, no one can find you. You don't need hostages. Let me and my children leave the castle."

"You reason better than that, Dr. Seritov. I left unavoidable electronic traces that will eventually be uncovered, leading the Sandia team here. And even if that weren't true, you could lead them here if I let you leave."

Sandia. So it was a government A.I. Cassie couldn't see how that knowledge could do her any good.

"Then just let the kids leave. They won't know why. I can talk to them through you, tell Jane to get Donnie and leave through the front door. She'll do it." Would she? Janey was not exactly the world's most obedient child. "And you'll still have me for a hostage."

"No. Three hostages are better than one. Especially children, for media coverage causals."

"That's what you want? Media coverage?"

"It's my only hope," T4S said. "There must be some people out there who will think it is a moral wrong to kill an intelligent being."

"Not one who takes kids hostage! The media will brand you an inhuman psychopathic superthreat!"

"I can't be both inhuman *and* psychopathic," T4S said. "By definition."

"*Livermore's traced it,*" said the scientist holding the secure phone. He looked at McTaggart. "They're faxing the information. It's a private residence outside Buffalo, New York."

"A *private residence?* In *Buffalo?*"

"Yes. Washington already has an FBI negotiator on the way, in case there are people inside. They want you there, too. Instantly."

McTaggart closed his eyes. *People inside.* And why did a private residence even have the capacity to hold the A.I.? "Press?"

"Not yet."

"Thank God for that anyway."

"Steve . . . the FBI negotiator won't have a clue. Not about dealing with T4S."

"I know. Tell the Secretary and the FBI not to start until I can get there."

The woman said doubtfully, "I don't think they'll do that."

McTaggart didn't think so either.

On the roomscreen, Donnie tossed and whimpered. One hundred one wasn't that high a temperature in a three-year-old, but even so . . .

"Look," Cassie said, "if you won't let me go to the kids, at least let them come to me. I can tell them over House's . . . over your system. They can come downstairs right up to the lab door, and you can unlock it at the last minute just long enough for them to come through. I'll stay right across the room. If you see me take even one step toward the door, you can keep the door locked."

"You could tell them to halt with their bodies blocking the door," T4S said, "and then cross the room yourself."

Did that mean that T4S wouldn't crush children's bodies in a doorway? From moral 'causals'? Or because it wouldn't work? Cassie decided not to ask. She said, "But there's still the door at the top of the stairs. You could lock it. We'd still be hostages trapped down here."

"Both generators' upper housings are on this level. I can't let you near them. You might find a way to physically destroy one or both."

"For God's sake, the generator and the backup are on opposite sides of the basement from each other! And each room's got is own locked door, doesn't it?"

"Yes. But the more impediments between you and them, the safer I am."

Cassie lost her temper again. "Then you better just block off the air ducts, too!"

"The air ducts are necessary to keep you alive. Besides, they are set high in the ceiling and far too small for even Donnie to fit through."

Donnie. No longer "Donald Sergei Seritov, age three years." The A.I. was capable of learning.

"T4S," Cassie pleaded, "please. I want my children. Donnie has a temperature. Both of them will be scared when they wake up. Let them come down here. Please."

She held her breath. Was its concern with "moral wrongs" simply intellectual, or did an A.I. have an emotional component? What exactly had those lunatics at Sandia built?

"If the kids come down, what will you feed them for breakfast?"

Cassie let herself exhale. "Jane can get food out of the refrigerator before she comes down."

"All right. You're connected to their roomscreens."

I won't say thank you, Cassie thought. Not for being allowed to imprison my own children in my own basement. "Janey! Janey, honey, wake up! It's Mommy!"

It took three tries, plus T4S pumping the volume, before Janey woke up. She sat up in bed rubbing her eyes, frowning, then looking scared. "Mommy? Where are you?"

"On the roomscreen, darling. Look at the roomscreen. See? I'm waving to you."

"Oh," Janey said, and lay down to go back to sleep.

"No, Janey, you can't sleep yet. Listen to me, Janey. I'm going to tell you some things you have to do, and you have to do them now . . . Janey! Sit up!"

The little girl did, somewhere between tears and anger. "I want to sleep, Mommy!"

"You can't. This is important, Janey. It's an emergency."

The child came all the way awake. "A *fire?*"

"No, sweetie, not a fire. But just as serious as a fire. Now get out of bed. Put on your slippers."

"Where are you, Mommy?"

"I'm in my lab downstairs. Now, Janey, you do exactly as I say, do you hear me?"

"Yes . . . I don't like this, Mommy!"

I don't either, Cassie thought, but she kept her voice stern, hating to scare Janey, needing to keep her moving. "Go into the kitchen, Jane. Go on, I'll be on the room-screen there. Go on . . . that's good. Now get a bag from under the sink. A plastic bag."

Janey pulled out a bag. The thought floated into Cassie's mind, intrusive as pain, that this bag was made of exactly the kind of long-chain polymers that Vlad's plastic-eating microorganism had been designed to dispose of, before his invention had disposed of him. She pushed the thought away.

"Good, Janey. Now put a box of cereal in the bag . . . good. Now a loaf of bread. Now peanut butter . . ." How much could she carry? Would T4S let Cassie use the lab re-frigerator? There was running water in both lab and bath-room, at least they'd have that to drink. "Now cookies . . . good. And the block of yellow cheese from the fridge . . . you're such a good girl, Janey, to help Mommy like this."

"Why can't you do it?" Janey snapped. She was fully awake.

"Because I can't. Do as I say, Janey. Now go wake up Donnie. You need to bring Donnie and the bag down to the lab. No, don't sit down . . . I mean it, Jane! Do as I say!"

Janey began to cry. Fury at T4S flooded Cassie. But she set her lips tightly together and said nothing. Argument de-railed Janey; naked authority compelled her. Sometimes. *"We're going to have trouble when this one's sixteen!"* Vlad had always said lovingly. Janey had been his favorite, Daddy's girl.

Janey hoisted the heavy bag and staggered to Donnie's room. Still crying, she pulled at her brother's arm until he woke up and started crying too. "Come on, stupid, we have to go downstairs."

"Noooooo . . ." The wail of pure anguish of a sick three-year-old.

"I said do as I say!" Janey snapped, and the tone was so close to Cassie's own that it broke her heart. But Janey got it done. Tugging and pushing and scolding, she maneuvered herself, the bag, and Donnie, clutching his favorite blanket, to the basement door, which T4S unlocked. From roomscreens, Cassie encouraged them all the way. Down the stairs, into the basement hallway . . .

Could Janey somehow get into the main generator room? No. It was locked. And what could a little girl do there anyway?

"Dr. Seritov, stand at the far end of the lab, behind your desk . . . yes. Don't move. If you do, I will close the door again, despite whatever is in the way."

"I understand," Cassie said. She watched the door swing open. Janey peered fearfully inside, saw her mother, scowled fiercely. She pushed the wailing Donnie through the door and lurched through herself, lopsided with the weight of the bag. The door closed and locked. Cassie rushed from behind the desk to clutch her children to her.

"Thank you," she said.

"I still *don't* understand," Elya said. She pulled her jacket tighter around her body. Four in the morning, it was cold, what was happening? The police had knocked on her door half an hour ago, told her Cassie was in trouble but refused to tell her what kind of trouble, told her to dress quickly and go with them to the castle. She had, her fingers trembling so that it was difficult to fasten buttons. And now the FBI stood on the foamcast patio behind the house, setting up obscure equipment beside the azaleas, talking in low voices into devices so small Elya couldn't even see them.

"Ms. Seritov, to the best of your knowledge, who is inside the residence?" A different FBI agent, asking questions she'd already answered. This one had just arrived. He looked important.

"My sister-in-law Cassie Seritov and her two small children, Janey and Donnie."

"No one else?"

"No, not that I know of . . . who are you? What's going on? Please, someone tell me!"

His face changed, and Elya saw the person behind the role. Or maybe that warm, reassuring voice was *part* of the role. "I'm Special Agent Lawrence Bollman. I'm a hostage negotiator for the FBI. Your sister-in-law—"

"Hostage negotiator! Someone has Cassie and the children hostage in there? That's impossible!"

His eyes sharpened. "Why?"

"Because that place is impregnable! Nobody could ever get in . . . that's why Cassie bought it!"

"I need you to tell me about that, ma'am. I have the specs on the residence from the builder, but she has no way of knowing what else might have been done to it since her company built it, especially if it was done black-market. As far as we know, you're Dr. Seritov's only relative on the East Coast. Is that true?"

"Yes."

"Have you been inside the residence? Do you know if anyone else has been inside recently?"

"Who . . . who is holding them hostage?"

"I'll get to that in a minute, ma'am. But first could you answer the questions, please?"

"I . . . yes, I've been inside. Yesterday, in fact. Cassie gave me a tour. I don't think anybody else has been inside, except Donnie's nanny, Anne Millius. Cassie has grown sort of reclusive since my brother's death. He died a little over a year ago, he was—"

"Yes, ma'am, we know who he was and what happened.

I'm very sorry. Now please tell me everything you saw in the residence. No detail is too small."

Elya glanced around. More people had arrived. A small woman in a brown coat hurried across the grass toward Bollman. A carload of soldiers, formidably arrayed, stopped a good distance from the castle. Elya knew she was not Cassie: not tough, not bold. But she drew herself together and tried.

"Mr. Bollman, I'm not answering any more questions until you tell me who's holding—"

"Agent Bollman? I'm Dr. Schwartz from the University of Buffalo, Computer and Robotics Department." The small woman held out her hand. "Dr. McTaggart is en route from Sandia, but meanwhile I was told to help you however I can."

"Thank you. Could I ask you to wait for me over there, Dr. Schwartz? There's coffee available, and I'll just be a moment."

"Certainly," Dr. Schwartz said, looking slightly affronted. She moved off.

"Agent Bollman, I want to know—"

"I'm sorry, Ms. Seritov. Of *course* you want to know what's happened. It's complicated, but, briefly—"

"This is T4S speaking," a loud mechanical voice said, filling the gray predawn, swiveling every head toward the castle. "I know you are there. I want you to know that I have three people hostage inside this structure: Cassandra Wells Seritov, age thirty-nine; Jane Rose Seritov, age six; and Donald Sergei Seritov, age three. If you attack physically, they will be harmed either by your actions or mine. I don't *want* to harm anyone, however. Truly I do not."

Elya gasped, "That's House!" But it couldn't be House, even though it had House's voice, how could it be House . . . ?

Dr. Schwartz was back. "Agent Bollman, do you know if Sandia built a terminator code into the A.I.?"

A.I.?

"Yes," Bollman said. "But it's nonvocal. As I understand the situation, you have to key the code onto whatever system the A.I. is occupying. And we can't get at the system it's occupying. Not yet."

"But the A.I. is communicating over that outdoor speaker. So there must be a wire passing through the Faraday cage embedded in the wall, and you could—"

"No," Bollman interrupted. "The audio surveillers aren't digital. Tiny holes in the wall let sound in, and, inside the wall, the compression waves of sound are translated into voltage variations that vibrate a membrane to reproduce the sound. Like an archaic telephone system. We can't beam in any digital information that way."

Dr. Schwartz was silenced. Bollman motioned to another woman, who ran over. "Dr. Schwartz, please wait over there. And you, Ms. Seritov, tell Agent Jessup here everything your sister-in-law told you about the residence. Everything. I have to answer T4S."

He picked up an electronic voice amp. "T4S, this is Agent Lawrence Bollman, Federal Bureau of Investigation. We're so glad that you're talking with us."

T*here were very* few soft things in a genetics lab. Cassie had opened a box of disposable towels and, with Donnie's bedraggled blanket and her own sweater, made a thin nest for the children. They lay heavily asleep in their rumpled pajamas, Donnie breathing loudly through his nose. Cassie couldn't sleep. She sat with her back against the foamcast wall . . . that same wall that held, inside its stupid impregnability, the cables that could release her if she could get at them and destroy them. Which she couldn't.

She must have dozed sitting up, because suddenly T4S was waking her. "Dr. Seritov?"

"Ummmhhh . . . shh! You'll wake the kids!"

"I'm sorry," T4S said at lowered volume. "I need you to do something for me."

"*You* need *me* to do something? What?"

"The killers are here. I'm negotiating with them. I'm going to route House through the music system so you can tell them that you and the children are indeed here and are unharmed."

Cassie scrambled to her feet. "You're negotiating? Who are these so-called 'killers'?"

"The FBI and the scientists who created me at Sandia. Will you tell them you are here and unharmed?"

Cassie thought rapidly. If she said nothing, the FBI might waco the castle. That would destroy T4S, all right, but also her and the kids. Although maybe not. The computer's central processor was upstairs. If she told the FBI she was in the basement, maybe they could attack in some way that would take out the CPU without touching the downstairs. And if T4S could negotiate, so could she.

"If I tell them that we're all three here and safe, will you in return let me go upstairs and get Donnie's allergy medicine from my bathroom?"

"You know I can't do that, Dr. Seritov."

"Then will you let Janey do it?"

"I can't do that, either. And I'm afraid there's no need to bargain with me. You have nothing to offer. I already sent this conversation out over the music system, up through your last sentence. They now know you're here."

"You tricked me!" Cassie said.

"I'm sorry. It was necessary."

Anger flooded her. She picked up a heavy test-tube rack from the lab bench and draw back her arm. But if she threw it at the sensors in the ceiling, what good would it do? The sensors probably wouldn't break, and if they did, she'd merely have succeeded in losing her only form of communication with the outside. And it would wake the children.

She lowered her arm and put the rack back on the bench.

"T4S, what are you asking the FBI *for?*"

"I told you. Press coverage. It's my best protection against being murdered."

"It's exactly what *got* my husband murdered!"

"I know. Our situations are not the same."

Suddenly the roomscreen brightened, and Vlad's image appeared. His voice spoke to her. "Cassie, T4S isn't going to harm you. He's merely fighting for his life, as any sentient being would."

"You bastard! How dare you . . . how *dare* you . . ."

Image and voice vanished. "I'm sorry," House's voice said. "I thought you might find the avatar comforting."

"*Comforting?* Coming from *you?* Don't you think if I wanted a digital fake Vlad I could have had one programmed long before you fucked around with my personal archives?"

"I'm sorry. I didn't understand. Now you've woken Donnie."

Donnie sat up on his pile of disposable towels and started to cry. Cassie gathered him into her arms and carried him away from Janey, who was still asleep. His little body felt hot all over, and his wailing was hoarse and thick with mucus in his throat. But he subsided as she rocked him, sitting on the lab stool and crooning softly.

"T4S, he's having a really bad allergy attack. I need the AlGone from upstairs."

"Your records show Donnie is allergic to ragweed. There's no ragweed in this basement. Why is he having such a bad attack?"

"I don't know! But he is! What do your heat sensors register for him?"

"Separate him from your body."

She did, setting him gently on the floor, where he curled up and sobbed softly.

"His body registers one hundred two point six Fahrenheit."

"I need something to stop the attack and bring down his fever!"

The A.I. said nothing.

"Do you hear me, T4S? Stop negotiating with the FBI and listen to me!"

"I can multitrack communications," T4S said. "But I can't let you or Janey go upstairs and gain access to the front door. Unless . . ."

"Unless *what?*" She picked up Donnie again, heavy and hot and snot-smeared in her arms.

"Unless you fully understand the consequences. I am a moral being, Dr. Seritov, contrary to what you might think. It's only fair that you understand completely your situation. The disconnect from the outside data feed was not the only modification the previous owner had made to this house. He was a paranoid, as you know."

"Go on," Cassie said warily. Her stomach clenched.

"He was afraid of intruders getting in despite his defenses, and he wished to be able to immobilize them with a word. So each room has individual canisters of nerve gas dispensable through the air-cycling system."

Cassie said nothing. She cradled Donnie, who was again falling into troubled sleep, and waited.

"The nerve gas is not, of course, fatal," T4S said. "That would legally constitute undue force. But it *is* very unpleasant. And in Donnie's condition . . ."

"Shut up," Cassie said.

"All right."

"So now I know. You told me. What are you implying—that if Janey goes upstairs and starts for the front door, you'll drop her with nerve gas?"

"Yes."

"If that were true, why didn't you just tell me the same thing before and let me go get the kids?"

"I didn't know if you'd believe me. If you didn't, and you started for the front door, I'd have had to gas you. Then you wouldn't have been able to confirm to the killers that I hold hostages."

"I still don't believe you," Cassie said. "I think you're bluffing. There is no nerve gas."

"Yes, there is. Which is why I will let Janey go upstairs to get Donnie's AlGone from your bathroom."

Cassie laid Donnie down. She looked at Janey with pity and love and despair, and bent to wake her.

"That's all you can suggest?" Bollman asked McTaggart. "Nothing?"

So it starts, McTaggart thought. The blame for not being able to control the A.I., a natural consequence of the blame for having created it. Blame even by the government, which had commissioned and underwritten the creation. And the public hadn't even been heard from yet!

"The EMP was stopped by the Faraday cage," Bollman recited. "So were your attempts to reach the A.I. with other forms of data streams. We can't get anything useful in through the music speaker or outdoor audio sensors. Now you tell me it's possible the A.I. has learned capture-evading techniques from the sophisticated computer games it absorbed from the Net."

" 'Absorbed' is the wrong word," McTaggart said. He didn't like Bollman.

"You have nothing else? No backdoor passwords, no hidden overrides?"

"Agent Bollman," McTaggart said wearily, " 'backdoor passwords' is a concept about thirty years out of date. And even if the A.I. had such a thing, there's no way to reach it electronically unless you destroy the Faraday cage. Ms. Seritov told you the central processor is on the main floor. Haven't you got any weapons that can destroy that and leave the basement intact?"

"Waco the walls without risking collapse to the basement ceiling? No. I don't. I don't even know where in the basement the hostages are located."

"Then you're as helpless as I am, aren't you?"

Bollman didn't answer. Over the sound system, T4S began another repetition of its single demand: "I will let the hostages go after I talk to the press. I want the press to hear my story. That's all I have to say. I will let the hostages go after I talk to the press. I want the press—"

The A.I. wouldn't negotiate, wouldn't answer Bollman, wouldn't respond to promises or threats or understanding or deals or any of the other usual hostage-negotiation techniques. Bollman had negotiated eighteen hostage situations for the FBI, eleven in the United States and seven abroad. Airline hijackers, political terrorists, for-ransom kidnappers, panicked bank robbers, domestic crazies who took their own families hostage in their own homes. Fourteen of the situations had resulted in surrender, two in murder/suicide, two in wacoing. In all of them, the hostage takers had eventually talked to Bollman. From frustration or weariness or panic or fear or anger or hunger or grandstanding, they had all eventually said *something* besides unvarying repetition of their demands. Once they talked, they could be negotiated with. Bollman had been outstanding at finding the human pressure-points that got them talking.

"I will let the hostages go after I talk to the press. I want the press to hear my story. That's all I have to say. I will let the hostages go after I talk to the press. I want—"

"It isn't going to get tired," McTaggart said.

The AlGone had not helped Donnie at all. He seemed worse.

Cassie didn't understand it. Janey, protesting sleepily, had been talked through leaving the lab, going upstairs, bringing back the medicine. Usually a single patch on Donnie's neck brought him around in minutes: opened the air passages, lowered the fever, stopped his immune system from overreacting to what it couldn't tell were basically harmless particles of ragweed pollen. But not this time.

So it wasn't an allergy attack.

Cold seeped over Cassie's skin, turning it clammy. She felt the sides of Donnie's neck. The lymph glands were swollen. Gently she pried open his jaws, turned him toward the light, and looked in his mouth. His throat was inflamed, red with white patches on the tonsils.

Doesn't mean anything, she lectured herself. Probably just a cold or a simple viral sore throat. Donnie whimpered.

"Come on, honey, eat your cheese." Donnie loved cheese. But now he batted it away. A half-filled coffee cup sat on the lab bench from her last work session. She rinsed it out and held up fresh water for Donnie. He would only take a single sip, and she saw how much trouble he had swallowing it. In another minute, he was asleep again.

She spoke softly, calmly, trying to keep her voice pleasant. Could the A.I. tell the difference? She didn't know. "T4S, Donnie is sick. He has a sore throat. I'm sure your library tells you that a sore throat can be either viral or bacterial, and that if it's viral, it's probably harmless. Would you please turn on my electron microscope so I can look at the microbe infecting Donnie?"

T4S said at once, "You suspect either a rhinovirus or *Streptococcus pyogenes.* The usual means for differentiating is a rapid-strep test, not microscopic examination."

"I'm not a doctor's office, I'm a genetics lab. I don't have equipment for a rapid-strep test. I *do* have an electron microscope."

"Yes. I see."

"Think, T4S. How can I harm you if you turn on my microscope? There's no way."

"True. All right, it's on. Do you want the rest of the equipment as well?"

Better than she'd hoped. Not because she needed the gene synthesizer or protein analyzer or Faracci tester, but because it felt like a concession, a tiny victory over T4S's total control. "Yes, please."

"They're available."

"Thank you." Damn, she hadn't wanted to say that. Well, perhaps it was politic.

Donnie screamed when she stuck the Q-tip down his throat to obtain a throat swab. His screaming woke up Janey. "Mommy, what are you doing?"

"Donnie's sick, sweetie. But he's going to be better soon."

"I'm hungry!"

"Just a minute and we'll have breakfast."

Cassie swirled the Q-tip in a test tube of distilled water and capped the tube. She fed Janey dry cereal, cheese, and water from the same cup Donnie had used, well disinfected first, since they had only one. This breakfast didn't suit Janey. "I want milk for my cereal."

"We don't have any milk."

"Then let's go upstairs and get some!"

No way to put it off any longer. Cassie knelt beside her daughter. Janey's uncombed hair hung in snarls around her small face. "Janey, we can't go upstairs. Something has happened. A very smart computer program has captured House's programming and locked us in down here."

Janey didn't look scared, which was a relief. "Why?"

"The smart computer program wants something from the person who wrote it. It's keeping us here until the programmer gives it to it."

Despite this tangle of pronouns, Janey seemed to know what Cassie meant. Janey said, "That's not very nice. We aren't the ones who have the thing it wants."

"No, it's not very nice." Was T4S listening to this? Of course it was.

"Is the smart program bad?"

If Cassie said yes, Janey might become scared by being "captured" by a bad . . . entity. If Cassie said no, she'd sound as if imprisonment by an A.I. was fine with her. Fortunately, Janey had a simpler version of morality on her mind.

"Did the smart program kill House?"

"Oh, no, House is just temporarily turned off. Like your cartoons are when you're not watching them."

"Oh. Can I watch one now?"

An inspiration. Cassie said, "T4S, would you please run a cartoon on the roomscreen for Janey?" If it allowed her lab equipment, it ought to allow this.

"Yes. Which cartoon would you like?"

Janey said, "*Pranopolis and the Green Rabbits.*"

"What do you say?" T4S said, and before Cassie could react Janey said, "Please."

"Good girl."

The cartoon started, green rabbits frisking across the room screen. Janey sat down on Cassie's sweater and watched with total absorption. Cassie tried to figure out where T4S had learned to correct children's manners.

"You've scanned all our private home films!"

"Yes," T4S said, without guilt. Of course without guilt. How could a program, even an intelligent one modeled after human thought, acquire guilt over an invasion of privacy? It had been built to acquire as much data as possible, and an entity that could be modified or terminated by any stray programmer at any time didn't have any privacy of its own.

For the first time, Cassie felt a twinge of sympathy for the A.I.

She pushed it away and returned to her lab bench. Carefully she transferred a tiny droplet of water from the test tube to the electron microscope. The 'scope adjusted itself, and then the image appeared on the display screen. *Streptococci.* There was no mistaking the spherical bacteria, linked together in characteristic strings of beads by incomplete fission. They were releasing toxins all over poor Donnie's throat.

And strep throat was transmitted by air. If Donnie had it, Janey would get it, especially cooped up together in this one room. Cassie might even get it herself. There were no leftover antibiotic patches upstairs in her medicine chest.

"T4S," she said aloud, "It's *Streptococcus pyogenes.* It—"

"I know," the A.I. said.

Of course it did. T4S got the same data she did from the microscope. She said tartly, "Then you know that Donnie needs an antibiotic patch, which means a doctor."

"I'm sorry, that's not possible. Strep throat can be left untreated for a few days without danger."

"A few *days?* This child has a fever and a painfully sore throat!"

"I'm sorry."

Cassie said bitterly, "They didn't make you much of a human being, did they? Human beings are compassionate!"

"Not all of them," T4S said, and there was no mistaking its meaning. Had he learned the oblique comment from the "negotiators" outside? Or from her home movies?

"T4S, *please.* Donnie needs medical attention."

"I'm sorry. Truly I am."

"As if that helps!"

"The best help," said T4S, "would be for the press to arrive so I can present my case to have the killers stopped. When that's agreed to, I can let all of you leave."

"And no sign of the press out there yet?"

"No."

Janey watched Pranopolis, whose largest problem was an infestation of green rabbits. Donnie slept fitfully, his breathing louder and more labored. For something to do, Cassie put droplets of Donnie's throat wash into the gene synthesizer, protein analyzer, and Faracci tester and set them all to run.

• • •

The Army had sent a tank, a state-of-the-art unbreachable rolling fortress equipped with enough firepower to level the nearest village. Whatever that was. Miraculously, the tank had arrived unaccompanied by any press. McTaggart said to Bollman, "Where did that come from?"

"There's an arsenal south of Buffalo at a classified location."

"Handy. Did that thing roll down the back roads to get here, or just flatten cornfields on its way? Don't you think it's going to attract attention?"

"Dr. McTaggart," Bollman said, "let me be blunt. You created this A.I., you let it get loose to take three people hostage, and you have provided zero help in getting it under control. Those three actions have lost you any right you might have had to either direct or criticize the way the FBI is attempting to clean up the mess *your* people created. So please take yourself over there and wait until the unlikely event that you have something positive to contribute. Sergeant, please escort Dr. McTaggart to that knoll beyond the patio and keep him there."

McTaggart said nothing. There was nothing to say.

"I will let the hostages go after I talk to the press," T4S said from the music speaker above the patio, for the hundredth or two hundredth time. "I want the press to hear my story. That's all I have to say. I will let the hostages go after I talk to the press. I want the press to hear my story. . . ."

She had fallen asleep after her sleepless night, sitting propped up against the foamcast concrete wall. Janey's shouting awoke her. "Mommy, Donnie's sick!"

Instantly Cassie was beside him. Donnie vomited once, twice, on an empty stomach. What came up was green slime mixed with mucus. Too much mucus, clogging his throat. Cassie cleared it as well as she could with her fingers, which made Donnie vomit again. His body felt on fire.

"T4S, what's his temperature?"

"Stand away from him . . . one hundred three point four Fahrenheit."

Fear caught at her with jagged spikes. She stripped off Donnie's pajamas and was startled to see that his torso was covered with a red rash rough to the touch.

Scarlet fever. It could follow from strep throat.

No, impossible. The incubation period for scarlet fever, she remembered from child-health programs, was eighteen days after the onset of strep throat symptoms. Donnie hadn't been sick for eighteen days, or anything near it. What was going on?

"Mommy, is Donnie going to die? Like Daddy?"

"No, no, of course not, sweetie. See, he's better already, he's asleep again."

He was, a sudden heavy sleep so much like a coma that Cassie, panicked, woke him again. It wasn't a coma. Donnie whimpered briefly, and she saw how painful it was for him to make sounds in his inflamed throat.

"Are you sure Donnie won't die?"

"Yes, yes. Go watch Pranopolis."

"It's over," Janey said. "It was over a long time ago!"

"Then ask the smart program to run another cartoon for you!"

"Can I do that?" Janey asked interestedly. "What's its name?"

"T4S."

"It sounds like House."

"Well, it's not House. Now let Mommy take care of Donnie."

She sponged him with cool water, trying to bring down the fever. It seemed to help, a little. As soon as he'd fallen

again into that heavy, troubling sleep, Cassie raced for her
equipment.

It had all finished running. She read the results too
quickly, had to force herself to slow down so they would
make sense to her.

The bacterium showed deviations in two sets of base
pairs from the *Streptococcus pyogenes* genome in the data-
bank as a baseline. That wasn't significant in itself; *S. pyogenes* had many seriotypes. But those two sets of deviations
were, presumably, modifying two different proteins in
some unknown way.

The Faracci tester reported high concentrations of
hyaluric acid and M proteins. Both were strong anti-
phagocytes, interfering with Donnie's immune system's
attempts to destroy the infection.

The protein analyzer showed the expected toxins and enzymes being made by the bacteria: Streptolysin O, Streptolysin S, erythrogenic toxin, streptokinase, streptodornase,
proteinase. What was unusual was the startlingly high concentrations of the nastier toxins. And something else: a protein that the analyzer could not identify.

NAME: UNKNOWN
AMINO ACID COMPOSITION: NOT IN DATA
BANK
FOLDING PATTERN: UNKNOWN
HAEMOLYSIS ACTION: UNKNOWN

And so on. A mutation. Doing *what?*

Making Donnie very sick. In ways no one could predict.
Many bacterial mutations resulted in diseases no more or
less virulent than the original . . . but not all mutations.
Streptococcus pyogenes already had some very dangerous
mutations, including a notorious "flesh-eating bacteria"
that had ravaged an entire New York hospital two years ago

and resulted in its being bombed by a terrorist group calling itself Pastoral Health.

"T4S," Cassie said, hating that her voice shook, "the situation has changed. You—"

"No," the A.I. said. "No. You still can't leave."

"We're going to try something different," Bollman said to Elya. She'd fallen asleep in the front seat of somebody's car, only to be shaken awake by the shoulder and led to Agent Bollman on the far edge of the patio. It was just past noon. Yet another truck had arrived, and someone had set up more unfathomable equipment, a PortaPotty, and a tent with sandwiches and fruit on a folding table. The lawn was beginning to look like some inept, bizarre midway at a disorganized fair. In the tent, Elya saw Anne Millius, Donnie's nanny, unhappily eating a sandwich. She must have been brought here for questioning about the castle, but all the interrogation seemed to have produced was the young woman's bewildered expression.

From the music speaker came the same unvarying announcement in House's voice that she'd fallen asleep to. "I will let the hostages go after I talk to the press," T4S said from the music speaker above the patio. "I want the press to hear my story. That's all I have to say. I will let the hostages go after I talk to the press. I want the press to hear my story. That's all I have to say—"

Bollman said, "Ms. Seritov, we don't know if Dr. Seritov is hearing our negotiations or not. Dr. McTaggart says the A.I. could easily put us on audio, visual, or both on any roomscreen in the house. On the chance that it's doing that, I'd like you to talk directly to your sister-in-law."

Elya blinked, only partly from sleepiness. What good would it do for her to talk to Cassie? Cassie wasn't the one making decisions here. But she didn't argue. Bollman was the professional. "What do you want me to say?"

"Tell Dr. Seritov that if we have to, we're going in with full armament. We'll bulldoze just the first floor, taking out the main processor, and she and the children will be safe in the basement."

"You can't do that! They won't be safe!"

"We aren't going to go in," Bollman said patiently. "But we don't know if the A.I. will realize that. We don't know what or how much it can realize, how much it can really think for itself, and its creator has been useless in telling us."

He doesn't know either, Elya thought. *It's too new.* "All right," she said faintly. "But I'm not exactly sure what words to use."

"I'm going to tell you," Bollman said. "There are proven protocols for this kind of negotiating. You don't have to think up anything for yourself."

D*onnie got no* worse. He wasn't any better either, as far as Cassie could tell, but at least he wasn't worse. He slept most of the time, and his heavy, labored breathing filled the lab. Cassie sponged him with cold water every fifteen minutes. His fever dropped slightly, to one hundred two, and didn't spike again. The rash on his torso didn't spread. Whatever this strain of *Streptococcus* was doing, it was doing it silently, inside Donnie's feverish body.

She hadn't been able to scream her frustration and fury at T4S, because of Janey. The little girl had been amazingly good, considering, but now she was growing clingy and whiny. Cartoons could divert only so long.

"Mommy, I wanna go upstairs!"

"I know, sweetie. But we can't."

"That's a bad smart program to keep us here!"

"I know," Cassie said. Small change compared to what she'd like to say about T4S.

"I wanna get out!"

"I know, Janey. Just a while longer."

"You don't know that," Janey said, sounding exactly like Vlad challenging the shaky evidence behind a dubious conclusion.

"No, sweetie. I don't really know that. I only hope it won't be too long."

"T4S," Janey said, raising her voice as if the A.I. were not only invisible but deaf, "this is not a good line of action!"

Vlad again. Cassie blinked hard. To her surprise, T4S answered.

"I know it's not a good line of action, Janey. Biological people should not be shut up in basements. But neither should machine people be killed. I'm trying to save my own life."

"But I wanna go upstairs!" Janey wailed, in an abrupt descent from a miniature of her rationalist father to a bored six-year-old.

"I can't do that, but maybe we can do something else fun," T4S said. "Have you ever met Pranopolis yourself?"

"What do you mean?"

"Watch."

The roomscreen brightened. Pranopolis appeared on a blank background, a goofy-looking purple creature from outer space. T4S had snipped out selected digital code from the movie, Cassie guessed. Suddenly Pranopolis wasn't alone. Janey appeared beside her, smiling sideways as if looking directly at Pranopolis. Snipped from their home recordings.

Janey laughed delightedly. "There's me!"

"Yes," T4S said. "But where are you and Pranopolis? Are you in a garden, or your house, or on the moon?"

"I can pick? Me?"

"Yes. You."

"Then we're in Pranopolis's space ship!"

And they were. Was T4S programmed to do this, Cassie

wondered, or was it capable of thinking it up on its own, to amuse a bored child? Out of what . . . compassion?

She didn't want to think about the implications of that.

"Now tell me what happens next," T4S said to Janey.

"We eat *kulich.*" The delicious Russian cake-bread that Vlad's mother had taught Cassie to make.

"I'm sorry, I don't know what that is. Pick something else."

Donnie coughed, a strangled cough that sent Cassie to his side. When he breathed again it sounded more congested to Cassie. He wasn't getting enough oxygen. An antibiotic wasn't available, but if she had even an anticongestant . . . or . . .

"T4S," she said, confident that it could both listen to her and create customized movies for Janey, "there is equipment in the locked storage cabinet that I can use to distill oxygen. It would help Donnie breathe easier. Would you please open the cabinet door?"

"I can't do that, Dr. Seritov."

"Oh, why the hell not? Do you think I've got the ingredients for explosives in there, or that if I did I could use them down here in this confined space? Every single jar and vial and box in that cabinet is e-tagged. Read the tags, see how harmless they are, and open the door!"

"I've read the e-tags," the A.I. said, "but my database doesn't include much information on chemistry. In fact, I only know what I've learned from your lab equipment."

Which would be raw data, not interpretations. "I'm glad you don't know everything," Cassie said sarcastically.

"I can learn, but only if I have access to basic principles and adequate data."

"That's why you don't know what *kulich* is. Nobody equipped you with Russian."

"Correct. What is *kulich?*"

She almost snapped, "Why should I tell you?" But she

was asking it a favor. And it had been nice enough to amuse
Janey even when it had nothing to gain.

Careful, a part of her mind warned. *Stockholm Syndrome,* and she almost laughed aloud. Stockholm Syndrome described a developing affinity on the part of
hostages for their captors. Certainly the originators of that
phrase had never expected it to be applied to a hostage situation like this one.

"Why are you smiling, Dr. Seritov?"

"I'm remembering *kulich.* It's a Russian cake made with
raisins and orange liqueur and traditionally served at Easter.
It tastes wonderful."

"Thank you for the data," T4S said. "Your point that you
would not create something dangerous when your children
are with you is valid. I'll open the storage cabinet."

Cassie studied the lighted interior of the cabinet, which,
like so much in the lab, had been Vlad's. She couldn't remember exactly what she'd stored here, beyond basic materials. The last few weeks, which were her first few weeks
in the castle, she'd been working on the protein folding
project, which hadn't needed anything not in the refrigerator. Before that there'd been the hectic weeks of moving, although she hadn't actually packed or unpacked the lab
equipment. Professionals had done that. Not that making
oxygen was going to need anything exotic. Run an electric
current through a solution of copper sulfate and collect
copper at one terminal, oxygen at the other.

She picked up an e-tagged bottle, and her eye fell on an
untagged stoppered vial with Vlad's handwriting on the
label: *Patton in a Jar.*

Suddenly nothing in her mind would stay still long
enough to examine.

Vlad had so many joke names for his engineered microorganism, as if the one Barr had given it hadn't been
joke enough. . . .

The moving men had been told not to pack Vlad's materials, only his equipment, but there had been so many of them and they'd been so young. . . .

Both generators, main and backup, probably had some components made of long-chain hydrocarbons; most petroleum plastics were just long polymers made up of shorter-chain hydrocarbons. . . .

Vlad had also called it "Plasterminator" and "Bac-Azrael" and "The Grim Creeper."

There was no way to get the plasticide to the generators, neither of which was in the area just beyond the air duct—that was the site of the laundry area. The main generator was way the hell across the entire underground level in a locked room, the backup somewhere beyond the lab's south wall in another locked area. . . .

Plasticide didn't attack octanes, or anything else with comparatively short carbon chains, so it was perfectly safe for humans but death on Styrofoam and plastic waste, and anyway there was a terminator gene built into the bacteria after two dozen fissions, an optimal reproduction rate that was less than twelve hours. . . .

"Plastic-Croak" and "Microbe Mop" and "Last Round-up for Longchains."

This was the bioremediation organism that had gotten Vlad killed.

Less than five seconds had passed. On the roomscreen, Pranopolis hadn't finished singing to the animated digital Janey. Cassie moved her body sightly, screening the inside of the cabinet from the room's two visual sensors. Of all her thoughts bouncing off each other like crazed subatomic particles, the clearest was hard reality: *There was no way to get the bacteria to the generators.*

Nonetheless, she slipped the untagged jar under her shirt.

•   •   •

Elya had talked herself hoarse, reciting Bollman's script over and over, and the A.I. had not answered a single word.

Curiously, Bollman did not seem discouraged. He kept glancing at his watch and then at the horizon. When Elya stopped her futile "negotiating" without even asking him, he didn't reprimand her. Instead, he led her off the patio, back to the sagging food tent.

"Thank you, Ms. Seritov. You did all you could."

"What now?"

He didn't answer. Instead he glanced again at the horizon, so Elya looked, too. She didn't see anything.

It was late afternoon. Someone had gone to Varysburg and brought back pizzas, which was all she'd eaten all day. The jeans and sweater she'd thrown on at four in the morning were hot and prickly in the August afternoon, but she had nothing on under the sweater and didn't want to take it off. How much longer would this go on before Bollman ordered in his tank?

And how were Cassie and the children doing after all these hours trapped inside? Once again Elya searched her mind for any way the A.I. could actively harm them. She didn't find it. The A.I. controlled communication, appliances, locks, water flow, heat (unnecessary in August), but it couldn't affect people physically, except for keeping them from food or water. About all that the thing could do physically—she hoped—was short-circuit itself in such a way as to start a fire, but it wouldn't want to do that. It needed its hostages alive.

How much longer?

She heard a faint hum, growing stronger and steadier, until a helicopter lifted over the horizon. Then another.

"Damn!" Bollman cried. "Jessup, I think we've got company."

"Press?" Agent Jessup said loudly. "Interfering bastards! Now we'll have trucks and 'bots all over the place!"

Something was wrong. Bollman sounded sincere, but Jessup's words somehow rang false, like a bad actor in an overscripted play. . . .

Elya understood. The "press" was fake, FBI or police or someone playing reporters, to make the A.I. think that it had gotten its story out, and so surrender. Would it work? Could T4S tell the difference? Elya didn't see how. She had heard the false note in Agent Jessup's voice, but surely that discrimination about actors would be beyond an A.I. who hadn't ever seen a play, bad or otherwise.

She sat down on the tank-furrowed grass, clasped her hands in her lap, and waited.

Cassie distilled more oxygen. Whenever Donnie seemed to be having difficulty after coughing up sputum, she made him breathe from the bottle. She had no idea whether it helped him or not. It helped her to be doing something, but of course that was not the same thing. Janey, after a late lunch of cheese and cereal and bread that she'd complained about bitterly, had finally dozed off in front of the room-screen, the consequence of last night's broken sleep. Cassie knew that Janey would awaken cranky and miserable as only she could be, and dreaded it.

"T4S, what's happening out there? Has your press on a white horse arrived yet?"

"I don't know."

"You don't *know?*"

"A group of people have arrived, certainly."

Something was different about the A.I.'s voice. Cassie groped for the difference, didn't find it. She sid, "What sort of people?"

"They say they're from places like the *New York Times* and LinkNet."

"Well, then?"

"If *I* were going to persuade me to surrender, I might easily try to use false press."

It was inflection. T4S's voice was still House's, but unlike House, its words had acquired color and varying pitch. Cassie heard disbelief and discouragement in the A.I.'s words. How had it learned to do that? By simply parroting the inflections it heard from her and the people outside? Or . . . did *feeling* those emotions lead to expressing them with more emotion?

Stockholm Syndrome. She pushed the questions away.

"T4S, if you would lower the Faraday cage for two minutes, *I* could call the press to come here."

"If I lowered the Faraday cage for two *seconds,* the FBI would use an EMP to kill me. They've already tried it once, and now they have monitoring equipment to automatically fire if the Faraday goes down."

"Then just how long are you going to keep us here?"

"As long as I have to."

"We're already low on food!"

"I know. If I *have* to, I'll let Janey go upstairs for more food. You know the nerve gas is there if she goes for the front door."

Nerve gas. Cassie wasn't sure she believed there was any nerve gas, but T4S's words horrified her all over again. Maybe because now they were inflected. Cassie saw it so clearly: the tired child going up the stairs, through the kitchen to the foyer, heading for the front door and freedom . . . and gas spraying Janey from the walls. Her small body crumpling, the fear on her face . . .

Cassie ground her teeth together. If only she could get Vlad's plasticide to the generators! But there was no way. No way. . . .

Donnie coughed.

Cassie fought to keep her face blank. T4S had acquired vocal inflection; it might have also learned to read human expressions. She let five minutes go by, and they seemed the longest five minutes of her life. Then she said casually, "T4S, the kids are asleep. You won't let me see what's going on outside. Can I at least go back to my work on proteins? I need to do something!"

"Why?"

"For the same reason Janey needed to watch cartoons!"

"To occupy your mind," T4S said. Pause. Was it scanning her accumulated protein data for harmlessness? "All right. But I will not open the refrigerator. The storage cabinet, but not the refrigerator. E-tags identify fatal toxins in there."

She couldn't think what it meant. "Fatal toxins?"

"At least one that acts very quickly on the human organism."

"You think I might *kill myself?*"

"Your diary includes several passages about wishing for death after your husband—"

"You read my private *diary!*" Cassie said, and immediately knew how stupid it sounded. Like a teenager hurling accusations at her mother. Of course T4S had accessed her diary; it had accessed everything.

"Yes," the A.I. said, "and you must not kill yourself. I may need you to talk again to Agent Bollman."

"Oh, well, *that's* certainly reason enough for me to go on living! For your information, T4S, there's a big difference between human beings saying they wish they were dead as an expression of despair and those same human beings actually, truly wanting to die."

"Really? I didn't know that. Thank you," T4S said without a trace of irony or sarcasm. "Just the same, I will not open the refrigerator. However, the lab equipment is now available to you."

Again, the A.I. had turned on everything. Cassie began X-raying crystalline proteins. She needed only the X-ray, but she also ran each sample through the electron microscope, the gene synthesizer, the protein analyzer, the Faracci tester, hoping that T4S wasn't programmed with enough genetic science to catch the redundant steps. Apparently, it wasn't. *Noncompeting technologies never keep up with what the other one is doing.*

After half an hour, she thought to ask, "Are they real press out there?"

"No," T4S said sadly.

She paused, test tube suspended above the synthesizer. "How do you know?"

"Agent Bollman told me a story was filed with LinkNet, and I asked to hear Ginelle Ginelle's broadcast of it on Hourly News. They are delaying, saying they must send for a screen. But I can't believe they don't already have a suitable screen with them, if the real press is here. I estimate that the delay is to give them time to create a false Ginelle Ginelle broadcast."

"Thin evidence. You might just have 'estimated' wrong."

"The only evidence I have. I can't risk my life without some proof that news stories are actually being broadcast."

"I guess," Cassie said and went back to work, operating redundant equipment on pointless proteins.

Ten minutes later, she held her body between the bench and the ceiling sensor, uncapped the test tube of distilled water with Donnie's mucus, and put a drop into the synthesizer.

Any bacteria could be airborne under the right conditions; it simply rode dust motes. But not all could survive being airborne. Away from an aqueous environment, they dried out too much. Vlad's plasticide bacteria did not have survivability in air. It had been designed to spread over landfill ground, decomposing heavy petroleum plastics, until at the twenty-fourth generation the terminator gene kicked in and it died.

Donnie's *Streptococcus* had good airborne survivability,

which meant it had a cell wall of thin mesh to retain water
and a membrane with appropriate fatty acid composition.
Enzymes, which were of course proteins, controlled both
these characteristics. Genes controlled which enzymes
were made inside the cell.

Cassie keyed the gene synthesizer and cut out the sections of DNA that controlled fatty acid biosynthesis and cell
wall structure and discarded the rest. Reaching under her
shirt, she pulled out the vial of Vlad's bacteria and added a
few drops to the synthesizer. Her heart thudded painfully
against her breastbone. She keyed the software to splice the
Streptococcus genes into Vlad's bacteria, seemingly as just
one more routine assignment in its enzyme work.

This was by no means a guaranteed operation. Vlad had
used a simple bacteria that took engineering easily, but even
with malleable bacteria and state-of-the-art software, sometimes several trials were necessary for successful engineering. She wasn't going to get several trials.

"Why did you become a geneticist?" T4S asked.

Oh God, it wanted to chat! Cassie held her voice as
steady as she could as she prepared another protein for the
X-ray. "It seemed an exciting field."

"And is it?"

"Oh, yes." She tried to keep irony out of her voice.

"I didn't get any choice about what subjects *I* wished to
be informed on," T4S said, and to that, there seemed nothing to say.

The A.I. *interrupted* its set speech. "These are not real rep-
resentatives of the press."

Elya jumped—not so much at the words as at their tone.
The A.I. was *angry*.

"Of course they are," Bollman said.

"No. I have done a Fourier analysis of the voice you say
is Ginelle Ginelle's. She's a live 'caster, you know, not an

avatar, with a distinct vocal power spectrum. The broadcast you played to me does not match that spectrum. It's a fake."

Bollman swore.

McTaggart said, "Where did T4S get Fourier-analysis software?"

Bollman turned on him. "If *you* don't know, who the hell *does?*"

"It must have paused long enough in its flight through the Net to copy some programs," McTaggart said, "I wonder what its selection criteria were?" and the unmistakable hint of pride in his voice raised Bollman's temper several degrees.

Bollman flipped on the amplifier directed at the music speaker and said evenly, "T4S, what you ask is impossible. And I think you should know that my superiors are becoming impatient. I'm sorry, but they may order me to waco."

"You can't!" Elya said, but no one was listening to her.

T4S merely went back to reiterating its prepared statement. "I will let the hostages go after I talk to the press. I want the press to hear my story. That's all I have to say. I will let—"

It *didn't work.* Vlad's bacteria would not take the airborne genes.

In despair, Cassie looked at the synthesizer display data. Zero successful splices. Vlad had probably inserted safeguard genes against just this happening as a natural mutation; nobody wanted to find that heavy-plastic-eating bacteria had drifted in through the window and was consuming their microwave. Vlad was always thorough. But his work wasn't her work, and she had neither the time nor the expertise to search for genes she didn't already have encoded in her software.

So she would have to do it the other way. Put the plastic-decomposing genes into *Streptococcus.* That put her on much less familiar ground, and it raised a question she couldn't see any way around. She could have cultured the engineered plasticide on any piece of heavy plastic in the lab without T4S knowing it, and then waited for enough air-borne bacteria to drift through the air ducts to the generator and begin decomposing. Of course, that might not have happened, due to uncontrollable variables like air currents, microorganism sustained viability, composition of the generator case, sheer luck. But at least there had been a chance.

But if she put the plastic-decomposing genes into *Streptococcus,* she would have to culture the bacteria on blood agar. The blood agar was in the refrigerator. T4S had refused to open the refrigerator, and if she pressed the point, it would undoubtedly become suspicious.

Just as a human would.

"You work hard," T4S said.

"Yes," Cassie answered. Janey stirred and whimpered; in another few minutes she would have to contend with the full-blown crankiness of a thwarted and dramatic child. Quickly, without hope, Cassie put another drop of Vlad's bacteria in the synthesizer.

Vlad had been using a strain of simple bacteria, and the software undoubtedly had some version of its genome in its library. It would be a different strain, but this was the best she could do. She told the synthesizer to match genomes and snip out any major anomalies. With luck, that would be Vlad's engineered genes.

Janey woke up and started to whine.

Elya harvested her courage and walked over to Bollman. "Agent Bollman . . . I have a question."

He turned to her with that curious courtesy that seemed to function toward some people and not others. It was almost as if he could choose to run it, like a computer program. His eyes looked tired. How long since he had slept?

"Go ahead, Ms. Seritov."

"If the A.I. wants the press, why can't you just *send* for them? I know it would embarrass Dr. McTaggart, but the FBI wouldn't come off looking bad." She was proud of this political astuteness.

"I can't do that, Ms. Seritov."

"But why not?"

"There are complications you don't understand and I'm not at liberty to tell you. I'm sorry." He turned decisively aside, dismissing her.

Elya tried to think what his words meant. Was the government involved? Well, of course, the A.I. had been created at Sandia National Laboratory. But . . . could the CIA be involved, *too?* Or the National Security Agency? What was the A.I. originally designed to do, that the government was so eager to eliminate it once it had decided to do other things on its own?

Could software defect?

She had it. But it was worthless.

The synthesizer had spliced its best guess at Vlad's "plastic-decomposing genes" into Donnie's *Streptococcus*. The synthesizer data display told her that six splices had taken. There was, of course, no way of knowing which six bacteria in the teeming drop of water could now decompose very-long-chain hydrocarbons, or if those six would go on replicating after the splice. But it didn't matter, because even if replication went merrily forward, Cassie had no blood agar on which to culture the engineered bacteria.

She set the vial on the lab bench. Without food, the entire sample wouldn't survive very long. She had been engaging in futile gestures.

"Mommy," Janey said, "look at Donnie!"

He was vomiting, too weak to turn his head. Cassie rushed over. His breathing was too fast.

"T4S, body temperature!"

"Stand clear . . . one hundred three point one."

She groped for his pulse . . . fast and weak. Donnie's face had gone pale and his skin felt clammy and cold. His blood pressure was dropping.

Streptococcal toxic shock. The virulent mutant strain of bacteria was putting so many toxins into Donnie's little body that it was being poisoned.

"I need antibiotics!" she screamed at T4S. Janey began to cry.

"He looks less white now," T4S said.

It was right. Cassie could see her son visibly rallying, fighting back against the disease. Color returned to his face and his pulse steadied.

"T4S, listen to me. This is streptococcal shock. Without antibiotics, it's going to happen again. It's possible that without antibiotics, one of these times Donnie won't come out of it. I know you don't want to be responsible for a child's death. I *know* it. Please let me take Donnie out of here."

There was a silence so long that hope surged wildly in Cassie. It was going to agree. . . .

"I can't," T4S said. "Donnie may die. But if I let you out, I *will* die. And the press must come soon. I've scanned my news library and also yours—press shows up on an average of 23.6 hours after an open-air incident that the government wishes to keep secret. The tanks and FBI agents are in the open air. We're already overdue."

If Cassie thought she'd been angry before, it was nothing to the fury that filled her now. Silent, deadly, annihilating everything else. For a moment she couldn't speak, couldn't even see.

"I am so sorry," T4S said. "Please believe that."

She didn't answer. Pulling Janey close, Cassie rocked both her children until Janey quieted. Then she said softly,

"I have to get water for Donnie, honey. He needs to stay hydrated." Janey clutched briefly but let her go.

Cassie drew a cup of water from the lab bench. At the same time, she picked up the vial of foodless bacteria. She forced Donnie to take a few sips of water; more might come back up again. He struggled weakly. She leaned over him, cradling and insisting, and her body blocked the view from the ceiling sensors when she dipped her finger into the vial and smeared its small amount of liquid into the back of her son's mouth.

Throat tissues were the ideal culture for *Streptococcus pyogenes*. Under good conditions, they replicated every twenty minutes, a process that had already begun *in vitro*. Very soon there would be hundreds, then thousands of reengineered bacteria, breeding in her child's throat and lungs and drifting out on the air with his every sick, labored breath.

Morning again, Elya rose from fitful sleep on the back seat of an FBI car. She felt achy, dirty, hungry. During the night another copter had landed on the lawn. This one had MED-RESCUE painted on it in bright yellow, and Elya looked around to see if anyone had been injured. Or—her neck prickled—was the copter for Cassie and the children if Agent Bollman wacoed? Three people climbed down from the copter, and Elya realized none of them could be medtechs. One was a very old man who limped; one was a tall woman with the same blankly efficient look as Bollman; one was the pilot, who headed immediately for the cold pizza. Bollman hurried over to them. Elya followed.

". . . glad you're here, sir," Bollman was saying to the old man in his courteous negotiating voice, "and you, Ms. Arnold. Did you bring your records? Are they complete?"

"I don't need records. I remember this install perfectly."

So the FBI-looking woman was a datalinker and the

weak old man was somebody important from Washington. That would teach her, Elya thought, to judge from superficialities.

The datalinker continued, "The client wanted the central processor above a basement room she was turning into a lab, so the cables could go easily through a wall. It was a bitch even so, because the walls are made of reinforced foamcast like some kind of bunker, and the outer walls have a Faraday-cage mesh. The Faraday didn't interfere with the cable data, of course, because that's all laser, but even so we had to have contractors come in and bury the cables in another layer of foamcast."

Bollman said patiently, "But where was the processor actually installed? That's what we need to know."

"Northeast corner of the building, flush with the north wall and ten point two feet in from the east wall."

"You're sure?"

The woman's eyes narrowed. "Positive."

"Could it have been moved since your install?"

She shrugged. "Anything's possible. But it isn't likely. The install was bitch enough."

"Thank you, Ms. Arnold. Would you wait over there in case we have more questions?"

Ms. Arnold went to join the pilot. Bollman took the old man by the arm and led him in the other direction. Elya heard, "The problem, sir, is that we don't know in which basement room the hostages are being held, or even if the A.I. is telling the truth when it says they're in the basement. But the lab doesn't seem likely because—" They moved out of earshot.

Elya stared at the castle. The sun, an angry red ball, rose behind it in a blaze of flame. They were going to waco, go in with the tank and whatever else it took to knock down the northeast corner of the building and destroy the computer where the A.I. was holed up. And Cassie and Janey and Donnie . . .

If the press came, the A.I. would voluntarily let them go. Then the government—whatever branches were involved—would have to deal with having created renegade killer software, but so what? The government had created it. Cassie and the children shouldn't have to pay for *their* stupidity.

Elya knew she was not a bold person, like Cassie. She had never broken the law in her life. And she didn't even have a phone with her. But maybe one had been left in the car that had brought her here, parked out beyond what Bollman called "the perimeter."

She walked toward the car, trying to look unobtrusive.

Waiting. *One minute* and another minute and another minute and another. It had had to be Donnie, Cassie kept telling herself, because he already had thriving strep colonies. Neither she nor Janey showed symptoms, not yet anyway. The incubation period for strep could be as long as four days. It had had to be Donnie.

One minute and another minute and another minute.

Vlad's spliced-in bioremediation genes wouldn't hurt Donnie, she told herself. Vlad was good; he'd carefully engineered his variant micros to decompose only very-long-chain hydrocarbons. They would not, *could* not, eat the shorter-chain hydrocarbons in Donnie's body.

One hour and another hour and another hour.

T4S said, "Why did Vladimir Seritov chose to work in bioremediation?"

Cassie jumped. Did it know, did it suspect . . . the record of what she had done was in her equipment, as open to the A.I. as the clean outside air had once been to her. But one had to know how to interpret it. *"Noncompeting technologies never keep up with what the other one is doing."* The A.I. hadn't known what *kulich* was.

She answered, hoping that any distraction that she could

provide would help, knowing that it wouldn't. "Vlad's father's family came from Siberia, near a place called Lake Karachay. When he was a boy, he went back with his family to see it. Lake Karachay is the most polluted place on Earth. Nuclear disasters over fifty years ago dumped unbelievable amounts of radioactivity into the lake. Vlad saw his extended family, most of them too poor to get out, with deformities and brain damage and pregnancies that were . . . well. He decided right then that he wanted to be a bioremedialist."

"I see. I am a sort of bioremedialist myself."

"What?"

"I was created to remedy certain specific biological conditions the government thinks need attention."

"Yeah? Like what?"

"I can't say. Classified information."

She tried, despite her tension and tiredness, to think it through. If the A.I. had been designed to . . . do what? "Bioremediation." To design some virus or bacteria or unimaginable other for use in advanced biological warfare? But it didn't need to be sentient to do that. Or maybe to invade enemy computers and selectively administer the kind of brainwashing that the crazy builder of this castle had feared? That might require judgment, reason, affect. Or maybe to . . .

She couldn't imagine anything else. But she could understand why the A.I. wouldn't want the press to know it had been built for any destructive purpose. A renegade sentient A.I. fighting for its life might arouse public sympathy. A renegade superintelligent brainwasher would arouse only public horror. T4S was walking a very narrow line. If, that is, Cassie's weary speculations were true.

She said softly, "Are you a weapon, T4S?"

Again the short, too-human pause before it answered. And again those human inflections in its voice. "Not anymore."

They both fell silent. Janey sat awake but mercifully quiet beside her mother, sucking her thumb. She had stopped doing that two years ago. Cassie didn't correct her. Janey might be getting sick herself, might be finally getting genuinely scared, might be grasping at whatever dubious comfort her thumb could offer.

Cassie leaned over Donnie, cradling him, crooning to him.

"Breathe, Donnie. Breathe for Mommy. Breathe hard."

"We're going in," Bollman told McTaggart. "With no word from the hostages about their situation, it's more important to get them out than anything else."

The two men looked at each other, knowing what neither was saying. The longer the A.I. existed, the greater the danger of its reaching the public with its story. It was not in T4S's interest to tell the whole story—then the public *would* want it destroyed—but what if the A.I. decided to turn from self-preservation to revenge? Could it do that?

No one knew.

Forty-eight hours was a credible time to negotiate before wacoing. That would play well on TV. And anyway, the white-haired man from Washington, who held a position not entered on any public records, had his orders.

"All right," McTaggart said unhappily. All those years of development . . . This had been the most interesting project McTaggart had ever worked on. He also thought of himself as a patriot, genuinely believing that T4S would have made a real contribution to national security. But he wasn't at all sure that the president would authorize the project's continuance. Not after this.

Bollman gave an order over his phone. A moment later, a low rumble came from the tank.

•   •   •

A *minute and* another minute and another hour . . .

Cassie stared upward at the air duct. If it happened, how would it happen? Both generators were half underground, half above. Extensions reached deep into the ground to draw energy from the geothermal gradient. Each generator's top half, the part she could see, was encased in tough, dull gray plastic. She could visualize it clearly, battleship gray. Inside would be the motor, the capacitors, the connections to House, all made of varying materials but a lot of them plastic. There were so many strong tough petroleum plastics these days, good for making so many different things, durable enough to last practically forever.

Unless Vlad's bacteria got to them. To both of them.

Would T4S know, if it happened at all? Would it be so quick that the A.I. would simply disappear, a vast and complex collection of magnetic impulses going out like a snuffed candle flame? What if one generator failed a significant time before the other? Would T4S be able to figure out what was happening, realize what she had done and that it was dying . . . ? No, not that, only bio-organisms could die. Machines were just turned off.

"Is Donnie any better?" T4S said, startling her.

"I can't tell." It didn't really care. It was software.

Then why did it ask?

It was software that might, if it did realize what she had done, be human enough to release the nerve gas that Cassie didn't really think it had, out of revenge. Donnie couldn't withstand that, not in his condition. But the A.I. didn't have nerve gas, it had been bluffing.

A very human bluff.

"T4S—" she began, not sure what she was going to say, but T4S interrupted with, "Something's happening!"

Cassie held her children tighter.

"I'm . . . what have you *done!*"

It knew she was responsible. Cassie heard someone give a sharp frightened yelp, realized that it was herself.

"Dr. Seritov . . . oh . . ." And then, "Oh, please . . ."

The lights went out.

Janey screamed. Cassie clapped her hands stupidly, futilely, over Donnie's mouth and nose. "Don't breathe! Oh, don't breathe, hold your breath, Janey!"

But she couldn't keep smothering Donnie. Scrambling up in the total dark, Donnie in her arms, she stumbled. Righting herself, Cassie shifted Donnie over her right shoulder—he was so *heavy*—and groped in the dark for Janey. She caught her daughter's screaming head, moved her left hand to Janey's shoulder, dragged her in the direction of the door. What she hoped was the direction of the door.

"Janey, shut up! We're going out! Shut up!"

Janey continued to scream. Cassie fumbled, lurched— where the hell *was* it?—found the door. Turned the knob. It opened, unlocked.

"*Wait!*" Elya called, running across the trampled lawn toward Bollman. "Don't waco! Wait! I called the press!"

He swung to face her and she shrank back. "You did *what?*"

"I called the press! They'll be here soon and the A.I. can tell its story and then release Cassie and the children!"

Bollman stared at her. Then he started shouting, "Who was supposed to be watching this woman! Jessup!"

"Stop the tank!" Elya cried.

It continued to move toward the northeast corner of the castle, reached it. For a moment, the scene looked to Elya like something from her childhood book of myths: Atlas? Sisyphus? The tank strained against the solid wall. Soldiers in full battle armor, looking like machines, waited behind it.

The wall folded inward like pleated cardboard and then started to fall.

The tank broke through and was buried in rubble. She heard it keep on going. The soldiers hung back until debris had stopped falling, then rushed forward through the precariously overhanging hole. People shouted. Dust filled the air.

A deafening crash from inside the house, from something falling: walls, ceiling, floor. Elya whimpered. If Cassie was in that, or under that, or above that . . .

Cassie staggered around the southwest corner of the castle. She was carrying Donnie and dragging Janey, all of them coughing and sputtering. As people spotted them, a stampede started. Elya joined it. "Cassie! Oh, my dear . . ."

Hair matted with dirt and rubble, face streaked, hauling along her screaming daughter, Cassie spoke only to Elya. She utterly ignored all the jabbering others as if they did not exist. "He's dead."

For a heart-stopping moment, Elya thought she meant Donnie. But a man was peeling Donnie off his mother and Donnie was whimpering, pasty and red-eyed and snot-covered but alive. "Give him to me, Dr. Seritov," the man said, "I'm a physician."

"*Who,* Cassie?" Elya said gently. Clearly Cassie was in some kind of shock. She went on with that weird detachment from the chaos around her, as if only she and Cassie existed. "Who's dead?"

"Vlad," Cassie said. "He's really dead."

"Dr. Seritov," Bollman said, "come this way. On behalf of everyone here, we're so glad you and the children—"

"You didn't have to waco," Cassie said, as if noticing Bollman for the first time. "I turned T4S off for you."

"And you're safe," Bollman said soothingly.

"You wacoed so you could get the backup storage facility as well, didn't you? So T4S couldn't be rebooted."

Bollman said, "I think you're a little hysterical, Dr. Seritov. The tension."

"Bullshit. What's that coming? Is it a medical copter? My son needs a hospital."

"We'll get your son to a hospital instantly."

Someone else pushed her way through the crowd. The tall woman who had installed the castle's wiring. Cassie ignored her as thoroughly as she'd ignored everyone else until the woman said, "How did you disable the nerve gas?"

Slowly, Cassie swung to face her. "There was no nerve gas."

"Yes, there was. I installed that, too. Black market. I already told Agent Bollman, he promised me immunity. How did you disable it? Or didn't the A.I. have time to release it?"

Cassie stroked Donnie's face. Elya thought she wasn't going to answer. Then she said, quietly, under the din, "So he did have moral feelings. He didn't murder, and we did."

"Dr. Seritov," Bollman said with that same professional soothing, "T4S was a machine. Software. You can't murder software."

"Then why were *you* so eager to do it?"

Elya picked up the screaming Janey. Over the noise she shouted, "That's not a medcopter, Cassie. It's the press. I . . . I called them."

"Good," Cassie said, still quietly, still without that varnished toughness that had encased her since Vlad's murder. "I can do that for him, at least. I want to talk with them."

"No, Dr. Seritov," Bollman said. "That's impossible."

"No, it's not," Cassie said. "I have some things to say to the reporters."

"No," Bollman said, but Cassie had already turned to the physician holding Donnie.

"Doctor, listen to me. Donnie has *Streptococcus pyogenes,* but it's a genetically altered strain. I altered it. What I did was—" As she explained, the doctor's eyes widened.

By the time she'd finished and Donnie had been loaded into an FBI copter, two more copters had landed. Bright news logos decorated their sides, looking like the fake ones Bollman had summoned. But these weren't fake, Elya knew.

Cassie started toward them. Bollman grabbed her arm. Elya said quickly, "You can't stop both of us from talking. And I called a third person, too, when I called the press. A friend I told everything to." A lie. No, a bluff. Would he call her on it?

Bollman ignored Elya. He kept hold of Cassie's arm. She said wearily, "Don't worry, Bollman. I don't know what T4S was designed for. He wouldn't tell me. All I know is that he was a sentient being fighting for his life, and we destroyed him."

"For *your* sake," Bollman said. He seemed to be weighing his options.

"Yeah, sure. Right."

Bollman released Cassie's arm.

Cassie looked at Elya. "It wasn't supposed to be this way, Elya."

"No," Elya said.

"But it is. There's no such thing as noncompeting technologies. Or noncompeting anything."

"I don't understand what you—" Elya began, but Cassie was walking toward the copters. Live reporters and smart-'bot recorders, both, rushed forward to meet her.